THE FOWLER'S SNARE

C.M.T. Stibbe

D1319514

KINGDOM WRITING
SOLUTIONS
West Sussex

Alternatively, the author can be contacted at her website at
www.cmtstibbe.com

This is a work of fiction. Names, characters, places and incidents
either are the product of the author's imagination or are used
fictitiously, and any resemblance to any actual persons, living or dead,
events, or locales is entirely coincidental.

ISBN-10: 0990600408
ISBN-13: 978-0-9906004-0-4

Printed in the United States of America

Library of Congress Cataloguing-in-Publication data
Stibbe, C.M.T.

Cover design by www.jwccreative.com
Maps by C.M.T. Stibbe

Published in 2014
Kingdom Writing Solutions
Rustington
West Sussex, UK

www.kingdomwritingsolutions.org

Praise for

THE FOWLER'S SNARE

Written historically with the knowledge of an archeologist and the passion of a troubadour, readers will be bound by the spell that C.M.T. Stibbe weaves from the very first page.
John Breeden II, Author of Old Number Seven

The author is well versed in historical fiction and is able to call upon a wealth of self-gained knowledge of ancient Egypt, the subject as huge as the land base it represents. I do love this book for the way it's written.
Neville Kent, Author of The Secrets of the Forest Series and One Off, Sir!

The author's research is excellent. Her description verges on the poetic and is in keeping with the superstitious and spiritual culture she invokes. A very powerful and poetic piece of literature.
Karen Charlton, Author of The Heiress of Linn Hagh and Catching the Eagle.

This is quite stunning - no other word for it. It's exciting, intriguing, sensuous, characters to care about, and what can only be described as visual artistry in the narrative.
Kay Christine Fenton, Author of The Fortune of Annacara.

A novel set against a richly described background of ancient Egypt that centers around the Pharaohs' annual chariot race where death is an all too easy outcome and the prize is something more than a beautiful princess. This is an intense novel that pits men against each other in a battle that is more psychological than physical. The result is gripping in a way that reminds me of Shakespeare's history plays.
Kristen Gleeson, Author of Selkie Dreams.

ACKNOWLEDGMENTS

I cannot express enough thanks to my proof-readers at the Script Doctor for their continued support and encouragement, and to Kingdom Writing Solutions for their mission and vision. I offer my sincere appreciation for the learning opportunities you have provided.

My completion of this project could not have been accomplished without the support of A. G. Gibson and John Gibson. To Teri Pickering for her many hours of editing. To my mother for her sacrifices and to my father for his grace. And to my amazing son, Jamie, for making me laugh, for your hugs and love, and for allowing me time to research and write. You deserve a Bentley!

Finally, to my loving, and supportive husband, Jeff: my deepest gratitude and love. I couldn't have done any of this without you. It was a great comfort and relief to know that you were there to offer suggestions and insight. My heartfelt thanks.

www.thescriptdoctor.org.uk

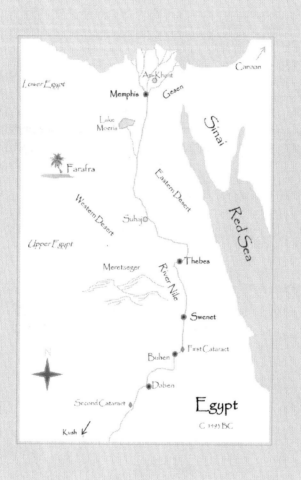

Canaan

Lower Egypt

Am-Khent

Memphis · Gesen

Sinai

Lake
Moeris

Farafra

Eastern Desert

Red Sea

Western Desert

Suhaj ○

Upper Egypt

Meretseger

River Nile

Thebes

Swenet

First Cataract

Buhen · Daben

N

Second Cataract ·

Egypt

C. 1493 BC

Kush

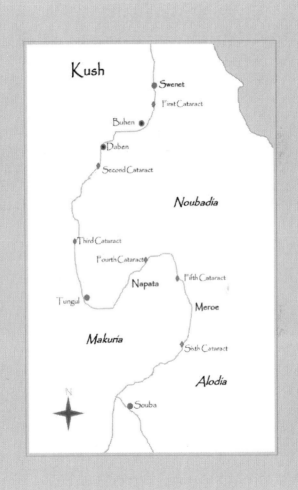

CHARACTERS

Ayize, fourth son of King Ibada of Alodia, House of Souba.

Harran, *Shasu* Prophet and Scribe to Pharaoh Kheper-Re.

Hatshepsut, Queen of Egypt, Great Royal Wife and sister to Pharaoh Kheper-Re.

Iutha, wife to Mkasa.

Jabari, Lieutenant to Commander Shenq.

Kanja, second son of King Ibada of Alodia, House of Souba.

Khamudi, Commander Shenq's houseman.

Khemwese, Bodyguard to Pharaoh Kheper-Re, formerly of the house of Meroë.

Kheper-Re, Pharaoh of Egypt, Son of Ra.

Massui, third son of King Ibada of Alodia, House of Souba.

Menkheperre, Prince of Thebes and son of Pharaoh Kheper-Re.

Meru-Itseni, Armor Bearer to Commander Shenq.

Meryt, wife to Commander Shenq.

Mkasa, Lieutenant to Commander Shenq, formerly of the house of Makuria.

Othene, Sorcerer to King Ibada of Alodia, House of Souba.

Pi-Bak-Amana, High Priest of the Temple at Suhaj.

Ranefer, Commander Shenq's housewoman.

S'haila, Imazi girl.

Saqr, son of Tarabin, prince of the Imazi.

Shenq, Commander of the *Kenyt-Nisu*, Pharaoh's most Honored Ones.

Tarabin, Bonelord of the Imazi.

Tehute, Captain to Commander Shenq.

Thutiy, Grand Vizier of Thebes.

Ulan, twin brother to Kanja and firstborn son of King Ibada of Alodia, House of Souba.

KANJA

Kanja strained against his chains, stretching his fingers out as far as they could reach. It was the sound of mourning that had woken him, a wavering sound that floated across the river. He imagined a procession of women along the banks of the Nile watching a funeral ship as it struggled against the current, carrying the dead king of Alodia.

"Father," Kanja murmured, smelling the sour stench of death.

Its better this way, a voice said, a voice that had been raging in Kanja's head.

It was the same voice that convinced Kanja to poison his father. But treason in Alodia carried the most ruthless of sentences. In three days, the prisoners would be tied between two horses and ripped apart, and what was left of them burned and scattered.

There was a yellow haze in the corner of the cell, a flame dancing in the nozzle of an oil lamp. It shed enough light on Kanja's surroundings to show he was not alone. Ulan, his twin brother, hung next to him.

"Brother," Kanja murmured. "Can you hear me?"

Ulan said nothing. Governor of Souba and firstborn son of King Ibada, he had skin the color of the soil and braided hair that hung to his waist. His stomach was purple like a plum and traces of pus streaked down to his navel. No doctor would help him now. So he slept as he hung from the shackles, a temporary relief from the horrors of the past two days.

Twisting to one side, the chains forced Kanja back against the wall and his neck burned from the weight of his head. A red shúkà hung from his shoulders and the remnants of a tribal collar, torn from his neck in the struggle, dangled over one breast. He cursed loudly. But no one heard.

That's why you're here, the voice said, persistent, bitter.

"Yes, that's why I'm here," he murmured, teeth gritted with anger. It made him feel inferior. He would need to respond to the voice otherwise it would needle him to exhaustion.

Memories of his father emerged now and then, blinding him like a mirror that had caught the sun's rays, and he retreated into the nightmares, reliving the pain of childhood. Prison was a familiar realm, a second home so to speak. His father locked him in the same cell from the age of eight, throwing scraps of leftover food until he could prove himself.

You will live like a dog and eat like a dog. Hunger will make a man out of you. Isn't that what he had said?

Only a coward would lock a child in a dungeon for talking back. Only a twin brother would bring stolen food and talk to him in the darkness. Ulan was never subtle. He was always caught.

Kanja was plunged into silence again, that interminable silence.

Your father refused to raise armies against Egypt. Don't you remember?

"I remember." Kanja wanted to please. He wanted a chance. "*I* can take Egypt."

Oh yes, and you will.

Kanja smiled at that.

He had proved himself at the age of fifteen when his father took him to Makuria, a sister kingdom. They ravaged its people and lands and he took a Makurae woman for a wife, dragging her from the rubble of a once glorious palace. Kamara, smooth-skinned Kamara. O gods, she had driven him wild.

He closed sore eyes and tried to swallow, arms splayed above his head and he began to ride a hot wave of shame.

"It was my idea to kill Baba, not yours," he muttered.

Ulan sighed as if he had already lost the will to live. Only the gold disks that hung from stretched earlobes glinted as he turned his head. "Water," he said with an old man's whine. His once laughing eyes were distant and clouded with tears.

Kanja saw the wound, quick and festering and cursed the guard that had caused it. "You need more than water, brother."

"Where's the sorcerer? Why hasn't he come?"

Kanja wondered why Ulan couldn't remember the sorcerer's name. He had a sick sensation Ulan couldn't remember anything. The sorcerer had a key and he had promised them freedom. *Now is the time*, the sorcerer said, *to escape oppression, to escape defeat.* Defeat was unthinkable. It only happened to the enemy.

"It won't be long," Kanja soothed.

"Thank you," Ulan said, turning his unseeing gaze to the floor. Beads of sweat glistened on his face and chest, and his plump lips trembled.

Ulan was thankful for everything. He was a gentle spirit in the gathering dusk and he had the gift of sight. But his mind was gone, drifting peacefully on an ebbing tide.

He'll be free soon. You'll see.

Kanja listened for footsteps, longing for them. The sorcerer would clap him on the shoulder like an old friend, pumping his hand and grinning like a whore. But it was another day before he came. And when he did, Ulan was dead.

Shadows flitted across the cell wall, shadows Kanja could barely see. He shivered with grief, sobbing and coughing. He felt nothing as Othene unlocked his chains, nothing still as he sucked on the nozzle of a water skin.

"Don't look at him, my prince," Othene whispered as he broke the chains. "Your father still lives."

"The mourning—"

"It wasn't for him. It was for your wife. They strangled

her to pay for your crimes."

"No," Kanja uttered. It wasn't true. It couldn't be. "She was with child," he sobbed, remembering how the sorcerer had lifted the curse of her barrenness. Kamara was brave enough. She would have fought back. She would have bitten the guard that touched her. "Did they—"

"No, no, my prince," Othene said, unlocking the shackles. "Your father will be sorry though. I laced his boosa and now he's sleeping like a baby. Only he'll wake up in an hour and want his sorcerer. So we must fly, my prince, faster than the desert hawk."

"Ulan," Kanja sobbed, seeing his brother's bowed head and sunken cheeks.

"Your father can have him. But he can't have you. There's a throne in a far off land and a princess," Othene whispered like the papyrus stems in a lonely wind, only there was an urgency to it. "We must ride to Makuria and then to Egypt. And then we will make you a king. I will tell you what to do."

Kanja closed his eyes to the darkness and when he opened them again, he heard the bleating of goats and he could smell acacia and cow dung. He thought he was dreaming. Turning sideways on a cot, he heard drums in the distance but it was thunder that cracked overhead and rain that pattered against the lattice roof. There was a gap in the wattle about the size of a man's hand and through it he could see the emblem of Alodia tapering in the wind, a black snake on a white pennant.

A fickle wind, he thought, listening to the sound of footsteps slapping through the puddles, villagers cloaked against the rain.

He thought of his wife as he lay on that bed and he whispered her name. But she was lost in the realm of the dead and her spirit trampled the desert where his house had once been.

Strong fingers kneaded his scalp, washing the long braids that hung down his back and a sliver of energy coursed through his tired bones, seizing him with a strength he was not expecting. Dark eyes caressed him with a hunger that matched his own and he pulled the young girl down beside him in the lamplight, safe in the sorcerer's house, safe within the enkang, the circular fence that surrounded the village. She reminded him of Kamara, the name he called out in a rictus of bliss.

It was some time before he saw Othene hovering in the doorway, hand wrapped around an ornate curtain. He was a striking man, hair cropped short and dyed with henna, the mark of an elder.

"Greetings, my prince," Othene said, hooked nose wrinkling with a smile. "You are well rested I see. You have been asleep for five days."

Five days. Kanja held down a hungry wail of sorrow still groggy from joyroot. "Ulan," he moaned.

"They put him in a wooden coffin and wrapped his body in goatskin," Othene said, head tilted to one side. "I saw it in a dream."

The burial of a traitor. *Yes, a traitor . . .* Kanja sobbed, hands balled in a fist. In his mind he saw one set of footprints in the sand between the acacia trees, heading toward the horizon where the moon met the earth. He saw Ulan with the sweetness of a child, walking alone in the shining mist and he wanted to call out to him. But there was no voice in his throat. Then he saw Kamara with a baby in her arms.

"Oh gods," he said, bile stinging his throat.

"Let them go," whispered Othene. "They will never rest if you talk of them."

Kanja understood. He looked down at the girl in his cot, tender and tearful. "Thank you," he said, as Ulan would have done. It was the last time he would be thankful for anything.

Othene crouched at the bedside, voice tempered with cunning. "We're near the outskirts of Tungul. We'll be in Daben before the month of Hathor because we run on the heels of the devil. And we have the Pharaoh's seal."

The scarab seal was forged, of course, like so many they had pillaged from the bodies of Pharaoh's noblemen in the wars. It was a way in, the only way he could see.

Kanja rubbed his forehead, weighing his options. They had already crossed the border into Makuria, a kingdom his father had conquered long ago, and Thebes was still a long way off.

"How many warriors do we have?"

"Six hundred."

"And my brothers?"

"I couldn't leave them behind, my lord. Your father would have drowned the runts."

One *runt* was a ten-year-old child and the other had no mind at all. Kanja thought for a moment, mind spilling with schemes. "And when we get to Thebes, what will we tell the watchmen?"

"We will tell them King Ibada is ill. We will ask for Pharaoh's help." Othene eased into a slow smile and patted Kanja's arm. "They won't suspect a thing."

Kanja closed his eyes, smelling the roasted flesh of a ground squirrel. He was hungry for food and he was hungry for blood. Egypt would be his only if he could breach the many gates of Thebes. Once over the border, they would camp between two ergs on the east side of the river where herders raised swine in the lower precincts. Kanja's men would have their fill until they were strong again.

"Have my warriors sworn allegiance to the heartland? Will they do anything I ask?"

"They will die for you, if that's what you mean."

"All of them?"

"All of them."

Kanja sensed the fluttering of Othene's pulse, the glare of his milky eyes. "What is it?"

Othene cleared his voice and stood. "They tell me your father changed the succession. They tell me the youngest will rule."

Of course he did. Kanja ran his fingers through the red-painted cornrows at his scalp, shaved above his ears and falling in braids below his waist. He felt a shiver of anger, praying every day to the god Apepi to shower his father with the darts of death. The succession would have gone to Ayize, King Ibada's youngest son, since the eldest was dead, the second was a murderer and the third was a simpleton.

"What else did they say?"

"The voices tell me many things," Othene said. "There's a Vizier in the house of Thoth, the Pharaoh's most beloved. He's the Keeper of Seals and Overseer of the Secret Scrolls. And he's a friend of mine. It will be easy to cut down the supernatural power that protects the Pharaoh."

Kanja laughed and then straightened. "What about the man they call *Kemnebi*. Do you know him?"

"His name is Commander Shenq in the Theban tongue," Othene said tersely.

"Shenq," Kanja intoned, saying the name over and over in his mind. "Roll the bones. Tell me what they see."

Othene let the bones slip from his hand, small bones, finger bones. "They see a curved sword and a tongue of steel. He is the Pharaoh's shadow. Half man, half spirit."

The name *Shenq* made Kanja nervous, more so than a bull with bloodied horns. His influence ran deeper than a goat brand and he was a blood-seeker, a tormenter of sorts. *I might even like him*, Kanja thought. "I'll make you Chief of Prophets if you spin your magic and give me Thebes."

Othene's eyes snapped to the girl, mouth coursing into a grin. "Will you take her with you?"

Kanja hadn't thought about it. He glanced at the nut-brown girl with the pale staring eyes. Were they pale? He couldn't really see.

"She has your power inside her now," Othene said.

"She thinks you're beautiful. They all think you're beautiful. People are drawn to you like a tiny bird with a broken wing. I warn them but they still come. And I tell them, this bird is a battle hawk. He will not be swayed by gaudy trinkets and lemon oil."

Kanja waved a hand and watched her go, a body rain-soaked and desirable, a body he would never see again. "My father burned these villages a long time ago. I was a child but I remember it."

"Over ten years ago there was a palace in Tungul with walls of silver," Othene said, battle-scarred hand resting on his chest. "Its pennants could be seen as far as the fourth cataract. There is nothing left of it now. The moon-warriors are gone and there are more Alodians living here than Makurae. How do you think we got in?"

Kanja laughed as a bolt of lightning split the skies. But his laughter turned to grief as he remembered Ulan and the wide-mouthed wound on his belly. Goat's milk and honey slipped down his throat, salving the sores on his tongue but it did little to repel a fresh wave of pain. "Half of me is dead."

"For a time, yes. But the potions will help you forget."

Kanja dressed in a red shúkà wrapped around both shoulders and tied with a belt. He squeezed the ornate grip of his war bow carved from a stave of wood and greased with pig fat. Thrusting his way through a curtain at the door, he heard a slow roar of thunder in the distance.

"When do we leave?" he asked as the rain spattered against his cheeks.

Othene stood by his side breathing in the sharp night air. "When the moon is black. When no one can see us."

SHENQ

Commander Shenq stood on the terrace of the prince's apartments, staring east over the desert at dusk. The great river stretched below him, coiling to the north, splitting and choking around a small island and fading into the yellowish distance beyond.

Vapors curled upwards from a small ewer balanced on a metal tripod. The scent reminded him of cedar oil and galangal, too rich for the likes of him. The day was murderously hot and a warm Peret wind stirred the desert sand, billowing out like a lady's veil. It was this same wind that stirred the Pharaoh's ensign above the first pylon, spirited and free. But Shenq's heart was full of dreadful murmurs as he counted each peal of the temple bell. It was the third hour.

"Uncle?"

Shenq heard the sleepy voice and stepped back into the cool darkness of the prince's bedchamber. "My lord?"

There was no answer and Shenq brushed a hand over the slender shoulder and the boy tensed and then relaxed. Perhaps he dreamed of salt sea air and the rattle of spears, and the many rivers of the northern lands.

"Sleep," Shenq urged, before padding back to the balcony.

Even the sky looked different from where he stood, stars somehow closer, somehow brighter. And when he looked down, he could see flickering torches in the first court and the beacons on the pylon gates. Ribald laughter trickled from the West Villas, lodgings for the nobles in the palace precincts. They were laying bets on the Kamaraan, the Black Races. *Black* because runners came back wounded and wretched, if they ever came back at all.

"Uncle . . ." the prince murmured and Shenq hardly gave him a second look.

The crow-like call of a night heron snapped him back to the starry skies and he watched the bird as it sped north along the slip, clutching a blue-finned perch in its talons. He was the only man alive who knew dark days were coming and whether they would come by boat or by land, and he carried the knowledge with a cold shiver. The walled city of Thebes was the kingdom of priests and the seat of Amun, a god that meant nothing to him.

A large sycamore stood sentinel by a t-shaped pool where a model ship bobbed up and down on the ripples. Beyond that was a wall twelve feet high and he could see the great river through a web of palm fronds. Moonlight shimmered off green waters and he counted the fishing boats as they moved silently downriver, sails rippling in a gust of wind.

Seven, he thought. Always seven. If there were any more, he would have raised the alarm.

"Uncle?"

Shenq turned only his head and saw Prince Menkheperre staggering towards him, wiping the sleep from his eyes.

"I can't sleep," Menkheperre moaned. "And the incense is making me sick."

Shenq grabbed the offending ewer and hurled it into the gardens. "There," he said. "That should do it."

The prince chuckled as he watched the lighted coals bouncing like fireflies across the flagstones. "Looks like we're in for a squall," he murmured, leaning over the balustrade and cupping his chin in a bandaged hand. "I hate the wind. And the sand makes me sneeze."

"It comes from the south, my prince," Commander Shenq said. "Whatever comes, we'll be ready for it."

"Did I wake you?"

"A King's warrior never sleeps, my lord," Shenq said, grinning.

"I had a bad dream. I dreamt I was in my room in Memphis and it was dark, except for a girl dancing."

"And that was a bad dream?"

"She was all white and floaty like a ghost."

"Did you recognize her?"

"Ra-*ther*. It was Satiah, the General's daughter."

"They say she's a beauty," Shenq said, brushing a long strand of black hair back over one shoulder.

"I don't like them flabby, not like father does."

"Plump, I think you mean," Shenq said, wondering why the boy was always so whiny. If he spent less time cataloguing beetles and scorpions, he might have an eye for girls.

A cloud hung low over the river like a cloaked horseman, flying feverishly through the ripples. Shenq thought he could hear the drumming of hooves but there was nothing there.

"There are over a thousand birds on the river," Menkheperre said. "Their tracks are like a foreign language, a secret code. Cuneiform I should say. And there's an omen in the heron's bark."

"It's a mating call," Shenq said tersely.

"My tutor took me to study the river yesterday. The levels have dropped too far since the flood. He says there might be a famine next year."

"Give it time. It's only Peret," Shenq said, retreating to his stool. He unsheathed a long-bladed knife and rested it on his lap. The grating of the whetstone soothed him as he ran the blade along its edge.

"Father will be relieved." Menkheperre slowly released a deep breath.

"Well, that's a good thing then. Your father, I mean."

"Yes."

"His temper will blow over in a day or two," Shenq encouraged. "A priest was throttled for giving false dream interpretations and your mother no longer bleeds."

"Then I'm all he has, his only living son."

"A *warrior* son," Shenq said, thinking fast. "The kingdoms of Kush will be yours one day."

"Kush belongs to King Ibada now."

"Yes but does it?" Shenq said, biting his lip. "There is the small matter of succession, the small matter that King Ibada's brother was once the rightful king. His sons died with him in battle, all except a child who had somehow mastered the shortsword and a shield, a boy as rigorous as his training and with twice the courage of the *Kenyt-Nisu*. He stood on board that ship all those years ago with his father's blood between his toes. He never cried. Such was his courage."

"And now he's a bodyguard," Menkheperre whispered, finger tapping his lips.

"Khemwese was once a Meroëvian lord, but he's no longer a free man. Not unless your father lets him go."

"One day he will rebuild Meroë," Menkheperre insisted. "He'll breed sons and Kush will one day be on good terms with Egypt."

"Perhaps," Shenq murmured. "Until then he has no home. Except Thebes."

"Father despises Kush. The kings are handsome and they breed sons. No matter how much he wants their territories he would never fight them himself," Menkheperre shrugged. "He'd send you."

"It's a poor reason to take several thousand heads, don't you think?"

"There's more than a few thousand. Harran keeps dreaming of blood, waves of it, pouring over the sand dunes and spilling into Thebes."

Shenq smiled fondly at the mention of the young *Shasu* prophet. "The blood he refers to are armies of Bloodmen, the scourge of Kush. They're known by the red sheets they wear and their braided scalps."

"They burned Meroë and Makuria over fourteen years ago," Menkheperre said, nodding. "And now they've leached as far as lower Kush."

"They'll leach as far as the palace gates unless someone puts a stop to it. Perhaps they do us a favor. Khemwese will get a chance to see his cousins again without making that long ride home."

Menkheperre chuckled at that. "Perhaps they'll sail on the river current and be here in the morning."

"King Ibada is not well enough to sail. But he has four sons old enough to carry spears."

"You know something don't you?"

"I know it's the year of the Kamaraan," Shenq said, pushing all talk of the Alodian Bloodmen out of the prince's mind. "Your father will pit his finest commanders against one another as he always does."

Shenq had so far succeeded in retaining the title of Great Commander of Thebes since his unusual skill with the curved sword had contributed mightily to each victory. And if he was honest, the scrawny runts he frequently raced were no contest at all.

"I should like to go—"

"Too dangerous," Shenq provoked, lips curling around the idea. He tapped the breastplate across his broad chest, enjoying the song it made.

"You could talk to father," Menkheperre murmured.

"The warriors of the Kamaraan don't drink wine served in silver goblets in the desert, my prince. No, we must dig for water. We must kill for food. And *shakāl* are no match for the best of hunters." Shenq hated the jackal-like creatures that roamed the deserts, black and sleek like the guardians of the dead. Their meat was chewy and hard to swallow.

"I want to go."

"Your father would never agree." Shenq already had a plan, only he hoped the Pharaoh would not see through it. "You're his only son."

"A *warrior* son."

Shenq met his eyes and nodded at the bandage on the boy's hand. "Splitting logs is not unusual for a swordsman;

it strengthens the arm. We don't breed puppies in the yard."

There was admiration in the boy's face. Menkheperre would learn to fight wars. He would learn to lead.

"Vizier Ahmose hunted *shakāl*," Menkheperre said. "He had one as a pet. They're good for hunting fox."

"I remember that dog. It's wrapped in linens now and stuffed in a burial jar."

"I have something for you," Menkheperre said, opening a cedar chest. He pulled out a sword with a curved blade and a sheath of the finest leather. Engraved on the pommel was the scepter of Thebes and there was a small star on the crossguard. So sharp was its edge it could take off a man's head with one slice. "Take it. You're my champion."

Shenq sucked in breath. "It's a fine piece," he murmured, slicing and cutting the air. He brought the khopesh to a halt but not before whittling a shard of wood from a table leg.

"It was forged in Irqata." Menkheperre sighed and bit his lip. "Ahmose asked me to keep it for you."

"It was his?" Shenq saw the rapid nod and placed the Khopesh on the table with both hands. "I'm honored he thought of me."

"So, you'll talk to my father?"

Shenq grinned. "I'll talk to your father."

There was a long moment of silence before Menkheperre spoke again. "Why won't he go hunting with us? The palace is stuffy and dark. I hate the dark."

"Your father is rather partial to it."

"Remember the Alodian traitor you killed last year. He died in the dark, didn't he?"

"I stabbed him in the back and pushed him down a well. No man would have survived it," Shenq said impatiently, recalling the traitor by the many faces he wore.

"No *ordinary* man."

"He was flesh and bone."

"What if someone found him?"

"They wouldn't know where to look."

Menkheperre tapped Shenq on the arm. "He's in father's tomb isn't he?"

Shenq shrugged. He didn't much care. "What's left of him, yes."

"What if King Ibada is watching us right now? What if he's dressed as a snake—"

"He's too sick to stand let alone dress up. He sent emissaries to Thebes a year ago to steal your father's gold. We killed them then and we'll kill them now."

Menkheperre forced a smile, though his face twitched with uncertainty. "Father clutches his belly and groans like a hag. He thinks he's about to die."

"Indigestion," Shenq muttered, recalling a loud gust from the Pharaoh's latrine.

"When we went to the shrine this morning, I saw a girl with golden hair," Menkheperre said, head aslant. "Father knew I liked her. So he sent for her and rutted her right there in front of me. She meant nothing to him."

"When your father slips away to the Great Fields, he'll ride with the lost. And when he falls, there will be no one to pick him up. It's a choice." Shenq was appalled but refused to show it. The Pharaoh was more *dog* than dog.

"But he doesn't care."

"No, but there'll be a time when he will. He's plagued with shadows and the darkest of these is ignorance. He rules the largest nation on earth but he'll never capture the imagination of the world. When you're Pharaoh, remember the girl with the golden face. These people fight for leftovers in the ashes of a nobleman's fire. They have no champion."

Menkheperre rubbed his temples as if they throbbed. "I don't want to be like father."

"You're a soldier," Shenq said, caution creeping into his voice.

He lifted the sword from the table and tilted the blade

to inspect the grain.

"What do you really think of him?"

Shenq hesitated, feeling a tinge of excitement. "He's a brother and a great king. But he's greatly off his feed."

Menkheperre began to snigger. "I asked him to help me dissect a frog yesterday only he came over all queasy. He said I had no right to kill it."

"I imagine it still bothers him."

"Reserve isn't the mark of a true soldier is it?"

"Not unless you consider frogs divine."

"Well he doesn't. So I thought it odd."

Shenq mused over the Pharaoh's state of mind. Three days ago, he found a Hittite girl in the library stealing books. He bent her over to give her a few lashings, saw how pretty she was and changed his mind. He had hardly left his bed since.

"It's quiet tonight," Menkheperre said. "Even the river horses have wandered too far inland."

"They're looking for grass." Shenq tasted the sour juice of frustration in his throat. He wanted to rush out beyond the city gates and slash a few enemies with his new sword. Instead, here he was in a vaporous den where the incense was heavier than his conscience.

"You should have gone home hours ago," Menkheperre said, waving one hand.

"Pharaoh's worried about your dreams."

"I had a dream about a dog eating a bird two days ago. There was nothing left but blood and bones."

"What do the diviners say?"

"They say it's just a storm." Menkheperre picked absentmindedly at the bandage on his hand. "What do you believe?"

"I believe in Harran's dream. I believe dark days are coming." The marrow of Shenq's bones seemed to creep with uncertainty, filled with sharp-knifed memories when women mourned their dead and washed bloodstained garments in the canals. "And I believe a warrior needs his sleep even if he's not old enough to shave."

Shenq looked at the boy with all the swagger of a man, room filled with the jewels Pharaohs like to wear. He had earned none of his wealth on the battlefield. "Best get some sleep."

"You'll be back at dawn then?"

"I'll be back at dawn."

Shenq re-sheathed the sword and slung it across his back. He walked through the palace corridors knowing Menkheperre would sleep better than his father. Pharaoh frequently stared at a star-studded ceiling, muttering like a madman and gripping an axe under his pillow.

He should be dead by now with all that worrying, thought Shenq, taking the reins of his horse from a stable boy. He swung his leg over the saddle and rode through the open courts to the parting cries of the night watchman.

A fresh breeze brushed against his cheeks and he was glad for the good clean air, not really thinking, just listening to the soft thud of the horse's hooves. Lanterns hung from the trees, pouring a sultry beam on the remains of a watchman's fire where pans of roasting meat and fresh bread were often cooked. Shenq rested one hand on a simple leather belt where he kept a skinning knife secreted on the nap side, forged of obsidian and sharper than an arrowhead. It came in handy some years ago when an enemy took all his weapons and forgot to take his belt.

There was a presence at the river's edge where grassy clumps twitched and bobbed in the shallows and something moved between them. There was no way of knowing if it was a dark rugged man taking a midnight swim or a wild dog taken beneath the water by a crocodile. He decided to go for the latter with all that splashing and hissing, and for a moment the breath caught in his throat. He could have sworn he saw the foxlike face of a man, grinning wanly from under a headdress of conch shells.

Shenq watched. He waited. And then all went quiet.

KANJA

Vultures quarreled over a carcass on the east bank, and their dusty-gray plumage was spattered with blood. One took to the skies and flew over a sandy erg, alighting near the opening of a goat-hide tent. Timber dwellings stretched from a central fire like the spokes of a giant chariot wheel and a large dung pile promised a belly full of scraps.

Kanja sat by the fire, slipping in and out of a trance. It was the joyroot that made him dream. He saw the bloodstained knife on his lap and wondered what manner of man he had just killed. A herald he thought it was, a runner from his father's palace. He kept a steady eye on the river paths just in case he saw a few more. They were bringing news of King Ibada and his runaway sons.

They won't get through, Kanja thought, caressing the miniature arrow stitched through his lower lip. Wrought in gold, the arrowhead was a blood-red gemstone from the southern mines.

"Ayize!" he said, catching sight of his youngest brother reaching for the vulture with an outstretched hand. "Don't feed it."

"He's hungry and his heart will tell the future," Ayize crooned.

The vulture had a rich robe of feathers and a clever eye. Kanja could understand the boy's interest. "Kill it."

"No! I won't kill him. He's found food for us every day."

Kanja eyed his brother thoughtfully. The bird had circled the skies with the accuracy of a divining rod and it wasn't all dead meat it found.

"Kill it," Kanja urged.

28

The bird's heart was what he needed to see into the future, to see his enemy. It was like the first bird he had ever killed as a boy, blacker than a dung beetle and talons curled over a fallen branch.

"Baba says they're sacred." Ayize shrugged, batting sand-caked eyes. "Baba says they're gods."

"If we eat the meat, won't we be sacred too?"

Kanja studied the boy with the hazel eyes and wide cheeks. His nut-brown braids were streaked with red dye and hung to his knees. He would be eleven in a month. *An innocent,* he thought, locked for a moment behind closed eyes. He began to see the dark-filled corridors in his father's palace and the bedchamber hung with scarlet drapes. He couldn't remember how many times he had tried to poison his father, how he had tried to smother him with a pillow because he wouldn't die. And when the guards came, they carved a hole in Ulan's belly wider than a yawn.

Ayize did not know who tried to kill his *Baba* and Kanja prayed he would never find out.

"We will find medicine for Baba, won't we?" Ayize said behind narrowed eyes.

Kanja nodded. "We'll find the medicine. Remember, we must be fierce and swift, and we must slay and destroy. The snake is our bond. Pray to him."

"I don't know what to say?"

Kanja loved that smile. "Say you are his servant. Say you will do anything he asks. Do it so Baba won't die."

Ayize lay prostrate in the sand and whispered the mantra with one eye open. He seemed to study the vulture with its waddling gait, beak covered in dung and insects.

"Do you miss your mother?" Kanja asked.

"I miss her stories." Ayize lifted his chin and narrowed his eyes. "Sometimes I cry for her."

"Warriors don't cry."

"Do you still see Ulan in your dreams?"

Kanja was surprised at the remark and nodded all the

same. "Always."

"Do you think he still sees us?"

"Every day." Kanja looked up at the sky and felt a tightening in his throat. He would have sobbed then but not in front of the boy.

"You are the voice in the moon, the light in the sun and the star in my heart. You are all things to me," Ayize said, lifting his shoulders, face covered in sand.

"Don't say that. Not now."

"But Baba said it to Ulan when he chose him. He said it when he put the crown on his head. You remember."

"Yes, I remember." Kanja sighed, wishing the guilt would go away.

"When will I be pierced?"

"When you kill that bird. And only if you promise to keep our secret."

"I promise," Ayize said, unhooking a small sling from his belt.

Kanja stretched out his muscular legs blackened by the sun and wondered how many crocodiles he had seen in the river last night. Two, three? He'd poked at least one with an arrow and all it did was hiss and grin and he wanted to smoke as many as he could find. He liked the meat. He liked the chase. And he liked the long-haired horseman he had seen on the path. He couldn't be bothered to follow him, but he would if he ever saw him again.

Ayize tore after the vulture and Kanja could hear the thrum of wings and the whorl of the sling. "Use your knife!" he shouted, chuckling.

The trees rustled in a brisk wind and the fire crackled, spitting ash across the desert floor. Goats stamped and flicked their tails in a nearby enclosure and there were pigs in the lower precincts, tasty when roasted.

The sound of the river lulled Kanja for a moment as he thought of Thutiy, Vizier and Keeper of Seals. A priest with pale-eyes—gray he thought they were—and skin smoother than polished marble. He was there when they arrived, falling prostrate on the ground as if he greeted a king. He had full access to the Pharaoh's revenue and the password of each city gate.

Kanja laughed at that. And he laughed when Thutiy told him about the princess, a girl more pleasing than a raincloud in the desert. How he had encouraged her with tales of the Bloodmen, a tribe so fertile they were sure to breed sons.

"I've told her to long for you in secret. And now she can't think of anything else," Thutiy said. "I have told her you are a noble commander. Egyptian princesses are permitted to marry commanders."

Soon, Kanja whispered, longing for her all the more.

Theban women were beautiful but they did not believe in the circumcision necessary to wives. He would have to cut her himself.

"Look!" The voice startled Kanja and he opened his eyes.

The head of a vulture hung from Ayize's bloody fist and there was a tiny red heart in his other hand. Kanja whooped, pumping the air with his fist. The boy was ready, small, but ready.

Othene appeared at the doorway of a nearby tent, sniffing loudly and patting a choker of beads. "May Apepi bring you health and happiness," he said, bottom lip adorned with cylinders of gold, the decorations of a diviner.

"Tell the great god to bring me this *Shenq*," Kanja murmured, thinking of the black leopard, seeing him in his thoughts, seeing him in his dreams. "What's his range?"

Othene sat down and stared upriver. "One hundred paces, easy, and more. They say he can launch three arrows one after another, smooth and true. He never misses."

"Bows?"

"Horn and ebony and strung with lion gut. But it's their arrowheads you need to watch. Hammered bronze and sharper than a dog's tooth."

"Are you afraid of him?"

"The men are. They say he can kill with his very eyes. I saw him on the river once. He stood on the Pharaoh's ship, watching the waves as if he could see what was under them. When the ship passed over there was hundreds of dead fish in the water."

Kanja felt his neck stiffen. He was the leader of the Bloodmen, a company more deadly than the Pharaoh's honored ones. When they raised their swords in battle all the enemy saw was a forest of curved blades held aloft in strong arms. Those same swords would test Shenq's spirit.

Letting the vulture heart slip through his fingers into the fire he said, "What do the ashes say?"

"The spirit speaks," Othene said, eyes rolling. His body began to shake and the beads at his throat rattled like the rasping coils of a viper. "A rider comes from the north. His sword will strike the snake . . . shadows with white faces."

"What does it mean?" prompted Kanja, crouching beside him. He respected the ways of the ancients.

Othene opened his eyes. "Death."

"*His* death you mean." Kanja snorted, feeling the chill of dead hands on his back. He was tired of waiting.

Othene's face took on a pasty glow. "You must drink muti and rub your body with fat."

"Don't tell me what to do. Tell me what you *see*!"

"Yellow eyes. They see you. They see me. And I see another prince, tall and proud. He is the foreshadowing of things to come."

The lost prince was a legend, of course, but it didn't stop Kanja dreaming of him almost as much as his wife's dying screams. His uncle had once been king of Alodia until he died on the battlefield and his sons surrendered their throats to Egyptian knives. If one had survived, he would be first in line to the Alodian throne.

"Are you sure?" Kanja said, staring at the sorcerer's hair, freshly hennaed and yellower than a vulture's beak.

"Have I not thrown bones and interpreted all your dreams, my prince?" Othene said, mouth full of empty chivalry.

Kanja gave an angry shrug and spat in the sand. "I want his beating heart in my hand. Find him!"

"I will ask the spirits," Othene said, closing his eyes again. "I see standing stones. I see a sword."

"He's already dead then. What an honor. What a relief."

Kanja snatched a human braid of hair that hung from Othene's belt. It was imbued with miraculous power and once hung from his father's head. The king had no power without it and he was bedridden now so it didn't matter. He closed his eyes and saw a man standing in the light of a full moon at harvest. His war cry was like a lion's roar and in his hand was a curved sword. Kanja thought he saw a star on the crossguard, simple as it was, but he had no idea what it meant.

"There's something else," Othene said in a low musing voice. "It's the season of the Kamaraan. They say the winner this year will have the hand of the princess. You should compete, my prince."

"And how will I do that?"

"I will do the dance of the snakes tonight. And it will come to pass."

HARRAN

Harran awoke from an afternoon nap to a foot against his shoulder. He turned on his pallet at the end of the Pharaoh's bed and thanked Commander Shenq. He would never have woken on his own.

Dressed in a tunic and *tallit*, he crept to the terrace, careful not to wake the Pharaoh. The mountains were somber in the gray light and he began to pray. The boughs of the great sycamore groaned in the courtyard below as a powerful twister swept across the plains, spitting out yellow sand as it went. He had seen the same spool of dust in a dream only this one had red flames in its belly and a war cry that would bring down the palace of the Great Bulls. The southern lands of Kush never slept and every year a war party attacked the border fortresses, slinking towards the many gates of Thebes.

As he tracked a black kite above the river mists with a green stem in its beak, he pressed two fingers to his lips in a phantom kiss and praised his Father in Heaven.

Have courage, child, it seemed to whisper as it slipped past on a dipped wing.

I'm ready, Harran said without words.

Ready for what, he didn't know but he could still smell the stench of charred embers from the dream he had. Vizier Thutiy seemed to think the sky would swallow the moon in twenty-five days and that the Nile would be swarming with frogs before the week was out.

Liar, thought Harran. He hadn't heard a croak.

He saw Commander Shenq out of the corner of his eye, nocking an arrow in a buffalo horn bow. He was standing on the corner of the balcony shooting rabbits again.

"It's started," Shenq whispered. "My captain found three dead men in the woods this afternoon. Bloodmen it seems."

"Pharaoh received a report from King Ibada three days ago," Harran whispered. "His four sons have escaped across the border."

"Escaped?"

"Two were imprisoned for trying to poison their father."

"Pharaoh didn't mention it."

"He wouldn't. He didn't want you shooting things in the desert and starting a war."

Shenq swatted a fly, trapping it in a tight fist. "Seventeen years ago, the Alodians wanted to unite all the provinces of Kush and let one king rule in Meroë. They would have been strong enough to go against Egypt then if we hadn't culled their numbers. If Ibada's sons are on our land, I'll find them." He tugged absentmindedly at the bronze bracer on his arm. "Did you hear drums last night?"

"Drums, sir?" Harran shook his head. "Vizier Thutiy has a drum. I didn't think he played it though."

"Seems he likes talking to the trees. Seems he's waiting for something."

Harran had seen him too. Strange eyes and a mouth that smiled too much, the Vizier often loitered in the herb garden crooning over his snakes. "He's been sniffing around the Pharaoh's library, sir."

"He's looking for these," Shenq said, tapping the sacred scrolls on the Pharaoh's gaming table.

Harran looked at the fat leather case brought in earlier by the master scribe. It was bound with braided thongs and sealed with the eye of Horus. "What does he want them for?"

"He wants to trade them for a kingdom." Shenq's golden eyes glowed as if he had just run a victory lap. "And one more thing, if Pharaoh mentions the Kamaraan, listen well and tell me what you hear."

It was that time again. Shenq had won the title for three consecutive years and there was a chance he would win it again. Harran glanced at the Pharaoh, spread-eagled in his bed. He had lost the greater part of the afternoon to a jug of sweet wine and there was a wad of linen in his mouth, all bloody from a bad tooth.

"Looks like rain," Harran said loudly. It rarely rained in the desert.

Pharaoh Kheper-Re sat up in bed, tugging at the linen poultice. Bloodshot eyes peered out from a tangle of hair as he hobbled to the table on the terrace like a blind man.

"Blasted drums," he said, sinking deep into his chair. "They kept me up all night."

"Drums?" Harran said.

"Yes, spirit-drums, you fool." Kheper-Re tapped the scrolls on his table with the flat of his hand. "You would have heard them yourself if you weren't so deaf."

"I sleep too soundly, my lord," Harran said, scratching a close-cut beard.

"I should starve you. You'd stay awake then."

Harran hoped the Pharaoh was teasing. He was looking forward to his supper. There was yesterday's bowl of stew left on the floor between the bed and the terrace, only the Pharaoh's cheetah had got to it first. The animal lapped and gulped so frantically, Harran hoped it was having a seizure.

He gazed over Shenq's lofty frame and long black hair. He was dressed in a *shenti*, a garment of black-dyed flax wrapped around his thighs, and from his belt hung an elaborate sash stamped with a cartouche of his name. Like the prized horses of the northern Bedouin with their refined heads and high-tailed carriage, an enemy would be in awe of such refinement.

"Will you swear on the book of Horus to give up your God? Will you?" Kheper-Re snatched a brightly colored flail from the floor and played it from hand to hand.

"You tried that one yesterday, my lord," Harran said, keeping very still. "And the answer was no."

Kheper–Re gave Harran a sour glance before looking up at the sky. "I never had bad dreams before you came. Not a single one!"

"If you recall, beloved Pharaoh, that's why you sent for me in the first place."

"I sent for you on Commander Shenq's recommendation. He said you could see into the future. He said you could read the stars better than my High Priest."

"Then the Commander forgot to mention it is HaShem that interprets, not me."

"What does your God say about the stars today? Why are they so different?"

It was amazing the Pharaoh could see anything at all; two squinty eyes no longer as sharp as they once were. *He can feel it too,* thought Harran, a shift in the wind, a change in the season. "An omen," was all he said.

"An omen?" Kheper-Re stared ahead as if he could see the dust cloud barreling towards him, sinking to earth. "Tell me the truth."

"Truth is sharper than a sword, my king. Can you bear it?"

"I am a god. I can bear anything." Kheper-Re looked on with his sad, black eyes. Only there was a rogue behind them, ready to jump out when least expected.

"I saw a great fire, my lord, one that devoured your city." Harran ran a hand through a wave of dark hair. "There were no survivors. Not one."

"You had the same dream last year," Kheper-Re said. His face was harder than rock and just as remote. "And now there's another?"

"This is the last of it, my lord. These armies are cutting a path towards Thebes. Who knows, they could have been hiding in the desert for months."

"There's no way in. The city walls are impenetrable.

Why is it danger clings to me like a parasite?"

"Remember HaShem and he will remember you."

"He doesn't know me." Kheper-Re came to his feet in one swift movement, fingers curled in a fist. "He's the God of your fathers not mine."

"He made you."

"Ptah made *me* from the rays of the sun. *You* were made from dirt."

Harran had stood long enough on that rocking ship. It was time to unfurl his sails. "How many times have you asked me where I get my joy? And how many times have I told you it comes from what I carry in my heart—"

"Joy? Where's the joy in your meager life! You sleep on floors, you eat nothing but scraps." Kheper-Re thrust out his chest, arms wide from his body. "I am Ra, Pharaoh of Egypt. Only kings live in palaces. Only kings are buried in the sacred mountains. Only I can read the sacred scrolls and determine the fate of Thebes. *That*, my boy, is joy."

Harran chewed on the end of a reed pen, temper roiling with every word. The scrolls were little more than myth and as for the priests he knew how they favored the east bank, how they frowned on the west. How they secretly considered themselves higher than the Pharaoh and built lavish tombs in their own names. "The grand Vizier must consider himself king then. He's built a tomb in the mountains far bigger, I understand, than yours."

"Liar! If it's blood you've come to see I'll give you blood!" Kheper-Re stumbled forward and swung the flail. The strike missed Harran as he spun out of the way and the flail swept across the tiles, thongs streaming out behind. "Next you'll tell me he took six fat virgins from my harem and a cartload of my best grain."

"Not women, my lord. It was six casks of dates and salt fish, and a chest of silver."

"Mustn't forget the silver," Shenq piped up from the balcony.

"He's too used to eating off my plate. I'll pull the

coward out from behind a wall and rip his head off with my own teeth," Kheper-Re said. "And then I'll stitch it back on with cat gut. He'll beg me to staunch the bleeding. I won't, of course."

Harran cleared his throat and wondered when the ludicrous tirade would stop. On and on it went until the Pharaoh began to shiver, knees knocking together like a dinner gong.

"He was a good friend and now he's betrayed me. How can he build a tomb larger than mine?" Kheper-Re sniveled as he cuffed away an angry tear. "Fetch me a blanket."

Harran gave the Pharaoh his arm and eased him into a chair. The stench of wine was strong in the air and bolstered by the sounds of belching. "Pride is the easiest route, my lord," he said, snapping his fingers at an attendant. "Never the safest."

"You are a good friend," lamented Kheper-Re, allowing the attendant to wrap the blanket around his knees. "I stand chastened and rebuked."

If it wasn't for the dribbling, Harran would have believed it. Kheper-Re was never more than a washed sow returning to wallow in the mire.

"The stars have predicted many things," Kheper-Re said, rolling up an empty sheet of papyrus and peering through it for signs in the heavens. "There are two bright ones on the northern horizon. It means someone's about to die."

"Then we must send an army to the southern borders," Harran advised, knowing Pharaoh saw little further than the quartz eyes of a stone lion. "Prince Menkheperre longs for battle, my lord. And he's old enough."

"Menkheperre is a frail boy who enjoys the rustle of books. He's a thinker. That's what the stars say. You try too hard, my precious friend. No one is going anywhere." Kheper-Re stared at his feet and there was a pout to his lip larger than a camel. "The Grand Vizier is building tombs you say? Send him in."

Vizier Thutiy was warming his bony rear by the central brazier, leaning against one of the four pillars that surrounded it. "How is our Great Bull today?" he whispered as he saw Harran approach.

"His tooth's bothering him. He's not in the best of humor."

"Nonsense. He's drunk," Thutiy said, waving two ring-filled fingers. "Tell me, you live in his apartments. You know his routine. Why, you even know what food he enjoys. Isn't that so, boy?"

Harran's mind was like a cloud of moths buzzing about his ears. The comment was more obliging than inquiring. "I scribe for him—"

"But you know when he eats and when he sleeps?" Thutiy said, headdress shimmering about his ears. "You interpret his dreams and translate his letters. He'll have no one else other than Commander Shenq and that Kushite there," he said pointing at Khemwese, the Pharaoh's bodyguard.

Harran knew the statement was an opportunity to exploit him, to find a scapegoat. But he was no whipping boy to fetch and carry. He wondered if the smooth-faced Vizier had any idea who he was, whether he remembered a boy that once cried for his mother, a boy that gripped the hand of his little sister until it was snatched away.

"I'm honored the Pharaoh has entrusted me with so much," he said with a little satisfaction.

"You don't trust me, do you?" Thutiy said, tilting his head to one side. "You think I'm Shaitan."

Harran put his hand up to restrain any talk of the one who avoids the light. But he couldn't stop the judging mouth, the pointing finger and the slander.

"That Kushite is just about as filthy as you are. How Pharaoh can stand the sight of you, I will never know! One would assume you both have a secret. One would assume our precious Pharaoh is afraid of you. Is he?"

"He's afraid of my God," Harran said, wiping the Vizier's spittle from his face. "Blessed is He who brings forth bread from the earth. No one is like Him."

"Liar! Your heart is blacker than soot—"

"Only the Holy One knows what's in my heart," Harran said, smiling.

"Do you want to swallow my dagger?"

Harran wondered if it was a trick question. So many were and they left him confused. "Let me think."

"Think? Your kind doesn't *think*," Thutiy said, tapping his head. "From now on, *Shasu*, you will refer to me as Good Master. You will say it over and over again until it's ingrained in that thick head of yours."

Harran wanted to block his ears from a voice as jarring as a pig's squeal only he kept blurting things out he knew he would regret. "A master is only good if he can truly love his servant."

"I should tell the Pharaoh how vulgar you are, how filthy your mouth is. You never learn."

"I would learn better if I wasn't led by a train of mules, my lord."

"You should be afraid of me. *Very* afraid."

"I'm afraid of snakes," Harran offered as he walked the Vizier to the Pharaoh's door. "Truly I am, especially the thick gray ones with black beads for eyes. There's nothing more deadly, more rapid."

"One of these days, I'll smother you in rotting fish and leave you outside for the dogs. It's only a matter of time." Thutiy straightened as they passed through the door and his voice lowered to a whisper. "What did our beloved Pharaoh eat today?"

"Eel and kidney pie," Harran said.

"Did he vomit?"

"He kept all his food down. Except the lentils. He hates lentils."

"You're sure."

"Quite sure."

"Quite sure *Good Master*," Thutiy corrected. He brushed past Harran, face twisted with rage. "Ah, glorious Son of Ra, may you live forever . . ."

Harran watched as Pharaoh held out his hand for the Vizier to kiss. He barely listened to the platitudes as a memory lodged itself in his mind, a sandstorm in the desert and a company of the Pharaoh's men. It was so long ago, he could barely remember his father's eyes, one brown, one green, or the scent of his wiry hair. They took him to Kush to work in the mines and they took Harran to Thebes to scribe for the Pharaoh. But it was his sister's screams he could still hear, animal-like as they faded into the distance. Meryt, sweet innocent Meryt, a virgin for the Queen's palace is what they said. And all the while a priest looked on, cracking a six-tailed whip. It was Thutiy all right. Harran would never forget eyes like that.

The vision dissolved and he was no longer a slave in the desert but the Pharaoh's most trusted Prophet.

"A falcon told me you had stolen treasure and hid it in a tomb," Kheper-Re said. "I didn't believe him, of course, because if you had, I would have stripped you naked and fed you to the jackals. You may be Grand Vizier but I am Ra, giver of life. The penalty of outdoing the Pharaoh is death. I am not as heartless as some people think; on the contrary, I am a compassionate man. But it is important I have your support."

"You have my support, Pharaoh, as keeper of the royal seals," Thutiy said, edging closer to the table.

"Who knows perhaps one day you will be keeper of nothing. Tell me, what are you building in the mountains?"

Thutiy said nothing for a moment and then groaned. "It was meant as a surprise, my lord. It is a glorious tomb for my glorious Pharaoh. A tomb with twelve gates."

"*Twelve?*" Kheper-Re gasped. "It must be deeper than hell."

"I wanted to show you the tomb at the Festival of Anubis, Great Bull. Now the secret is out, I would like to

42

wring that falcon's neck if I could catch him."

"You will never catch him. He has golden wings and lives in the heavens. Isn't that so, *Shasu*?"

Harran felt like nodding, although it had never once occurred to him that he was anything like an angel. He decided not to make any sudden movements that might make the Pharaoh suspicious and besides, the joyroot was beginning to wear off.

"And where will you be buried, Vizier?" Kheper-Re rubbed his jaw with a finger.

"Oh, I have a small nook above the tombs of the artisans. It is hardly bigger than a burrow in its current state."

"Then I insist you shall be buried with me," Kheper-Re offered. "My father stopped the tradition of taking servants with him to the underworld and replaced them with *shabtis*."

"The little wooden slaves are an excellent substitute, Pharaoh," Thutiy quickly returned. "The sealing of good men in a tomb is such a waste."

Kheper-Re gave a freakish smile and shook his head. "*Men*, yes, but not Viziers. I think you would serve me well. Let's hope for your sake you die before me. Come, we must not keep Amun waiting."

Kheper-Re worked hard to show he was sober. But the chair pitched sideways as he vacated it and he shot forward like a dart from a blow-pipe. Scrunched on a rug, his hand was wrapped around his privates and the sound of cackling bubbled from his throat.

"To the shrine, my lord," Harran pressed in a good-natured lilt. He held out his hand and pulled Pharaoh to his feet, hoping no one would hear the Commander's gargling laughter. "The sun is already on the horizon. The divisions of Ra await you."

"I might be attacked on the road," Kheper-Re said with a lowered head.

"No one has ever been attacked on a straight road,"

Harran whispered.

"The people don't want to see me. Not like this."

"There are crowds out there, people who love you," Harran assured, hoping the avenue was teeming with more than just angry farmers throwing rotten fish.

"Then I will give them my last drop of blood, my last meal," Kheper-Re said. "Well, maybe not my last meal. Too much honey is bad for the teeth. Isn't that so?"

"They would need a great deal of it," Harran said, trying to straighten Kheper-Re from a stoop. "As it stands, most have never eaten honey. Nor have they tasted wine."

"Are they mad?"

"They're poor," Harran said.

Thutiy grinned savagely and pushed his way forward. "Out of my way, shepherd and get your filthy hands off the Son of Ra." He took Kheper-Re's arm and led him through the great hall followed by the Commander.

Harran gave a helpful smile and bowed. He hated the cloying smell of incense and the tedious monotones of priestly chants. Instead, he shared a look with Khemwese that gave rise to a snort of laughter. It was then his eyes darted to the table.

The sacred scrolls were gone.

SHENQ

Shenq had a few secrets of his own as he rode with two of his men through the city gates towards the river path. He stared at the emblem of Thebes emblazoned on the palace pennants and hanging limp on its pole. It was the scepter of the fourth Nome—a symbol of authority—and it would stay that way if he could help it. His sword was plenty sharp enough to scare Vizier Thutiy if he found him by the water's edge with a snake curled around one arm. Last he knew, he was burning rats and chanting a mantra to awaken a storm.

Storm? What storm? The only storm Shenq knew about was the khamāsīn and that was four months away during the Festival of the New Moon.

"Clear night, sir," he heard Captain Tehute say. "Good for snaring a bird or two."

Shenq sensed the drift of Tehute's thoughts. He longed to race in the Kamaraan. "Talking of snares, there's always game in the desert. You'll both ride with me in the Kamaraan. That I promise."

"Thank you, sir," Meru-Itseni said, teeth flashing behind a wide smile.

"You understand the risk?"

Tehute spoke first. "My sister looks after the child now my wife is dead. They don't need an old man like me."

Meru-Itseni bit his lip and turned his face to the ground. "When I go home every night I feel like a young god. My wife waits for me in the courtyard, sure she can hear me coming over the honking geese. I am full of love for her. She runs barefoot to meet me, calling my name and wrapping herself around me in a way that's always new."

"And your son?" Shenq asked, imagining the tiny child with a wooden horse in one hand. Jabari's horse. He carved all the toys for the village children.

"He waits until I walk under the gate. And then he takes my hand like a man and says, 'how was your day, father?' And I always tell him. 'Better for seeing you, my son.'"

Shenq shivered as if a cold breeze caressed his spine. He couldn't help but think of the small child, how he would be if his father never came home. In that same moment, he yearned for a boy of his own. "Get some sleep. I want no yawning in the palace tomorrow."

Meru-Itseni and Tehute saluted and wheeled their horses around. Shenq watched them canter towards the village, leaving him in a wake of dust. He patted his horse, caressing the black stripe that ran down its back. The animal nickered now and then and Shenq whispered his name.

"Marees, what do you see?"

The horse lifted his head and snorted, and Shenq twisted in his seat to study at the path behind him. A sand rat darted between the trees carrying a lizard in its mouth. There was nothing else in the shadows, nothing he could see.

His mind tumbled with visions of a horde of tribesmen who might one day sit outside the city gates, drinking blood and conjuring demons. There were no traitorous men to let them in but there was one who held the keys to the city gates.

Vizier Thutiy had risen rapidly from the rank of Overseer of the Gold and Silver Houses, taking over old Vizier Ahmose duties after he died. He would have taken over his villa, too, if it hadn't been for the sharp end of Mkasa's sword and a few well-chosen words. The moon-warrior wasn't about to surrender his childhood home to a court flatterer.

Shenq's spine stiffened when he thought of Mkasa. The

warrior was brave and curious, a little too *curious* in his opinion. He had glanced more than once at Shenq's child-wife and if he was tempted to do it again there would be a rattle of harsh words.

Putting aside all jealousy, he watched the moon as it danced on the water and he heard the rapid whinny of a black kite overhead. Pale mists rose up from the reeds, thick enough for a man to hide in and he saw a flicker of light through the trees. It was hard to say what it was, a fire maybe or the ferryman's torch giving off the stench of pitch and sooty smoke.

As the ground sloped towards an overhang of sycamores, he heard the harsh call of an egret as it rose out of the water, long legs trailing behind. But a slender dart struck it through the belly, bringing the bird down with a splash. Shenq could not make out the color of the fletchings nor could he see a hunter in the shallows.

He reined his horse around, eyes scanning the marshes and the winking stars in the night sky. Lovers frequented the canals now and then, wrestling naked in the silt. But there was a mood in the air so threatening; it slashed at his thoughts like a sand cat raking the dirt with its paw.

Content to watch from his shadowy nook, he heard the squealing of a beaten piglet and saw seven warriors at the water's edge hauling a crocodile through the shallows. A man stood nearby, stick poised in mid-air. He used the lure of the piglet's screams to attract the crocodile to a line of bait.

Shenq felt the prickling then, the knowledge that danger was close. Dismounting, he took the bow from his shoulder and ran through the reeds. Crouching ten paces upriver and head craning for a better view, he saw three reed boats crossing the river, riding the current with powerful oars. Two warriors moored them to an old tree root and their hand signals indicated the need for secrecy. They were dark-skinned, *hebony* by the look of them and their hair was long and woven in braids. Disks of ivory covered a defined point at the hairline, nestling at the center of each forehead.

Bloodmen and Snakers, Shenq thought counting seven of them, bodies a shine of water.

They bound the crocodile's jaws and smeared its eyes with mud. It became suddenly still as if the vapors from a nearby brazier had smoked it to sleep. A warrior took out a knife and cut into the chorded belly, holding up a bloody finger to a boy on the verge of manhood. Three smears on the boy's forehead and the warriors whooped.

Kissed by blood, Shenq thought. A real man now.

They chattered freely as they divided the meat, skewering it over the brazier. There was a musical strain to their language similar to the tribal Makurae and where Makurae favored hues of malachite, these men preferred the colors of the rising sun. Their quivers were painted with snakes and their bows were made of horn braided with brightly colored wool. These were no ordinary men. They were noblemen, richly ornamented with glass beads.

Shenq was close enough to hear them talking and he inclined his head to listen.

"Did you know the sycamore is the hardiest of all trees? It can weather any storm," said a man dressed in a hooded cape.

"I don't care about trees. I don't care about storms," said a young warrior with a bow on his back. "You said the moon would go black and now it's brighter than a thousand lanterns."

"It will go black, Mongaka. I swear by Apepi's teeth."

"What about the gates," the warrior said, pointing at the walls of Thebes. There was a gold ornament in his lip that glinted each time he spoke. "Open them."

"You'll see a hundred open gates before the battle's done. Haven't you seen a hundred miracles since leaving the Redlands? Lucky I should say."

"Lucky," the other repeated, nostrils widening to a scent.

"And I'll teach the princess how to love a Bloodman, how to satisfy a real man."

Moonlight fell in dusty shafts through the trees and the young warrior squinted at them. "What is it that protects the Pharaoh, a man that fears battle and wins no victories?"

"Wisdom, my friend. It is all in the texts. But there's a price to pay."

"Name it."

"I want the title of High Priest of Thebes. You see, I want just as much as you if I am to risk my life to get it."

The young warrior shot the hooded stranger a smile. "So you want comfort in this new life. Then I will guarantee it."

"A very wise decision," said the other, bowing his head. "You are no longer a Tausmen. You are a king. I will be back in a day or two with the magic scrolls. I trust your sorcerer will read them carefully." The man disappeared into a thicket, whistling under his breath.

The sorcerer came out from the shadows, a bald man with a horsehair wand. "He'll never give them to you. He'll keep them himself. One day the serpent will turn round and bite him. There's always a price. How far is the great Mongaka willing to go?"

"As far as it takes."

"You have no soul."

"I have you, my good luck charm." The younger warrior kept sniffing the air, finger rubbing the wooden limb of his bow.

He knows I'm here, thought Shenq. *He can smell me and I can smell him.*

He watched for many hours, feeding off their movements and their gestures. He could almost read their minds by the time he found his horse and cantered downriver to his villa. The fluid tongue of the natives was well known in Thebes and so were their terms of respect. Mongaka meant *master* in Alodia.

49

Bellowing to his houseman, Shenq heard the gate open revealing a brightly lit courtyard and a pool beyond.

"You're late," the old man said.

"There are wild men in the marshes," Shenq said, handing Khamudi his bow. "Hebony with braided hair."

"They're from Souba," Khamudi said. "They bring oil from Dongola and Faras. Fine-looking so the women say."

"How long have they been here?"

"Two weeks, Maaz, maybe three."

"Where are they camped?" Shenq took off his clothes and motioned for a bucket of water. He felt the first sluice against his body and the scrub of salt on his back.

"South of the lower precincts on the east bank where all merchants camp."

"They're not merchants, old father. Bloodmen I should say. They don't lack for courage and they're far from home. Send for Mkasa. Tell him to meet me here at dawn."

Shenq stepped into the cool waters of his pool, resting his head against the stone rim. *Filthy Alodians, riding north under a different guise.* Tausmen . . .

They were once Tau's men. Only Tau the Alodian, headman to King Ibada, was a rotting corpse, dangling on the end of a rope. Who was leading them now?

Shenq remembered how Lieutenant Mkasa had already surrendered the smallest finger on his string hand when he was held captive in the mountains. He was unlikely to surrender the city of Thebes to the snake-worshipping Bloodmen at any cost.

I'll take him with me, Shenq thought since Mkasa understood many of the ancient dialects of Kush. He could speak them like a native.

He padded through the hall, glancing at the shadows cast by the oil lamps that danced up and down the walls. Meryt lay curled on his bed, silken hair spilling over a pillow. He would never forget their wedding day, the birdsong and the scent of blossoms in the garden. They had walked arm in arm under the lintel just as the sun began to sink like an eye peering over the rim of the mountains. The villa was filled with floating lights and fireflies, and happy voices that meandered through the gardens. It was a place between two worlds, a secret place where he could hide. And he would never forget those sweet pale eyes, a timeless beauty that reminded him of a sculpture. Small wonder she trembled at his touch. She was so young . . . *so terribly young.*

He lay down beside her, listening to the sounds of the night and billowing drapes. The gap between them seemed suddenly vast, inaccessible, and when he reached out and traced a finger along her spine, she murmured, "Husband."

And then, "Is it you?"

MKASA

Mkasa stood on his terrace and looked up at the moon, shiny like a silver plate. When he saw its face, he imagined his birthmother dressed in a blue shúkà and shawl. She was long dead now, wandering the celestial plains with the sons of Makuria. When he scrunched his eyes closed, he could still see the fires and he could hear his sister's screams, those wild raging screams. The tribesmen left her covered in blood and barely breathing.

Come, my precious boy. Come with me. The man who came to fetch him had big hands and a kind heart. "My wife will be a mother to you. And you shall have brothers."

The man had many sons as Mkasa recalled. Five of his own and another orphaned on the battlefield just like him.

Brothers . . . It means family. It means I belong.

He sighed loudly, heart sore for the man that had brought him to Thebes. He was the same man that had given him the largest villa on the west bank. He chuckled at that. And now he was to join brother Shenq at dawn and take the ferry to the east bank. There were royal visitors to entertain, sons of Alodia or *Bloodmen* as the people called them.

"Husband," Iutha said, face groggy from sleep. "Can't you sleep?"

"No," Mkasa grunted. He had hardly been to bed.

"Did you dream?"

"I always dream."

A month had passed or was it more? Mkasa thought his heart would split in two. The sight of Shenq's wife was almost more than he could bear, the occasional smile, the occasional look. She was enchanting, sparkling green eyes and long flowing hair. He had taken that first plunge in the market place, nodding politely and offering to carry her basket. He found himself hoping that she would say something to encourage him, anything, the merest word. But the house-woman was always with her, ushering him to one side with an impatient wave.

"I spoke with the great falcon," Iutha said, pushing a mass of dark curls from one shoulder. "He has given me a commission."

"Osiris only speaks to those who are about to die," Mkasa reminded, glancing at her swollen belly as he walked back to the bed. Her dark eyes studied him and there was pity in them.

"It was a vision, my lord. It was unbelievable—"

"As most of your stories are."

"My lord, it was a dream sent from the gods," she said, reaching for him. "I dreamed of warriors from the black kingdoms. Listen. You can hear the drums."

"I hear nothing." Why did he suddenly hate her? Why did he think of her as a foul spit of a woman serving none other than the devil? "Be careful what you say, my love. Be careful who you serve."

"I serve *you*, my lord."

"I wish it were true."

"You're cruel," she said, frowning.

Mkasa nodded. He couldn't argue with that.

Iutha was the only daughter of the man he called *father* and Mkasa married her out of obligation. A Queen's maid for thirteen years, she sewed the royal gowns and bed linens. They were childhood companions, inseparable until the Pharaoh tore them apart with his jealousy. There were rumors that he had taken Iutha's mother to his bed and the same rumors said Iutha herself was now a royal bedmate. Mkasa refused to believe it until her belly became plumper than a wineskin. She had lied about her virginity all those years ago and she was lying now. Those lies had hacked away at Mkasa's pride and, bit by bit, he became more distant riding out in his chariot and screaming until his lungs began to burn with sand. It had taken the edge off the pain but never the enormity of it.

"Do you know what it is to tell the truth, woman?" he asked her.

"I do."

"Then do it."

She gave him a sideways glance and scowled. "You have never forgiven me, have you?"

No, he had never forgiven her. She told him the Pharaoh had taken her against her will. But he had seen her staring off into the distance, eyes glassy with tears. Her lies had gusted in like an ill-wind across the desert and now she was bedridden with fever and chills. He could get no sleep because of her racking cough.

"Don't let the gods rule your life," Mkasa murmured, running a finger down the side of her tearstained face. "Remember, there is a better God in heaven than the ones in Thebes."

"You will be imprisoned for saying such things," she whispered, coughing. "The High Priest will have none of it."

"The gods are nothing more than scraps of wood with holes for mouths. Yet you bow to them and take offerings."

"As you should," Iutha pressed. "Hathor is the goddess of motherhood. She says I shall have twins."

"I pray you live." Mkasa couldn't help himself. Twins had taken many a mother out of the world.

"And if I should die," she said, stiff with terror, "will you take another wife?"

Mkasa half smiled at that. "If it pleases you."

He knew it wouldn't. She would sooner starve than see him married to another. Iutha was a princess in her own right. She could have married the son of a Viceroy rather than a barbarian with silt-colored skin.

"You're mine and I'm yours," she whispered.

He would have repeated the words a year ago. Now he

stared down at red-rimmed eyes, hating the sound of her sobs. He could not understand why she desired him, why her hands so often found his. And when they did, he felt like a drowning man no longer knowing which way was up and which way was down. He felt lost in a cloud of mud, kicking, kicking, kicking, until he broke through the surface, gasping for air.

"My poor, Mkasa," she said, wiping her eyes and stroking the stump of a finger on his drawing hand. "Will you grieve for me as Shenq does for his wife?"

"He grieves for her?" Mkasa felt a stir of hope in his belly.

"She doesn't love him. She never has. I see her look away. I see her flinch. How does that make you feel, husband?"

It made him feel light-headed if he was honest. "You're mistaken."

"You know she doesn't love him. You know, don't you?"

Mkasa knew Meryt was a virgin when they married, an innocent. "She's shy that's all."

"But will Shenq ever win her heart?"

"What's winning got to do with taking a wife. The courtship is a battle well fought. The wedding night is a battle well won."

"Women are not won with spears and arrows," Iutha cradled her belly, head tilted to one side. "We are won with patience."

"How do you know all this? Did your mother teach you?" Mkasa felt the heat rise in his cheeks. "Or did the Pharaoh?"

"Don't . . ." Iutha pressed a finger against his lips. "Pharaoh may rule the Two Lands, but he doesn't rule me."

"But you think of him from time to time?"

Iutha lowered her face. "Everyone knows how much he loves women and everyone knows how much he wants a son. When he commands, we obey. One day you will understand."

"What is there to understand? Pharaoh takes what he sees. And he saw you." *She made sure of that*, Mkasa thought. With her pale skin and flinty eyes, she had a way that turned a man's head.

"You have no idea—"

"If the babes you carry are bright-skinned, then I'll know. And there's always so much blood after a gelding, my lady." Mkasa thought of the Pharaoh's pleading eyes and a scream or two. He would never hurt Iutha but he would divorce her if he had to. "Are you afraid?"

"No, my lord. Girls have always seen more blood than boys," she said, wiping away a tear. "You weren't there. No one was there."

It was true. Mkasa was not there to save her. But Pharaoh was as handsome as he was cruel and girls were like dung flies drawn to the biggest pile. "He's impressive, our beloved Pharaoh. He's the richest man in the world. Perhaps the lady Meryt has cast a glance here and there."

"She has not," Iutha said. "None of us have."

"Then who does she love?"

"Not you, beloved," Iutha crooned, leaning in closer. "She could never love a Kushite. Not the way I do."

The word *Kushite* was too general a term for his liking but he would forgive her that much. He was a son of Makuria, a royal city that once stood on the banks of the river Nile.

There was a knock on the door and his houseman entered with a smile on his face. "Commander Shenq's houseboy has come with a message, my lord. He wants you to ride with him at dawn to the eastern desert. He wants you to talk to the Bloodmen."

"There, you see," Iutha murmured, "warriors from the black kingdoms. Can't you hear the drums?"

Mkasa could hear nothing except the hollow sound of the wind and the whisper of trees, and he waved his attendant away. Sometimes he saw the scarred face of Tau the Alodian and sometimes he dreamed of him. Tau's armies were self-governing, killing their own comrades on a whim.

"Lie down," he said gently. "I won't share your bed. Not until the babes have come."

"You won't share my bed then."

Mkasa felt her head against his shoulder and he caught the light purr in the back of her throat. Her skin was pale, no longer the rich shade of autumn leaves and her spirit had lost its fire. They used to lie entwined on the bed as if they would never let go. But all that was forgotten now.

Yes, he would grieve after she was gone. She was like a sister to him, the sister he had once loved and lost.

And then he heard the drums.

KANJA

Kanja pressed his feet into the deep Sabaean carpet and stretched. He could still hear the drums pounding in his head, dusk drums, dawn drums, any drums. Sunlight seeped beneath the leopard skin drapes that covered the door and the silhouette of his gray mare made him smile.

"Shh . . . Nura, my love," he said, patting her fine head. She was the only female to share his tent.

He glanced at Massui, a brother younger by two years, sleeping on a mat beside him. He had droopy eyes and wide face suggestive of a different mother, and he was a simpleton, stronger than an elephant with no ambition of his own. It was fear that kept him idle and so he slept as often as he could. And then there was Ayize, hands covered in vulture's blood and sleeping like a baby. Kanja was envious of the boy's reputation, his unusual charm. It was no wonder his father favored him.

"You will have your piercing," he whispered, stroking Ayize's back.

Grabbing his bow and quiver from an attendant, he ventured outside to a sky bathed in the russet colors of dawn. The central fire had all but died, fiery nuggets fanning outwards in a sudden gust of wind. There was no sign of Thutiy, the one who promised gold and the password to the city gates. The snake-charming wretch must have lost his nerve.

Never follow me, Thutiy once said. *You'll perish if you do.*

Why? Kanja wondered. He was as fleet a shadow and just as quiet, and if he followed Thutiy all the way to the palace, he might overhear a few passwords along the way.

He took a glass jar of joyroot and held it up to a blazing torch. It was the color of wolfsbane, and after a few gulps there were no more memories. He could see circles of moonlight in the glowing embers and he laughed wildly, hankering for a few snakes of his own.

It had been two months since his army arrived all coated in dust and sweat. Thebes was a magnificent city, gardens rich with blooms and villas so large hundreds could live in them. The market was bursting with colorful spices and exotic oils, and the women were beautiful. They were eager to share his bed wanting nothing in return. But there was a princess behind those high walls and he was willing to pay a bride price of thirty oxen and three hundred head of cattle if he had them.

He nodded to Yuku, a tracker by trade, squat and broad with a chest-full of scars. Najja, the stargazer stood beside him, chin painted red and harnessed with beads. He had one pale eye that gazed off in the distance and cheekbones you could cup in one hand. He was handsome so the women said. They were both part of the forty-nine, a group of gallant warriors of the royal house.

There was only stale bread and salted fish in the stores, and Kanja flicked a fly from a haunch of pork. The meat, spitted the night before, hung from a wooden frame and several maggots had already tunneled into the greasy flesh.

The creatures of death, he thought. Maggots had no business in fresh meat. He was suddenly aware of the sorcerer behind him and wondered why Othene had to tiptoe about in the darkness.

"What do you want?" he said, wishing he was somewhere else.

"We have visitors, my prince, visitors from the city." Othene scratched the inside of his left wrist where the tattoo of two red-painted eyes stared back at him.

Kanja turned to look at Othene, barely holding his patience at bay. "Don't call me, *prince*. And cover your arm."

"Yes my . . . Yes, Mongaka," Othene said, bowing.

Kanja listened for the crowing of the rooster but there

was nothing but silence. Hurrying outside, the torches shed light on a warrior wearing a blue shúkà with disks of lapis in his ears. Braided hair hung down his back and heavily adorned fingers gripped the haft of a Theban forged spear. He was Makurae by the look of him, a brother so to speak. The second was tall, eyes like fire and the handle of a khopesh peeked over one shoulder. His uniform bore the black and gold insignia of the Pharaoh's elite, breastplate covered by a collar of precious stones.

"Kemnebi," Kanja said, hand tightening around his belt. He had never seen him in the flesh but he knew who he was.

"It's Commander Shenq," the Makurae corrected, head aslant.

Kanja felt a twinge of anger. The boy was not his equal. "Who are you, Makurae?"

"Mkasa, son of Ahmose, Vizier to the Pharaoh." Mkasa's eyes flicked to the gold snake coiled around Kanja's arm.

An equal of sorts, Kanja thought, wondering how Mkasa belonged in such a royal household. Weapons honed, belts oiled, the boy was well outfitted and strong, and the smallest finger was missing on his drawing hand.

"Kanja, spearman to King Ibada," he said, tapping his chest. He wanted to lie about his heritage and pretend he was a Bedouin but his style of dress had already given him away.

"Peace be with you," said Shenq, speech fluent and entrenched in the accent of the natives. He wore a bronze bracer on his bow arm and leather sheaths on three fingers of his left hand.

His style is anything but Theban, thought Kanja, aware of a black leopard pelt draped over olive skin and long glossy hair. He had never seen anything like it. The creak of leather and the snort of horses behind the tents was an indication of how noble these men were. No wonder Thutiy was in hiding. Several thousand of the Pharaoh's men had surrounded the camp.

"Is that your watchman?" Shenq said, shooting a warning glance at Massui half-asleep on the ground. "If it is, I kicked him on the way in."

"He's a simpleton, Commander," said Kanja, setting his jaw. "We revere his kind."

Shenq looked Kanja directly in the eye. "Do you have permission to camp here?"

"We have a seal."

True, they had crawled over the dunes too far east of the river to be seen by the border guards and Kanja was damned if he was going to let a pampered noble drive him out.

Dark eyebrows drew together in a frown and Shenq seemed to hesitate for a moment before replying. "Show me."

Kanja glanced at Mkasa. "*Adui*," he hissed in his native tongue as he brushed past. The boy was sure to know the word for *enemy*.

The Makurae would have some knowledge of the six dialects of Alodia unless he'd been torn from his mother's womb before he had a chance to learn them. His eyes were small and luminous, as if they hid a smile.

Kanja rummaged in the darkness of his tent until he found the small leather pouch under his pillow. He felt a presence and turned slowly. The moon-warrior stooped under the cowhide flap, eyes brushing over the sleeping boy and the dead vulture on the ground.

"What are you looking at?" Kanja said in the tongue of his ancestors.

The Makurae shook his head, gaze clouding.

Kanja reverted to the language of Thebes. "Do you deny your ancestors?"

"My ancestors are the pride of Thebes." Mkasa seemed to study the arrow piercing on Kanja's lip and his forehead puckered and then relaxed.

"You have no relatives in Makuria then?"

"It was so long ago. Perhaps you remember it better than me. There was once a palace in Tungul and a village on the east bank. I can still hear the songs of the grain-gatherers and the warriors' drums. Then one day a pack of Bloodmen raided it and then they burned the women and children. There's no singing now."

Kanja clenched his jaw. His father took him on a plundering tour of Makuria when he was a boy. There were tight little villages near the river and big-breasted women that burned so fast it excited him. He could still smell the stench especially when they roasted hog-meat. This Makurae was as broken as the rest of them, only he was smart enough to have run away. "Don't you want your freedom?"

"What I *want* is none of your business," Mkasa whispered, glancing back at the Commander who was some distance from the tent.

"All men want something." Kanja peered across the tops of the tents, seeing a spiral of dust in one of the aisles. The Commander's men were taking prisoners. "You're no more than a thief, Mkasa son of Ahmose."

"We're alike you and I."

"Go to hell!"

"Then we go together."

Kanja offered Mkasa the pouch. "Better take this to your Commander. He might be wondering where we are."

"He's a clever man. I would watch him if I were you."

"Oh, I intend to, brother. I intend to watch him night and day." Kanja's eyes fell on that stump of a finger and smiled. "How did you lose your finger?"

"I lost it to a Bloodman. Only he never lived to tell the tale."

Kanja followed Mkasa to the campfire, catching Shenq's dark expression as he examined the seal.

"This is as genuine as the smile on your face," Shenq said, turning it over in his hand. "Why are you here? Better climate?"

Kanja felt himself flinch. "King Ibada is dying," he said trying to curb his rage-filled voice. "I was asked to find a doctor in Thebes."

"And so you brought six hundred armed men along for the ride?"

"I brought these men to fight sand-warriors, Commander. There are tribes living near the stone quarries of Swenet. They took our livestock."

"Those tribes are puny peasants too hungry to fight. It's remarkable you weren't massacred," Shenq returned, glancing over his shoulder at a goat pen. "Seems you took all they had. Tell me, how do you lead?"

"By my wits."

"Perhaps I should throw myself on your mercy."

"You would be treated better than you have treated me."

"Desperate times require desperate actions. Tell me, did you bring a letter from King Ibada?"

"A letter?" Kanja shrugged, nostrils open to the scent of citrus. He dared not think of his father's muffled screams behind a silken pillow just in case Shenq could see into his thoughts. "He gave me no such letter."

"Oh come now. You're too smart to lie. Kings always furnish their heralds with letters and their commanders with orders. The last herald had a letter. The Pharaoh read it himself."

"Heralds?" Kanja said, resisting the temptation to sweat. He thought he had killed them all.

"Yes, *heralds*, with exciting news."

"What news?"

"I knew you'd ask."

The rising sun had cast fingers of light along the desert floor, illuminating the Commander's eyes. They tunneled into Kanja's, never straying from his face.

"It seems three Alodian princes are missing," Shenq said. "You haven't seen them have you?"

"We are also from Alodia—"

"So I see," Shenq said, mouth flickering in a half-smile. "Wasn't the King's second son called Kanja? How many others share his name?"

"Well over half the city," Kanja said, studying the man with eyes like fire. No man had ever outsmarted Shenq and no man could outrun him. He likely sensed the lie.

"You've just missed the Festival of Hathor," Shenq said, searching Kanja's face. "It would have taken your mind off battles."

"But we haven't missed the races," Othene said, stepping forward.

"For a kingdom so far south, I'm surprised you've heard of them," Shenq said, studying the mystic.

"Heard of them?" Othene said. "Everyone's heard of the Kamaraan. If only you knew us better you might consider us worthy contestants. These are superior fighters. Highly trained like your *Kenyt-Nisu*."

"And why would King Ibada send his very best to find medicine? Any one would think he expected war."

Kanja watched Shenq thoughtfully. There was a gleam in his eye, an inner light. The Great Commander of Thebes was either amused or angry, he couldn't be sure. Shenq just stood there, eyes locked with the sorcerer in some imaginary battle.

"I understand only seven men compete against each other," Othene continued. "It's a shame outsiders cannot be chosen. It would be a great honor."

"You don't know what you ask." Shenq said, glaring at Othene. "Who are you?"

"I'm a diviner, a conjurer of snakes."

Kanja glanced sideways at the sorcerer. He was glad Othene's wrist was covered with a leather wristband. The tattoo was the mark of a royal guardian.

"You are welcome to eat with us," Othene said, eyes flicking towards Kanja. "We have smoked meat and date wine."

"My men will keep yours company for the time being,"

Shenq said, lifting his head suddenly to the warbling of a lark. "They will stand guard at the camp boundary."

"We have brought oil and elephant tusks for the Pharaoh, may he live forever," Othene said, giving a curt nod.

"You will bring them to the palace tomorrow although I cannot guarantee an audience with the Pharaoh," Shenq said, turning his head to look at an enclosure of goats and cows. "Do you have swine?"

"A few hogs," Othene said. "The rest have been butchered."

"It's sacrilege to eat pork in the upper precincts," Shenq said. "You will purify yourselves before coming to the palace. And you will bring no weapons."

"Yes, sir," Kanja offered, suddenly finding his voice. He glanced at Mkasa whose glassy eyed stare seemed to shoot right through him. "You will fetch me then . . . to the Palace?"

"I will be honored," Mkasa replied.

Kanja studied the Commander as he mounted a dun horse, black tail feathering in the wind and a dorsal stripe down its back. Housed in an open sheath on Shenq's back was a khopesh sword. The hand-guard hung from two hooks and a strap kept the grip in place. It would be easy to unsheathe and swing over one shoulder. *Irqatan-forged*, he thought.

"We'll be back at noon tomorrow," Shenq said as he reined his horse back around. "My soldiers will stay with you. It's the least I can do."

Kanja watched them leave through a cloud of dust, sensing a battle more grueling than he previously thought. "I assumed the seal was good enough," he grunted.

"It was good enough to get us over the border, Mongaka," Othene said, shrugging. "It should have been good enough to get us through the city gates. I've read the stars. I see the leopard in the dark of the night and I hear his heartbeat. There is only one way to hunt him. And that is to trap him."

"And the princess?" Kanja murmured, screwing up his face.

"When she sees you, she will refuse you nothing. Her heart will be your heart. She is the key to unlock all gates."

Kanja knew about his face and the strength of his body, how it tempted the women. He was tired of them pawing his body like they had never seen a man before. All he cared about now was rushing out after Shenq with a well-greased bow. It would be quicker than running a race. Instead, all he could hear were the shallow grunts of a wounded leopard in his whimsical mind. There was nothing there except the Commander on a dun horse, body shifting rhythmically from side to side.

"I'll race for the ancestors," Kanja murmured. "I'll do it for Ulan."

KHEPER-RE

"Greetings, Pharaoh, may HaShem protect you," Shenq said, bowing.

"*Horus*, you mean," Kheper-Re interrupted, stroking a sad-eyed terrier on his lap no larger than a dinner roll. "I can't find the scrolls, Shenq. I've looked everywhere."

Shenq lowered both his head and his voice. "Your Grand Vizier took them, my lord. Since he is their keeper it does seem fitting. Only I got to thinking. If a man is able to build such a grand tomb in the mountains for himself, wouldn't the same man be helping himself to the treasury?"

"It's all rumor, Shenq."

"Perhaps it is rumor as you say, my lord. But just to be on the safe side, I exchanged the leather case and what he did take was the text of Pharaoh Nefrikare and his dancing pygmy."

"Pygmy . . ." Kheper-Re swallowed hard.

"Yes, my lord, little men from the land of trees and spirits."

"I know what they are!" Kheper-Re yelled, lurching forward and pitching the small dog from his lap. He couldn't think over the frenzied yipping and gave the animal a nudge with his foot. "Where are my scrolls? The real ones, mind?"

Shenq waved at an elderly attendant and shouted, "Laundry. Basket."

The old man lifted a gnarled hand and cupped an ear. He nodded and then shuffled off towards an explosion of dirty linens in the corner of the room.

"He's lost his mind," Kheper-Re said, feeling a throbbing vein in his forehead. "It's bad enough he's strayed from the wash-house and now he thinks he's Overseer of my wardrobe."

"He *is* the Overseer of your wardrobe, my lord," Shenq said, crossing arms decorated with golden armbands. "It's Djoser."

"Oh," Kheper-Re said, screwing up his eyes for a better look. "So it is."

He coughed bitterly from behind a cloud of smoke and winced. Another tooth had blackened with gum-worm and he dreaded the large metal tongs. "It's the great falcon that looks after our comforts. And talking of comforts, where's my squatter?"

"It will be installed tomorrow, my lord."

"Good." Kheper-Re said, thinking of his chariot-shaped lavatory.

"The sculptor has made a marble bowl, my lord, cut ingeniously into the footplate and scented with rose water. I pray it's to your liking."

Kheper-Re barely nodded even though he was longing to try it out. He would dream of the wind in his hair and the screech of horses. *So much better*, he thought, than scurrying across the sands in a contraption ready to catapult him to his death.

"There's a snake in the garden," said Shenq, looking over the balcony.

Kheper-Re followed Shenq's gaze, sensing a flash of anger. He stared at the angular planes of Shenq's face, the curve of his lips and its mocking smile. And for the first time in his life, he was horrified to admire someone so heartless. "Do you know why I made him Grand Vizier of Thebes?"

"I can't imagine," Shenq said, lips suddenly pressed into a white slash.

"Because I trust him."

"Ah, then you're not the only one who's taken an interest in him."

"Don't work so hard to undermine him, Shenq. You

waste your time."

"But I have so much time to waste."

"Listen," Kheper-Re almost hissed, "just because there are no wars to fight, doesn't mean you can look down on the pride of Thebes and pass judgment. He's my cousin."

"Several times removed," Shenq reminded, "by a baker's daughter in a back alley."

Kheper-Re hunched beside an oil lamp. He was tired of poring over miserable tithes where farmers frequently surrendered the worst of their stock. Where they hid the best of it no one knew. Except Shenq. He knew everything. "Vizier Thutiy is tutor to the princess," he said. "But of course you know that."

"The princess has learned many legends, my lord, but none half as entertaining as the rumors from Alodia. It appears King Ibada's Bloodmen sire over ten thousand sons a year. That's quite an army if you ask me."

"What? Did you say they *sire* over ten thousand sons?"

"The Vizier says each man is hung like an ox, my lord," Shenq said, stooping forward like a buzzard. "An *ox*!"

Kheper-Re felt a pang of embarrassment. He knew very little about the size and stamina of Bloodmen, and if he wasn't mistaken Shenq was trying to taunt him. "How do you know?"

"Ask the Vizier for the source of his information, my lord. We can only pray it's false."

"It's nonsense. All of it," Kheper-Re muttered, rubbing his chin.

Although, it could be true . . . Alodians were handsome, so his sister said, and his daughter was already besotted with a shadow. What would happen to Egypt if their beloved Pharaoh no longer deposited his life-giving seed in noble wombs? The river would not rise and the people would starve. And according to the court physician, the royal member had not *risen* much since the last flood.

The attendant continued to root and rummage through the basket and for what, Kheper-Re couldn't imagine.

"Stop that racket!" he yelled, hoping the man had found something of value to sell at a handsome profit.

Djoser threw up his hands in a gesture of surrender. "Your scrolls, Nisu," he said, gripping a leather-bound case. The old man staggered towards him and laid them on the table.

Kheper-Re glowered at the Commander with the long black hair. His waist was cinched with a golden sash and the head of a leopard was embroidered on the widest pleat. It was the order of his rank. "Tell me, what prize should I offer the winner of the Kamaraan?"

The opulence of the royal bedchamber seemed to capture Shenq's interest, eyes floating over the walls as if he was inspecting his troops. "A large tomb in the western desert or the hand of the princess, my lord. No man will ride for less."

No man is worth a tomb, Kheper-Re thought, not unless he was a god. And why was Shenq so concerned with tombs? "The princess it is," he said.

"Good choice, Son of Ra," Shenq said, bowing.

Kheper-Re fumbled through his memories. There was not one man who represented the warrior god Montu in quite the same way. But was Shenq loyal? "What if I'm not the Son of Ra?"

"If you're not the Son of Ra," Shenq said with a sideways grin, "then who are you?"

Kheper-Re dropped his voice to a whisper. "I'm just the son of a Commander and a harem girl. My sister is the one filled with the blood of kings, the true life-blood of Egypt. Even the omens say it. See, the roaring lion has hunted me down and now I'm as good as dead."

"It suits you then to put on the rags of pity," Shenq said, hovering above him with an aura of menace.

There now. Let's see if how far that rumor spreads. "It suits me to forget."

Sometimes Kheper-Re felt so drunk he had to lean on Shenq's arm and this was one of those times. Shenq nodded but there was a glower of mischief in those sharp eyes.

He thinks I'm a frail-boned man with nothing to show for my reign. He's probably right. "Tell me, what does that sweet girl call you? All wives call their husbands something, a pet name?"

Shenq furrowed his brow. "Husband?"

"That's what comes of marrying a shepherdess." Kheper-Re felt a terrible sense of foreboding even as he saw the mocking smile. "They're as cold as a nightmare. I told you not to marry her. But no, you ran off with the stinking wench and now you're sorry. I'll tell you this, I spoke with Vizier Thutiy today and you know what he said? He said, sell her to highest bidder. Those merchants out there would barter a fine arabi horse for a girl like that."

"My lord, they're not merchants."

"Have her followed," Kheper-Re said. "She has a lover, that's what it is. You know what we do with unfaithful wives?"

Shenq sighed loudly. "What do we do with unfaithful wives, my lord?"

"We cut out their tongues and parade them naked around the market place. And that's before we burn them."

"My wife pleases me. I want no other." Shenq's face screamed of anger and there was a knot on his brow deeper than a scar.

"Then you're a fool! Perhaps I should beat the insanity out of you." Kheper-Re stared at the solemn face, realizing Shenq was no stranger to scars. He had a deep furrow on his right shoulder and another on his thigh.

"She is the light in my darkness. I thank HaShem for her."

"Is she with child?" Kheper-Re couldn't help himself.

"She's sickly in the mornings and she craves olives and honey. All the midwives agree it must be a boy. They say when a mother craves olives it's always a boy."

Stop—saying—that! Kheper-Re wanted to shout out, hands curled into a fist. He struggled for all it was worth, but the fact that the girl was with child made victory impossible. "It could be a girl. It could be stillborn. It could be a *monster!*"

Shenq merely bowed his head and brushed away a stray lock of hair from his eyes. "Then I pray for a healthy infant."

Kheper-Re couldn't help wondering if he should say a prayer. But the gods never heard him when he did. He brought the best of offerings to the god Min, but no amount of worshipping the orgiastic seed-planter had done him any good.

He ushered Shenq forward with an impatient hand. He wanted to beat the stuffing out of such a confident spirit. "Hapuseneb knocked down a wall in the temple this week without my permission. He said he did it to lengthen the existing sanctuary. I would have flogged him if he wasn't High Priest. They have no respect. Not one!"

Shenq offered a small dip of his head. "My lord—"

"I'm not just an ornament to add majesty to any ceremony. I'm the builder of the realm. *These*," Kheper-Re said, resting two fingers on the scrolls, "are sacred documents only I can touch. Do you know what I hate, Shenq? I hate dead fish, especially one that owns one third of Egypt, is exempt from paying taxes, chief of the sacerdotal order and next in line to the throne. The kind of fish I don't like. And to punish him, I will promote *Shasu* to Chief of Prophets."

"A bitter draught to swallow," Shenq said without smiling.

Kheper-Re glanced down at Harran, head bent on his task. He seemed to be scratching cuneiform symbols on his tablet, blind to the promotion he had just received. "I shall fly my falcon tomorrow," he muttered. He had pretended a glut of illnesses to stop any opportunity for war and, as for the chariot, it was with great reluctance he hunted at all.

"Is that wise, Pharaoh, with your leg and all?"

"My leg?" Kheper-Re asked, spinning an empty cup in circles on the table.

"You were limping yesterday."

"Much better," Kheper-Re said, sticking out a leg for good measure. He couldn't remember which one and it was too late to withdraw it. "The Vizier has found me a match, one of the daughters of Queen Ati of Punt. The dowry was exceptional. The girl, sadly, was not. Her skin is as red as a grape and she has an odor."

"Keep her indoors, my lord. Too much sun and a grape becomes a raisin."

Kheper-Re wondered if mounting her would be as grueling as climbing a sand dune—too much effort and a lot of shift. "I thought *you* might like her."

"My lord," Shenq said, almost laughing. "One wife is quite enough."

Kheper-Re saw the cold, hard eyes staring back at him. If he could bet on it, Shenq wanted to tell him some high-handed tale about the High Priest and a temple boy, only there was bound to be a prank behind it.

"Tell me, what rumors do my nobles spread? And no lies this time."

"Talking of your Grand Vizier, he was enjoying another dip in the temple pool this morning. He was whispering with his attendant . . . rather loudly."

Kheper-Re chuckled. Only Shenq could hear a mouse fart. "What were they saying?"

"They were wondering how frequently you vomited."

Kheper-Re was fascinated and appalled. Torture was the only punishment for men like that. They wanted him dead. They *all* wanted him dead. But his Vizier?

"And before I forget, there is news from the custodian at Suhaj," Shenq said, licking his lips as if he was thinking for a moment. "King Ibada has renamed his successor since his eldest son has died and the others have gone missing."

"Missing?" Kheper-Re felt increasingly alarmed at the prospect of anything valuable going missing. "How many sons does he have?"

"Three, since one has recently died."

"Ibada was a fool when he refused to give me his oath. I'm tired of his quarrels, tired of his pillaging and tired of his inability to rule his own nation without creeping north and trying to take over mine! A divine warning would put a stop to it."

"You do it so well."

Kheper-Re wagged a warning finger. "He sent one of his mongrels to haunt me last year, to steal my gold."

"The mongrel is dead, my lord, by my own hand."

"Oh, I don't doubt that he is, Commander. But Ibada has some explaining to do if he wants to keep his throne. I seem to recall he's fond of trickery and witchcraft." Kheper-Re was pleased at his imposing voice. He would have patted his own back if he could reach that far. "I'll geld him if he so much as shakes a wand in my direction, do you hear?"

"Talking of King Ibada," Shenq said with a smile that somehow did not reach his eyes. "Those merchants you keep talking about are Bloodmen. They were granted entry because they had a royal seal."

"They're common peddlers," Kheper-Re said, squinting at the seal in Shenq's hand. It was larger than most and made of turquoise.

"My lord, there are over six hundred of them."

"*Six hundred?*" Kheper-Re barely whispered. He felt something lurch in his belly, possibly his breakfast which threatened to re-appear. "What makes you think these are Ibada's men?"

"Because they're here."

Kheper-Re trapped a sob in his throat. "He sent a herald a few weeks ago. I didn't mention it because I knew it would anger the Queen."

"You didn't mention it because you knew it would anger *me*."

Kheper-Re thought for a moment. Was he so transparent? "You would have rushed off with ten thousand armed soldiers to wage war on Bloodmen and sorcerers, a war you had no hope of winning."

"Come now, isn't a sword mightier than a magic wand?"

Kheper-Re wanted to nod. Sorcerers were liars and their wands no more than cut-off branches with a few decorations to please the eye. None could make a wish come true. "What shall we do with them, Commander? What shall we do with these *Bloodmen*?"

"It would be wise to question them. Justice must be seen to be served."

"There's no justice here, my friend. If they're waiting to be served then send them a warrant."

"There's something else," Shenq said rather cagily, or so Kheper-Re thought. "Young girls are flocking to the east bank. It seems these rearing cobras are spreading more than their hoods."

Kheper-Re almost regurgitated a piece of fish. "Fornicators," he muttered, tapping a foot on the tile floor. "I pray to Set they're not filling precious wombs with foreign spit! They're unfit to live on my land let alone rut half the village. It would give me great satisfaction to slit a few hundred throats and lop the Alodian tree of its finest warriors. It's enough they got past the border. Someone will pay for this."

"Give me the word, my lord."

What if there were more than six hundred, Kheper-Re thought. What if there were forty thousand of them reclining in their tents and eating roasted beef? *His* beef. "I hate stupidity. It deserves the foulest of punishments. Don't you agree?"

"There are a few exceptions, my lord."

"There are no exceptions, Commander. The most celebrated minds in the kingdom don't need to sweat and struggle to find one. There's a breach in the border six hundred men wide and the only person responsible is *you*."

"I have my uses, my lord."

"Your rank falls directly under General Pen-Nekhbet and since I have retired the incontinent old fool, the border fortresses are yours."

"A promotion? Then I stand corrected."

Shenq's words puzzled Kheper-Re and he felt another nudge of disgust. Shenq was known for his sour disposition and he needed handling, rather harshly.

"You didn't think of your sweet young wife when you failed me. Such a lovely thing. She's at my mercy after you die. But since my father thought so highly of you, I will give you a choice. It is a beggar's choice, one suitable for a traitor. I want these savages off my land, do you understand?"

"I think we understand each other perfectly, my lord."

Kheper-Re smiled inwardly. The weasel was likely thinking up a plan to wriggle out of his punishment. "And you can forget about strategy, Shenq. It's never that simple."

"I disagree. Your father often scribbled simple plans in the sand. They were most effective in winning wars."

Kheper-Re realized he was looking at Shenq as if he was a strange mural. "I propose a fight to the death. You against their leader."

"If it pleases you, my lord. The Kamaraan is a worthy opportunity. Seven of their best men against seven of mine."

It was a stunning idea even if Kheper-Re hadn't thought of it himself. The Alodian seven would be the best they had, the higher ranks so to speak. It would be most revealing. "And while you play cat and mouse in the desert, I'll burn the rest of them."

"Very good, my lord." Shenq bowed his head, offering

little more than a glazed look behind half-lidded eyes.

Kheper-Re wanted to starve Shenq into submission but he knew his childhood friend had the stomach of an ox and the fire of a lion. He had sent him on a foray a year ago to rid Egypt of a threat. The prisoner he did bring home was the highest-ranking commander in Thebes. It was scandalous. They tied the wretch to a stake in *plotter's field*, a wasteland on the north side of the palace set aside for burnings. It was especially hot that day as Kheper-Re recalled and it would have been a three-day torture to reap information on Ibada's armies if it hadn't been for a farmer's scythe glinting in a bed of reeds. The man was ablaze within moments, swaying on his post as if gyrating to music. Kheper-Re hated burnings. He couldn't stand the smell.

"You may not come back, Commander."

Shenq half smiled at that. "I always come back."

KANJA

Kanja awoke suddenly from a deep sleep and threw the blanket from his sweating body. He was still groggy from joyroot and thirsty for more. Firelight flickered under the cowhide drape and there were whispers beyond it in the darkness. It was the sorcerer's voice, a torrent of moans like the endless purr of a cat.

Najja lifted the drape and stuck his head into the darkness. "Moon's high, my prince, high enough for a stroll."

They served him well these shadow-hunters, stalking prey and peeping in windows. And it was the *peeping* that interested him the most. "A stroll?" he said.

"The Vizier has a gift for you, a *royal* gift."

Kanja poured himself another cup of wine and winced as he swallowed. He had an appetite for gifts. "Did you see her?"

"I saw her jewels, if that's what you mean."

Kanja yawned and stood on stiff legs, drawing a heavy breath, and he shivered as a crisp breeze swept across the desert, fanning the flames of a dying fire. Othene let out a long groan, neck craned to the sky as he crouched, arms hugging his belly as the wind whined through the camp.

He sees something, Kanja thought, straining his eyes to the shifting shadows, wondering if they played tricks on him. His spirit was troubled and there was an unmistakable feeling that something was watching him, something that whispered in his ear with hot sticky breath. His back bristled as if a needle-sharp quill drew a word there.

So close to the enemy you cannot see, said a voice. *The real enemy . . .*

Kanja knew his army continued to sleep, a deep unearthly sleep. The cold night air did that to a man, warm under his covers, ears dead to the sounds of an intruder. But something did intrude, more in Kanja's thoughts than amongst the dark avenues between the dwellings. He knew he couldn't see it. But it was there, stalking, coming closer.

He walked through the tents, hearing the soft tread of his warriors behind and wondered if the thing in the darkness could see him now. He could almost see the vapors as they curled towards him, and he couldn't bear the sound of them, those chattering, fluttering things.

He tried to run only his body pitched forwards and the pain in his stomach was from an unseen fist. Gasping for breath, he lashed out at the threat, stroking the air with an empty hand. And then he saw it. Two ancient eyes, ghostly white eyes full of sadness and hate.

You know what I am, it said before he asked. A black menacing presence he knew from childhood.

Gray scales oozed with pus and there was a stink that made him retch. He had no choice but to draw a lasting breath or he would drown in that mist. It was a man's voice that made the thing vanish and with it went a screaming horde. Kanja could see their wings, their trailing talons. But he couldn't see their ghastly faces.

"Mongaka!" Yuku said, running forward. "What did you see?"

Kanja spat in the sand and then straightened. He felt a dull throb in his stomach and a bitter taste in his mouth. By the look on Yuku's face he had seen nothing, not even the screaming swooping things that banked to the west over the mountains like a thick gray cloud. There must have been close to a thousand sent to raid and kill, and if Kanja wasn't careful, they would be back again when he was alone.

"Nothing," he said, raising his chin.

I'm dreaming, hallucinating, he thought, heart returning to a steady patter. Perhaps it was the sweet-smelling oil on his body that attracted the creatures in the first place. They had surely stuck to him like flies to honey.

"The Vizier promises women from Mitanni and Hebron, my prince," Yuku said. "They're eager to share a couch and a roof to keep the sun off. Some big, some small . . ."

Kanja tried to hide his rising excitement. He was thankful he didn't have to stink of sweat and dust after climbing a wall where a ragged score of guards would be waiting for them to drop to the other side. He barely heard the drone of Yuku's voice but he liked the sound of these girls, some reedy and slender, and some bigger than bush pigs. He preferred the *bush pig*, all fleshy and soft to the touch, and he hoped for a generous haunch of it when he got behind that wall.

The moon shone overhead, brighter than a silver scarab in the sky as they crossed the river in a small reed boat. Crocodiles slipped into the water from a nearby sandbank, paddling downstream towards the great bend in the river. Something had rallied them, a carcass perhaps, and their gray-armored bodies sped onwards with the current. Majestic villas graced the banks, walls painted with birds and lotus ponds, and fields lay beyond them all silent under an inky sky.

The Vizier's villa was close to the palace gates and there was a ship moored at the foot of the ramp with large staring eyes on its bow. There were torches on the jetty all the way to the water, flickering and snapping in the wind.

A girl waited for them at the gate, arm a jangle of bracelets. "The Vizier welcomes you to his house," she said, painted eyes scurrying down Kanja's body. "He would like you to bathe."

She can't stand the stench of me, Kanja thought, following her through the house.

A fountain played in the center of the garden where a burst of irises and blue-headed cornflower shuddered in a light breeze. Long drapes danced amongst the columns, brushing the painted tiles and teasing two small cats with their tassels. There was a strong scent of lotus blossom that made him heady with desire and the rush of a bird's wings startled him as a black kite lifted from an architrave and ascended into the sky.

"A good omen," Najja whispered, scratching his pierced nipples and sniffing the wind. "We're in good hands."

Kanja wanted to laugh. He was aware of a powerful feeling of lust the more he thought of those hands. Steam poured from the double doors of the bathhouse and the pool was decorated with green tiles and potted lilies. Two large silver flagons poured fresh water into a bubbling pool scented with sweet smelling oils.

Women tugged at Kanja's clothes, and he was naked before he could smile. He wondered how clean a man could get with all that washing; the maids were vigorous with the scrubs. He sat tall and rigid like the king he was, looking up at the pillars and their palmiform capitals. Thutiy had done well for himself. Too well, he thought.

"I will conquer this city. I will own every part of it, lands, men, women—"

"It's a mighty thing to prove," Najja said, looking up at the high walls. "You must fight the Commander and his weasel words."

Kanja knew the Commander played him like a spinning toy and with every day that passed a new torment took over the last. Those strange eyes were in each dream, counting every weakness he had. *If I lose, I'm doomed to loneliness. And that will never do.*

"He killed my uncle and cousins. He did that with a sword. Some might say I should forgive and forget. But I won't. Let them blabber and whisper in their elegant tongue. They'll soon meet a better master."

"Vizier Thutiy has been a good master," Najja said. "He's filled the Pharaoh's harem with many a princess and the treasury overflows with dowries. It takes a sharp mind to think up these things."

"Where is he, that snake of a man?"

"Here!" Vizier Thutiy shouted as he swept into the bathhouse. "Greetings, my lords."

"You have ears like an owl," Kanja said, scowling.

"And so I should. I can always hear prey in the undergrowth."

"What news?"

"Commander Shenq graced me with his presence this morning. I gave him no food or drink so he didn't stay long. Apparently, I am a thief. Apparently, he can't prove it."

Kanja felt a chuckle rise in his throat but he refrained from laughter. "Your treasure is well hidden, I hope."

"Very well hidden." The Vizier bowed his head, eyes never leaving Kanja's.

"And the scrolls?"

"I thought it safer to send them to Suhaj, my prince, what with the Commander following me night and day. Nothing is sacred."

Othene was right. The conjuring fool had fallen in a pit of his own making. "And in return, the High Priest will give us a token?" Kanja asked.

"You have my word. As for the Commander, he has nothing of value to give. I'll wager he'll have to do more than just sing for his supper. Let us have music and wine," Thutiy said, clapping his hands. All of a sudden the bathhouse was full of flustered servants, carrying silver goblets of blood-red wine and trays of eel and figs.

"Leave enough room for desert," Thutiy said, winking. "I will leave you to sample what will one day be yours. This house, this kingdom, who knows? Perhaps the whole world."

Kanja lay back against the tiles scarcely touching a plate of figs and, somewhere in the distance, a harpist struck up a tune. Girls pampered with strong fingers, kneading juniper oil into the muscles at his neck and there was a tale behind each smile, some eager, some shy. He wasn't sure which he liked better, *eager* perhaps.

Long ago, he floated in a deep-tiled bath and memories of his father broke through the gaiety, piercing like a bee sting.

Do you even know what a shadow-hunter is, boy? Invisible, that's what he is. That's why I keep you locked up in the dark. You'll eat fish-heads until you vomit. And then you'll eat vomit until your bowels give way.

They locked him in that stinking dungeon for smiling at King Ibada's new wife. Kanja was twelve at the time and he chuckled now as he thought of it. He did more than smile at that large romp of a girl. He found comfort in her big nursing breasts and he could have stayed there all night if it hadn't been for a one-eyed headman who dragged him through the corridors by his hair. Even he had a smile for the new Queen. They all did.

A rush of cool air woke him from a deep sleep. There was no sign of his warriors or the women and at first he thought he was dreaming. The doors were open and on the threshold he saw a silhouette of a woman with beaded hair and a headdress of rosettes. Her face was small and fine, nose slightly hooked. She held all the wisdom of the Pharaohs.

Swords and spears won't hurt this one, he thought, glancing at a tight black gown.

"Greetings Commander Kanja," she said, bowing her head. "I am princess Neferure, daughter of Ra."

Kanja already knew those almond eyes, the tilt of the chin and the collar of a thousand jewels. "You have traveled some distance, princess."

She smiled at that. "Less than a quarter of a mile and so much faster in a carrying chair."

Kanja had never been this close to a highborn princess of Thebes. She was not beautiful but there was something about her that drew the eye. "I hope you didn't whip those poor bearers into a frenzy. How many did you have, four, six?"

"Six," she said.

"Tell me, princess of Thebes, do you often greet guests in your Vizier's bathhouse?"

"No," Neferure whispered.

"Of course you don't. And anyway who's to know."

"My father would know. He could burst in at any moment and you would be horsemeat," she said.

"We both know that's not true. Your father's too drunk to care and your mother is in bed with your tutor."

"You should kneel," she said, walking to the lip of the pool.

"Is that wise?" Kanja was already waist deep in hot water and it was high time he got out.

"I shall decide what is wise," she said, steam rising between them. "You're a common soldier and I am a princess of Egypt."

Kanja saw the coquettish tilt of her chin and it stirred his warrior spirit. He would have her whether she wanted him or not. "And you came all this way to see a blood warrior up close."

"I came all this way to see what the cats are purring about." Her smile was as intoxicating as a rare perfume. One whiff of it and Kanja knew he would be hypnotized. "They were wrong," she said. "There's nothing special about you."

Kanja stood and took a strip of linen from side of the pool. He slowly blotted the water from his chest knowing where she was looking with those large black eyes.

"Is it true your kind feels no pain?" she asked.

Kanja wondered where she had heard such a ludicrous thing. All men felt pain. "Does a snake feel pain?"

"Oh," she said. "Then you cannot love."

Kanja almost choked at that, throat closing around his words. "I said nothing of love."

"Then why are you here?"

"I was summoned." He wrapped the linen around his

waist and stepped out of the pool. "Careful, snakes bite."

She took a step backwards to allow him room. But only a step. "I've been bitten once before and should have died from it."

"But you didn't die."

"No," she murmured.

"Come closer. You'll see me better."

"I can see very well from here, Kanja of the three kingdoms, if that's who you truly are?"

"Who else would I be? A traitor?"

"If you are I should hate to die."

Is this some clever trap to snare one? "You're safer with me than half a hundred men. There's nothing here to hurt you."

"You don't understand. I'm betrothed to a child-prince. Menkheperre will be cruel just like his father. That's how it is with sons."

"Not all sons follow their fathers." *Not all sons try to kill their fathers.*

"Walk with me," she said, giving a high-pitched whistle.

A handmaid with black painted eyes came running from the garden and bowed solemnly. Over one arm she carried a fine linen tunic and in her hand she carried green leather sandals overlaid in gold.

"Dress him," Neferure instructed.

Kanja felt the caress of linen over his head and soft fingers at his feet. He held out his arm and she gave him her hand, and they walked through the gardens in the crisp night air, stars twinkling overhead. He felt a pang of hunger, though food was furthest from his mind.

I'll bed her and forget her, he thought, and then the thing that drove him mad with desire would pass.

There was a well on property with winding steps leading to a glistening maw of water. The princess took him there to lean over the lip and when she shouted, her voice rattled off the stone walls. It was a strange dark place and if Kanja truly believed in monsters, this is where they lived. His father's headman was a monster. He drowned in a well so they said.

"This is where Vizier Thutiy entertains his officials," she said, pointing to a row of offices within the walled compound. "He has four grain silos and seventeen horses, and his flowers are the best in Thebes. After father's of course." She translated the inscriptions on the limestone jambs of the front door, *Vizier Thutiy, beloved of the Pharaoh, fair judge and keeper of the law.* Kanja almost choked on her words.

Thutiy was the biggest liar in Thebes.

A large anteroom with a porter's lodge opened up into the main hall where eight columns painted with lily-shaped capitals supported a ceiling of brilliant blue. Drapes shuddered in a cool breeze and two metal braziers burned brightly as if someone had added an infusion of incense.

"The Vizier's audience chamber," Neferure said, leading him to a smaller room off the main hall with a raised dais and a carved guilt chair. "He looks quite splendid on good days."

Kanja wanted to ask her about the bad days but he held his tongue. A man surrounded by such wealth hardly had *bad* days. He was a king in his own right. Nearly.

"And here," she said, leading him through a second door surmounted in blues and reds, "is the veranda."

He could smell roast fowl and freshly baked bread, and he saw a table spread with platters of calf meat and liver, and dishes of lentils and moonfish. Cushions and rugs were set out on the tiles and couches to recline on, and there was a rectangular pond in the garden shimmering in the moonlight.

Najja and Yuku had a girl in one hand and a cup of wine in the other. Kanja wanted to balk at their laziness, their recklessness, but he wanted their loyalty more. *Give them a hint of what's to come and they'll die for you.*

He sucked down a plate of liver and drank four cups of wine. Neferure talked and talked, and he had no idea what she said. He didn't want her love, not if he had to betray her in the morning. All he wanted was Thebes and he would bait her until he got it.

"You must wear gold, only gold," he heard himself say. In truth, her eyes made his blood rise and his resistance was beginning to wane. "Gold is for Queens."

"And father has so much of it," she murmured.

Kanja was pleased to hear it. "Every occasion is made better with wine," he said, handing her a cup. "And this is one of Siwa's finest."

She seemed to look at him through narrowed eyes, face tilted slightly to one side. Wind buffeted against the stone grills in the windows and all he could think of was the storm. *It's coming*, he thought, yellow mists and barrages of stinging sand. It was the very breath of Thutiy's snakes. Hissing, rasping.

"Have you ever seen the snake god?" he asked.

"No," she said, lying back on a deeply cushioned couch. "What does he look like?"

"A snake," Kanja teased, "with fangs as long as my finger."

Neferure stared at the upturned finger and gave a small smile. "No one's ever seen him. Only father."

"Your father's seen everything. I wonder if he sees me through those heavy lidded eyes and wonders what I might do." *Kiss her and be done with it,* said the voices.

"What will you do?"

"This," he said, lurching forward and catching her round the waist.

He pressed his lips down on hers, sliding one hand down her spine and pausing at the small of her back. She smelled of lotus and sweet spices, and he wondered if he could love her. It was a hot-blooded kiss, a long one, and he knew she would pretend some annoyance at his forwardness. He let go of her suddenly and shuffled back a little.

"You shouldn't have done that," she said, raising a

hand to ward him off. "I am a daughter of Ra. The guards—"

"Are drunk and your father . . . Where is your father?" Kanja said, looking around the veranda.

"He sleeps." Neferure said.

"How careless when he has such a noble guest." Kanja noticed a flicker of a smile on her face and suddenly regretted his words.

"You? Noble? You're no nobler than my handmaid."

"Your handmaid could be the Kandake for all I care. And she's such good company," Kanja said, glancing briefly at the girl astride Yuku's stocky waist. "At least she's in love."

Neferure looked uncertain and then she sighed a little. "I want to be in love."

"I can love you." *For a few nights,* Kanja thought. He took the measure of her relief and then, "You've had lovers before."

"I've kissed a man," Neferure said, spreading her fingers out in a fan against her breastbone. "But there was nothing in it."

You've kissed more than one, he thought, staring at the curve of her hips. With all her beauty and jewels not one wisp of truth came from those shimmering lips of hers. He would make her angry. He would make her cry.

"Perhaps you're right," he said. "There was nothing in the kiss."

"*His* kiss," she corrected.

"Any kiss."

"No," she implored. "There are kisses and there are kisses, some sweeter than others."

"And you would know?"

"I would." Neferure lifted her chin and that crooked nose. "And you have loved so many girls. Do you even know their names?"

"None," he said, reading the disappointment in her face.

He didn't much care for jealousy, the ugliest of all emotions. He felt the saliva in his mouth and the tingling in his fingers, and he glanced away for a time. He thought he saw a woman in the shadows, eyes glistening with tears. She seemed to blend with the trunk of a palm tree as if she was part of the spiny bark. There was only one he loved, only one he worshipped and he wondered if it was her spirit he saw.

"Don't you wish your father could see you now?" he said, taking Neferure's hand.

"*You* see me. Perhaps that's enough," she said, voice twined with desire.

He kissed her again, only this time he could taste the mint on her breath and the jasmine in her hair. He could hear the faint murmur of the wind through the palm fronds and a whisper of grasses by the pond.

Kamara used to smell of jasmine. My Kamara . . .

He couldn't say her name aloud but he thought of her every time he loved. It was the only way he could get through the pain.

Neferure returned that kiss and there was passion in it.

MKASA

Mkasa held Iutha back with a muscular arm. Her breath smelled of sour wine, face twisted with threats. He had no wish to slap his wife but this time was different. There was a pitch to her screams, bitter, devilish as if her body had taken on another spirit. He held a warning finger to her lips but she was too fast for him. The scouring pain on his right cheek was sharper than a scorpion sting and he caught her wrist then, seeing the blood beneath her fingernails.

"You animal!" Iutha shouted, though for what Mkasa couldn't imagine. "You go to Shenq only to see *her!*"

"I go to Shenq because I have been summoned. Come with me."

"I won't. I won't see you staring fawn-eyed at that girl."

"It's only for tonight, my love. And the Commander will pick his men for the races."

Mkasa braced himself with all the strength he had and a flutter of shame lodged itself like a pinecone in his stomach. His only desire was to run to the Commander's house and away from her accusing face.

"Bar the door behind me," he said, wondering if any Bloodmen had followed him home. They were lighter on their feet than he was. "Promise me you'll bar the door."

She nodded, wiping away a tear. "These babes twist and turn. They wear me out."

"You torture yourself," Mkasa said, gesturing to his attendant. "Lie down and rest. It won't be long now."

Iutha watched with those pretty eyes of hers, finger pointing below his belt. "I pray that child of hers isn't yours."

Mkasa tilted his head, stunned at her words. "Gods

woman, are you drunk? I love no one else."

"Liar!" Iutha screamed, waddling past a horizontal loom she could no longer bend down to use.

Iutha's rages had broken Mkasa's resolve and he found himself lying more frequently now. But he still longed for her in his quiet times. "Say what you like," he shouted after her. "I have never broken my vows."

The attendant handed Mkasa his bow. "She threw a vase at me yesterday, my lord," he cackled. "Lucky I ducked."

Mkasa couldn't keep the snigger from his face. Bali's dark eyes still sparkled beneath thick eyebrows. He was a native of Thebes, born in one of the Pharaoh's granaries so his father said.

"Your seal," Bali said, passing the chain over Mkasa's neck. The underside was polished to a shine and there was a fish on the face with a bright green eye. "Better you wear a blue shúkà tonight. We live in hungry territory now."

Pharaoh required all his soldiers to wear a *shenti* and a headdress in the palace. Now Mkasa's braids hung loose down his back and the dark blue sheet hugged his frame just like the tribesmen in the south. He embraced the old man, feeling shoulders bonier than bats wings and he heard the dolor in his voice as he said goodbye. Only a few more *goodbyes* and he might never see Bali again.

"Better use the wall," Bali said with a grimace.

Mkasa could see why. Iutha barred the front door with a scowl on her face and he wasn't in the mood to push her aside. Sprinting to the garden wall, he edged his bare feet into each groove and pulled himself up. The desert was a flicker of torches in the purple evening sky and across the river he imagined the Bloodmen dancing to the beat of their drums. He could hear the sound if he listened and sometimes he imagined the sparkling palace at Tungul and its deep blue pools.

Dropping his weapons on the other side, he vaulted over the wall and rolled as he hit the ground. His belly was a tangle of emotions as he watched the tops of the trees as they swayed in a singing wind, a wind from heaven to waken his soul.

Meryt. Her name was on his lips day and night if only he could forget it.

In his sullen silences he heard the music of the *Shasu* and the clear voice of a woman he had grown to admire. When he dreamed it was always her face he saw. It was wrong of course. A man could not love two women.

There was a roasting pit opposite the Commander's gate where they smoked hog and drew lots for the crackling. It was here the warriors met, patting each other on the back as ribald stories floated on the breeze. Shenq stood amongst them, a man to empower all men, a fighter of life's inescapable battles. Mkasa had never known a better brother except Harran, a man gifted to melt a heart of stone and a joy that stirred the deepest part. He was absent, likely manacled to the Pharaoh's ankle.

Jabari's long neck reached over the rest and he waved an oily bone. "Tell me about the leader of the Bloodmen," he said, drawing Mkasa to one side. "What's he like?"

"Kanja," Mkasa whispered, staring at the setting sun and a flock of terns that bickered on the river. "It means *one from outside*. There's a boy in his troop, eleven, twelve may be. He had a dead vulture in his hand, a ritual kill. They use the heart to see into the eyes of the enemy. Ayize is his name, *let it come*."

Jabari lifted a hand to ward off the flies. There were more rings on him than in a cow's ear. "Did you recognize them?"

"How should I?" Mkasa snapped.

"Think," Jabari persisted. "A scar, a weapon, *anything*."

Mkasa closed his eyes, dragged once more into the nightmares of childhood. He heard the screams again and he saw his sister's beautiful face. Nabukha . . . She was fourteen years old when she died. *Fourteen*, he wanted to say but his lips were stuck around the memory. He saw shadows gyrating in front of a large fire, dancing and shrieking, and pumping the air with their spears. Only it wasn't an ordinary fire. The logs were women, lovely Makurae women, screaming behind a veil of smoke. And if he thought hard enough, he could see the very color of their eyes and the jewelry they wore.

Jewelry . . . He remembered a king wearing a crown crested with ram's horns. He wore beads and cowry shells, and gold piercings in his lip.

"Kanja had an arrow through his lip. Gold it was with a bright red tip."

Jabari snapped his head up, eyes piercing like a stitching awl. "Only nobles wear those."

"No," Mkasa murmured, not daring to trust his suspicions. "He can't be a prince."

"If he is, he's insane," Jabari broke in. "You know what Commander says. He says, 'beware the bush pig. His tusks are not easily seen.'"

Mkasa tasted a sour tang in his mouth and his throat burned. "They'll never get beyond the city gates."

"They've already got past the border." Jabari wiped his mouth, grease streaking down his chest.

"I'd like to row the river and burn the entire camp with the help of a few friends. We could float Kanja's body on the northern current until it sinks altogether. Only it would be just my luck if the birds screeched over it as it drifted ashore. If he is a prince, I would hang for it."

"They can't hang you. You're royalty."

"Their sorcerer can read minds."

"He can't read minds."

"He can read mine."

"He's a yellowhead. He's only interested in himself." Jabari said, snapping the bone and sucking out the marrow.

"Whatever happens to me, promise you'll look after Iutha."

"Nothing will happen to you," Jabari said. "Unless you

go killing in the dark without the Commander's permission. You'll lose all those ribbons of yours."

"*You* can read minds."

"I can read yours," Jabari whispered with a grin.

"I'd rather do my killing on a full stomach."

"There's ox inside," Jabari said. "I found it near the temple. With a halter over its head and a few tugs, it was here in no time."

"You'll be hanged one of these days," Mkasa said, chuckling. He saw a faraway light in Jabari's eyes only it wasn't as bright as it was before. "You still love her don't you?"

Jabari sighed loudly. "A lieutenant has no business courting a princess. I took her riding once that's all."

"You taught her to fight, to use a bow, a chariot—"

"That's all I was good for. She has a tutor to teach her the rest. Better get that ox while it's still hot."

Mkasa dipped his head beneath a leafy bough and walked to the villa with Jabari behind him. He could hear a lyre and the sound of pipes, and the dominant tremor of drums. The dances were southern, ancestral, and he knew them all in his deep heart's core. The tantalizing scent of thyme floated from the gardens and a string of cow-bells chuckled beneath the gate.

Khemwese stood at one corner of the terrace spear in hand. "Greetings, brothers," he said, bowing at the neck. Boar tusks hung from silver rings in his ears and dangled as far his jaw.

"Greetings," Mkasa said, hooking arms with the giant. There was a quiet dignity about him he admired. "Pharaoh let you go I see."

"He sleeps like a cat up a tree. The higher he climbs, the deeper he sleeps."

"What's he drinking these days?"

"Mandrake and chamomile to honor the gods. It'll be several hours before he opens his eyes."

"One day his eyes won't open. One day Kush will call

you *lord.*"

"My time has not yet come."

"But it will come," Mkasa said, wishing it would hurry up. "How can you let him run you ragged like an errand boy?"

"I am an errand boy." Khemwese grinned and inclined his head. "For now."

Mkasa gave him a friendly cuff on the shoulder. "HaShem be praised."

He knew of HaShem because his father often spoke of him. That's how it was with family. But Khemwese? He believed because Harran said things in that confident voice of his and the words echoed through the gardens and the inner courts of the Pharaoh's apartments like the piercing sound of bird song. Khemwese had turned his back on the snake gods and the crocodiles, and he had grown to love the Name.

"I hear there's a side of ox inside," Mkasa said, licking his lips. "A rather big one."

"It took a long time to cook," Khemwese said, "and less time to catch. Jabari is an excellent hunter. He should be rewarded."

"He will be," Mkasa said, "with iron bracelets for his wrists and feet."

"Perhaps a bite of cheese and a loaf of bread will help ease the conscience."

"Ah," said Mkasa, looking at Khemwese's wide-faced smile. Cheese and bread was the last thing on his mind. "Let me pass and I won't say a word."

Khemwese winked and stood aside, revealing a garden filled with dancing women. Mkasa saw Meryt in a gown of pearl, twirling to a stirring pipe and its mournful tune. He hardly felt his feet move in time to the drums like a thousand heartbeats in the earth and he never saw the Commander and his warriors as they pressed forward for a better view. Meryt spun closer and closer, hair slapping against his arm and he wondered what she would be like to touch, if her lips were soft, eager. There was no batting of eyes nor did she look his way. Instead, she dipped him a small bow and left the dance floor, beckoned perhaps by an unseen hand.

It was some time after dinner before Mkasa entered the house through the open terrace. He hoped no one had sensed his eagerness, his curiosity. He found a fresh side of ox wrapped around a spit and he was about to rip a small shard of flesh from its back when he heard the rustle of robes behind him. And there she was, veil ebbing and flowing in a current of air.

"Cousin," she said, leaning forward to kiss him on the cheek. "You dance well."

Words caught in Mkasa's throat for a time as he savored eyes greener than the river. Meryt was splendid in a bodice of nacre intertwined with roses, a gown so strangely opaque, he couldn't see a stitch of skin through it.

"Congratulations, my lady," he stammered, finding it hard to talk and think at the same time.

A faint smile touched her lips and she barely bobbed her head. "You are a moon warrior tonight, I see."

"Just for tonight, my lady."

Meryt's gaze flitted around the room, never settling on him for long. Sometimes her fingers played with her necklace, sometimes they gripped at the sides of her gown. A woman grown, she was fifteen now and his heart hammered just a little louder.

"Do you miss Makuria?"

"I hardly remember it."

He saw the flush that crept along her cheek and the chin that dipped downward. She paused and waited for him to speak, only he delighted in the silence. "This is my home, my lady. And you are my family."

"How is Iutha?"

Sour, hostile, suspicious. "Longing for the babes to come," he said. "I pray it's an easy birth."

She nodded rapidly, lips wide over white teeth. "Pharaoh's astrologer said the moon will be swallowed by the sky. Then the whole world will turn black. Have you ever seen it?"

"The priests say strange things happen when the moon goes black. Like dogs eating children and milk turning sour in the udder. One year an ox plowed through a stable, killing fourteen arabi stallions and then drowning itself in the river. No one would eat the meat for fear of going mad themselves."

He hoped she could read the dread in his voice. But all he saw was a pair of dimples in her cheeks.

"It's all so strange—what you say," she said, looking down. "But then the priests are fond of stories. They can trace their heritage right back to the gods. And even the gods are false."

"You're so beautiful." Mkasa breathed deeply, smelling the scent of rose water in her hair.

She seemed to look at him as if noticing he was there for the first time. "I have so looked forward to our supper. My husband has invited all those he expects to race with him in the Kamaraan."

"It's an honor," Mkasa said, grinning.

He longed for the races, the sound of the war horns, the creaking chariots and the wind against his cheeks. But most of all, he longed for one last sight of her. She would be the last face he would see before he died.

"You will be the pride of Thebes," she said, "all of you. Your names will be on every door post. You will not be forgotten."

An oil lamp brooded and sputtered nearby, drapes swaying in a gust of wind. The lights seemed to dim with every breath and he was frozen with desire, unable to shrink from her as he should. A torrent of black hair hung down her back, shinier than a skein of silk and he wanted to reach out and touch it.

"You'll miss Shenq when he is gone?" The question

was absurd under such circumstances. The Kamaraan was dangerous and she was likely terrified.

Her lips parted in silent agreement and she nodded hesitantly. "He will come home."

"But what if he doesn't?" Mkasa's finger traced her cheeks, softer than the inside of a rabbit's ear. "I will be your champion then."

She stepped backwards, eyes flashing open in surprise just as the drums stopped.

Mkasa pressed a finger against her lips, wanting to take her in his arms to lie beneath two burgeoning roots of a sycamore. Pleasure washed over him, bringing a warmth and sweetness he had never known and he hoped never to break free of the dream. "I would do anything for you, *anything*," he whispered.

"Be gone, you fool," the voice made him turn suddenly and there was Shenq armed with a scowl.

Mkasa saw the stare, colder than the kiss of sea spray. "I meant nothing," he said, holding up his hands, palms outward.

"If my lady were to crook her finger, would you come running?"

"I would," Mkasa said, without flinching.

"Then you're a very brave man. I welcome fearless men especially where you're going."

Mkasa had no idea what Shenq meant and rather hoped he wouldn't find out. As far as he knew, he was going to the east bank at dawn to make friends with a chieftain.

"Are you ready, Mkasa of Makuria? Are you ready to take on the devil himself?"

"I'll take my chances." Mkasa could hear the defiance in his voice even as he said it.

"Your chances are the same as mine." Shenq whispered. "I think that's fair don't you?"

HARRAN

Harran stood behind the Pharaoh's throne, watching the prince's favorite cheetah as it stretched out on its back. It was beautiful, though, with a set of canines longer than his middle finger. He thought the beast would look better from a distance and he edged back a little, pretending a smile of admiration.

"This race," Pharaoh Kheper-Re said, patting the Queen's arm beside him. "It must have obstacles."

"Oh, it will, my lord," Vizier User said, wiping the gloss from his forehead. "I have the plans. I think you'll like them."

The princess sat beside her mother, occasionally looking up at Vizier Thutiy whose hand rested protectively on her shoulder. Thutiy was a known storyteller, an embroiderer of myths, and one of his stories had clearly made her blush.

"I hope these Alodians don't win." Kheper-Re massaged his legs as if he could ease some life back into them. His cheeks glistened with gold ore and his eyes were thick with kohl. "They might, you know."

"The route is dangerous, my lord," User said, "more dangerous than in previous years. They may have to use the Ma'arav pass to get to the white desert. We must not forget the Imazi control the eastern gateway."

Harran knew the Imazi were a nocturnal tribe, pale-skinned as if their bodies were drained of blood. They lived in large caverns beneath the western desert, surfacing only at dusk to hunt.

"My grandfather signed a treaty with their bone-lord," Kheper-Re said. "He even gave him his twin daughters. They were beautiful so my mother said. Lord Tarabin has permission to trade with Thebes. He won't lay a hand on my men."

"Not unless they touch the sacred *shakāl*," User reminded.

"*Shakāl?*" Prince Menkheperre interrupted, leaning forward in his chair. He was dressed in blinding white although somehow the ensemble looked better on his father. "How exciting! I would like to see them, father. I would."

"Read your books, boy," Kheper-Re growled, giving the prince a puzzled look. "That's all you need to see."

"Imazi are fond of their meat," Queen Hatshepsut reminded. "Have you not seen their crowns, their armor? They skewer their enemies over an open fire and eat the flesh right down to the gristle. I saw a crown once. It was made of the bones of men's hands."

"That is true," User said with a little less warmth in his voice. "But the Commander is a resourceful fellow. He'll know what to do."

"My mother tried to marry me to an Imazi princess once," Kheper-Re said. "She somehow got the notion that uniting the two nations would bring color to their cheeks. The women are beautiful, yes, but they're cold to the touch. The wretched girl would have eaten me first. I soon put a stop to that."

"Very wise, my lord," Harran said, narrowing his eyes as the sun began to rise. "The Queen is your first. She should also be your last."

There was a long pause where no one spoke and no one paid it any mind except Harran. The Pharaoh was distracted, eyes scanning the walls as if he could find a single thought amongst the painted reliefs of his ancestors.

"More wine, my lord," Harran whispered.

"Yes, yes, I should like to try the seal of Aten. It is a superior vintage."

Vizier User waved to the cupbearer and glanced at Harran fondly. "There are those that follow the adage that if they fail to find favor with the Pharaoh, they will be destroyed. My father preferred straight-talking folk like your prophet here. Harran is not afraid to tell the truth, my lord. Even if it costs him his life."

"Your father was a very great man," Kheper-Re said, lip quivering as if the memory was painful. "*His* father was a shepherd."

User stiffened. "Who's to say that shepherds cannot be leaders of men, my lord?"

"Leaders of sheep, you mean." Kheper-Re cleared his throat, face redder than a boil. He peered into his cup, bearing his teeth. "This wine is worse than dog piss."

"I might add," User said, seemingly before the Pharaoh had any notion of slapping his cupbearer, "that these plans are similar to ones my father drew. After all, pitting Commanders against each other for the title of Commander-in-Chief of Thebes was his idea. But with your permission I have decided to grant the teams a boon. The first team to arrive at each temple must bring back a token, my lord, of no less than twenty deben in gold."

"Ah," Kheper-Re said, bowing his head in agreement. "You have surpassed even your father, Vizier. A great notion. They will do doubt kill each other for these tokens. I like it."

Harran strained to see the map on the Pharaoh's lap and twice he found the Queen's eyes staring up at him, so black he could almost see his own reflection. Instead, he glanced at User, the second eldest son of the late Vizier Ahmose. He was stocky and as bald as an egg. Installed as Pharaoh's representative after the death of his father, he had proved both honorable and learned.

"The Kamaraan will begin in Thebes and cross the western desert to the great oasis," User continued, small eyes blazing with ideas. "But there are natural hazards, my lord, quicksand and hostile tribesmen to mention a few. And the High Priest of Suhaj is a foul degenerate with an iron wand."

"Ebony, actually," Kheper-Re corrected, "and smaller than mine."

User frowned before bowing his head. "He speaks holy words and utterings, but father said he was soft in the head."

"I'm sure your learned father never said that. Pi-Bak-Amana is a magician, mightier than most. He once had a magic box that spewed blue smoke," Kheper-Re said, head resting on the back of his chair. "Only it was stolen."

"*Wagered*, my lord. Our High Priest has the Box of Heka in the sanctuary of Amun. Thebes holds the world's magic now, my lord."

"*I* hold the world's magic."

"I don't mean to intrude," Hatshepsut said, without looking anyone in the eye. "If the teams leave at the same time, surely they would much sooner turn around and kill one another than race. There would be no excitement in that. What do you say, Prophet?"

"For form's sake," Harran said. "We should allow the Alodians to go first. I think a day should do it. Commander Shenq has good shooters and drivers. They'll soon catch up."

"Good shooters," Kheper-Re repeated, setting his jaw and eyeing Harran as if he was confused about what day of the week it was. "There was a time when I was the greatest of all. I could shoot hog and deer, and reload faster than any man. I drove my own chariot with the reins about my waist. I didn't need a driver. You should have seen the frames of meat I brought home. The streets were full of people cheering and throwing garlands. You remember."

Everyone did and so did Harran. The exhausted animals were herded into a bay of cliffs by the charioteers and all killings were awarded to the Pharaoh whether he loosed an arrow or not. Kheper-Re's eyes were bad now and he had no form at all and, as for driving, he had a keen-eyed tutor to crack the whip and a few bad jokes.

"If the winds come," Hatshepsut continued, "won't the

riders be blown north to the White Desert?"

"Now that would be entertaining," said Kheper-Re, sucking on a date. "This race could take weeks."

User held up a hand and nodded slowly. "Commander Shenq has traveled the white sands many times, my Queen. He was attacked by a large group of sand-warriors at Sitta. He found his way back then."

Harran caught the Queen's eye as she looked up at him. He knew exactly what a deer felt like in the path of a leveled weapon. "Every self-respecting warrior trains daily, my lady, so they can carry four year-old heifers and inflict wounds with a flick of a finger. The Commander is no exception and his mind is a well of tricks."

"Well said," replied Hatshepsut, eyes rolling down Harran's face as if she could no longer meet his eye. "Vizier, we want the best of heralds. We want the best storytellers. I want to hear everything, *see* everything."

"Our heralds will run behind the teams, my lady. And when they bring back the dead, they will bring back news."

A loud tap on the door brought Commander Shenq to the audience chamber in four long strides. His *shenti* was belted with a black sash edged in red and blue, and braided tassels fell to his knees.

"Greetings, Great Bull," he said, head lowered. "The Alodians are awaiting your pleasure. They bring gifts, if it pleases you my lord."

"Send them in if you must though I would prefer it if they were arrow fodder," Kheper-Re muttered.

Shenq saluted. "They will be, my lord. I have excellent shooters in my company."

Kheper-Re seemed to wince at the remark and then nodded. "Bring them in. And on the way out remind them where Alodia is."

Lieutenants Mkasa and Jabari entered, breastplates glinting with precious stones. They escorted seven Alodians, skin shiny with oil and chins painted red. Adorned with beads and feathers, their shúkàs were little more than linen sheets wrapped over their shoulders and falling to their knees. They were a curious breed, Harran thought as he watched them, eyes bouncing from man to man. When they prostrated themselves before the throne, none kept their eyes on the floor.

"Rise," Kheper-Re said, ridding himself of the plans. He shot a glance at ten bearers carrying elephant tusks and chests of spices and unguents.

Vizier User stepped forward and bowed to Kanja. "Behold now His Majesty Pharaoh Kheper-Re, He Whose Royalty Is Divine, Strong Bull, Rich In Power And Protector Of Ra. Hear his voice."

"State your names," Kheper-Re said, looking the warriors over. He seemed to fidget in his seat as introductions were made and he glared at Kanja and the boy at his side.

"May I congratulate the Great Bull of Egypt and his Queen," Kanja said, bowing. His eyes settled on the princess as if she was a fly in a spider's web and his lips glistened with fresh saliva. "Princess Neferure," he said, bowing again.

All eyes turned to the princess whose face showed the subtlest of greetings. Her chest hitched beneath a translucent sheath and her kohl-painted eyes examined Kanja as if he were an unusual breed of horse. She was dressed in crimson and gold, and her hair was thicker than a priest's bell-pull. Harran saw the lust then like a smoldering coal and he knew the girl would never look back.

"She is a jewel," Kheper-Re said. "You may feast your eyes all you want, my illustrious savage. But she goes to the winner, you understand."

"I understand," Kanja said, gazing at Neferure just long enough to make the Pharaoh blanch.

Clever though, Harran thought as he saw Kanja avert his gaze briefly to incite Neferure's curiosity. He seemed to hide behind a façade of vivid colors, taking care not to show his feelings.

"We were not expecting a company from the south," Kheper-Re said, hand resting on Hatshepsut's arm and looking about as if his eyes were following a scurrying mouse. "Where's my cushion?"

"Gracious majesty," Kanja began voice thick with the drawl of his clan. "We were given a seal by your late Commander Osorkon, administrator of Buhen and principal of the border fortresses. But I understand it's no longer valid."

"It was never valid. The Commander you speak of was a traitor. We burn traitors and scatter their remains to the four winds." Kheper-Re beckoned to the attendant with some impatience. "Ah, here comes my cushion."

Commander Shenq walked forward, hardly giving Kanja a second look. "Commander Osorkon mentioned King Ibada before he died. Seems they knew each other very well."

"King Ibada knows many nobles in Egypt," Kanja said, tilting his head. "He is a well-loved king."

Was, Harran thought, sensing a prickling in his belly, a warning. The warrior was strong, body ripe with muscle and tattoos that indicated he was a higher caste than just a spearman.

"Tell me, how *is* King Ibada?" Shenq said.

"Ill," Kanja shook his head and the rings in his ears rattled as he spoke. "That's why we came to Thebes. To find a doctor."

"What's wrong with him?" Shenq said with an unfocused gaze.

"He vomits blood."

"Does he have a taster?"

"All kings have tasters."

"We received no word of your arrival," Shenq said. "Commander Osorkon has been rotting in hell for over a year and here you are with four hundred men."

"I have been sent to extend the hand of friendship,

Commander, and to appeal—"

"Friendship? You call the destruction of Makuria *friendship*?"

"The war was over ten years ago. I wasn't aware Makuria fell under the protection of Egypt," Kanja said, eyes flitting towards the princess.

"It does," Shenq said. "But of course you knew King Ibada destroyed it all, villages, livestock, lands. South winds blew slaves north to Egypt and there's no knowing if Makurae royalty cuts stone for the Pharaoh under the blazing sun. Or if the Pharaoh's cupbearer is indeed a prince."

Kanja eyed the cupbearer with some trepidation and then laughed. "I would know a Makurae if I saw one."

"As I would recognize an Alodian prince if he were a spit-throw away."

Harran shivered. There was another prince standing by the Pharaoh's door, meeker than a milk cow. It was lucky no one mentioned him.

"King Ibada's campaigns were before my time, Commander," Kanja said, glancing briefly at Mkasa. "Even so, I was told the Makurae were terrorizing the Alodian farmers along the borders, burning their fields and stealing children. If it wasn't for King Ibada's spies, Alodia would be a pile of ash."

"Do you hunt?" Shenq said with a sidelong glance.

"I have been hunting since I was a child," Kanja said, exchanging a look with Othene.

"You don't look like a hunter."

"I have been hunting for twelve years."

"*Twelve years*," Shenq murmured, nodding. "You look so young."

Harran knew Shenq was familiar with the Alodian rites of passage, how the warriors shaved their heads when they came of age. Kanja had elected to keep his hair long to look younger than he was.

"I have killed over two hundred elephants and

numerous leopards," Kanja said, lifting his chin a little higher. "But never the black leopard."

Shenq smiled that characteristic smile, white teeth flashing behind bold lips. "The black leopard is tricky to hunt. Only kings can bring them down. Take that boy there. I'll wager a fine arabi horse he has royal blood. And if he does, the leopard's his."

"I see you share great affinity with the creature. Perhaps you even share his manners." Kanja kept a heavily ringed hand on Ayize's shoulder. "The insignia of my clan is the vulture, Commander. Ever caught one of those?"

"Scavengers and demons. I wouldn't waste my time on them," Shenq said, turning to face Othene with a tired smile. "Tell me, sorcerer, how many demons does it take to be in the presence of evil?"

Othene fixed Shenq with a frosty stare, lip dripping with gold. "Only one."

"And you would know."

A trickle of laughter came from Shenq's men and Harran confined his to a snort. Othene had no idea what he was up against.

"These men are stronger than you think, Commander," Kanja said with a smile that expected to win Shenq over. "Stronger than their guardian spirits."

"Then I propose a challenge just to see how *strong* these spearmen are."

Kanja blew out a series of short breaths, eyes darker than death. Sometimes those same eyes flicked towards Khemwese, studying him behind a squint. "What are you proposing?"

"You may dance in the flames of a traitor's fire," Shenq said, smiling, "or you may run the Kamaraan. The winner will earn the title of Commander-in-Chief of Thebes and the hand of the princess. He will also take house and lands from the loser. That includes wives, my friend."

Harran flinched when he thought of his sister bartered to a rout of wolves. Once a lady's maid and attendant to the Queen, she was now married to the great Commander of Thebes.

"Do you have a wife?" Shenq said as if he enjoyed the crossfire. He had enough arrows to defeat hell.

Kanja shifted on his feet, shooting a glance at the princess. He took his time to answer and when he did it was no more than a sigh. "She's dead."

"Then you have nothing to barter with."

"I have cattle and pasture."

No one else saw the silent communication between Kanja and Vizier Thutiy. But it was loud enough for Harran. There was something between them, a subtle shake of the head, a look. If he wasn't mistaken, they had met before.

"Commander-in-Chief is a generous reward. But to marry a princess . . ." Kanja murmured, lips stretched over white teeth. "I accept the challenge."

"To race you mean," Shenq said over another ripple of laughter.

"To race," Kanja said, nodding.

Neferure reached for another cup of wine and raised it high. But there was a tale behind those eyes, thick and dark as if she already knew the power of the scorpion's sting. Her heart seemed afire with a dangerous longing but there was something else that made Harran grimace. It was a raw-boned power, the kind girls had over men they never really wanted.

Harran smiled. Kanja had truly met his match.

"You have a sorcerer to lead the way and I have a prophet," Shenq said, folding his arms and cocking his head. "I'll wager my best horse you'll never return. Surely the traitor's fire is quicker. Less painful."

Prophet? Harran had not expected Shenq to choose him and he barely heard Kanja's voice as it tried to gust away the whispers in his head. *Race . . . in the Kamaraan? Him?* He flashed a look at Khemwese and all he saw was a mellow smile. *Blessed are you Lord, our God, King of the Universe, for*

*sending me someone who knows how to use a spear. And Father?
Just one more thing. If I do have to go, be my shield and my guide.
And let Khemwese do the fighting. He's so much better at it than I
am.*

"Your prophet is a star-gazer. My sorcerer can read
minds." Kanja glanced at Harran with those black eyes of
his, mouth set in a tight grin. "I'll take my chances."

"You underestimate our Chief of Prophets. He saw you
coming—"

"He has good eyes then."

"—In a dream," Shenq continued.

Kanja's posture seemed to stiffen and there was a bead
of sweat on his chest that streaked down the narrow
channel of his abdomen. Harran rather suspected the sly
glance Kanja gave him was one of fascination rather than
hatred, and he wondered if he would have admired Kanja
had they not been enemies.

"The races will begin on the first day of Meshir," Shenq
said. "Pharaoh will provide horses and chariots. The rest is
up to you."

Kanja cleared his throat. "Why concern yourself with
the *rest?*"

"Because," Shenq said in a tone that suggested Kanja
was quite the simpleton. "You are not familiar with the
chariot and as for the hurdles, there are ancient temples
run by mad priests and deep wells of poisoned water."

"As I said, Commander, I'll take my chances."

"And Imazi," Kheper-Re whispered, leaning forward in
his chair. "And *shakāl.*"

The Pharaoh's drawn out rendition of the desert
dangers almost made Harran laugh. And by the look of it,
Shenq was holding back a chuckle himself.

"Vizier Thutiy," Kheper-Re said, waving his cup.
"These are fine young men don't you think?"

"Indeed, Great Egypt," Thutiy said coming out from
behind the princess's chair. "And so I must pray to Amun
that your Prophet is as well-equipped as theirs. It would be

a shame to wager so much with so little."

Harran suddenly felt like a leper with no arms. He tried to keep his face a mask even though his belly churned with dread and he felt faint. *The heat*, he tried to tell himself. And the incense which seemed to get thicker by the moment.

Kheper-Re ignored the jibe with a good-natured nod of his head. "Henceforth, they shall be known as the Bloods. My team will be known as the Hawks after the very crown of Egypt." He gave Hatshepsut a light tap on her arm, eyes flicking to the door. The women stood and bowed, retreating to the Queen's apartments.

"Vizier, escort the Bloods back to the east bank and bring them ox and wine from the temple. They shall have a feast before they ride."

"Very good, my lord," Thutiy said, bowing.

Kheper-Re gave Kanja a long hard stare as he departed and only the young Alodian boy returned it with a small smile and a polite nod.

"I thought the heathens would never leave," he said as the doors swung shut. "They're striking and regal. I say these races will be the most brutal we've had yet."

"I see the heart of a snake, my lord," Harran offered, stroking his beard. He didn't like the look of Kanja or his sorcerer. One was young and reckless, and the other a tired old man desperate for riches. If he wasn't mistaken, the sorcerer stared at Kanja with a bite of jealousy.

"Well said, Prophet," Kheper-Re replied. "I hardly think this *Kanja* has been wallowing about in the river like a frisky hippo. He's been watching the palace for months."

"I have an idea," Harran offered. "Well, I think it's a good idea." Several pairs of eyes were wide with anticipation and Harran swallowed a tiny glob of spit. "Royal marriage treaties insist princesses marry princes. If this Kanja of Alodia is a spearman he clearly doesn't qualify. He must prove kingship before he can take our beloved daughter into his tent."

"Ah," Kheper-Re murmured, lips suddenly widening into a grin. "You shall have five goats and a herder's cottage. I'll kick out the herder and you can have his cottage."

"There is something else, my lord," Harran said, feeling sorry for the herder. "Vizier Thutiy has some knowledge of the southern kingdoms. He may know these warriors very well. Isn't that so, Commander?"

Kheper-Re stroked a powdered cheek and stared at Shenq. "How well?"

"I have been following the Vizier for some time, my lord," Shenq said. "Seems he's been promised a title in return for favors."

"Favors?" Kheper-Re said, taking a few good swallows of wine. "What kind of favors?"

"Girls."

"And where does the Vizier find these *girls*?"

"They come from the village and from the palace, my lord."

"The palace—"

"Princess Neferure has offered herself as a gift. She is quite smitten with our red guests."

"She's a fool!" Kheper-Re barked.

"A very useful one," Shenq said. "He may tell her who he really is."

Kheper-Re snatched more wine from the cupbearer's tray. "He's nothing but a savage. He'll kill her first."

"Not if he wants Thebes. And who wouldn't love such a beauty," Harran encouraged, thinking fast. "She can speak nine languages and play the harp."

"Do you think he cares?" Kheper-Re groaned, dazed and stiff. "He'll chew her up and spit her out! That's what dogs do. He won't get Thebes. He won't get my throne. And if he lays *one* hand on her, I'll skin him myself."

Harran gave an exaggerated shudder. He knew the Pharaoh expected it. "The Commander's right, my lord. This *dog* might be ready to whisper his real name in a fit of passion. And if he is a prince, we'll send him home under armed guard. Imagine how grateful King Ibada will be. Imagine how much gold he might give in return."

Kheper-Re was silent for a time, grunting now and then, and mumbling sounds of disapproval. "No doubt you'll want more goats before you leave."

Harran was overjoyed at the sin offerings. He would spatter the blood against the altar and burn the fat for HaShem. "I would be most grateful," he replied, wondering how to enlarge the tiny goat pen he already had. He began to pray in earnest for the wisdom of the Most High to be like the small rain on the tender herb.

"And you." Kheper-Re turned to Shenq. "The priests will work the Heka and you'll take the magic box to Suhaj. The High Priest will give anything to have it back. *Anything*, you understand?"

"My lord." Shenq cleared his throat. "This is most generous."

"Generous? There is nothing *generous* about it! I won't see my kingdom lost to the enemy. You will stand in for the prince," Kheper-Re said. "And you *will* win. I don't want my daughter marrying a red-painted heathen and we don't want Egypt going to the pigs. Is that understood?"

"Yes, my lord. Though there is one small issue," Shenq said, face aslant like a brilliant bird of prey. There was a conspiracy of silence between them until he spoke again. "The rules of the Kamaraan do state that there can be no substitutes. The prince must ride."

KANJA

Kanja paused and lowered his bow. He could see little of the river beyond the dense thicket where slivers of moonlight barely penetrated and it was too dark to make out a track beneath the detritus. He hid behind the spiny trunk of a palm tree, listening to the breeze as it caressed the silver discs at his forehead.

There was a light coming from the river and below it a boat cutting a swift course towards the east bank. White robes revealed three priests fighting the rage of the river with long painted oars and a fourth stood at the stern swinging a lighted torch from side to side. Water spattered against the ram figureheads both fore and aft, and Kanja could make out a hooded figure in the deckhouse reclining behind silken drapes. He sensed a flash of excitement as a priest gave shout and four Alodian warriors leapt down to the river's edge to pull the boat in.

Neferure sprang into his thoughts and he liked what he saw, though not half as much as the precious stones that twinkled amongst a torrent of hair. If Kanja wasn't mistaken, Thutiy had interpreted his nightly trysts as infatuation and he had brought the lady with him. She stood ten paces behind him, heavily veiled.

"Thutiy," Kanja hissed, stepping out from behind the tree. "Where have you been?"

"Forgive me. The lord Commander came to my house again last evening."

"What does he want?"

"He *wants* to know whose side I'm on."

Kanja saw the puckered brow and the pained expression. "He knows nothing."

"He knows *something*," Thutiy whispered. "He asked for

the keys to my house and worse, he asked me to surrender my title. He said I had no business being a Vizier, not if I was thieving from the treasury."

"Are you?"

"I took a few gold statues. Enough to pay for my passage to Suhaj."

"You're leaving."

"I must go tonight if I am to live."

Kanja wondered if Thutiy knew a good deal more if only he chose to share it. The Pharaoh loved him well enough and he was curious as to why Thutiy needed to steal at all. "What have you brought?"

"The princess. I told her father she would serve in the temple for three days with the priestess of Hathor. That way the soldiers won't come looking for her. I can only imagine what she wants but for Amun's sake don't ruin her. She's not a harlot."

"It's bad enough she comes so willingly. Don't slander her as well," Kanja murmured, eyeing a twist of black hair that peeked beneath her veil. He had three days to enjoy the girl and Thutiy to thank for it.

"I've brought yeast, henna and linseed," Thutiy whispered, beckoning to the warriors to empty the boat. "There's frankincense and mandrake for pain, and wine to mix it with."

"Any gold, silver?"

"I took what I could." Thutiy gave an easy nod. "I'll keep company with the spell-caster until you send for me."

"And I shall build you a tomb greater than any High Priest before you," Kanja intoned, drawing himself up to look noble. The bone disk at his forehead seemed to fascinate Thutiy as well as the wool threads in his hair. "Send greetings to Pi-Bak-Amana. Tell him to work the serpent's magic. Tell him to summon it to the skies."

"It will be a privilege. Amun be with you," Thutiy whispered, looking furtively through a fan of leaves.

"And with you," Kanja said.

114

The Vizier sprinted away through the undergrowth, a watery phantom surging between the trees, a phantom Kanja hoped he would never see again.

"Princess," Kanja said. "May Horus bless you a thousand times."

"Commander," Neferure whispered, eyes lively beneath a sweep of lashes.

Gods, she's beautiful, he thought, eyes trailing her hair, her neck. She was strong, willful perhaps. He liked that in a woman.

Taking her hand, he walked back to the camp, hearing the sound of mellow drums in the distance. Twice, he paused to listen to the shrill whistle that announced the departure of a black kite from its roost and twice he saw the bird in the starry blackness.

An omen, he thought imagining the serpent of the skies. It would come soon to purge the land with fire. He thought he had seen one once, wings a membrane of skin, large-toothed jaws and a long tail. Some said the creature could breathe fire, burning up the desert and sucking up the waters of the great river.

But it was a myth.

His eyes caught the sign of fresh hoof prints in the mud by the water's edge leading to the ridgeway on higher ground, a drover's road. The tracks belonged to a horse proceeding at a careful walk, one that had stopped for a drink while its rider caught his breath. The width between the near and off hooves determined a broadchested breed with a striding gait, one like the Commander had.

The glow of firelight shuddered against the tents as they entered the campground and Kanja could hear the pounding of the rawhide drums. He nodded at Shenq's soldiers at the boundary, amused at their ignorance. They likely thought the veiled woman was nothing more than a harlot.

"You will dance for me," Kanja said, longing to take her right there. Protocol denied such a rash move. She was a princess. She deserved a tent.

"It is my pleasure," she whispered, struggling to maintain a modest smile.

"My house is yours." Kanja beckoned with a sweeping hand. *And so is my bed.*

Neferure took off her veil and stood before the roaring fire, feet tapping the earth in time to the drum, curling and twisting like warp on a pegged loom. The wine would take away all nervousness and she would be dancing naked if he had his way.

Othene tapped him on the arm with a cup of warm milk and herbs. "I had a dream, a moon dream. I heard a voice crying in the rain. A child's voice."

Kanja drained the cup and tensed, feeling sweat pooling on the small of his back. He hoped it wasn't Ulan. Without the Alodian burial chants to lead a soul to its celestial home, the spirit would wander on the plains until it found an animal to indwell. *Better my horse, O precious brother,* he sighed, wanting Ulan with him always. He loved his mare with her wedge-shaped head and small muzzle. She was the only female left he truly loved.

"Tell me," he urged, almost losing his legs. The potion was more powerful than the last. When Othene's hair turned the color of straw, he knew he was past caring.

"He said there was a storm coming," Othene said. "He said there were dogs, so many dogs."

Kanja sat on a log and stared at the ground. He dreaded the loping *shakāl* and he could almost feel the choke of teeth around his throat. "Drone the mysteries and send in those storms. Better now than later."

"Whatever pleases you, my prince."

Kanja watched the girl dance, sensing a desire so feverish he almost didn't know where he was. "Have you ever wanted a woman more than war bow?"

"No," Othene said flatly.

"Then you have never truly loved. Loving a woman is better than battle-bliss. Better than when your dagger bites and twists, better than the snarl of an open throat."

He dropped the cup as the muscles in his legs began to twitch and he stood hesitantly at first, feeling the ground beneath bare feet. He walked towards Neferure with only one thing on his mind and he cared little at the sound of popping bone when he grabbed her by the wrist.

"You're hurting me," Neferure said, trying to wrench her hand free.

"You wouldn't be walking if you were hurt." Kanja released his hold and passed his arm around her waist instead. "You danced for me. Now you're afraid of me?"

"Not afraid," she said, dark eyes widening.

No, not afraid, he thought. She wasn't above torturing him with those milk-white thighs of hers and he wondered if she had merely been sent to trap him. He shook his head, not wanting to hear another word. She was like a beautiful snake, coiled and shimmering, waiting to rise up and spit.

"Come," he murmured, dragging her into his tent.

"You have no right—"

"I have more rights than you know, girl."

"I'm a princess," she snapped.

"And I'm king of the world," he said, seeing a raised hand that seemed ready to beat him in earnest.

He anchored that hand before it slapped him. There she was, dark and glorious and all he wanted to do was break her pride. He glanced at a flickering oil lamp in the center of the tent where a thick dowel stretched from floor to roof and a length of rope hung from a rafter.

"Savage!" she cried, body suddenly shaking when she saw the rope.

"Then I must behave like one."

"Touch me and I'll kill you," she said, drawing a dagger from her belt. It was a beautiful dagger, curved and glinting with precious stones.

Kanja laughed deep from his belly and he felt a surge of excitement as she rushed on, blade held in a downward lunge. He blocked her all the same, twisting the knife from her hand. He wanted to push her down amongst the thick carpets until she was half-forgotten and helpless like a pinioned bird. Then he would be sated, holding her tightly, whispering, cajoling until she fell quiet from her whimpering. Only this girl was different. She wanted his very soul.

"Why did you come here?" he said, trapping both her hands in one of his and prizing the dagger from her grip.

"A common man would never touch a princess," she said trembling, mouth aquiver. "A prince wouldn't hesitate. I know who you are, Kanja of Souba. If you were truly a spearman, how would you know about fine wines or that they even come from Siwa?"

Kanja placed the dagger in his belt before lunging for the rope. He pressed her against the dowel and tied her to it. The little harlot had only been bullied by her father to get him to admit he was a prince. A feeble snare if ever there was one.

"You tried to poison your father," she said through bitter tears, "you and that brother of yours. And then you tried to smother him. You can't keep me here. You can't!"

"Lies, all lies!" he said, truly believing it. "No one knows you're gone. Last the Pharaoh heard you were taking offerings to the temple."

"Thutiy's a traitor," she sobbed. "And you . . . you have no heart."

Kanja felt his fists ball in frustration and his mind screamed as he tried to hold back. Her eyes motioned behind him and he turned, frozen by another pair of eyes.

Ayize.

The boy had seen it all and there was hatred in that look. His mouth was pressed in a white line as he sat in the corner, knees pulled up against his chin.

Kanja paused for a moment, forehead beaded with sweat. "Hate me all you want, brother. Now our war begins."

MKASA

It was twilight when Mkasa left his house. His wife's plaintive voice still echoed along the twisting path, a bitter sound over the rippling river. The scuffle of swamp hens alerted him to a nest of floating reeds and the rustling trees made him shiver. If the Commander's gate was locked he knew he could climb the wall with his bare feet. He could climb a sheer rock-face if he had half a mind to.

"Greetings. You're early," Khamudi said, pushing the gate open.

"Early?" Mkasa gave a shy smile. He knew Shenq was still at the palace, reluctantly waiting for the prince to fall asleep. It would be an hour or more before he came home that night.

"You came to make eyes at a young girl. Beware the flail, my lord. It's never far behind," Khamudi said, patting his own rump.

Mkasa heard the sound of a grinding pestle. Ranefer was mashing a bowl of chickpeas in the kitchen, tutting in mild annoyance. "Master's not here," she said as he walked towards her. "He'll welcome you with a hug before he cuts your throat."

Mkasa put an arm around her and took a small pouch from his waist. Two gold rings spilled out onto the table, glinting furtively in the torchlight. "My mother's."

"You're a fool," Ranefer said, mouth tightening as she worked the pestle. "You have a wife at home."

"Childbirth always goes hard when there's two."

"Ah, then you're justified," Ranefer said with a shudder. "Poor girl, all alone in that house. You should be ashamed of yourself."

Mkasa was ashamed even when he picked up the rings

and walked through the house. Behind the drapes on the terrace a young girl sat, embroidering a shawl. She was dressed in a purple gown embellished with amethyst, a weave so fine it could have been woven from thin air. He walked towards her, catching the musty aroma of palm wood in the hearth.

"Greetings, my lady," he said gently. "I've brought you something."

"For my husband?" Meryt asked, looking at the rings in his upturned hand. A jewel-studded shawl slipped from her bare shoulder and she tugged it back into place.

"For you," he whispered, coaxing with an anxious voice.

Mkasa saw her tremble. He saw both hands wound tightly together as if she could not take them. "You're afraid of him," he said.

"He has never been unkind to me."

"Then why do you hide?" Mkasa was familiar with her hiding places, a hollowed out tree in the garden, a laundry hamper. "You do hide, don't you?" he pressed.

"I was afraid of him once," Meryt said, eyes suddenly distant. "He came to me over a year ago in the women's garden and offered himself as a husband. I hardly knew him then."

"And now?" Mkasa advanced slowly, holding out a hand as he would to an unbroken colt. He could lie to her and say the Commander was a licentious man with an arsenal full of women. But it wasn't true.

"And now," she said, taking his hand and standing, "he is my champion."

"Do you love him?"

The question seemed to startle Meryt and she looked up at the torches burning along the walls, eyes floating this way and that. "Little-by-little, I do."

"You have *my* heart," Mkasa whispered.

It was a bold thing to say as he pressed her hand against his chest. He did not expect an answer and when it came his heart throbbed so loudly he thought she might hear it. "You are more precious to me than our City of the rising sun. I am bound to you, my lady."

"Then you are no better than a prisoner," she said ruefully. "A man in chains."

"Those are chains I welcome," he said.

There was a chill in the air though he wondered if he had imagined it, and a tart fragrance about her with a hint of lemons. It was the same scent Shenq wore.

"Iutha was the Queen's companion. She . . ." Meryt's voice trailed off as if she dared not talk of her and Mkasa dreaded what she might say.

"She lay with the Pharaoh before she was given to me," he said. "It's his child she carries not mine."

"Pharaoh takes what he wants," Meryt said, refusing to go silent beneath his gaze. "He takes it over and over again. And there are bruises and red eyes. And so many tears."

Mkasa scowled at that and bit his tongue. "Her tears are not for me nor are her dreams. Do you dream?"

"Sometimes," Meryt said, "but yes, I dream."

"*You* are in my dreams. It's your face I see not hers." Mkasa knew such dreams would never come true unless Shenq died in the race. He could die. All of them could die. The very thought lit a spark in his mind. "Promise me . . . promise me if your husband dies, you'll marry me."

Meryt shook her head and took back her hand. "You have a wife."

Every time Mkasa thought of Iutha it was like chewing on a piece of gristle. "If Iutha dies in childbed, will you marry me?"

"She won't die," Meryt murmured, veil a shimmer of purples and blues. "She has the Queen's nurse to care for her."

"*If* she dies," Mkasa persisted. He sucked on his bottom lip, waiting in the silence, waiting for the girl to tell him what to do.

Meryt pulled the shawl up over her head, sweeping the extremities over both shoulders. "I know about dreams," she said walking towards the terrace. "They're lies. All lies."

"What are lies?" Shenq strode in from the garden and bobbed his head beneath the drapes.

"Dreams, my lord," Meryt said.

Shenq took her hands in his and kissed them, eyes feasting on her for a time before nodding at Mkasa. "Greetings, cousin. You're early I see."

Five warriors gathered behind Shenq, Khemwese, Jabari, Harran, Meru-Itseni and Captain Tehute, all dressed in the black and gold trimmings of their company. Mkasa bowed his head, feeling a knot in his belly bigger than a man's fist. He would hide his fear if he had to.

"The Kamaraan begins in two weeks," Shenq said, ushering them to his table. "I suggest we begin training tomorrow, Pharaoh's orders."

"The Pharaoh has lost three commanders in the past six years," Meryt said, with a worried frown.

"That's because I killed every one, my lady" Shenq said to a round of laughter.

Mkasa heard the rustle of leaves on the terrace and something in him wanted to bolt towards the river path and away from all this madness. There was a change in the air he couldn't define as if the warriors were turning into demons.

"Lieutenant Mkasa brought me these," Meryt said, holding out the rings for all to see.

"How generous," Shenq said. "They're worth a year's supply of beef."

The house rang with joyful laughter and they all reclined amongst a nest of cushions where goblets of blue glass were laid out on a short table. Ranefer brought in bowls of soup and ostrich eggs, honeyed ribs and square baked loaves.

Mkasa's ears were tuned to the snapping of the fire in

the grate and the murmuring of voices but none of it concerned him. He searched for eagerness in Meryt's expression, a flicker of devotion. But she was timid and her eyes rarely found his without dipping to the floor. It was like staring into a pale flame, lost in the magic of it, and he hardly noticed Jabari poking him playfully in the ribs.

"Don't stare, brother," Jabari whispered. "Not at another man's wife."

"I wasn't staring."

"You were. Commander sees *everything*."

"Does he know how you used to visit the princess? Does he know how often you vaulted over that balcony at night?"

"Probably." Jabari sipped his wine and sighed. "It was a month ago when she cried, when she told me she couldn't see me anymore. She told me she didn't love me."

Mkasa fixed his eyes on his friend, feeling a rush of pity and then anger. "Her eyes deceive her, brother. If they keep looking to the east, she'll be nothing more than a *huna*."

"A king's whore?" Jabari said. "Not her. Pharaoh must have given her a commission."

Mkasa hoped he was right. Pharaoh was ruthless when it came to enemies. And the Alodians were enemies. He listened to the chatter of the men, sometimes hearty, sometimes solemn, and he breathed in the rich scents of the gardens, wondering why he felt so gloomy.

"Jabari says there are wild dogs in the dunes, sir. Bigger than foxes and smarter than men," Harran said, bouncing a curled knuckle against his lips.

"*Shakāl* have eyes the color of the moon and a pelt softer than a baby's head," Shenq replied. "If we kill one, the pack will take revenge. And they know who to follow."

"And the quicksand?" Harran said, face alight with simple things.

"There's a shimmer on the sands only a hunter can see

and the horses can smell danger for miles. We have seven good men, counting our beloved prince. He will be dressed in bronze plate and treated as an equal."

"Sir?" Mkasa said, counting the number of warriors at the table. Including the prince, the total was eight, one more than the Pharaoh has assigned. He tried to pour himself some wine but there was none left in the jug. "Have you selected all your men?"

"I have." Shenq entwined his fingers in Meryt's and turned casually towards Mkasa. "You'll find more wine in the kitchen."

Mkasa found Shenq's houseboy in the open-air kitchen dinking barley beer through a straw. He was usually a cocky boy with a smile that almost reached his ears, only tonight he wasn't smiling.

"There," Shepses said, pointing to a jug of wine on the floor. He scampered behind the grain silos and disappeared into the shadows.

Mkasa took four large gulps from a cup tied to the lug handle of a large jug. He looked up at the starry sky and saw a swirling mist hanging in the air like a ladies veil. He could see the spine of the great mountain range to the west and to the north, he imagined the wetlands of the delta where the moon commanded the tides, water lapping against the shore. It was quiet as he drained another cup, captivated by its sweetness.

"What do you know of these Bloodmen," a voice said.

Mkasa whirled towards the sound and there was Shenq behind him with a flail in his left hand. "They won't touch the hide of a jackal or drink water that flows south, sir. They're afraid of horse's eyes and cattle with broken horns. The beetle that rolls dung across the sands is an omen, a death chime—"

"And they're excellent marksmen," Shenq said. "They have night-eyes. If they can bring a bird down at night then we're well matched wouldn't you say?"

"Yes, sir."

"You asked me if I had picked my men," Shenq said with a careful tilt of his head. "I have one too many. So I got to thinking. It's much easier to destroy a fortress from inside its walls, don't you agree?"

"Yes, sir."

"We believe the youngest of the Bloodmen is the crown-prince. If it's true, we need to bring him home before they kill him."

Mkasa was conscious of a particular strain of evil clawing inside his chest. He was afraid. More than he had ever been in his life.

"If I had a man willing to steer these savages into a pit of their own making, Thebes would be a safer place," Shenq murmured. "I know what you're thinking. Riding with a pack of demons will cost you your sanity, even your life. That you would give anything to be on my team . . ."

Mkasa felt his body sway like a barley stalk and he hardly heard the words, those terrible words. He was lightheaded, more so than when he first arrived. It was the wine.

"They will take you in willingly," Shenq continued, "especially with the scars of shame on your back."

"I'd rather die a Theban, sir." Mkasa felt his forehead pucker and the tickle of sweat on his cheek. "And Kanja won't take me. He's no fool."

"Of course he'll take you. He's the very seed of evil. He wants to win, doesn't he?"

Mkasa sensed the familiar prickling of fear. He knew Shenq was right. Kanja could do with a native, one that knew the desert better than his own hand. "Please, brother . . ."

"God sends only His best."

Mkasa felt strong hands as they pressed him against the wall. The wine was thick with joyroot, enough to remove the after-burn but not the pain of the flint-shards as they bit into his flesh. On and on the flail struck his back until it was torn to shreds. When it was over Shenq looked him in the eye.

"Go to the temple of Isut and give these jewels to the priest," he said, handing him the two rings Mkasa had brought for Meryt. "He has more need of them than my wife. I've requested milk and cattle for Kanja. You won't go empty-handed."

Mkasa heard the crack in his resolve even as he tried to recover. The rings were once his father's and now Shenq was punishing him for it.

"It will take all a warrior's cunning to come out of this alive. Take this," Shenq said, unsheathing a gold hilted knife from his belt. "Say you stole it from the Pharaoh's Commander. Say you have been stripped of your titles and possession. That should do it."

Mkasa began to shake and he saw the pathetic form of Shepses beside the silos with a hand across his mouth and glistening eyes. They all knew.

Jabari approached with an empty quiver. "It wouldn't do to take weapons," he said. "We can't send you off with a full hand."

Mkasa felt his knees buckle and he put out a hand to steady himself. "Look after Iutha. It's you she'll turn to when I'm gone."

"I'll go to her tonight and I'll tell her you're a hero. You will come home." Jabari sighed, teeth tracing his bottom lip.

Mkasa turned towards Shenq with a half-smile and bowed his head. "You think too highly of me, sir. Pray to HaShem. I don't think He knows who I am."

KANJA

Kanja sat on a freshly-hewn log with Othene on one side and Massui on the other. He was already heady with wine and the drums droned out the voices in his head. Girls danced in front of the fire, bellies glistening with sweat and precious stones, and sometimes they leaped and sometimes they shrieked. A troop of bearers paraded through the campsite, frames piled with food and jugs of wine. There was goat's cheese wrapped in ox tongue and ribs drenched with date wine.

"Our Pharaoh is most generous," Kanja said, tearing the flesh from a goose leg with his teeth. "He sends the best of his stocks to fatten us up. What can he possibly want?"

"Your brothers are afraid to eat it." Othene warned, raking a hand through his yellow hair. "They think it's poisoned."

"Poison! Poison!" Massui moaned, swaying from side to side.

Kanja glanced at Ayize cross-legged on the ground. He stared long enough to get the boy's attention and there was a scowl on that sad young face. "The milk-men will eat it first. Let's see if they dream and vomit."

Othene shouted at a group of herders, urging them to eat. He turned then and placed a hand on Kanja's shoulder. "So our little princess has accused you of poisoning your father."

"She's doesn't know what she's saying," Kanja said. "He's sick. Do you hear that boys? *Sick*. And we are here to find medicine, the best!"

Both Ayize and Massui nodded, eyes wider than cups.

Truth was, Kanja could never let her go. Not now that

she knew who he was. "She thinks she can play me like a harp," he said, voice faint. "She's a fool to think it."

"Fool! Fool! Fool!" Massui cried, ticking the words off on his plump fingers.

"Calm yourself, sweet brother," Kanja said, patting Massui on the wrist.

Near the fire, a bearer cast a narrow-eyed look at Kanja and bowed his head before leaving. He was a giant of a man with a belt edged in gold and a sword at his hip. It was a bronze khopesh with an inscription below the crossguard like the ones the Meroëvians wore. Kanja wanted it as soon as he saw it. *A prince's sword,* he thought, riveted to its silvery sheen. A bolt of jealousy nearly brought him to his feet.

"No," Othene said. His eyes were glazed from the visions and when he spoke there was a dream-like quality to his words. "He's one of Shenq's riders."

"How do you know?"

"See his breastplate?"

Kanja did. It was a corselet of precious stones decorated with disks of deep greens and reds and in the center was a plate engraved with a name. Only he couldn't read it from where he sat. It was the tusks in the warrior's ears that brought a prick of conscience. They were Meroëvian-crafted with their silver caps and hooks. "I thought all my cousins were dead," he whispered.

"This one's no cousin. His bones are too thick. And those tusks could have been bought from a merchant."

"Uncle Kibwe-Shabaqo had thick bones."

"Not like his."

"What are those necklaces," Kanja said, pointing at the gold pendants the bearers wore.

"They are gold flies, symbols of bravery and amulets of fertility."

"I want one."

"Then kill for it."

Kanja sighed loudly. He had no stomach for bloodshed

tonight, and the drums were making his head sore. There was something in the sorcerer's words that made him tremble and his eyes found Najja's. The stargazer stood beside the storage hut, sharpening an arrow and there was wisdom in those tapering eyes. He shook his head more than once, only a slight shake, too small to discern.

"I hear whispers," Othene said, waving his wand. "There's a Prophet amongst their riders with the authority on earth to tell dreams. I would kill him first if I were you."

"Kill him! Kill him!" Massui repeated, pumping the air.

Kanja nodded, skin crawling with goose bumps. He had chosen his riders, Othene, Massui, Najja, Yuku and Ayize, but that was only six.

It was then he saw Mkasa under the sycamore tree, eyes glistening in the wind. His back was marred with open sores and his lips hesitated on the verge of a whisper.

"What happened?" Kanja said, walking towards him and hooking arms.

"They beat me. They took away my house, my lands, my wife. They said I was a traitor for stealing this." Mkasa held out the knife, jewels winking in the firelight.

"Give it to me," Kanja said, tilting the blade and studying the grain. "Where did you get it?"

"From the Commander's belt," Mkasa said with a curt nod. "While he was sleeping."

Kanja grinned. He was proud of the Makurae, a kindred spirit in an orphaned world. "You're no longer theirs. You're mine now. Sit and tell me about Shenq. Tell me how to break him, how to break his soul."

"There is no soul to break. Only an iron heart that is as cunning as it is fearless. He's the Pharaoh's royal sword and he will cut you down and lead as he always has. A sword like that can never be sheathed, not so long as a single enemy remains in the world."

"And the Pharaoh?"

"Kill the Pharaoh and you kill the sun."

Kanja chewed on the inside of his mouth, tasting blood. The Makurae would need a reward to tempt him or a spell to break his armor.

"The princess is here," Kanja said, lungs filled to their fullest. He could almost smell a dark fleece of hair and the sweat on her skin.

"She's here?" Mkasa said.

Kanja imagined her soft flesh against his only he would never admit to dreaming of her. But he did every night until he awoke trembling. "Share her with me."

"I have a wife," Mkasa murmured.

"*Had*," Kanja corrected. "I hear there's a filly in the Commander's stable all ripe for the plucking."

"She's a jewel, all beauty and grace."

Kanja caught the misty-eyed look of wonder, a flicker of sorrow. *He's in love. The poor blind fool is in love!* And then a thought came to him. "You shall have her if we win."

Mkasa shook his head. "I cannot hope to win her—"

"If you cast the first arrow, you shall have the girl you love." *There. The victim is never the first to know.* "And if you kill Shenq, I'll make you Nomarch of the North. Ride with us?"

The Makurae hesitated before giving him a triumphant glance. "I would be honored."

"What is your talisman?" Kanja said, eyeing the gold disc around Mkasa's neck.

"HaShem," was the quiet reply.

Kanja had never heard of *HaShem* nor had he seen his likeness on the temple walls. But something about the name began to intrude on his consciousness. "Where's his shrine?"

"In here," Mkasa said, patting his chest. "He's the voice in the wind."

"Wind, wind, wind," Massui echoed, grinning.

Kanja smiled at his brother as the drums began to pound and the soft sound of pipes whirled somewhere in the back of his head. He was aware of a hand on his shoulder and the odor of boy-sweat. Ayize flopped down on the log beside him and cleared his throat. "I want to ride with Mkasa."

"You can ride with whoever you want." Kanja took off a beaded shoulder strap and let it hover from one hand. "This is for you, for your brave heart." Ayize mauled the air in response just as Kanja snatched it back. "Promise me, you'll be brave. You won't cry out?"

"I won't cry out." Ayize snatched the strap and hung it diagonally across his chest.

"Drink this," Kanja said, offering a cup of wine. "It will kill the pain."

He remembered the steep spike of fear before his first piercing. But all he could remember was the effusive spark of a firefly, a world of whispers. The drug was potent, removing even the remotest tendril of panic and although he had somehow walked, he could not remember feeling his feet.

Ayize's eyes become distant and his head snapped upwards just in time to see a comet as it arced across the sky, blotting out the stars and the beatific moon.

"A sign!" Othene shouted. "A sign of kingship."

Massui said the words over and over again, head lolling forward on his chest. A streak of spittle dripped from the corner of his mouth and his eyes were suddenly half-closed. He would sleep in the dirt for a time like he always did, waking refreshed for a new day.

Kanja heard the whimper as needle punctured flesh and he saw Ayize recoil briefly. But the pain would be nothing compared to the joy of manhood and the boy would one day stare at his reflection in the river and marvel at its majesty. Only Alodian nobility had such piercings, raising themselves above the tattooed herd.

He scooped Ayize in his arms and nodded at Othene. "Take the Makurae to your tent and tie him up."

He heard Othene cracking his wand over one thigh to urge Mkasa on. There would be an array of ram's skulls for the warrior to look at and a pot of healing salve if he was lucky.

"I see arrows," Ayize murmured as Kanja carried him to bed, "so much blood."

"There is no blood," Kanja said, almost hearing the whoosh of arrows over the pulse of the drums. He laid the boy amongst the cushions and covered him with a blanket.

"Your blood," said the sleepy voice.

Kanja knelt there for a time, watching the boy sleep. He felt powerful and empty at the same time. The princess was half-asleep, arms tied behind her and lips glistening from the drug he had given her. She leaned against the wooden pole, head slumping on her chest and there was an eerie tone to her murmuring he didn't much like.

"Liar," she whispered.

He took a fresh swallow of wine, heart shuddering as if the old one had been replaced with something new. He had no words for it but he knew what had taken root, cravings he could never shake off. He remembered the very first thing he ever killed, a young vulture, almost as tall as he was. Tracing the arc between the missile and the target, he calculated the distance in his head, feet shifting as he drew back on the bow. He could still feel the tension in his fingers as he watched the bird, cold and indifferent just like his father.

It took forever for the arrow to reach the apex of its arc. Even the whispering of the grasses culminated to a high-pitched hiss and Kanja was paralyzed on his feet.

The arrow struck. The bird fell.

Kanja began to pant, seeing black birds and white-skinned sorcerers in his mind and he was damned if he was going to dream about them again.

A large crack of thunder peeled overhead followed by a humid stillness. He felt a nudge of pity as he watched the princess, legs trembling beneath her. He crouched at her side and cut the bonds at her wrists and ankles, and she fell sideways to the ground.

He stroked the unruly curls and he kissed her forehead. "You will see through our eyes, my princess. You will hear through our ears. And you will bear many sons in my name."

He knew the evocative words had the effect he was striving for. They would change the girl from the inside out and she would forget her ancestry. Her face became a distant blur as he dragged her to his bed and he gripped onto one thought.

I have seen the vulture. I have seen the way.

He awoke to the sound of a crowing rooster, one arm pillowing the back of his head. He was naked but for a sheet across his waist and he felt the warmth of a girl beside him, wishing they were a tangle of arms and legs.

She refused you again and yet you are striking, son of the gods, the voices said.

He was more striking than any other man. Except Shenq, of course, and the thought made him sick. He decided to drink his way to the finish line and as much as it clouded his wits, it was the only way he could forget. He reached for the dagger Mkasa had stolen from Shenq and kissed its shiny blade.

"Today we race," he said to Ayize. "Tomorrow we rule."

He reached for his shúkà as the boy lifted his head from a nest of pillows. He was too tired to speak, too drowsy from the wine.

The princess stirred, groaning suddenly. She lay in his bed, wrists tied and there was dried blood on her hands. He cut her loose and she lashed out just as he thought she would, spinning out of reach, hair cascading over her face.

Kanja edged towards her, dagger flashing from one hand to another, smoothly, swiftly. She was sharp-witted but not enough so it seemed for a dagger. He flung his legs over the bedroll as she slunk back towards the wall of the tent, watching him with those dark eyes. His teeth were clenched in a tight grin as he looked behind her at a pile of horse blankets and the thud was louder than he predicted as she fell back against them.

Her body shook beneath his, arms trapped above her head and restrained by a strong grip. He felt a knee close to his groin and the thrill of the instant was more intense than he imagined.

"I swear to you," she said. "If you take me against my will, I'll kill you," her voice broke as she said the words and she began to sob.

"Now that I would like to see," Kanja murmured, kissing her cheek.

He gazed down at a suspicious, pinched-eyed face and he wondered how much sin she could swallow in one day. Some women yielded girls, some boys. A man would never know just by looking at them.

He pulled her up and tied her to the pole, tilting her face upwards with a finger. "Stay here, my jewel. Don't go wandering off, now. The boy will kill you if you do."

Her mouth puckered for an instant and he could almost imagine the hook in her lip. She would question his cruelty for a time and then begin to pursue him. They always did.

"They'll come looking for me," she sobbed, "and they'll kill every man in this camp—"

"They won't come looking. You're in the temple, remember? That *is* what you told them, wasn't it?"

He bent down to kiss her and she resisted at first, voice whiny with contempt. But it did little to improve the cold gaze he knew he had and, covering her mouth with his, he plunged into the past, tasting the full lips of another before he broke away.

Patience quickly soured to rage and he slapped her without wanting to. He heard her quiet sobbing as he walked from the tent, seeing a web of clouds in the sky, dark and threatening almost to the horizon.

Approaching the fire, he found a mullet and three moonfish lying on the coals, skin blistered and steaming in the morning sun. Othene prodded the embers with his spear, moaning a chant or two.

Disturbing the dream-weaver was not Kanja's intention so he relieved himself against a tree, flicking off the last drops before tucking himself away. And as he did so, he thought of Mkasa. *You're neither a lackey nor a drifter. So I'll draw you in, my friend, and as soon as you look beyond the stars, I'll clip your wings.*

He would do more than clip his wings; he would kill him when the time was right. The warrior was hitching his chariot to the wrong horse if only he knew it. And now he was hitched to a wooden frame in Othene's tent and sleeping like a baby.

He could kill you, a voice said. *He could stand behind you with a bow in one hand. What then?*

Kanja wanted Mkasa where he could see him, where he could take a dagger and open him up like a fig. And the seal that bounced against the warrior's chest was beautiful, powerful too. If Kanja was honest, he was afraid of it.

He turned to find Mkasa standing by the fire, face pinched in pain. He wore a red shúkà and his skin was freshly oiled. "How are your wounds?"

"Othene said they would seep and begin to draw."

Kanja could smell blood and a trace of vomit. "You'll never forget," he purred.

"I don't suppose I will."

Kanja held his breath before speaking. "Go and say goodbye to your wife. Tell her we leave tonight."

Mkasa bowed, eyes dark and brooding. Kanja watched him saunter along the avenue of circular-shaped tents and out into the desert beyond.

If he's an honest man, he'll come back. And if he doesn't . . .

Sometime in that overcast morning, a stout wind rose from the dunes and spiraled round and round, dust sheeting the green fields and turning them brown. The sun was a pale disk in the morning sky and there was a haze on the horizon that made Kanja nervous. He drank another cup of wine and then felt a wash of pain in his belly and doubled over. There was a buzzing in his ears before he collapsed. Waving away kind hands, he lay there and slept for a time until he heard the voice.

"Mongaka!" Najja shouted, eyes glaring. "The girl's gone."

"What?" Kanja slurred.

"Ayize. He cut her lose."

SHENQ

Shenq looked up at the sun, large as a flat loaf and blotted out by a veil of clouds. The smell of fish and onions wafted from a small fire at the water's edge where a young family delighted in the offerings of a meager meal.

"Pharaoh wept when he heard the news of Vizier Thutiy," he said to his armor bearer. "Gone to Suhaj, I'll wager. He won't get sanctuary, of course. Not with a pile of old crone's tales."

Meru-Itseni gave a deep laugh. "Did Harran find the plans, sir?"

"He copied what he could. Looks like we'll be going north to Mara'av in two days."

"Imazi country," Meru-Itseni said, tapping the leaves with the haft of his spear. "My wife travelled to Mara'av with the royal wet nurse. They were asked to deliver a footling. There was nothing they could do for the mother. But the child lived. She was a half-blood, a Darkeye."

"One of us," Shenq murmured.

"Imazi whelps are whiter than the walls of Memphis, sir," Meru-Itseni said. "But this child was sallow-skinned and blue-eyed. My wife had never seen anything like it."

"Tell your wife to come and see my Meryt. She could do with a friend."

"She would like that, sir. There's more food in your house than mine."

Shenq let out a wheezing chuckle as if he had just swum the width of the river and all the while he thought of his sweet child-wife. How he had chased and she had run.

If you don't go in with a fight, you don't go in at all, he thought.

He pictured every strand of her hair and eyes that

shimmered with the brilliance of the sun. He had repainted his villa for her, wooden columns in blues and greens where ibis took flight across the walls and the floors came alive with fish and lotus ponds. There were mirrors of polished bronze and rugs thick with the hide of the southern panther, and fountains that dripped with the scents of honeysuckle and safflower. He remembered the day he brought her to his house, walking along the river path with Khemwese to guard them. She should have been carried in a golden litter not treading those tiny slippers into the dirt.

"Sir. These Bloodmen, what are they like?"

"You'll know them by the stench of horse sweat and you'll see their arrows before you see them. The best way to deal with a Bloodman, I've learned, is to speak as magnanimously to him as he speaks of himself."

"Devils," Meru-Itseni said.

"There's only one devil. The rest are just demons."

Shenq thought he heard the sound of keening above skittering leaves but it was the bubbling call of a little egret. His nostrils opened to the smell of pitch as the front gate of his villa came into view, torches crackling in their metal brackets. The sky was surmounted by threads of purple and near the horizon was a wedge of geese.

"These are for you," Shenq said, rattling two golden flies on the palm of his hand. "You have cleaned my weapons and kept them sharp. And you have been a good friend to me."

"Sir," Meru-Itseni bowed and took the flies. "I am truly honored."

"Time you had a few more pendants on that choker." Shenq tapped his own collar where twelve flies chimed at the touch. "For honor, bravery and spirit. Peace to you," he said, waving the warrior off with a nod.

"Peace to you, sir." Meru-Itseni pressed his heels into his mount and cantered south along the river path whistling a tune. When Shenq could no longer see his stocky frame in the river mist, he went inside.

"Quiet isn't it, Maaz?" Khamudi said, as he unbuckled Shenq's breastplate and khopesh.

"For now," Shenq said, sizing up his houseman.

The old man's arms were pocked with gooseflesh in the cold night air and there was a faint whiff of wine on his breath. He was a spirited man, fingers stripping off Shenq's bracer and thumb rings as if undressing a child.

"I sent your warriors home," Khamudi whispered. "Lucky there's not one sniffing around my mistress. I would have nocked an arrow in his general direction but my eyesight is not what it was. I can do little more now than lance a boil on my son's—."

Shenq slapped a hand over Khamudi's mouth and shook his head. His wife was likely close enough to hear. "Wash me!"

He felt the smack of water from a full bucket and the scrubbing of salt against his thighs. His mind purged the frustrations of the day as a fresh tunic hung from well-oiled skin.

The drapes on the terraces wafted to and fro in a current of air and he saw a slender silhouette behind them.

"Meryt," he whispered, jogging towards her.

"My lord," she said, smooth cheeks spangled by a shimmering veil.

"I have something for you." Shenq pulled out a necklace so blue he found himself thinking he had never truly seen the color.

He saw the shine of white teeth as he fastened the catch at her throat and he felt the brush of lips against his cheek. A friendly kiss, not a lover's kiss. No matter how often he argued with himself that his pleasure was hers, guilt pecked at him like a crow on the roadside.

She loves another.

The voice came out of nowhere, callous and distant. It wasn't true.

But she looks at him.

Had she? He couldn't remember a time when she had. Her generous nature was to blame not a rabid desire for love especially outside the bounds of marriage. Meryt had little experience of desire in their brief year together.

"Were you waiting for me?" he asked, taking her soft, pale hand in his.

"Yes, sir," she said, eyes fixed on him as if he would suddenly pounce. It wasn't a definite *yes*, a faint *yes* as if duty-bound and then . . . "Pharaoh has sent for me."

Shenq escorted her through a pair of ornate pillars to a couch, mind roiling with anger. "He shan't have you. After all, he has plenty of maids to master his knee and those nomadic hands of his. Has he forgotten you are no longer his ward? You are a wife now, *my* wife."

"Yes, my lord."

"You're safer in my house than his."

He wanted to kiss her then but held back. It is said that maids enjoy laughing more than fondling and if it were true, he would need to amuse her.

"Pharaoh has an aura about him, a presence," he said, pouring a cup of blood red wine. He looked up at the rafters on the ceiling, groaning from a sudden gust. "It lingers long after he is gone. Fortunately we are able to throw open the doors to let it out."

Meryt giggled and skittered to a pile of cushions nestled by a low crackling fire. Shenq sat down beside her feeling the warmth of her shoulder next to his.

"He lives in a world of whims," he continued, visualizing a drunkard playing piggy-back with a harem maid. "Yesterday, he dreamed of shooting a prize buck, dressing him out and dragging him back to the palace where his nobles went wild with envy. It's not like he goes hunting elk or poking around the woods every time he feels the urge. He's spends half his day on the couch, gripping a burning torch and smoking the hairs off his legs."

Meryt curled forward, clutching at his arm in laughter

and gasping for air. "I was afraid of him once," she said. "He asked for things men shouldn't want before they're married and his eyes would linger on a girl the way a husband would."

"A maid's smile can ruin a man faster than a gelding knife and he's lost more than his pride. Not once have I seen him turn a plump fish over a fire nor has he ever caught one. I should never have saved his life," Shenq said, glancing at a ewer pitted with holes.

"You saved his life?" Meryt said in an uncertain tone, sipping her wine.

"He was twelve at the time, swinging a dagger, arms wide, wanting to prove himself. So prince Wadjmose threatened him with a word, parrying his dagger in the air. Kheper-Re knew it was too late to withdraw. It would have been cowardly and besides he had already made the challenge. For all his side-stepping and thrusts, he lost in his rage and Wadjmose would have run him through if I hadn't used that ewer to shield him," Shenq said pointing. "And all the while Kheper-Re was wailing to his gods. It wasn't his day."

"Does he fight well now?"

"Only with his wife," Shenq said with a whisper. He longed to drag the wretch through the thorns even now.

"They say he has visions."

"I wouldn't call them visions," Shenq murmured, almost hearing the hissing of the Pharaoh's tongue as it cut the air. "More like fantasies. And why wake a tyrant when he's dreaming."

He felt her grab his arm more than once, face dimpled with smiles and delighting in his stories. The fire in the hearth hardly flickered and he had no wish to rekindle it. She would come closer if only to feed from his warmth.

"How is my brother?" she asked.

"Harran is an honest man, strong, sane. He has so much of you in him. He chooses honor over blood, God over king. But Pharaoh will never come second. He'll think of some way to punish him."

"Pharaoh may knock him down," she said. "But God will raise him up."

He passed an arm around her waist, gazing at a smooth throat and trying to ignore the explosive hammering in his head. His warriors cleaved to him like an arrow nocked to a bowstring. But Meryt was the arrow that leaped into the air, dancing to a rhythmic hum.

"Exquisite," he said, finger caressing the necklace he brought her. He heard the swallow deep in her throat, cheeks on fire. "These stones are larger than any I have ever seen. Even Lieutenant Mkasa has none like this. Tell me, why would he bring you jewels?"

Meryt chewed at her lip and swallowed. "He wanted me to promise that if anything happened to Iutha or to you, I would marry him."

Shenq felt his posture stiffen, refraining from flashing a cold smile. His heart was filled with hatred for Mkasa, a fresh wound and bleeding still. "What did you say, my lady?"

"I said, no."

"Then I'm glad I horsewhipped him for daring to dream."

He skimmed over her bright face, too innocent to understand how clever this red enemy was, turning brothers against sisters, wives against husbands, sons against fathers. There would be no compromise and it caused a chill down Shenq's backbone as if a ghost had pushed past without touching him. He stood and pulled her to her feet.

"He's bold. He plays a dangerous game. I pray he's quicker with a sword than me or he'll have to watch his back."

She shuddered. "So much is expected of you."

"Then I had better sleep with one eye open."

He reached for her hand and she let him hold it. She was his first real love, the others were hopeless imitations desperate to evoke feelings he never had and he was tired of coming out hungrier than when he went in. Meryt's eyes spoke to him, things he wanted to hear and he wondered if she ever thought the same, whether she dreamed of kissing him, lying naked with him. Pressing their bodies so close, they could never be close enough . . .

"It's the sorcery I fear the most. It's the one thing that has preyed on my mind in these last few days."

"The enemy may be cunning, my lord. But they don't have HaShem."

The very sight of her brought a lump in his throat and there was something mystical in the brief moments they shared. "There is one forfeit, my sweet love. If I should die, you will once again become the Pharaoh's ward. It is his wish."

"I should be grateful."

Careful, would have been a better word and Shenq pondered the empty stare, the flat voice.

"You will come back?" she said, with a slight intake of breath.

He nodded. He had too much to lose.

She smiled at that and his loins stirring in their familiar way, arousing old instincts he would no longer need to fight. She was as pure as the honking white swan on the water swimming by itself under a twinkle of stars, God's handiwork in a fine-stroked painting. He barely noticed the snapping logs in the hearth as he laid her on the bed, flames curling around charred logs. He didn't want it to stop. And praise God, neither did she.

MKASA

Mkasa felt Iutha's small hand in his as they waited on the pier at dusk. He looked south at the bend in the river and saw a boat lit with torches. The curved prow beat a path towards them, oars dipping and leaving a trail of gold beads along its beam.

"There," she said, eyes filling with tears and patting his chest with admiration. She was beautiful then in her gold and red, a strong face amidst a cluster of dark curls. "You will be like a god tonight," she said. "The Pharaoh has much to thank you for."

For bringing the princess safely home? Yes, he has much to thank me for. Mkasa found the poor girl sobbing by the river, pacing in circles and rubbing her wrists. She was sorry for loving the Alodian Commander and she was sorry for Thutiy's lies. There was a small reed boat by the jetty and he rowed her to the west bank. She was safe now in her father's house.

"Come with me tonight," he urged Iutha, regretting their quarrel.

She shook her head, face scrunched in a mask of fear. "I won't celebrate your death. And I won't stand beside a Blood. Look at you with your beads and war paint. "

"At least I didn't steal from the Pharaoh's treasury and run squealing to Suhaj."

She was quiet at that, eyes glowing like a hunter's moon, no doubt committing every detail of him to memory. When he conjured images of her now, he could see her weeping over his bloodstained carcass when they brought his body home.

"I wish I could tell you how lonely it is. How cold it is without friends. Even God has forsaken me."

"*All* have forsaken you. The people think you've deserted them. They think you've abandoned the Pharaoh. You have abandoned me."

Mkasa was dying inside. "Pray for me," he said, chin lifted to the storm clouds overhead.

Rolling his jaw forward and back, he felt the beaded harness tighten at his brow, thongs passing under his freshly painted chin. The Seal of One hung from his neck, a polished disk nestling between his pectorals and his father's war bow hung neatly from his shoulder. It rubbed against his back and he winced now and then, eyes watering from the pain.

There was a sturdy wind in the long-tailed reeds as the boat drifted towards the jetty of his father's house, oars lifted as they came alongside. Footsteps beat against the wooden planks, urgent steps.

I will never see you again, he thought not daring to kiss her. But he was driven to hold her, arm curling around her shoulders. A hand lightly touched his arm, a hand he wanted to brush away with terrible and foreign words. "Sir," he said without turning.

"It's time," Commander Shenq said, eyes scanning the scars on Mkasa's back. He turned to look kindly at Iutha. "Blessings to you sweet lady."

"How dare you! How dare you take him from me! From all of us," she whimpered. "They almost killed him."

Mkasa felt a surge of shame, drawing breath as he waited. He had no idea what the Commander would do but he prayed in the quiet of his heart.

"They almost killed the princess," Shenq said, gathering her to his chest. "If it wasn't for your beloved husband, she would never have made her way across the river." He stroked her hair with a sinewy arm. "Sister, God has need of him."

Mkasa trembled as he left that place, feet heavy on the deck of the boat. He felt her eyes burn through his shoulder blades as he stood rigid at the stern and all he could hear was the water trickling about the hull as they paddled forward. No sense in looking back, not until she was lost in the misty light.

"Study this," Shenq whispered, pressing a map into Mkasa's hands. "I think you'll find it familiar."

Mkasa beckoned for a lamp and examined the map. More than twelve years ago his father had taken him on a tour to escort exiles to Farafra, an oasis village in the western desert. It was a popular merchant route where golden dunes dominated the skyline and rugged cliffs stretched as far as the eye could see. Three shrines perched on a natural rock shelf and served a single purpose. Defense. But on that night so long ago, intruders crawled across the valley floor carrying bone swords across their backs. Their skin was whiter than the desert around them, whiter still than the caverns they lived in.

"You waste one good man in the company of thieves. How do you expect me to survive?" Mkasa asked.

Shenq glared at the seal. "Show the Imazi *that*, my friend, and you'll bring them to heal. They won't touch a seal-bearer. You have my word."

Mkasa remembered how they shied away from Vizier Ahmose, arms drawn across their faces. They shouted in the language of the shadow-world, trembling at the talisman of the fish. He was suddenly soothed by the pounding of the drum and he watched the rowers bent into each stroke, driving the boat on with grunts and moans. The moon had cut a swathe down the center of the river, and he couldn't remember a time when he had breathed air so fresh.

"Your father was convinced the Imazi clan was immortal because they never aged." Shenq sounded certain. "But they do die and when they do, their bodies are left above ground for the *shakāl* so their spirits will live. Human flesh is a delicacy. If you are captured, there are underground lakes and rivers in their world. Follow the streams and you'll find a way out. And make sure you keep the boy alive. That's an order."

"Yes, sir."

"When you get to Farafra, look for black arrows. That way you'll know where I am."

Mkasa's mind began to wander, imagining the billowing drapes of a bed where a woman quivered with desire, sated and happy with the bliss they shared. But it wasn't Iutha's face he conjured. No, it was never hers. It was one that looked up at him with the urgent desire of a child, eyes green and gold. Her husband stood beside him, black hair trailing in the breeze, and it was her husband that had banished him.

"I deserve to die," he muttered as they approached the palace jetty.

"You don't deserve death," Shenq said. "It's is too great a punishment. I should have hacked off your manhood and fed it to the pigs."

Mkasa chuckled. He wanted to hate Shenq. He wanted to reach over and rip out his throat, only he loved him more. They had spent too many years as playmates to throw it all away.

"I'm sorry," he almost sobbed.

"You will be if you don't win this race."

Mkasa handed Shenq the map. "How big a fool do they take me for?"

"Rather a big one," Shenq said, grinning like a jackal. "Pharaoh has given orders to burn the camp. It will be a pile of bones by nightfall."

Mkasa enjoyed Shenq's company as they walked side by side. The aroma of pitch from the procession torches reminded him of when his father first brought him along the avenue of sphinx, flames crackling between the recumbent statues. Ahmose would often regale them with stories of a time when the Pharaohs were mightier than the gods. The painted images on the entry pylons were indeed majestic but the reigning monarch was anything but.

"We'll part here," Shenq said as they stood in the first

court. "I'll return the map, you find the Bloods. It won't do to avoid Kanja."

"He's probably drunk, sir."

"He's smarter than you think." Shenq looked long and hard at Mkasa before saluting. "God go with you."

"And with you, sir."

Mkasa watched the royal grooms as they brought out nine horses from the Pharaoh's stables, all caparisoned with the Alodian colors of sunset and equipped with rawhide shields. Two each were hitched to three chariots and three more were laden with weapons, blue blankets for the dead and what appeared to be a coil of fish netting.

Fish? There are no fish in the desert, Mkasa thought, wondering if the nets were meant to catch *shakāl.*

Shenq slipped away through the second gate, muscle heaped upon muscle, a glossy sword on his back. Whether or not it was divine strength that separated him from ordinary men was a mystery but he was sheathed in an impenetrable armor.

When Mkasa entered the great hall, nobles stared with wide searching eyes and they parted to make way. They had never seen him in Alodian red and some even began to hiss to a round of laughter. He heard Iutha's voice then, cursing and spitting. *The people think you've deserted them. They think you've abandoned the Pharaoh.* He could barely hear the lute that struck a tuneful air or the whispers, and his stomach turned at a whiff of perfumed incense.

Meryt advanced towards him with the royal wet nurse, her body supple as a reed and hair tumbling down her back. He couldn't tear his eyes from the trusting smile.

"Lady Meryt, Nurse Inet" he said bowing to both.

"Shalom," Meryt replied, face coloring like a rose.

He repeated the *Shasu* greeting, ears straining for her next words.

"You look just like them." She seemed to shiver, pulling a veil close to her shoulders. "Doesn't he look like them?" she said to the nurse.

"Indeed he does," Inet said, giving Mkasa a bright-eyed smile. "Come and hug me so I know it's you."

Mkasa took the nurse in his arms and over her shoulder he studied Meryt's breathtaking youth, an otherworldly spirit. She did not know the power she had. "I do this for Pharaoh, for Thebes," he said. "I do it for you."

He felt Inet draw back and he saw her disapproving glance. "You'll do it for the Commander, boy. Or you'll regret the day you ever hung from your mother's teats."

"It's my last night. Why would I care?" He smiled at the nurse and then Meryt. "Don't be afraid, my lady. Thebes has stout walls and towers, and warriors glowering from the gatehouses. You're well protected."

He felt suddenly hot, too hot to breathe. She kindled such a burning in him he had to remove his gaze just long enough to make eye contact with Commander Shenq, a true conqueror. He had likely returned the map to the Pharaoh's apartments, secreting it beneath a voluminous pile of tributes. But the territorial scowl on his face made Mkasa tremble. He was no longer on the same side and tempting vengeance was not what he had in mind.

"My ladies," Mkasa said, bowing.

He walked towards the Queen whose dignified air and confidence far exceeded that of the Pharaoh. Her wig was glossy with oil, dressed with a diadem of precious stones and her unique style still caught the eye as did the cobra at her brow. A wreath of fresh flowers and persea leaves made from a twist of papyrus and trimmed with linen, rested on her lap. There were cornflowers, bitterweed and blue lotus curled around the collar, and red berries from the nightshade herb.

"Your majesty." He greeted her with a deep, silent bow. The Pharaoh hardly acknowledged him, muttering to his astronomer about the position of the Sopdet, the dog star, and stuffing the remains of a flat-loaf in his mouth.

"Approach," Hatshepsut whispered. Her eyes occasionally floated to Senenmut, Chief Steward and astronomer to the Pharaoh. He was a stocky youth with a face creased with smiles. "Tell me, are the Bloods as skilled as the *Kenyt-Nisu*."

"Oh, yes. They have lived on the land for many years. They are a cousin tribe to the Makurae."

"They're sinister and untamed. No manners to speak of."

"The palace of Alodia is unlike this, your majesty. The walls are decorated with wild animals and hides not seen in these parts. The nobles are selected by the many visions they have, the animal quests they return from. They are a breed unlike the Egyptians."

"Superior perhaps?"

Mkasa was surprised at the question. She could hardly be weighing his loyalty after all these years. "*In*ferior, my lady."

Her gaze started at his throat and became trapped at the beads at his neck. "Good answer, cousin. I see you have been well taught."

"Well enough to trap a demon when he sees one," interrupted Shenq who stood suddenly by his side.

"He'll see many. I wonder if he will become too fond of them to kill them," Hatshepsut said.

"Our beloved Makurae is not fond of anything, my Queen. You have my word on that."

"They'll kill him."

"He'll keep his eyes down and bow his head a lot. They'll forget he's there and take more mind to their horses," Shenq assured.

Hatshepsut lifted the wreath. "Wear this for me tonight, sweet cousin. It will remind you of home."

Mkasa stooped before the throne and let her slip the fragrant collar around his head. He felt those delicate fingers as they caressed his cheek and he saw the tears in her eyes. *Come back,* her lips seemed to say.

"Mkasa, you red-faced heathen!" Pharaoh shouted, dismissing Senenmut with a scowl. "What have they done to you? Paint and beads, and a horse's harness for your head. Neigh for me, will you?"

Mkasa chuckled. "Inside a vulture's nest, I must be a vulture too."

"Then be a cunning vulture, cousin," Kheper-Re said, arms reaching, hands flapping. "It seems the stars are favorable tonight. In the spirit of good faith, we have allowed the barbarians a head start. I doubt they'll make good use of it with all that wine in their bellies. You go like a man dancing on quick sand. Bring the boy home. But if you both die, Shenq will be thrown into a brazier and roasted."

Mkasa stood back from the Pharaoh's embrace, unable to wipe the smirk from his face. Shenq would pay after all. "I am most grateful, my lord."

"My eyes might be failing, cousin, but my ears are all the sharper for it. These duskies spread vile heresy. They worship the enemy of Ra, a slithering tyrant. They do it with orgies and trances and wands of human hair. Theirs is another world, a torment to me."

"Whatever torments you, my lord, torments me."

"It torments me that they tie up my precious daughter and violate her sacred body. If it wasn't for you and that Blood-boy, she'd be carved into little pieces and hung from the trees. We cannot prove they are Alodia's princes, not without a court case. Not without weeks of waiting for Ibada to come and identify them. No, we must be seen to be just. So we'll believe they're the spearmen they say they are and we'll let them race. Perhaps they'll find Thutiy, our royal runaway. Go in peace and bring back the boy. The rest may rot in the desert for all I care."

Mkasa saluted and walked towards the first court, still smelling the Pharaoh's rich scent on his cheek. Within four hours, dawn would streak along the eastern horizon in its bright and casual way and Shenq's men, sober and competent, would hurtle through the flatlands gaining on the Bloods in less than half a day.

He found himself lost in the reflection of a wide-bellied jar set on a pedestal and filled with incense pellets. An unfamiliar face stared back through its brassy sheen, a heathen in shades of red.

Have I sunk so low?

He closed his eyes for just a moment, imagining the creaking oars of his father's boat, bow cutting through emerald waters and foam glistening in its wake. Green and blue pennants fluttered in his mind, crisp sails swollen with God's breath. But it was the royal standards he heard, wind whipping the poles and halyards, sand scouring his legs. A wave of curiosity rippled along his spine and he turned instinctively.

"Harran," he said, almost stumbling backwards.

Harran had a quiet strength, one that dominated a room full of noise. But Mkasa couldn't remember seeing him in the great hall, supping with the rest of them. He likely kept to himself, bobbing back and forth in prayer in the dark of an adjoining garden.

"Shenq asked me to pray with you, brother," Harran said, pulling at the collar of his tunic, hair disheveled in the wind.

They bowed their heads in prayer, Harran speaking in his *Shasu* tongue. Mkasa was thankful for the scent of blue lotus to send him on his way and the wind that hummed a joyful tune.

"Since Egypt has the only blade of grass for miles, it attracts," Harran said, hesitating as if trying to find the right words, "a greater evil. One that has grown out of pride and defiance. Her people are scorpions, hiding under rocks and coming out at night. Remember, your refuge is in here," he said, hand patting his chest.

"I'm afraid" Mkasa confessed, no longer wrestling with his emotions.

"You are man, not spirit," Harran said. "Nothing wrong with fear. A fearful man is a wise man. A patient man is wiser still."

"But the sorcery, the magic—"

"There's a lot of it about," Harran said, grinning. "By the way, HaShem does know you. Very well. So I'll see you soon."

Mkasa let out a long loud breath. "Yes, I believe you will."

He turned briskly and walked to the first court. The mare his father had given him pawed the ground with one hoof, draped in the red colors of the Alodians and fastened between the traces of a chariot. She stopped when she saw him, nostrils flared and head bobbing as if the ribbons in her silver mane irritated more than the flies.

What have they done to you? he thought, patting her neck.

He cinched the fringed saddle pad and glanced over at her companion, a bay stallion with a dished face. It was the smell of sweat and wine, and a vicious clap on the back that announced Kanja, chest covered with a wide collar of teeth interspersed with leopard's claws.

"Greetings brother," he said, squeezing the hilt of a silver knife.

"Greetings," Mkasa returned. He hoped Kanja had not seen him in the garden with Harran. He hoped he was too drunk to care.

"You weren't at the celebrations. I looked for you." Kanja appeared drowsy. His eyes were dull in the torchlight, mouth agape.

"I went to my villa, remember?"

"How is Iutha?" Kanja said, face slightly inclined as if keeping his men in the periphery of his vision.

"Tired but well." Mkasa scratched his ear where disks of blue malachite adorned the lobes. He wanted no more thoughts of her, keeping the pasted smile on his face.

"Ayize will ride with you. His choice." Kanja's gaze seemed to scuttle up and down Mkasa's body as if inspecting his garb.

Mkasa was racked with pity as he looked down at the boy, brown eyes thick with wonder. It was a dangerous

153

decision to run the race, one Ayize had made on a flippant whim.

Horns broke into a riot of song as the great doors swung open. The avenue of sphinx was ablaze with torches. People cheered and waved, children straining between the legs of soldiers. Pharaoh Kheper-Re walked from the gardens with the Queen, followed by Commander Shenq. From his right hand hung three large scarab seals pierced with leather thongs

"Warriors mount!" Shenq bellowed, sporting a wry smile. He played an arrow through the fingers of his left hand, black goose feathers thrumming in the wind.

Mkasa jumped on the footplate, wide enough for two bins of arrows. He squeezed the reins, gazing down at Ayize's whitened knuckles as they curled over the front-guard.

"Behold the Bloods!" Shenq cried to the crowds, as cheers went up from the nobles. "Place your bets!"

A shower of rose petals hit Mkasa in the face and he spat them away with a grin. He listened to the Commander's voice, praying he would hear it again.

"Take the northern caravan route to Mara'av, and then head west to Farafra," Shenq said, handing the seals to Othene. "The High Priest has welcomed contestants for many years and his armory is well stocked. Show him a seal and he will show you his storerooms. A beacon will be lit for the team that arrives first and the High Priest will give that team a token.

"Return by the eastern caravan route down to the river city of Suhaj. I pray you get there before the sky swallows the moon. All dead men must be accounted for and left where they fell. Any missing will count against you. All teams will then ride towards the rising sun to the Pharaoh's palace. The first team to deliver their tokens to the Pharaoh, wins."

Mkasa looked up at the moon, a slender crescent in the night sky. He knew he had a week before the same moon waned and then it would be the fourth month of Peret, the beginning of the fifty-day storms. The desert terrain was uneven and carpeted with scree, and there would be packs of *shakāl* scuttling between the dunes, half-dog, half-spirit.

"Begin on my mark," Shenq cried, black arrow raised.

As the Commander's hand lowered, Mkasa urged the horses forward and they strained briefly in the traces before lurching to a gallop behind the others. The wind rushed at his cheeks, pounding them with excitement and he looked down at his companion, a fresh-faced boy whose lips were curled in an ear-piercing shriek.

Anxiety seeped into terror as Mkasa smelled a sickening odor on the wind, an odor he recognized. Burning flesh and timbers so subtle it reminded him of childhood. Throwing a cursory glance over his left shoulder, he saw the sky aflame with the colors of dawn. Only it wasn't dawn. The Alodian camp was on fire.

He turned to look at the Commander one last time, seeing his bright face in the darkness. *If there is a god that delivers, if there is a god that saves, then rescue me now.*

KANJA

Kanja was tired of the rough terrain where the rawhide lashings of his chariot wheel had worked loose and the pole creaked unsteadily beneath them. They found a well near a small oasis and bartered for wood and goat's milk in the village. After half a day, they yoked up the horses and veered west towards the mountains and the sandy plains. The moon hung in the sky brooding over the dunes below and all the while the wind whispered over the sands like a horde of rumoring spirits. Kanja gestured to Othene to let the reins fall slack over the front guard, easing the horses to a walk.

Ayize will never reign, he thought, hardly giving the boy a second look. *Not after what he's done. Traitor. Vile little traitor.*

Yuku and Massui whispered in their chariot, laughing at old times and occasionally pointing at sand flurries. Mkasa kept his team reined in beside Kanja's with Ayize's sleepy head against his arm. Twice the Makurae looked at the horizon behind them and twice he scowled. If Kanja had read it correctly, he was likely nervous at the lack of friends.

"Food!" a voice bellowed.

The sound brought Kanja back to the present. He saw Najja astride a black horse dragging a second laden with weapons and water-skins. There was a beaded strap over one shoulder and on his head was a lion's mane greased with sheep oil and ochre.

"Good shot," Kanja said, seeing two dead rabbits and three foxes strung from Najja's saddle.

Najja flicked a hand in Mkasa's direction. "It's his turn next."

Kanja glanced at Mkasa and grinned. There was an

intrepid soul behind that face and he was conscious of a stab of jealousy.

"I was just a child when my father took me to Makurae," Kanja said, breaking the monotony. "I was just a child when he asked me to send a flaming arrow into a school house. What would you have thought of me then, Mkasa of Makuria?"

"No less than I think of you now," Mkasa said.

Kanja sucked down a wrench of shame. The response was too swift, too honest. He snapped his fingers, ordering Mkasa's chariot to fall in behind him. He no longer cared if Ayize heard the truth. The child would fear him as much as the rest.

"And what would you think of me if I told you children ran from the burning hut with flames on their backs?" he cried, head craned round behind him.

"I pity you for the memories."

There was an echo in the words as if they bounced off the mountains. All he heard was horses' hooves as they clacked against marl and the vibrations under the footplate. The moon's face was clearer than he had seen it in a while and he was surprised to find the lowlands bathed in a hoary light and brighter than he would have liked.

Othene nudged him, a grim face scouring the dunes and glancing behind at the tracks in the sand. "Dog," he said, pointing at the piles of excrement in the sand. "They were here three hours ago, maybe four."

Kanja had no idea how the sorcerer knew without digging his finger into the crusty remains. He gazed at the western mountains rising out of the sands, pasty against a dark sky and overlooking a series of flat-topped dunes. A dump of scree perched on a craggy shoulder, a variegated landscape so breathtakingly barren. "What hour is it?" he shouted to Najja.

"Moonset," Najja called back. "Horses are tired, Mongaka, and so is the boy."

"Every hour wasted is one hour earned by the enemy,"

Kanja muttered, sensing a flutter of unease. "We'll camp up there," he shouted to his men, pointing at a hillock, sprouting with grass.

They huddled together against the cold, tents no more than blankets draped over ropes and boulders to anchor them. There was a crisp scent in the air that reminded Kanja of pomegranate. Or was it figs? They ate a small meal of bread and cheese, and roasted fox and rabbit over an open fire. Kanja knew it was foolhardy. Shenq's men would likely see the smoke and the curling flames, but he was too hungry to care. He sent Yuku to keep watch on the crest of a small hummock and told him to stay awake until dawn.

He dreamed of Thebes that night and he saw golden heads of barley rustling in a brief wind. He dreamed of a girl with long black hair and the peek of a dimple on her naked back, and when he reached out, all he could feel were feathers and claws. Wrenching away the saddle blanket, he saw a dead vulture lying on its back with a black arrow in its belly.

Hawks . . . they could have killed us!

Kanja unsheathed his knife and reached for Najja, telling him to rouse the rest. Looking over at the hummock where Yuku kept watch, he cursed through gritted teeth. The warrior had fallen asleep.

Can't blame a drunkard. It was the fire, you fool.

Kanja began to think he was hearing things, a sharp whistle on the wind or was it a high-pitched scream. He heard no footfalls but his own as he crept through a clump of grasses, seeing nothing but a grayness about the skies he didn't like. The horses were nickering and biting, and he stumbled over to sooth them.

"Nura," he whispered, running his hand along the mare's back and stopping dead at the croup.

There was a slash in her buttock as long as his arm and a streak of dried blood beneath it. At first he thought it was *shakāl* until he studied it closer. There were no side-by-

158

side notches as in a dog's claw but a single track as if it had come from a knife. He grabbed a water skin and cleaned the wound, dabbing it with strong-smelling ointments from his pack.

"What is it?" Ayize cried. "What's happened?"

"Be quiet!" Kanja said, tightening his grip on the knife. He looked for Yuku and slapped him across the face. "Move. Now!"

He pushed through his men and snatched up his blanket, kicking the dead vulture as far as he could. Wild dogs could have scented all the blood by now, moving like the wind in the rusty glow of sunrise. It was not as hot as the day before and after half a day of riding, they found a few abandoned cottages and a goat left to roam the streets.

"Where are the drovers?" Kanja murmured, muscles quivering.

"Something must have frightened them away," Mkasa said in that flat tone of his. "See the well? Too many flies."

Kanja dismounted and sauntered towards it. A cloud of flies hovered over the brim and he swept them away with an angry hand. Peering over the edge, he sucked in a ragged breath. There in the water was a dead vulture, belly ripped down the middle and a black arrow in its chest. He jumped back and moaned.

"Spirits. *Dog* spirits," Othene said, suddenly by his side.

"No. If *shakāl* roamed these parts, they would have stripped the carcass bare. Look for yourself."

"*Kemnebi*," Othene said, seeing the arrows. "He could have killed us all."

"But he didn't. He wants to play. Just like big cats do." Kanja looked the sorcerer in the eye and grinned.

For all Kanja's outward boasting, he was more fearful than he had been in months. The terrain was flatter than an old hag's breast and he could see nothing moving in any direction. Taking the goat, he laid it across his horse's neck and took off for the open road. They slaughtered it when they found the remains of a smoking fire and they drank the milk and roasted the cuts.

Othene threw his bones. "I see geese. Seven," he cried, holding up a fist. It meant the Hawks were to the west of them, ahead by all accounts.

They buried the remains of the fire and the carcasses, and pressed on through the late afternoon. Dusk seemed to hem them in between high dunes and narrow valleys and the chariots hindered their progress. If his men travelled slowly then so did Shenq's and Kanja saw no sign of the other team, not even a shadow.

"We'll camp behind that ridge," he said, knowing his voice was flavored with exhaustion. He was sick of riding and he was hungry.

Najja continued to scour the skies with unforgiving eyes. He was a natural star-reader and a boon to their course, neck sheathed with more rings than a snake's tail. He twisted in his seat to scan the northern horizon. Something was coming and it was closing in fast.

Kanja saw a cloud of sand, rising behind a high dune that stretched from east to west. It was too dense for a sandstorm, indicating a herd of animals or a company of men. He held up a hand, listening to the soft murmur of the wind as it swept across the plains. His mare champed on her bit, nostrils open to an unfamiliar scent and the horse at her side scuffed the ground with one leg, withers twitching. They were vulnerable to attack on the open road and it was too far to run for the hills.

Kanja ordered his men to dismount using their chariots as a barricade, bows to the ready. The horses were skittish and likely to bolt, and Kanja gestured to each driver to hold their heads. A welter of impulses seized him as he waited, fighting down visions of what was behind the dune.

He saw the first *shakāl* as it clambered over the summit and then a second and a third. Large creatures with silky coats, long ears and a gliding gait adapted to the shifting sands. He nocked an arrow, hearing the creak of the limb as he drew back the string. The first struck just below the collar and the second pierced a milky eye. All three collapsed in the sand and, as far as he could make out, there were no more behind them.

"Be ready," he shouted, suspecting a surge to follow over the brow of the dune.

Najja dropped back a pace and turned a full circle, scanning the plains and Mkasa placed a protective hand on Ayize's shoulder, pushing him down behind the chariot. Kanja respected the gesture even though he felt a familiar burning in his chest and the pain of a clenched jaw.

It's safe now, the voices said.

"No, it's not safe. It's never safe," Kanja muttered.

When he could wait no longer, he walked slowly towards the first dog, crouching and caressing the soft fur. The second dog shuddered as a trail of steam broke suddenly from its open mouth and the third gave off a high-pitched whine. Najja unhooked a mace from his belt and smashed the skull with one swing.

"Over there," Mkasa shouted, pointing.

Kanja saw a flash of light. Pairs of lights. Eyes.

"Move!" he croaked, his voice barely above a whisper.

They ran towards the chariots, mounting horses and footplates and streaking to a gallop. Kanja looked sideways at Othene whose eyes were tapered against the wind, one hand beating the reins against the front guard and the other cracking a whip in the air. Behind them was a cacophony of howls and he could see the sorcerer's terror as the creatures began to close in.

He hardly heard Mkasa's deep throated yell before they reached a sunken bed of loose silt. But it was too late. The horses skidded to a halt, sinking knee-deep in quick-sand.

Kanja leapt from the footplate just in time to see his men swerving to the left and right to avoid it. Unhooking the bow from his back, he nocked two arrows aware of three other warriors by his side. Blocking all thoughts from his mind, he took careful aim at the rush of barred teeth and snarls. The creatures were met by a rain of arrows and the air was thick with whines.

To Kanja's surprise the remaining dogs padded gingerly towards their dead, sniffing the air briefly and sensing only what dogs sense. It was like looking into the faces of the ancestors, dead men whose spirits had never found their way home. Then they howled in unison before streaking back over the dune and out of sight. Over seventy-five carcasses lay in the sand and Najja went in amongst them with his unforgiving mace.

"They'll follow us," said Mkasa, panting. "It could be three days before we see them again. But they'll follow us."

Kanja shook his head, one hand carving through his braids. "We'll shake them off."

"No, you don't understand. They're blacker than a sorcerer's cat in the dark. We'll never see them."

Something in Mkasa's words disturbed Kanja and he took a sharp intake of breath. *Dogs don't feel. They don't have a mind to feel.* What was he thinking? "Bring me three dogs. I want their pelts!" he shouted.

"We can't touch them!" Mkasa shouted. "It's bad enough we killed them."

"I *said,* bring me the dogs," Kanja insisted, flicking a hand at Najja and dismissing Mkasa with a wave.

"They're *bitches,*" Ayize corrected and stalked off towards Mkasa.

Kanja wondered why the boy mentioned the gender. A dog was a dog in his world with their solemn looks and chuffing. But a horse? He took one last look at the mare, ears twitching at the distant sound of baying dogs. She whinnied, nostrils enlarged and eyes rolling and there was no time to end her misery. The more she struggled, the more she sank.

"Wake up," Massui whined at the mare. "Wake up!"

"Leave her," Kanja said, heart-sore and afraid. "Can't you hear those howls? They're coming closer. Listen."

Massui nodded. "Dying . . . dying," he moaned, face

covered in a slick sheen of fear.

Kanja knew what he meant. The howls were like mourning women, scratching their faces and tearing their clothes. "Go and help Najja load the dogs," he said. "Now!"

Kanja held his breath, studying slopes of gray marl and golden sands, and a mist that hung on the crest of a nearby dune. He could hear the faint trickle of water from a riverbed nearby.

"Lead the horses single-file," he said, glaring at Ayize. He wasn't finished with the boy, loathing his large-eyed stare.

They urged their horses on at a gallop and headed towards the mountains where the chariots labored over jagged rock and glistening stones. Thin, sharp gusts rippled across the region and the howls drifted towards them on a lazy wind.

Storm's coming, Kanja thought, seeing a patch of threatening clouds in the west. The wind was coming from the south. It might blow past them if they were lucky.

Najja and Othene took the first watch as the rain subsided, sharp squalls bringing only a shower here and there. Their bellies were pressed against the incline of a sandbank, chins resting on the summit and Najja was shrewd enough to tie the Makurae to a chariot wheel so they could get some sleep. Yuku drained the last of the wineskins and began to wretch, yellow saliva streaking from his mouth. Kanja hoped the warrior had a little more race in him.

He wrapped himself in a leopard skin pelt, listening to the munching of harnessed horses and the whistle of water through their teeth. In the darkness his tears ran freely, knowing the *shakāl* were ripping the hide off his beautiful horse as he lay there. It was past sunup before someone shook him and a warm pancake of fat and honey was thrust in his hand.

"Dust," Ayize cried, hand flattened over his brow.

"Over there!"

"Gods, why didn't you wake me," Kanja murmured as he stood.

He urinated down a rabbit hole, lifting his eyes to a churn of dust in the distance. The warriors urged the horses into the traces as thin clouds hovered over the far off hills and Kanja thought he heard the distant rumble of thunder.

"Lead on!" he cried taking up the rear and signaling to Massui ahead of him. He noticed his brother's heels were blistered from the long march and his shins were covered in sores. He felt a pang of sorrow and chided himself for not having dressed them.

They led their horses through a small ravine carpeted with scree so sharp that it pierced their feet and made them bleed. Veering down a moat carved in the sand, they remained parallel to the ridges along a continuous path. It was some time before they mounted their chariots, Yuku riding behind Massui on a packhorse since Kanja's team were gone.

Ayize stood by Mkasa's side, chatting about the sand drifts and the direction of wind and, from time to time, his eyes would lock on the Makurae with a smile that stretched to his ears.

"You look tired," Kanja shouted to Mkasa, wondering how anyone could sleep tied to a chariot wheel. "How long to Farafra?"

Mkasa inclined his head to study the horizon, eyes scrunched in the glare. "Three days or more, depending on the winds."

"Then we had better get a move on."

Kanja flicked his reins, urging his horses to a gallop. He was thirsty, having had only a few swallows of water and a cup of sour milk. He could hear the wheels clipping against loose rock as he took the lead, taking flight across the plains to where the sky met the earth, bluer than a baby's eye. But the yellow haze they had seen on the horizon dissipated into the open stretches and Kanja began to doubt it was ever there. Suppose Shenq was still far behind. Suppose the cloud was just a sandstorm waiting to plunge down on them at any moment, burying them into the sands forever. Suppose it was a herd of antelope . . .

Hummocks of white sands burst through the speckled terrain but at no time did he see the tracks of chariots or a broken spear with fletchings of black. He was forced to slow the horses to a walk, cursing the Pharaoh loudly for the wheels they did not need.

For two days they saw only foxes and snakes, shooting geese in the sky and roasting them over a fire. At night they rested on the leeward sides of the sandstone hills, overlooking the mountain crests each channeled with drifts of sand.

Najja and Yuku skinned the *shakāl*, tacking out the hides until they dried, and Othene sucked down a mixture of wine and joyroot, surrendering himself to a day-long trance. Wells were scarce and the few they found were lined with doum and acacia wood, giving up enough water to last them for a day or two.

By the third day, the oasis of Farafra was sighted in a large valley flourishing with date palms and bubbling springs, and three small shrines perched on a rock shelf looking out across the desert. As the sun dipped behind the western hills, Kanja led his team down the avenue of rams towards the temple of Ptah. Children threw garlands of flowers and women danced in the streets as they rode past. Flames crackled from a beacon high up on the pylon roof, pedestal garlanded with red streamers.

Kanja stared down the avenue where a horn sounded in one long note, signifying the sinking of the Atum, the sun disk. He saw four priestesses shaking sistra and twenty priests carrying a curtained litter which they set down before the temple gates. The Chief Priest, a giant bull of a man, peered out from behind the embroidered drapes, jaw freshly shaved and body wrapped in white linen.

"Greetings in the name of Ptah," he said, blinking rapidly and biting a plump lip. "Welcome to Farafra."

Kanja bowed. "I'm Kanja, spearman to King Ibada of Alodia and these are my brothers," he said, hand sweeping over the rest. "We bring incense for the great god."

"Ah," the priest said as if it made no difference.

Kanja offered an unguent jar in the shape of an ibex with a cartouche on its left shoulder. *Ibada, King of the five nations of Kush,* it read.

"Who's the boy?" The priest's eyes flitted to Ayize as if he had found a priceless gem.

"A vizier's son, my lord," Kanja said, reading the priest's curiosity. "An excellent bowman."

"Family then."

"A distant cousin."

"I see," the High Priest said, wiping a nose speckled with veins. "Is this all you have?"

Kanja was incensed. It was all he had been given. "The great Pharaoh of Thebes, may he live forever, is most generous," he said, hand across his breast. "He has allowed seven of my men to compete against seven of his in the Kamaraan, my lord."

"Indeed. You must have luck on your side or a merciful opponent." The priest settled back against his cushions. "The winds are treacherous at this time of year. You may be forced north to the white sands."

"We are a match for it," Kanja said with a scornful chuckle, "and the Imazi are easily convinced."

"Convinced?" the priest interrupted with a half-laugh. "Of what? They hack men to pieces and eat their flesh. I can't imagine what would convince them otherwise."

"We are celebrated hunters, my lord," Kanja said, patting the beaded strap across his chest.

"I pray you are vicious enough. There are worse things out there than Imazi my fine friend. Oh, and by the way, we received a message from Alodia over a week ago. It seems King Ibada has lost his sons. You haven't seen them have you?"

"Sons?" Kanja exhaled through his teeth, jaw set in a vicious grin. He started to speak only he was met with a raised hand.

"No matter," the priest said, wrinkling his nose. He scanned the warriors with a look of incredulity. "I extend my protection and my hospitality. There are three barrels of wine in the sanctuary and three oxen freshly slaughtered. You're welcome to them. And the token, of course, is yours."

Kanja gestured to Othene. "My sorcerer has a rare gift, my lord. It comes all the way from Alodia."

"Ah, a wooden doll," the priest said, handling the effigy with tapered eyes. It was a spindly thing, long legs and kinky hair.

"Not just any doll," Kanja corrected, knowing the statue was as worthless as the wood it was whittled from. He had two more in his pack. "A sorcerer's doll."

The High Priest handed it to an acolyte as the litter was lifted off the ground. "You may purify yourself in the pool. And then you will dine with me."

Kanja bowed again, smelling the stench of his own sweat as a burst of rain broke through the clouds. "My lord, did some men ride through here? Theban perhaps?"

The priest looked down at him and shook his head. His eyes brushed over Mkasa and the seal over his chest. The frown was unmistakable. "None that I know of, only wine merchants and they were on foot. There were soldiers here during the month of Ta-ab for the festival of Sekhmet. But none since."

"You said soldiers?" Kanja said, bending his ear to the priest's observation.

"They are long gone now. This is the only oasis for miles around. We are always expecting someone."

The High Priest continued to smile, teeth yellow beneath a plump lip and he beckoned to a priestess more handsome, Kanja thought, than a man. They followed her through the sanctuary where high pillars reached to a painted ceiling and pink-veined statues of Ptah blinked in the torchlight. Eyes of chalcedony followed them from every nook where seated cats and cows peered out from the shadows. But it was the sacred lake that delighted Kanja the most, torches blinking at the water's edge and the moon dancing between the ripples.

A priestess washed away the grime and dirt from his body, feeding him with wine and honeyed figs and he listened to the soothing tone of the harp. He merely watched as Mkasa and Ayize wandered through the groves, pointing at the moon as if they saw a sign in its silvery smile. But Kanja cared nothing for the moon as he gazed down at the naked belly of the girl he was about to rut and if he wasn't mistaken, there was a white stone in her navel so clear it was like a drop of water.

"Brother." The voice took him by surprise and he turned to find Massui shaking as if he was the bearer of bad tidings. His plump thighs were speckled with water, knees knocking against one another.

"What is it?" Kanja said through gritted teeth.

"Snakes!" Massui said, pointing at a pillar of sand.

Kanja stood and stared out at the desert. A plump twister advanced over the dunes and he smiled, thinking of Shenq's men tumbling like ants in its wake.

"The magic is working, my sweet brother," Kanja said, patting Massui's arm. "They won't get far. Not in this."

SHENQ

Shenq watched the red beacon burning at the pylon gates and he watched Kanja's men bathing in the temple pool. His team had arrived in Farafra at dawn, dismantling their chariots behind the temple. A few well-paid heralds were willing to haul them as far as a tanner's barn on the outskirts of Thebes and Shenq would recover them on the way home.

He stood in the shade of the olive groves, tracking a target through a veil of leaves. Meru-Itseni stood by his side, leading a donkey laden with wine skins. They were both dressed in the tob and coat of the Bedouins, headdresses tied with an igal of camel wool.

"They'll be thirsty what with all those vultures we left for them, sir," Meru-Itseni said. "There isn't a fresh well between here and Thebes."

Shenq heard the birds fall silent as a strong breeze tickled his cheeks. "Tell me what you see."

"There's a method to their grouping, sir, a social order," Meru-Itseni said. "They're noblemen for sure. If we've set our snares correctly, these are Ibada's sons."

The sun had burned off the morning haze and Shenq knew it would be hotter than before. Harran had led them to Farafra, dream after dream. He would often stop for a time and sniff the air, raising his hands to the winds and closing his eyes. Shenq wondered what mysteries the prophet saw and what prayers were in his heart. He was imposing in his humble way.

"See how Othene stares at his Mongaka? It's like two dogs with a juicy bone. They're enemies not friends," Shenq said.

"It's too quiet, sir. There's not a bird in sight."

"Windstorm," Shenq said, pointing to a gray plume against the darkening skyline. "It's coming this way."

Shenq watched Kanja wishing he was a pile of ash and stumpy bones. The warrior was naked except for a knife-garter at his thigh and he seemed agitated, finger pointing towards the column of sand. He ushered the warriors towards the temple gates with a flat hand, shouting at Ayize and leaving Mkasa to shift for himself. Only one remained behind, sucking on a wineskin, eyes rolling into the back of his head.

"If Mkasa can live through this, he can live through anything," Meru-Itseni whispered.

Shenq looked at his bearer, taking heed to his measured tone. "Ibada broke the Makurae. He took their lands and raped their women. Mkasa's hatred is deeper than ours. And hatred is what keeps him hungry."

"He's more than just a gaming piece, sir. He's your brother."

"*All* of you are brothers."

In that brief moment, the leaves shook with the sudden force of the wind, sand and loose twigs whipping through the air. Shenq felt the hem of his tunic lifted by the squall and he pressed the donkey closer to the tree trunk. All he could hear was groaning branches and the pounding of debris as it passed through the oasis and the desert beyond, and he hoped his warriors had the sense to ride it out in the shrine. It was some time before the winds died completely and a black kite wheeled and mewed in the dusky skies. He heard a snapping twig and a rustling of leaves. Mkasa passed within twenty paces, eyes flicking in all directions and fingers playing with the seal at his throat.

Meru-Itseni slipped a black arrow from his quiver and handed it to Shenq. There was a quiet hum as the arrow flew, striking the trunk of a nearby tree. Mkasa seemed to hear the hard thud, lips drawn back over large white teeth, and his eyes followed the direction of the shot as he pulled the arrow free.

"I hear them chattering in the night, sir," Mkasa whispered when he found them. "They talk of winds and magic and giant birds. Alodian boys are often called Kanja, Massui, Ayize. Common names. It's the sorcerer that gives them away. When he took off his leather wristband to wash, I saw the mark of a king's guardian on his left wrist. Two red-painted eyes."

"What are the others like?"

"Massui likes the smell of morning bread, sir, sweets mostly, and Yuku takes a swallow of wine when no one's looking. Najja does nothing but sharpen his weapons and read the stars, and the sorcerer wanders off all by himself. His eyes are sharpest at night."

"And Kanja?"

"He watches the boy, sir. He never sleeps."

"I expect he told you to kill me."

"Yes, sir".

"You better get on with it then."

Mkasa grinned at that. "Sir, how long must I ride with them?"

"As long as it takes to bring me the boy. *Alive.*" Shenq took two wineskins from the baskets and handed them to Mkasa. "The wine of the gods, my friend."

"If the winds come, Kanja knows you'll likely ride through the Mara'av canyon, sir. He said it was the fastest route for a fool."

"There's no fool like an old fool," Shenq murmured. "We'll be leaving in a few hours. Let Kanja think we're ahead. There's nothing foolish about that."

"He's good with knives, sir, and he never misses," Mkasa said tiredly.

"Keep Ayize close," Shenq said, thrusting a medicine pouch in Mkasa's belt. The welts on the warrior's back were still pink and raw. "If the Khamāsīn comes, find a hole. A deep one."

Mkasa scampered off into the night, scars deeper than a cattle-brand. The kite screeched overhead and Shenq saw its speckled underbelly, wings stretched out in descent. He was charged with a feeling of unease as it alighted on a nearby tree, head inclined to movement.

"We're being followed," Shenq whispered, hearing the snapping of twigs. His first impulse was to load his bow but he knew the nature of their pursuer for the glutton he was.

Meru-Itseni turned a full circle where he stood, scanning the trees with a trained eye. He nodded as he tugged on the donkey's tether, tightening a strip of cloth across his nose so only his eyes were visible.

They walked towards the edge of the trees, looking back towards the temple putting as much distance as they could between themselves and the lake. Shenq could smell the sour stench of vomit through his shaal and he heard the scuttle of a rabbit in the undergrowth as they spilled from the woodland onto a drover's path. The shrine was straight ahead, door flanked by two sputtering torches, and his men were safe inside a place only a priest would enter.

Shenq drew his dagger, trying to wrap his mind around a sound like the recurring *zrip zrip* of the reed bunting. Only it was a man not a bird, and he twisted round to face him.

Yuku stood in the shadows, rubbing a thumb across the blade of his knife. A natural predator with an eye for snares, he was too drunk to notice the hoot of an owl or jump when a rabbit cowered on the path. His eyes were transfixed on the shrine, doorway aligned with the rising sun and crowned with the image of Apepi.

"Greetings," Shenq said, accent thicker than a coating of dust. He noticed a slight tremor in Yuku's knees and if he wasn't mistaken, the warrior was near collapse.

"Where are you from?" Yuku seemed to recognize the accent.

"Siwa, though my tongue is forfeit if I don't speak the language of the Pharaohs," Shenq said, voice a rumble. He had the alarming notion the warrior could speak it better than he. "And you?"

"Kush."

The term was too general in Shenq's opinion and he watched the warrior as he lowered his chin without an inkling of recognition. His eyes were narrowed from the smoke of the torches and he was thirsty by the look of him.

"My master is a headman," Yuku slurred.

"A headman," Shenq repeated, moving forward a few paces. Yuku's braided hair was spectacular, only when he looked closely it was graying at the temples and crawling with lice. He might have been handsome once if it hadn't been for the drink.

"There's a sorcerer with him." Yuku looked at Meru-Itseni and then back at Shenq as if trying to get the measure of them. "He says the south will destroy the north. He says the vulture will destroy the leopard."

"Those are dark words," Shenq said, giving him a sour glance. "But I've never seen a vulture take a leopard unless it was wounded."

Yuku's eyes widened as if he was trying to keep himself awake. "I've killed a few leopards, but never a black one. Not like my master."

"Does this headman of yours drink wine?" Shenq said, trying to put a rising nausea to rest. He wanted to know more about the leopard but he had a stash of poisoned wine to get rid of and a few men to kill.

"I've nothing to barter with." Yuku hesitated. He scratched his head more than once, gold rings jangling at his neck.

"You have a good knife."

Shenq heard the clatter of the knife as it fell at his feet. "Southern forged," he said, crouching. He tilted the blade back and forth, admiring the snake-like handle. "I have sons you see, and my youngest asked for a knife. Not that he's old enough to use one but there's no harm in asking."

Yuku seemed to like that and laughed; only it was a

nervous laugh like when a man breaks his last spear on the battlefield. He took the wine and pointed to the door of the shrine.

"The serpent of the Nile," he slurred, "Sometimes it moves. Sometimes it speaks."

Yes, we all see shadows in the wine. Shenq hoped none of his men were playing the fool and he fought down the urge to look behind him. Yuku began to tremble, half-turning before he saw Shenq's raised hand.

"Tell your most illustrious master we send him greetings," Shenq said. His khopesh was still covered in its sheath and peeking over one shoulder, and if he drew it now it would only give him away.

Yuku nodded and sauntered towards the woodland with his load, disappearing in a swathe of palm fronds.

Shenq entered the shrine and looked his men over with a smirk. He caught Jabari's glance as it flashed in his direction, a warning not to go alone. "Prepare the horses and wait for me at the west boundary. I have a job to do."

He set out at a brisk walk with Meru-Itseni at his side. They stalked Yuku through the trees as far as the temple precincts, taking care to stay in the shadows.

The grounds were eerily quiet and through the canopy of leaves the sun was bright enough to see through the yellow dust. When they reached a small clearing, there he was crouched in the long grass, sucking on the wine skin and clutching his belly.

"He'll start to feel thirsty before he becomes delirious, sir."

Shenq gave a quick nod, hearing the ghastly sounds of retching. "Then they'll find him in the morning without a scratch on his sorry carcass."

MKASA

"I've brought wine," Mkasa shouted, pushing open one of the big double doors of the temple.

He padded down the main sanctuary in bare feet, feeling plush leopard skins between his toes. From somewhere in the distance, the echo of a male voice and a few well-ordered responses indicated the evening call to worship. The priests would be filing into the small sanctuary soon to put their patron god to bed.

"What did you barter with," Kanja said. He stood before the altar swinging an axe.

Mkasa forced a smile and held out the wine skins. "Arrowheads. Vintage of the gods, so the merchant said."

Kanja shook his head and muttered before dropping the axe on the floor. He snatched the skins in two tight fists and there they hung like freshly slaughtered hens. "Best get rid of it, my friend. They're likely poisoned."

Mkasa almost gagged as he watched Kanja stalk between a forest of columns where a wide swale of shadows seemed to swallow him whole. Frail lights flickered on every plinth, lamps brighter than a thousand *shakāl* eyes. And then he heard the splash of wine on the flagstones, only it wasn't half as bad as the clatter of that heavy axe on the floor.

"The merchant was an evil spirit," Kanja shouted from the darkness.

An evil spirit? Mkasa felt his stomach roll. Last he saw, Shenq was dressed in flowing robes and smelling of lemons. "He was wealthy by the look of him," he said, voice hitched to a whimper.

"He must have turned you over like a dog."

"He didn't touch me," Mkasa grunted.

"Take a brother with you next time," Kanja walked back to the altar. "Yuku out there?"

"Yes," Mkasa lied. "He's with the horses."

"Fetch him."

Mkasa made for the door in less than ten strides, hearing the patter of feet behind him. He knew it was the boy, running to keep up.

"He knows you're lying," Ayize murmured. "You are lying, aren't you?"

"I might be."

"Are you?"

"Walk on," Mkasa warned, feeling too many eyes burning into his shoulder blades.

When they reached the first court, dust skittered across the stone slabs and the trees groaned under the weight of a fresh wind. "The yellowhead keeps summoning the winds," he said, walking briskly towards the gate. "If he's not careful, there'll be a hurricane."

"He's a sorcerer not a yellowhead." Ayize winced. "What is a yellowhead?"

"A man who loves himself. He puts more henna on his head than on his clothes."

Ayize blotted a small trickle of blood from his piercing. "When he throws bones you laugh at him and when he goes into a trance you say he's just hallucinating."

"He's a fake. Why your father allowed such a man to roam his halls, I'll never know. Perhaps King Ibada was too weak to care. Perhaps someone was trying to poison him." Mkasa saw the boy's upturned face and open mouth and he wanted to laugh. "Your brother was the father of all that. And yet here you are *the chosen one* like a bone between two dogs. I wonder if he'll let you live, my prince."

Ayize stiffened, eyes widening. "I'm not a prince."

"Of course you're not."

"Kanja wouldn't hurt me—"

"You've plowed this field before in your own mind.

176

Don't tell me you haven't."

Ayize grimaced and stopped walking. He reached a hand out to steady himself, fingers wrapping tightly around Mkasa's arm. "That's what the princess said. That's why I let her go."

"You're a wise man. You'll be rewarded for what you did."

"I might be dead before I get that reward. *You* might kill me."

"Are you afraid of me?"

"I've never been afraid of you. If you wanted to kill me, wouldn't you have done it by now?"

"No. I'd wait until we were alone together. Perhaps in a wood," Mkasa said, looking over at a stand of trees beyond the main gates. "All men love a good fight. I'm no different."

"You are. You have the eye."

"No one has the eye. Not even the yellowhead. He's so full of greed it'll kill him unless he kills it first."

Ayize cupped a hand around his mouth and whispered, "He can change into a bird, a scorpion. He could have been the *shakāl* in the desert. Mother said he could change into anything."

"Better hope he can change into a cow. Then you can milk him for all he's got."

Mkasa listened to the pounding wind and the thrum of the linen shades that kept the sun off the courts. The sounds reminded him of the creaking ship his father once had, sails snapping in the wind, prow slicing through the foam. He longed for the river and the distant honk of geese, and he longed for the sadness in his heart to go away. Instead, he watched the priests as they filed along the avenue of rams between the sputtering torches and the smoke.

"Kanja wouldn't hurt Baba," Ayize said.

"You know he did," Mkasa muttered, wondering why the boy was so stubborn. "He drank with harlots and thieves. Strange how you Alodians love one another."

"He's a prince. He has rights."

"He has no rights!" Mkasa hissed. "He betrayed his own father. How much will he betray you?"

Ayize shuddered. "Mother told me how Ulan loved my Baba. How he rubbed his feet. How Kanja fed him broth."

"But did she tell you what else they did?" Mkasa felt a rush of bile to his throat and his stomach tightened. He didn't want to tell the boy what he knew, how much Shenq had told him. But he was charged to attack from the inside, to plant a seed of doubt in the boy's mind. "Your brothers smothered him with a pillow and your mother screamed for the guards."

Ayize opened and closed his mouth, eyes riveted on Mkasa.

"Heralds brought news of your brother's crimes. That's why Pharaoh invited Kanja run the Kamaraan. To punish him fairly. After we left, Pharaoh ordered the men you left behind to clean and sharpen their weapons. Then he burned the camp and all your men. He made sure all bows and swords were returned to King Ibada along with horses and other valuables. He wanted no part in the betrayal. There are no traitors now. Egypt has nothing to be ashamed of."

"All of them?" Ayize said.

Mkasa could only nod as they walked through the trees, eyes tracing the swaying grasses and stopping suddenly at a family of chicks that scuttled across the path. He hadn't been so skittish in months only today there was something bitter in the air, the faint smell of *death* if he could give it a name. "I could be lying."

"I know when you lie. The insides of your eyes go red and you sweat."

Mkasa chuckled and nudged Ayize off the path under the shadow of a palm tree. It was safer there in the darkness and he thought he heard running water.

"These are your people. But they'll massacre each other

for power. Watch out for Kanja. He's full of cunning and envy. You'd better let me dress that wound," Mkasa said, jabbing the air for emphasis. "Or you'll be dead in a few days."

He found a small stream at the edge of the oasis and sat Ayize down beside it. Gently squeezing the puss from the wound, he bathed it in water and a smear of honey from his pouch. It would scab overnight.

"I saw Kanja with the princess," Ayize said. "I saw what he tried to do. It's not love, not when you force a woman is it?"

"No, it's not love," Mkasa said, sitting down beside him.

"What do men and women do? In the darkness, I mean."

There was damage in that sad face and it suddenly dawned on Mkasa there was always the damage you couldn't see. The same boy that left Alodia was not the boy that stared at him with those sorrowful eyes.

"Well, there's love and there's love," he said not knowing how to explain it. "The best of these is a love that grows deeper, stronger. Satisfying like a burst of rain on a parched land, like running through a field of grass and never stopping. You never want it to end."

Ayize blew out a mouthful of air. "You've loved a woman like this?"

Mkasa shook his head. "I was given to my adoptive sister in marriage. Father's wish."

"Do you love her?" Ayize steadied his voice with effort.

"Yes." Mkasa thought of Iutha for the first time since they left and he swallowed down a lump of grief.

"But not like that," Ayize said.

"No, not like that."

There was another woman in Mkasa's dreams, a haunting little spot in his memory. And when he thought of her, sighs came from deep in his throat and his heart ached. He felt like he had taken an arrow in his spirit even as he recalled the high painted columns of the Commander's house, the vines and the chrysanthemums. He could see row upon row of juniper and wormwood in the herb garden and he hoped he would see it again. Especially her.

"Many will die tomorrow," Mkasa said, inhaling the heady scent of the soil. "But not you, not if you stay close to me."

"I'll stay very close then," Ayize whispered, face brightening.

"If you had any sense, you'd make a dash for it."

"And where would I go?"

"Find *Kemnebi*. You'll be safe with him."

Ayize gave an impatient huff. "I thought you hated him."

"Sometimes we're safer with our enemies than with our brothers." Mkasa felt goose bumps along his arms as he said it. "And sometimes we're just better off dead."

He narrowed his eyes to the distant fields where oxen pulled carts and a donkey brayed in protest. He knew there was a rage in the boy's head so dark, he would never see through his tears.

Mkasa led the way through the grove towards the temple, conscious of the sharp scent of vomit. Beneath the sputtering torches, he saw the wineskin abandoned on the path before he saw the body. The skin was already purple and blue and covered in blotches, almost unrecognizable except for a peek of gray at the temples and a torn red shúkà. Shenq had snared the first bird with a wineskin and it wouldn't be long before he snared the rest.

KANJA

Pipes wailed and drums pounded, and so did Kanja's head. Shadows seemed to hunker in the High Priest's gardens and he thought he saw an arrow spinning on its axis, cresting through the trees. It was a black kite banking past, feathers brushing the leaves overhead.

Magic, he thought, muscles suddenly tense.

His mind was full of images of the god Shu sitting on the edge of the moon and blowing gusts from his fat cheeks. But there was no wind now, only the soft whisper of a breeze between the statues of Ptah, fanning the flames of the braziers. He ducked beneath the boughs of a large sycamore, garlanded with calcite bowls and flickering with tiny lights. He could smell quail and emmer bread warming over a snapping fire and he could see the High Priest sitting on a high-backed chair with legs of paw and claw.

"Welcome, clan-brother," the High Priest said. "I was expecting you."

Kanja sat on a folding stool, inlaid with gold and ebony, and there was a low table between them laden with ostrich eggs and dates, and jugs of blood-red wine.

"What is your name," the High Priest said.

"My name?" Kanja felt a light shiver between his shoulder blades and took a swallow of wine. "You already know my name."

"I journey on the wind, my friend. I know a prince when I see one. Oh, you must forgive my intrusion. It all started with the Magus spell, a most unusual spell. He cast it from these very gardens. Sometimes we see shadows of lost friends, shadows of new. And sometimes we see demons of our own conjuring. But you have filled my heart with unknown things."

"What things?"

"I see poison and I see a king. Ah, the elderly are such a burden aren't they? Can't say I blame you. But you see Ulan wasn't willing was he? And Kamara never had a choice. If you tell me your name, I can bring them back. Let's start at the beginning, shall we?"

Kanja felt the roar and scream of his battling wits. He could hear soft eddies in the air and he could see the yellow veins in the sycamore leaves. Flowers drizzled from their spreading limbs, soft as swans down, and there was a young black bird lying on a bank of moss, flowers flirting at its feet. It was too far away to touch and Kanja was in a lock-step neither moving forward nor back. He thought he heard its stony caw in the distance and the flapping of its leathery wings. But the vulture was dead. *His vulture.*

"How you tumble and wrestle," the High Priest said, refreshing Kanja's cup. "Why don't you just touch it?"

A ray of moonlight broke through the foliage revealing wings that weren't black, wings shimmering with blue and purple and green. Kanja wondered if the bird would suddenly lift into the sky and be gone. But it didn't. He swallowed a sharp lump of dread even as he reached for it. It was his first kill. A boy never forgets his first kill.

"It can't be?" he said.

"The very same. You were sad then. But see, now it lives."

The feathers seemed to ripple on a crosswind as Kanja reached for it. But in his heart he knew it was dead. The creature had barely enough strength to lift its head and the eye blinked only once. That's how it was with magic. Fickle. False.

"What are you?" Kanja snapped.

"I am a thousand years old," the High Priest said, holding Kanja with a glittering eye. "I am the master of darkness. Worship me and Thebes will be yours."

Worship him and you will die . . . the voice persisted. Najja's voice.

Kanja wanted to fight the vision. He wanted to break out and run. He wanted to scream. And in the midst of it all he saw his father, lying on a bed of blood and sweat, a sorry husk of a man with hardly a breath in his tired old body. "Help me, child," he whispered.

No, I won't help you, Kanja thought, knowing the old man would rise up like the phoenix and peck him to death. He knew trickery when he saw it.

"You are cruel, Kanja of Souba. Can't you see your father needs you?"

"He doesn't need me. He hates me. Always has."

"Locked you in a cell, didn't he? Fed you scraps from the kitchens."

Kanja didn't want to remember and he drained his cup. "It's Ayize he loves."

"You're afraid of the boy. You're afraid he's the shooting star that will take your birthright. You should kill him. Tonight, if you're smart."

Kanja felt his head throb from the wine and his belly was tangle of nerves. "He's only a boy."

"Today, yes. But what will he be tomorrow? You think he dotes on you. You think he waits for you like a little dog for his master? Better not take little dog's bone unless you want a fight."

Kanja rose suddenly from the stool and hurled the cup of wine through a sea of flowers, leaving a trail of petals on the flagstones. He ran through the courts to the sanctuary and lay panting on the cold hard floor. It was all he could remember until the next morning when he heard the spatter of rain and a shriek of wind. There was a crowing rooster at one end of the temple and a jarring horn outside. Torches lit the sanctuary, casting fluttering shadows against the pillars and the acrid smell of incense helped him to breathe.

He lifted his head from the floor, a cold flagstone he had somehow used as a bed. Unhooking the knife from his garter, he dragged the tip across the stone floor, striking a spark with the tip. The noise woke a girl beside him, black dress cast aside in a moment of passion. He called her by name and slapped her thigh. He wanted to be alone.

He stood and walked over to Ayize and crouched on the hard stone floor. The boy was asleep on his side. He always slept on his side. The knife seemed to shudder in Kanja's hand. It would be so easy. So merciful. He raised it over the boy's head, aiming for the tiny tremor in that soft brown throat.

"Mongaka," Najja hissed, grabbing Kanja's wrist. "No! No more killing."

Kanja turned to see Najja's tear-stained cheeks and he heard the sobs. His mouth was a twist of grief and the sun was hardly up.

"It's Yuku," Najja murmured. "He's dead."

They found him crumpled in a heap on the path, one arm torn from its socket. Kanja could only imagine what had happened to it with wild dogs rooting in the woods, howling and barking.

He kept stumbling over the rotting image in his thoughts, a bloated carcass picked clean by creatures with rushing wings and scales. But he knew nothing like that existed, nothing that bellowed yellow smoke and burned like lightning. It was the wine that had killed Yuku just like he knew it would.

Othene weaved a path towards him, a dark shape in a flicker of oil lamps and face beaming like the grinning dead. "I've left a marker beside the body and three deben of silver for the heralds. They'll bury him well."

They won't. Nobody said anything about paying the heralds and they'll take the gold for themselves. Kanja's first impulse was to slap Othene across the face, but the sorcerer was only doing his job. Besides, he had been up all night securing provisions for their journey and the horses were already stamping and snorting in the first court.

"Can you hear the winds, my prince?" Othene said voice hoarse from his mantras.

Kanja snatched his *shúkà* and belt, hearing the reed mats slapping against the transom windows. He had no desire to praise the sorcerer for his magic nor did he want to see sand scurrying about the courtyards.

"These are no ordinary winds," Othene said, rubbing his hands together. "Come, see for yourself."

The east doors seemed further than Kanja imagined and every step was an effort. As he pulled them open a yellow mist hung in the air and he could only just make out the pylons at the entrance of the first court.

"These mists will keep us hidden from the Hawks," Othene said, taking a calming breath.

Yes, and they'll keep the Hawks hidden from us. Kanja gave a slow smile. There was a strange grimness in Othene's eyes and he could feel that menacing, silent prelude to the breaking of bad news. "And?"

"Najja found an old shrine near the village," Othene said with the same serious expression. "He said it was filled with hay and horse dung."

Kanja wished he could redeem time and he wished he could leap on the back of his horse and bolt after them. "There'll be no tracks, not after the windstorm."

"They left without chariots, my prince."

Kanja hardly heard Othene's words. He had flirted with the same idea since they had already lost one team. He could see Shenq on that golden horse of his with a twist of cloth between his ears, nestling like a coiled snake. "No more mercy, old father. If they don't need chariots then neither do we."

"The winds will blow the leopard west to the canyon of the cave men." Othene tapped his head. "I always dream."

"There's another power out here in the desert." Kanja stepped back and crossed his arms. "It's not magic. Not like yours."

"The *Shasu,* you mean?"

"You know what I mean. Can he see me?"

"Of course he can't see you. There's only one voice in

his head."

Kanja nodded slowly. "Be careful how you stir the winds. The Makurae says one small voice is more powerful than many."

He waited a few heartbeats, gazing at the statue of Ptah, *the master of justice,* with his gold striped scepter. The more Kanja thought about Yuku, the more he wanted blood. He snatched the token from the altar and wrapped it in his pack.

"Oh, I quite forgot," Othene continued. "The High Priest would like a word."

"What kind of word?"

"I think you said a few too many last night." Othene bowed stiffly and walked down the steps to the first court, robes catching in an eddy of dust.

Kanja pulled his bow over his head and slung it across his chest. He found the High Priest in the library, poring through a cluster of scrolls in a reed basket.

"A Snaker perhaps, a spearmen, no," the High Priest muttered, plucking a document from the basket and unrolling it on the table. He stabbed it with a finger. "A herald brought this."

Kanja nodded tightly, faking an interest. "And *this* is?"

"A writ. Plain and simple." The High Priest looked him right in the eye. "You do understand that all armed warriors from an enemy state must have orders. You *do* have orders?"

"I am not here to do battle. I'm here to run a race."

"Some may disagree given your extensive armory." The High Priest confined his laugh to a snort, eyes fixed on Kanja's belt. "An axe, a bow and several knives is somewhat extreme, especially in the sanctuary. A rider must leave his weapons with the overseer. They are not permitted in the temple. King Ibada had a son called Kanja and another called Massui who, if I recall, was born with a defect. What was it? Speech, sight, mind? And what was the youngest called?"

Kanja cleared his throat, feeling a rise of irritation. He imagined the High Priest was a grunting pig, belly scraping the ground. *Hog-man can hardly move,* he thought, heartbeat growing loud in his ears. *Hog-man is unarmed.* "All newborns are named after royal princes. I was no exception."

The High Priest smoothed out the papyrus with both hands, eyes squinting at the script. "This writ says I am to arrest any suspicious persons. And I find you suspicious."

"On what grounds, my lord."

"On whatever grounds I see fit. You are not a spearman. I can see that."

"I'm very good with a spear, my lord."

"Your tattoos tell another story. You're a Snaker."

The darkness behind the High Priest seemed to creep about the room and Kanja could see the lacy wisps of dying oil lamps and the yellow glow of demon eyes.

Demon eyes?

Surely not. It was the joyroot, filling his mind with the many apparitions it carried.

"King Ibada is a beloved brother of mine," the High Priest said with a sneer. "You didn't know that did you?"

Kanja took the measure of that porcine belly and the fat little pins beneath it. "King Ibada is a fine king," he said, running out of flattery. "If I were his son, I would be honored."

"I wouldn't admit to being his son if I were you." The High Priest's eyes shifted about as if they followed his ideas. "There are archers behind those pillars and dogs at the ready."

Kanja refused to believe it. The only thing he could smell was the goose fat on the High Priest's arms, thickly smeared to keep the sun off. "My father is dead," he said. "And he was hardly a king."

"Then you have lost the very heart of your kingdom."

Kanja frowned, feeling the chill of dread in his bones. *He knows who you are,* the voices whispered.

"Are you hiding?" The High Priest crooned, rolling up

the writ. "You shouldn't have come if you're hiding."

Let the arrows fly, the voices said. *Quickly, before it's too late.*

Pulling an arrow from the quiver on his back, Kanja rushed forward and plunged it into the priest's chest. He did the rest with his silver knife and the fat old man slumped forward, head smacking against the table.

Kanja didn't wait for a legion of priests and barking dogs. He tore the writ from the High Priest's grip and ran through the sanctuary, rousing his men with a shout.

Othene took the scroll from Kanja's hand and gave it a cursory glance. "Pharaoh will have a copy of this writ before the week's out. It gives a list of all our names, our horses, our tattoos—"

"The High Priest is dead."

Othene gave a small nod and grunted, "We'll never get out of here. They know we're killers now."

"That's what we do," Kanja said, snatching a headdress from Othene's arm and wrapping it around his head. "Follow me!"

He sprinted to the first court and looked up at the high walls. It was quiet except for a barking dog in the village and the sweeping wind beyond the gates. The priests were in the shrine at the east end of the avenue of rams, called to worship by the horns at dawn.

Mkasa brought a horse around in a wide circle and beckoned for Kanja to mount. The packhorses were weighed down with water and weapons, and a third that had once belonged to Yuku carried wood and fresh goat's milk. Kanja gave a sideways smile at Massui, encouraging him to mount his horse.

Poor fool, he thought, loving him all the more.

Najja drew the locking bar of the eastern gate just as the sun appeared over the horizon. A sudden silence swept along the crest of the walls and they listened to the sistra in the distance and the deep-throated chants.

"They're coming closer," Ayize said, reining in his horse.

Kanja swung his axe in a wide arc and pointed it in a westerly direction. "Ride as fast as you can!" he shouted.

Despite his suspicions, the voices in the back of his head whispered a warning. *Shenq's too far ahead. You'll never catch up. And the dogs are out there, same as before.*

Kanja dreaded the same unrelenting desert, and he dreaded Shenq's men who hid amongst the dunes in silent ranks. He urged the stallion to a canter, charging past a steward with waving arms and he snubbed him with a vulgar gesture, rousing his dull-witted brother to a howl of laughter.

They reached a good speed down the avenue of rams before the priests came on, some scattering behind the statues, some shouting in their guttural tongue. One pulled a knife from under his arm and brought the razor-sharp blade down on the horse's shoulder. Kanja heard the arabi scream before he tumbled from its back, rolling clear as he hit the flagstone path. The axe slipped from his hand and skimmed out of reach, and he heard the dull ring of metal against stone.

As he spun to face the priest, he saw another axe glistening in the sun. With one savage blow to the neck the priest's head fell from his body and Kanja watched it slowly at first as if he simply dreamt it.

Najja held his axe aloft, cheek glistening with blood. "I'll kill all of you! Every one of you!"

The priests looked on with bulging eyes, moaning and whimpering. Some clawed the air as if to run and some backed away in quick, jerky steps.

"Get the horse," Kanja muttered as he struggled to stand.

"Leave him," Najja said. "The animal's as good as dead."

Kanja cursed and spat, and motioned to Ayize. "Bring me your horse. You can ride with him," he said, nodding at Mkasa.

He wanted to kill the boy right there and then if he was

honest. He wanted to gut him slowly and hear him wail.

I'll do it tonight, he thought, *when no one's looking.*

Hour upon hour they trudged in a southeasterly direction through a thin wall of dust where the sky had disappeared altogether and the horizons were lost. Nothing broke through except a fox and Kanja struck it swiftly with his sling, leaning down from his horse to retrieve it as they passed. He had a nagging sense they were being followed by a creature with a sharper mind than his and he glanced at the fox, blood dripping from its nostrils.

Jumpy, are we? said the voice with a trace of humor.

Kanja listened to the horses' hooves as they snapped over carpets of gray rock and powdery sand, and he hoped to catch a glimpse of something.

See, what did I tell you? There's nothing there.

Until a dog began to sing, an echoing howl that would never stop and out of the swirling mists they came snapping and snarling. Kanja urged his horse to a gallop no longer caring where they went. He barely saw Massui straight ahead swirling an axe, cheek glancing off the side of a large dog with glowing eyes. He heard a scream in the yellow mist and cursed the gods as he pulled an arrow from his quiver. Aiming at where he had last seen the dog, he heard nothing but the rush of wind and the whisper of the arrow as it sped through the air.

Madness, he thought. He could have struck anything.

He thought he saw Mkasa, axe raised in the thick of them. The dogs were too fast on their feet, dodging each strike and beating a retreat before coming back on them again.

Kanja felt a sharp pain in his thigh as claws scraped along his calves and his horse stopped suddenly, rearing and shrieking. The breath was knocked out of him as he hit the hard-packed sand and all the while he stared into the eyes of a creature deadlier than a man's sword. He shielded his face from the saliva as it dripped on his thigh and he could hear the snarl as the creature retreated. And then the desert was silent except for the shriek of horses and the war cries of his men.

Kanja rolled on his side smelling the stench of burning flesh. He tried to stand but the effort forced him down, and he tried again, this time seeing the earth as it waved beneath his feet. The saliva had penetrated an open wound and he retched as he knelt, spewing up liquid the color of ash. Maggots, the size of a man's finger, weaved amongst the slime and he gasped at the hand on his shoulder rigid like a dog's claw.

Mkasa's face began to bend as if it was a reflection in a rippling pool, lips curling and teeth the size of a horse. Kanja was forced to his feet by a strong arm only he couldn't feel his legs.

"Has he been bitten?" a voice said.

He never heard the answer. The world went black for a time until he was jogged awake by the horse beneath him, smelling sweat and blood on its flanks. He reached for his water skin but there was no sign of it and his throat burned with the taste of sand. He heard Mkasa shout and through the mist he saw Othene, Ayize and Najja all unharmed and out of breath as they drew alongside. But Massui was bleeding badly, blood dripping from his ankle. The warrior was too simple to understand and too feverish to care. Kanja heard him chuckle loudly, a long drawn out sound that never drew breath and he was alerted to a sense of loneliness as if he would never hear that chuckle again.

A canyon came into view nestled between two escarpments of gold and silver. It was sand and scree, of course, and as barren as the desert they had just come from.

"We're too far north," Mkasa said, whistling through his teeth. "The southern tip of the white sands is only a day away. We must find a cave."

He gestured for the men to dismount and they led the horses through the mouth of the canyon as the sky became stippled with the first blush of evening. Climbing the slopes to a series of caves, Kanja noticed the first were too shallow to shelter in but the third was deep enough for a blazing fire. He could feel the prick of stitches in his thigh and he heard Othene's silky voice. The wine he drank was warm and bitter, and the cave became a haze of whispers.

When he awoke, he could see Najja plucking a dog's tooth from a man's leg. The same man screamed and the sound carried into the thick night air. Othene stood on a narrow ledge at the mouth of the cave scattering seeds in the breeze. His hennaed lips moved and sometimes he just stared as if he saw something no one else could see.

Inside, the warriors laughed and supped on fox and rabbits. Two voices whispered beside him and he listened to their earnest chatter.

"The *shakāl* took a chunk out of the half-wit's leg," Mkasa said, hands raised to the open fire. "He'll be dead by morning."

"He won't die. The sorcerer burned out the corruption. Why do you think he screamed?"

"He *screamed* because the sorcerer gored his leg with the tooth before he took it out."

"Liar!" Najja unsheathed his knife.

"The odds don't favor your side, not if you kill an honest man."

"I won't kill you, brother. That would make me a coward as well as a murderer."

"You were a coward when you burned my village and you were a murderer when you burned our women. King Ibada made us watch until every last one crumbled to dust. You can't begin to understand how every day I wondered if I would be tortured or killed. If you ever call me *brother* again, I'll kill you."

"Quiet!" Kanja muttered, watching a dead snake blistering on a small pan. "Bring me food."

The meat was warm and flakey against his lips, and he saw Ayize hold up the severed head, thrusting it at Massui with a loud *hiss*. The laughter carried into the night just as he feared it would. "Will we ever outrun the *shakāl?*" he said to Mkasa. "Will we ever be rid of them?"

"*Shakāl* do what all wild creatures do. Hunt and kill," Mkasa murmured, voice tapering to a sigh.

"They're not like other wild creatures."

"No, they're smarter. There are fifty dogs in each drove, and each *drove* has its own pack-leader. A thousand eyes watch you at night and they'll herd you in until there's no way out. And just when you think you're safe, they're right there behind you crunching on dead men's bones."

Kanja shuddered and wondered if Mkasa was trying to scare him. The howling was bad enough until he realized it had stopped. "How does *Kemnebi* hunt them?"

"He doesn't. No one does."

"But if he did, how would he do it?"

"Instinct, smell, terrain, same as any hunter. He can smell a man long before he sees him and he'll wait all night if he has to. He'd sooner die than fail, if that's what you mean."

No, there was much more. It was something to do with those instincts of his. And then there was the prophet, the man with child's eyes. The voices in his head reminded him that *Shasu* buried their dead in a valley, a dark place where the sound of mourning could be heard at dusk.

"The *Shasu*," he murmured, eyes heavy. "What's his secret?"

"His God is bright and determined," Mkasa said. "He's everywhere. Can't you feel Him?"

Kanja could and began to shiver under the blanket. It wasn't always harassing little spirits that bothered him, flitting about with bared talons and hurling a curse or two. He could easily get his fist around their wiry little necks. This was something much bigger. Something he couldn't see.

"Well then," Kanja said, giving way to nervous chuckling. "Let's see how clever this God is."

KHEPER-RE

Kheper-Re opened his eyes, his dream already fading. He thought he still heard the groans of lovemaking, feeling a fondle here and there. And last of all, the sounds of girlish giggles floating across the courtyard and up into the starry sky. He nursed a secret hope of reclaiming the dream at a later stage and finishing what the girl had started. He couldn't say what had awoken him, possibly a poke in the ribs.

At least now he was sitting on a dais between his sister and his daughter in the first court, waiting for the heralds to come home. There were lesser wives behind him, one in a golden gown with eyes of onyx, one he loved more than the rest.

Aset . . . The girl in his dreams.

"If you don't mind me asking," he said, leaning towards Princess Neferure and hiding a yawn behind a hand. "Where did you get that goose leg?"

"I was given it," Neferure whispered between bites. She was tearing the flesh off with her teeth like the savage she was and throwing the bones on the floor.

"I think we should go back to having tasters." Kheper-Re watched her lips hover over the rim of a fresh cup of wine. "Ask that man over there. He's been making eyes at you all evening."

"They're wrestlers father, part of the entertainment. But of course you wouldn't know since you slept though most of it."

Kheper-Re squinted at two men locked together all muscle and sweat, one dressed in black for the Hawks and the other in red for the Bloods. The Hawk blocked a strike to his hip and all of a sudden he appeared to lose his footing, sliding to the ground in a cloud of dust.

Careful now, Kheper-Re thought, musing over the warrior's dexterity and poise. "Strong, aren't they?"

"I've seen better," Neferure whispered.

"You can't fight. Not like that."

"You doubt me, father. I can do more than you think."

Kheper-Re squinted at her in the lamplight, wondering what lies she had told. "When the heathen tied you up, did he touch you?"

"Of course he touched me, father. How else would he have tied me up?"

"You know what I mean."

"He kissed me . . . rather passionately."

Kheper-Re shuddered, wondering what else he did. "I didn't ask you to discuss the merits of a kiss. I asked you to find out who he was."

"Kanja is his name. And yes, he is a prince," Neferure said through clenched teeth. "He is honored by the wars he fights, by the hands he takes."

"I will not pray to the gods for his return. No, I will pray for his death. It's the only reward for a beggar like him. I should have killed him before he left. But where's the fun in that?"

"He's well decorated for his victories. You should see his—"

"I've been decorated too, I think you'll find. There have been no wars since my coronation except a squabble in the south and a minor raid in the north. I was there. You were not. Eleven out of fourteen competitors were hacked to death during the last Kamaraan. Kanja won't come back. And you will marry the prince and have sons."

"How, father? Menkheperre has never had a wet dream."

"You're right. He's had more maids than you've had gowns." Kheper-Re grabbed a bowl of beans which he mistook for a cup of beer and proceeded to sift a bulb of garlic between his teeth. "I had you followed."

"Why, father?"

"Why? Just a feeling. Fathers are allowed to have feelings."

"I've done nothing wrong."

"You know all about soldiers. Take Lieutenant Jabari for instance," Kheper-Re said, staring off into the distance. "Oh wait, you already have."

"He pursued *me*, father." Neferure lifted her chin and lowered her eyes. "Not the other way around."

"You should hear the gossip in the guardhouse. Apparently, you're married to pleasure alone."

Neferure bristled at that. "They're all liars."

"That's a lot of guards, my girl," Kheper-Re said, looking at her with mock disgust. He even tried a grimace.

"What do they know of love? Stinking, sweating men," she said, two fists hanging by her side.

"Jabari's clean so all the women say. He's also an excellent shot."

"He's faithful, father, which is more than can be said of you."

"Like father, like daughter. What a precious team we make. Are you still in love with him?"

"A little."

"Only a little?"

"Oh, father, what does it matter?" Neferure blew through her mouth. "There is another I love, a lion-heart, a *Bloodman*."

There it was, plain to see. The poor girl had fallen in love with her captor. "I envy your youth. I can't pretend to match it. I was like the sun once in all my gold and grace, and the streets were alive with the sound of my name. Even goats were said to bleat it across the fields."

"Father, don't you see?" Neferure whispered. "The people don't love you. They're afraid of you. How many men have you mutilated and now call *eunuch* because of your jealousy! And how many nobles have you turned out of their homes to make way for better men?"

"A few," Kheper-Re agreed. He was glad she had noticed.

"Why must you be so cruel?"

"Cruel? I'm not cruel. Your darling father has a nose for traitors. They hide in plain view where all the traitors hide."

"I never hide, father. I'm not afraid of you."

"You should have been born a boy," Kheper-Re said, patting her knee.

"Perhaps I am inside," she said, almost sobbing.

Kheper-Re wanted no more talk of traitors and held a finger to her painted lips. Besides, too much excitement and she would be green-faced and throwing up all over the slabs.

He could just make out silver tableware in the middle of the courtyard, all piled in a basket and adorned with black ribbons. So far, no one had thrown any in the basket for the Bloods and he hoped it would stay that way.

"Brother, the heralds," Hatshepsut whispered, pointing through the open gates.

"Where's my supper?" Kheper-Re muttered, gold cuff knocking over a cup on an attendant's tray and spilling wine all over his *shenti*. "No one's given me any supper."

"The heralds are here with *news*," Hatshepsut said, as if the last word would entice him away from his stomach. She grabbed a flatbread off a passing tray and laid it on his lap. It was modeled in the shape of a horse with two raisins for eyes.

"I hope its good news," Kheper-Re said, studying the horse. He didn't much like the look of its upturned mouth and the swelling between its legs. It was all hallucinations. No point in worrying if it's just hallucinations.

"All hail Amun, giver of life," the herald said, prostrating himself before the dais.

"Rise to meet the sun!" Kheper-Re shouted at the herald. At least, he assumed it was a herald. The man was as blurred as a mirage and stank of rotting milk. He motioned to the priests to swing their smoke-filled censors over the glistening man, still covered in desert filth. The stench would take hours to dissipate much like dog excrement clinging to a sandal.

"May your seed flow, O divine Son of Ra" the herald said, grabbing a cup of wine which he quickly gulped. "May Amun light your path this day and may Hathor bring you a thousand years."

Kheper-Re nodded, hoping his seed did flow. So far it had bred a trough of infants too hideous to speak of and he knew, of course, why they were so hideous. Harran had told him. They were *hideous* because they were the product of incest.

"My name is Yunre, my lord," the herald said. He was round-faced and merry, body rippling with muscle.

"Tell me, Yun-*re*," Kheper-Re said, sniffing. "Who's winning?"

"Hard to say, my lord. On the first night, the winds misted the desert plains and we found the teams tough to track. The Bloods have a sorcerer with a fist-full of bones and he's conjured a mighty storm."

"What of the Hawks?" Kheper-Re said, trying hard to keep the scowl from his face.

Yunre began to pace from side to side, arms out by his sides. "On the first night, the Hawks took off their breastplates and sleeves, and stripped the horses clean of their plumes. Dressed in leather-strapped armor, we couldn't see them for sand. And they're as quick as cats.

"Two days later we saw the Bloods. They were all skin and teeth. Looked like they'd been fasting, my lord."

"Hah!" Kheper-Re lobbed his goblet in a perfect arc and watched it clatter to the floor, glowering like an angry eye. "For the Hawks!" he cried.

There were loud cheers and the chink of jewel studded daggers, and attendants ran about retrieving all the spoils for the baskets. There was a maid in the corner dressed in ivory linen with rosebuds around her neck. She looked nearly as splendid as he did, *better naked*, he thought, and splayed on a deep crimson blanket. He'd ask for her when the festivities were over.

"Fill the cups!" Kheper-Re held up a hand as a hundred goblets rang together.

"The nobles have had enough, my lord," Hatshepsut assured through gritted teeth. "Soon they'll be ripping around the courts looking for a way in."

Kheper-Re had already considered inviting them into his apartments for a quick snorter despite all the nasty things they had been saying about him. They seemed like a nice crowd and sorry too, especially the farmer who had swallowed a goat testicle for a punishment, although he begged not to do it again.

"On, on," he shouted at the herald, emptying his cup on the first toast.

"The wells were full of dead birds, my king," Yunre said, "shot through with black arrows. Kanja cursed the gods and had to suck the very blood from his arm. Horus knows it was the only thing his men had to drink. Truth is, they probably bit themselves half a hundred times and should have died from it."

Laugher swelled up like a sea and echoed off the walls. The nobles bawled and yelled and another pile of gold hit the Hawk heap. Even the Queen leaned forward in her chair, mouth pressed in a white line as if she suffered a glut of saddle sores.

"It was dark and there was a rush of wind across the plains," Yunre said. "The Hawks crept between the tents of the Bloods and slashed Kanja's prized mare. It wasn't until the following afternoon a pack of *shakāl*, slaver dripping from between their teeth, tracked the scent of blood and healing salve. They were filled with arrows before they got there and the Bloods did well to escape them. But they lost two horses and a chariot in Sheb-ah Swamp."

Kheper-Re heard a round of gasps before raising a

hand to silence them. He had visions of two arabi horses in the ghost bog, legs sinking as far as the gaskin and screaming in agony. He recoiled at the thought and grabbed a bowl of roasted quail wings to crunch on.

"Commander Shenq found the horses wedged in a shallow bed of quicksand and collared to a chariot," Yunre affirmed and the crowd sighed with relief. "He has two more packhorses to his team."

"Two more, do you hear?" Kheper-Re shouted to the crowds. There was a roar of delight, of course, just like he expected.

"The Hawks push their horses hard, my king, and the Bloods are forced to match the pace. Our Commander's like a fowler. He adjusts his bait to every bird so he can bring them in one by one."

A fowler, yes . . . Kheper-Re felt a sudden rush of euphoria as he waved for another cup of wine. He decided to throw in the title deed to the palace in Memphis just as the nobles wagged a dozen tongues, hurling fish bones and goose legs. It was all they had left.

"The priests lit a beacon in Farafra," Yunre said, hesitating for greater effect. "The Bloods took the first token."

Kheper-Re felt a pinch of embarrassment as the room fell silent. "Anyone dead?"

"Bloodman Yuku is dead, my king. It was Hawk killing."

The mood turned clumsily to a round of cheers. Kheper-Re had barely eaten his breakfast and the wine had gone to his head. Shadows seemed to shift between the columns and the statues of the gods stared down at him with their dark stone eyes. He was filled with a familiar sense of dread and fiddled nervously with his little bread horse.

What if they lose?

Neferure laughed. "Kanja has hardly been here a few months, father, and now he almost reigns."

"A week, a month, what does it matter? And no, he won't reign. He's the very seed of evil and there's no medicine for that." Kheper-Re tore the head off the bread horse and chewed loudly.

"Admit it father, you're afraid. There's a chance he might win," Neferure said, falling back into a moody silence. "And then I'll have to marry him."

"You accuse me falsely, girl. And remember, loving a traitor is treason."

Neferure blanched and lifted a single eyebrow. "Seems like the Hawks are losing."

"Not so, my lady," Yunre corrected. "Our fowler is well ahead, setting his snares on the open road."

"There, see!" Kheper-Re said, smile tightening and twisting. "My beloved Commander fights with an iron sword, not just for play."

"We haven't seen him face-to-face, my lord," Yunre sounded distracted. "Not after the bloods killed so many *shakāl*. The creatures will not rest until the last man is dead. Such is their nature."

Kheper-Re briefly closed his eyes as he recalled Shenq on the battlefield, sword cutting through the air, horse rearing under him. He heard strange echoes then, small and shrill like a child at play and he wondered if Shenq still lived.

If the Bloods are just as cunning, then he could be dead. Or torn to pieces by a shakāl and trampled by his horse.

A sudden terror filled him and he held his breath, hands balled into a fist. He thought he could hear a faint rustle of leaves, a man calling his name. Bread squelched from inside one hand and when he looked down all he could see were two doughy buttocks and a flattened tail.

It was a sign.

SHENQ

Shenq twirled an Alodian arrow between his fingers as he followed the blood trails to the cliffs. He prayed Mkasa was still alive and Ayize too. They had found a *shakāl* struck by an Alodian arrow and Shenq's men had the sense to leave the carcass where it fell. Kanja had meddled in their natural order and the blood-sniffing man-eaters would follow his tracks just as Shenq had done. *Shakāl* out-smelled man and interpreted the height and depth of the sounds they heard. And they were out there, somewhere.

They had almost run out of water and Shenq was weaker than he cared to let on. The light began to fade and a whistling wind from the south cut through the mists, clearing the way to the canyon at the gateway of the rising sun. His instincts told him Kanja was hiding up there in one of the many caves, only Shenq had no desire to open himself up to an ambush and decided to camp nearby.

His horse nickered and threw up his head. *Water.*

To the south of the canyon was a bay sheltered from the winds and a stream that fed into a pool. A steady trickle journeyed down to a dried-up riverbed, disappearing finally into the cracked earth. The slope above was not as steep as Shenq thought and, as the horses drank, he kept his eyes on the face of the slope. The scree was rough and jagged, and a climber would need to make certain of each step before reaching for the next.

Khemwese and Harran took the first watch, lying on a hillock to survey the eastern desert. Their lighthearted banter made Shenq angry and he hissed a curse in their general direction. Taking a small rug from his horse's back, he made a tent out of a length of rope tied between two rocks. He gripped the Box of Heka under one arm, wrapped in goat pelt and rabbit fur trimmings and he wondered what caused such a whirl of activity in his head. He couldn't sleep no matter which way he turned. The nights were colder than usual and he heard the sound of Kanja's horse, snorting and pawing the earth.

"She can smell him," said a voice in the darkness. It was Tehute, crawling out of his tent on all fours. He was rubbing his thigh vigorously since the age-old arrow wound was clearly bothering him. "I'll load her up with weapons. That should put a stop to it."

Shenq rubbed his hands, breath misting in front of his nose. "What's up there?" he said, looking towards the crest.

"Caves. Deep enough for men and horses. I saw a trail of blood in the sand," Tehute murmured. "They're up there, sir."

Shenq began to chuckle. He couldn't help himself. "Kanja would do well to sleep with one eye open. He's a fool to think we're not far behind."

"He's drunk on joyroot," Tehute sighed. "Last Kamaraan, your driver drank two cups of it before they cut off his leg. He never felt a thing."

Shenq remembered the last race with a grimace. He could still see the enemy chariot sliding athwart his course, arrows pinning his driver in the chest. The driver was hurled beneath the wheels, bones snapping as he hit the ground. All Shenq could do was take up the reins and steer into a hedge on the border of the great river. He hoped for a soft landing on the other side. But he was mistaken. As the horses burst through, the chariot gave a sickening lurch forward. He saw what was coming and grabbed an overhanging branch just as two horses and the most elaborate of the Pharaoh's chariots dropped fifty feet into the bed of the river.

"Six horses died in that race," Shenq recalled. "Beautiful arabi horses."

"This will be my last race, sir." Tehute sighed loudly. "Any more and they'll beat it out of me."

"You're never too old. I can't imagine a race without you. I can't imagine a battle without you either."

"I've taught you everything you know. Now teach the boy. Remember, he may not heed good words, but he'll heed good wisdom. You'll thank me one day for all the yelling, the horsewhipping and the half-rations. And you'll thank me for hauling hogs and cleaning sties. That's where you got your strength and humility." Tehute looked at Menkheperre asleep in a makeshift tent. "He'll thank you too."

Shenq wondered why Tehute looked so wistful and patted him on the shoulder. "Wake Jabari and Menkheperre. I have a hunter's thirst for action."

Tehute shook both warriors with his foot. "On your feet," he muttered.

They ascended the slope of the rocky saddle, slowly at first, to measure the shale. It made little noise underfoot as they pushed for the summit and the shrieking wind concealed the shift of rocks. Shenq looked to his right over a narrow ledge. He could see Khemwese and Harran several feet below lying across a stumpy dune and staring out into the desert. They were talking about HaShem if he could bet on it.

Joined at the hip, he thought, wondering what one would do if the other died.

"There," whispered Jabari, crouching behind a boulder. He pointed across the canyon to a glow of firelight where a man stood at the mouth of a cave. Both hands were raised to the moon.

"What's he doing," Shenq said, lying flat on his belly.

"Summoning the winds, sir. He's calling out to the god, Shu."

Shenq felt his forehead crinkle and his eyes shifted from one side of the canyon to the other. "If his voice gets any louder, he'll rouse the Imazi."

"You don't believe he's a sorcerer do you?" Menkheperre said, placing a hand against the leather bands at his chest.

"Perhaps I'm missing something you're about to point out."

"Well, it's the winds, you see. They're fiercer this year than last. And then there's the moon."

"What's wrong with it?"

"It's not as round as it was a week ago."

For the first time since they left Thebes, Shenq saw it again, a bright orb whose upper edge had somehow disappeared. Old feelings of terror made him jumpy and he could almost see a pair of leathery wings draped down Othene's back. He had never seen the demon of darkness but he would know him by sight.

"That's not magic," he scoffed. "Sorcerer's can't conjure darkness nor can they change the moon."

"Vizier Thutiy said the sky would swallow the moon," Menkheperre reminded, caressing the fly collar below his neck. "That's magic if you ask me."

Shenq picked up the awe in the warrior's voice. "He ran off to Suhaj with the ancient texts. That's stealing if you ask me."

"The High Priest has been after those texts for years. He thinks he can speak the magic and destroy my father."

"I say good luck to him," Shenq said, studying Othene across the canyon.

Stories of pygmies were hardly worth a harlot's bangle and he wondered what the High Priest would make of them, a dwarf with a massive brow. He was hostile when he put his mind to it, only he might be more gracious when he saw the magic box in Shenq's pack.

"See how he throws the seeds," Menkheperre said. "He knows the winds are coming."

"All diviners do that," Shenq said. "They chant, they moan, they rock their heads from side to side. They're all skilled in their trickery. But they don't fool me."

"And if the sky does go black, what then?" Jabari asked.

"We'll be dragged down into the guts of the earth by the Imazi and cooked," Shenq said. "They like dark meat."

"I don't care if they prefer goats," Jabari muttered. "They won't be gnawing on my bones for supper. Promise me something. If they catch us, don't let them eat me."

Shenq grinned. "No chance, my friend. You'll be buried with the best of them when your time comes. My tomb's plenty big enough."

A stout squall entered the canyon, bringing with it the rich tang of mountain rain and the moon was brighter than a ship's bell. Shenq watched as Othene parted his robes and urinated in the sand.

"Load that bow, boy," he whispered to Menkheperre. "See if you can shoot his pecker off."

Menkheperre lowered his face in his hands to stifle a bout of laughter and by the time he had got a hold of himself, Othene had already disappeared into the fiery glow of the cave. Another warrior took his place using a spear as a walking stick. He sniffed the air and cast a furtive glance at the opposite slope.

"Massui," Shenq muttered. "*Shakāl* can scent further than five dunes and they'll be sniffing that bloody leg about now."

"I want to be like you," Menkheperre murmured. "I've thought about it long and hard."

"You don't know what you're saying."

"I know what it costs. And I've sworn the oath."

"You're a boy of twelve, my lord, not a warrior. Not yet."

"I have to kill someone, don't I?"

Shenq shrugged. There was a giant of a possibility on the opposite slope.

"Easy prey," Menkheperre said, following Shenq's gaze. "There's nothing half as deadly as a black goose feather."

Shenq knew the prince had more talent than any

bowman and twice the energy. But if he missed, the arrow would glance off Massui's right shoulder and disappear into the cave. He betted on three arrows to do the job with the moon as bright as it was. The boy would likely miss on the first try. "We'll just lie here and watch then."

Menkheperre notched an arrow with a black shaft and he raised his bow and drew. The first arrow tore through the air with a muffled hum and buried its head in a pile of loose rock. He cursed as he loaded a second, watching his restless target through narrowed eyes. The arrow slotted nicely into the hollow of Massui's throat and the third ripped through his chest. Massui coiled into a twisted knot and hit the ground with a loud smack. He choked and gagged, and no one heard.

"Now you're a warrior," Shenq whispered, impressed by what he saw.

Menkheperre did not answer and Shenq knew why. The first kill always did that to a man even after the rush of victory. He would be sad and lonely for a time until he felt nothing at all.

The wind of the approaching storm sighed eerily like an old crone drawing her last breath. Shenq could feel something coming closer and closer, and his eyes darted about, lips pressed together. *And here I am wondering what to do with the rest of my day*, he thought until he heard a snarl.

"Down there," Jabari whispered. "In the shadows."

Loping dogs swept along the valley floor and the jet-black fur of the alpha male shimmered from shoulder to tail. His jaws locked onto Massui's throat for some time until he was sure he was dead.

"Beautiful . . ." Menkheperre murmured.

"And deadly," murmured Shenq. All he could see was a nice fur rug and a pot of stew.

"The gods will have revenge on the ones they killed."

"The *shakāl* will have their own revenge," Shenq said, "and we can leave the gods out of it." He knew the boy wanted a pup and it would only be a matter of moments before he scurried down the hill, scooping one up in his arms and crooning over it like a baby. "They'll drag the body through the canyon and out the other side. His bones will be picked clean by morning. All except his head."

When the dawn came so too did the rain. It was a brief downpour that barely covered the north side of the cliffs, falling aslant on a brisk wind. The fire in the Alodian cave had long since died and Othene stood at the entrance, looking up and down the valley floor as the sun spilled in from the east.

"Looks like he's lost something," Shenq said, hiding a smirk.

For an eternity Othene stood there with baleful, smoldering eyes, studying the terrain and the skies. It was all Shenq could do to remain motionless, each breath seized in his throat until a big voice echoed against the cliffs.

"Find him!" Kanja limped down the mountain with a thick bandage around his leg. "He can't have gone far."

Najja and Ayize strapped on their belts and bows, and led the horses down. Mkasa walked with heavy, ponderous steps, toying with his seal and letting the sun catch on the mirror side.

"He knows we're here," Jabari said, watching a flash of light. "And he knows Massui's dead."

"They'll follow the tracks and go north for a time." Shenq said, watching Najja crouch, hand hovering over the scree. "Then they'll head east."

Shenq led his men back to camp. "Give the animals water and wait with the Captain," he said to Jabari and Menkheperre.

He quickly formulated a plan in his mind and went in search of Harran and Khemwese. He could hear them even before he found them, whispering about demons and a net to trap them in.

"Any sign of them?" he said, crawling up the rise of the hillock.

"Not yet," Harran said.

Shenq imagined a drove of *shakāl*, gnawing bones and sucking on the marrow. He scanned the entrance of the canyon bathed in the warm glow of the sun's first rays. Najja was the first to appear, hand over brow, surveying the silent, empty plains. Twice he sniffed the air, eyes flicking from left to right and Shenq wondered what he sensed.

"The *shakāl* dragged a man over that dune last night, Maaz," Khemwese said. "I saw the light in their eyes and then,"—he paused, looking down at his hands—"a hissing sound."

"Like whispers," Harran said, making a face. "He's been hearing it since sunup."

Shenq's pulse began to pound in his ears and he drew a deep breath. He studied Mkasa and Ayize as they curbed their horses behind Kanja's but there was no sign of Othene. Perhaps he was hiding in the canyon, dreading what he might see.

The howls were distant at first, ranging from low growls to high-pitched wails. Closer they came, scurrying like a colony of scorpions and spilling over the dune. Najja urged his horse forward at a gallop, bow lifted, eyes measuring his range. He was a tall gangling man, face shaded by the lion's mane headdress he wore. The spear impaled two dogs before he reined his horse around, galloping back to where Kanja stood with his bow at the ready. The *shakāl* came on with pearls of foam on their tongues and arrows crested two at a time, shrieks echoing against the cliffs. But they stopped suddenly as if responding to a silent command, a flash of light that shimmered across the sands.

The seal.

Shenq saw it again, a burst of light so sudden it was a miracle he could see it at all. The dogs fell back far enough to reveal what they had brought, a carcass so hideous it was nothing but a shine of blood attached to a man's head.

Kanja dismounted and ran towards his brother and when his knees hit the ground, he wailed and screamed at the top of his lungs. The *shakāl* looked on for a time, wind ruffling their smooth black coats. They were crouched on all fours, snouts raised and twitching.

When the mourning ceased, they lifted their heads and howled the song of victory.

MKASA

Mkasa tucked the seal under his shaal as they galloped away from the setting sun. He felt the boy, warm against his back, both astride one horse and as close as they could be. It was the only road through the canyon, towered on both sides by flat-topped cliffs. When he looked up, he caught a glimpse of smoke and wondered if there were Imazi beacons along the crest. All he could hear were horses' hooves and Ayize's quiet sobs.

Even Mkasa felt a twinge of pity when he wasn't laughing behind a hand. It was Shenq's men that had killed Massui. He could tell by a few bloodstains left amongst the rocks and a clean Hawk arrow.

Lucky the others hadn't seen it, he thought.

Kanja rode in front of them, horse kicking up clods of sand. Every fragment reminded Mkasa of a swoop of black swallows, only these ones screamed taunts and pecked with needle-sharp beaks.

Keep watch, a voice cautioned, a voice just like his father's. He would if he could keep his eyes open. He hadn't slept a wink in days.

"Ayize," he whispered, tapping the boy's hands around his waist.

"Where are we?" Ayize jerked back suddenly, almost losing his balance.

"Ma'arav," Mkasa murmured, dreading the Gateway to the West. "The winds have blown us off course."

Two towers stood on opposite slopes, gray and threatening, and positioned so that travelers coming from the east must pass between them. White banners fluttered overhead decorated with a jackal-headed snake, and through the loopholes Mkasa thought he saw pale faces watching from the darkness. He knew they were deciding whether to let the riders pass and there would be a price to pay if they did.

Ayize coughed quietly. "They'll come out of the shadows. We won't make it."

Mkasa knew the Imazi were like a wind out of nowhere and there was a dark strain in the air he couldn't explain. "Your brother has gold and spices to pay them. We'll make it."

"What if it's not enough? What if they want a horse?"

"Then we'll give them a horse."

"I don't like it. We should turn around."

"We're fast, remember?"

"Yes," Ayize said, swallowing hard. "We're fast."

"And we're ready." Mkasa slipped two arrows from his quiver and unhooked his bow. "Remember, if anything happens, run!"

Mkasa thought he saw a flicker of light in one of the loopholes but it was only the pale glow of the sun. They were exposed to arrows from both sides, boulders scattered along the hills and high enough to hide behind. An eerie silence crept along the path behind him and he looked over his shoulder more than once. All he could see were shadows shifting back and forth, a trick of the light perhaps as the sun sped through the valley floor like a tidal wave. He was glad he had his father's seal—a flash of light to blind the jackal.

"I heard something," Ayize said with a slight wheeze to his voice. "They're here."

And they'll fill us with arrows, Mkasa thought, trying to keep Ayize's mind off the eerie whistle of the wind and the nickering of their horse.

"Othene says the white desert is full of sinkholes," Ayize said. "He says you can't see them until it's too late."

"Trust your nose, your gut. Watch and listen."

Mkasa smelled a fresh scent that reminded him of home. Iutha would be crooning over her belly and dangling her swollen ankles in the pool. He regretted slapping her and he wished he had kissed her goodbye. There wasn't time. There was never time.

"He's singing again." Ayize peered around Mkasa's shoulder at Othene ahead of them. "He's always singing."

"He'll get a sore throat."

Ayize chuckled as the sorcerer muttered to evil spirits even as he sat astride his horse. He gripped the horsehair wand in one hand, chanting at the top of his lungs. What he hoped to get out of that dreadful moaning, Mkasa couldn't imagine and he hoped the spirits he summoned were useless without fire. But there was something in the tremor of his voice that alarmed him, something urgent.

"Kanja tried to kill you in the temple," Mkasa said, looking over his shoulder. "I saw it."

Mkasa felt Ayize shudder only the boy never had time to answer. An unfamiliar voice rang out in the hills and Mkasa nearly tumbled from his horse. The animals shied and flicked up their heads, whinnying and stamping in fear. Three men emerged from the slopes behind the towers and Mkasa took their measure with a glance: men clad in bone breastplates and sleeveless jackets of fur. Their leader, a man with gray-veined eyes, bore a sword of hammered obsidian and on his head was a rack of antlers.

"Stop!" he cried.

"The Tarabin," Mkasa whispered and the spit went sour in his mouth. "My father took me to see him when I was nine. He's got no heart, no soul. They say he's like the moon in all but innocence and there's mystery behind that face of his."

"Greetings," the Tarabin cried when he saw them. He scrutinized the pelts over the packhorses and the shell disk on Kanja's forehead. "I am Tarabin lord of the deadlands. And you are?"

Kanja hesitated for a moment and narrowed his eyes. "Kanja, spearman to King Ibada, leader of the Bloods."

Tarabin tilted his mighty head, eyes studying Kanja all

the more. He was both striking and hideous, face pinched as if he tasted something sour. "I cannot fathom why you remind me of Ibada. It's not your face or your skin, but in your every gesture."

There was something about the way he said it that made Mkasa cringe as if scorn and fascination had coiled together like a snake charm. He let his eyes follow the intricate designs of Tarabin's weapons, the silver handles and the engraved gemstones, and the thick muscular legs that supported it all. It was meant to frighten him. It should have frightened Kanja.

"We only wish to pass," Kanja said. "We bring gold and spices."

"Off your horses," Tarabin grunted. "All of you."

Mkasa pulled Ayize off the horse. He looked green and ready to bolt, and Mkasa was at a loss as to how to comfort him.

"Kneel!" Tarabin shouted.

They knelt.

"Where are you bound?" Tarabin said, tilting Kanja's chin upwards with the tip of his sword.

"To Farafra at the Pharaoh's command," Kanja explained.

"Farafra," Tarabin repeated, lowering his sword. His forehead began to pucker below a sharp widow's peak and his hands were partly covered in leather where each knuckle was reinforced with metal. "Better you die here than there."

"Die?" Kanja said over the grunting of a horse as it defecated.

"You killed the *shakāl*." Tarabin stressed the last word as his rheumy eyes gave Kanja's weapons a cursory glance. "You don't much care for them do you?"

"We were attacked—"

"This is their territory. You should have been mindful of that."

Mkasa watched from behind Kanja, gauging the

distance between him and the next man. If he was careful, he could cut the medicine pouch from his belt. There was a vial inside that was as rank to smell as it was to taste and he hoped Shenq would find it in the dirt.

He looked first at the man at Tarabin's side, wearing a helmet of bone and a fox's head. He seemed content to fletch an arrow as he stood there, impassive to the proceedings and sporting a smile that suggested they would all kiss his blade before nightfall. The third warrior gnawed at a skewered rat, still hot by the steam that came from it. Bracelets forged from the vertebra of an ancient animal clattered on his arms, each graven with unusual metals.

"You killed fifty bitches and eleven dogs," Tarabin said, looking at the pelts hanging over the packhorse. He was strong, he was confident and he eyed them viciously. "The bitches are most precious. They were in whelp."

Mkasa held his breath only for a moment, musing on the splendor of such a man. His hair reminded him of a pearl radiating a host of colors from every fiber. If it wasn't for the childlike faces of these Imazi warriors, he would have betted on a thousand years apiece. But he was too afraid to bet. All three were night-warriors, more dangerous than Kanja by far.

"They killed my brother," Kanja moaned. "They took his body—"

"To strip the flesh. That is what they do," Tarabin said with a curled lip. "You killed an entire drove. Seems you owe *them*. Give me the boy and I'll let you through."

"No," Kanja interrupted. "Take our horses, weapons, whatever you want. But don't take the boy."

"Precious is he?"

"He's sick," Kanja replied with bright-eyed confidence.

Mkasa wanted to reach out and reassure Ayize, he wanted to tell him it would be all right. Instead, he kept picking at the medicine pouch with the tip of his knife until the thongs finally gave way. It slipped to the ground between two flat stones, camouflaged as if it were part of the landscape.

"Bitches are precious to dogs," Tarabin said. "They're the hunters of their clan. I'll take the boy unless you can think of anything better."

"He's not worth the dust he came from," Kanja insisted.

"You must take me for a fool. I know choice meat when I see it. Do you know what we do with traitors? We skin them alive and hang them in the gallery." Tarabin shook his shaggy head and burst into a peel of laughter. "It's not all work in our court. If the harvest is good, we serve the best meat and the best wine. And we dance."

"If you want the best meat, take *him*," Kanja said, pointing at Mkasa. "He's the prince of Alodia, the traitor you seek."

Tarabin sniffed and peered around Kanja's shoulder. "And you are?"

"Mkasa, son of Ahmose," Mkasa said, not knowing where his voice came from.

"Stand!" Tarabin yelled, before turning to his men. "There's a tale for later. I remember an Ahmose . . . he was a seal-bearer, brilliant and dazzling like this boy."

He was so much more. Mkasa barely nodded, and bowed. *And so am I.*

"See how he plays me?" Tarabin said. "He must take me for a god."

Rat-Eater laughed at that, spitting out bits of meat before drawing himself up in an attempt to keep his dignity. His silver hair flayed out behind his waist, shimmering like water on sand. "He should be on his knees then, lord. Like the others."

Mkasa suddenly remembered Shenq's words. *An attacker should be admired. After all, he drew his sword first.* "Aren't you a god?" he said.

"Of the underworld perhaps. I'm no more *god* than you're Alodian. Tell me, why do you ride with these men?"

Mkasa felt the stiffness in his joints more than he had over the past few days and his battle-numb mind refused to believe what he had just heard. He was dressed as an Alodian and could easily pass as one, but he realized he had little chance of survival against a man with a dog's sense of smell. "I ride with them because they're my brothers."

"You would swear it on your mother's name, no doubt," Tarabin said with a grim twist to his mouth. "If your leader won't fight for you then neither will I."

"Let him fight Saqr," said Fox-hat, whose breath would have knocked down an oryx at fifty paces.

Mkasa bowed his head. Saqr meant *falcon* in the Imazi tongue and he hoped the warrior they spoke of had none of those sharp-witted characteristics. "I would be honored, my lord."

Even as he said it, Mkasa's throat squeezed shut. White eyes stared back at him, pupils no more than a thin slit in an eddy of gray veins, and there was a sound like the rush of a thousand chariots in his head.

I know who you are, a voice said.

Mkasa nearly jumped. He tried to fill his lungs with the crisp morning air, wishing he could float away from the dark sinister presence.

"You're brave Mkasa, son of Ahmose." Tarabin said, eyeing him with a sideways glance. "I reward brave men."

Mkasa hoped it would be a big reward, one that allowed his skin to remain on his bones.

"Fight Saqr and I will make you a night warrior," Tarabin said. *Lose, and you'll swallow my sword.*

Mkasa heard the murmur that followed, quiet as it was. The idea of swallowing swords drifted up from his memory, a cruel shadow from childhood. The Imazi spitted their captives with swords and hung them over an open fire, and he could still hear the screams if he thought hard enough.

Forbear, he told himself, half-wondering if Tarabin

could hear him through that thick skin of his.

"You will find the Desert of Tables a miraculous place," Tarabin said, face inclined to Kanja. "But you will have no peace there, not with the moon like it is."

Mkasa wondered what it was about the moon. It was ragged on one side as if something had taken a bite out of it.

"Leave the son of Ahmose if he's the best you have," Tarabin said, teeth big behind wide lips. "And ride. *Ride* as far as you can before the winds come!"

Ayize swung his leg over the mare's back, eyes searching the canyon for a way out. He stared down at Mkasa, mouth trembling as if his grief was all locked up inside and he mouthed two words before wheeling the horse around.

Run, Mkasa almost murmured. But the words were lost in the dust that separated them.

Mkasa saw only their heads as they pressed forward, urging their horses to a gallop even through the demanding terrain. He had no time to interpret Ayize's words and besides, he was too nervous to try. His gut churned with unease as he heard the wind cantering about the rocks. It would be the last time he would hear it.

And it was the last time he would see the boy. He had failed.

"Quickly," Tarabin said, holding out a hand to usher Mkasa up the slope. "We must get below ground before the storms."

Mkasa glanced wistfully out into the desert. There was a dust storm in the distance, a spinning column, cutting a path towards them. In the tunnels, they wouldn't feel a thing even as it thundered overhead. But Kanja's men would be thrown from their horses and worse if they didn't find a hole to hide in.

He clutched the limb of his bow, thankful it was still on his back. Surely if they wanted to kill him they would have stripped him naked for the vultures. Rat-Eater circled behind him, raking the turf with his spear and all the while he murmured and grunted.

"Can't be too careful with traitors about," Tarabin explained, snapping his fingers to hurry him up. He nodded to Rat-Face and caught what looked like a pebble in the palm of his hand.

The climb was slippery on the scree and twice Mkasa stumbled, steadying himself against boulders. Tarabin seemed to glide up the hill as if he had done it fifty times in his sleep and there was a snarl to his lip as he snapped a second warning. There was a wand crowned with human hair in his belt and an axe with a burnished cheek. They were the color of human bones, all polished to a shine.

Tarabin stopped mid-way up the slope and brushed aside a curtain of old roots at the mouth of a tunnel. A wooden gate creaked on its hinges, revealing a corridor cut into the rock.

"Welcome to the city of Ma'arav," he said, sniffing frequently as if storing scents in his memory like animals did. He barely nodded to the doormen before padding off down the shaft, a soft sandy slope lit with an array of sputtering torches.

"Are you loyal to your leader, Mkasa?" he said, voice echoing against white-washed walls painted with ancient images.

"He's not my leader," Mkasa returned. *Kanja's nothing but a lean figure in red stalking the desert like a brilliant bird of prey.*

"You're right. He is not your leader. Your leader is *Kemnebi*, rival of rivals. They say he's faster than serpent spit."

Mkasa flinched when he heard the name and his skin began to dew with sweat just thinking about him. He had met many formidable men in his time but none as fearsome as Shenq. He missed him if he was honest. "Have you met him?"

"I see him in your heart. It's close enough."

Mkasa marveled at the deep powdery carpet under his

tired feet until he was interrupted by a horn blast from the center of the earth. There was a host of white men down there in the darkness, ready to steal his soul.

"We won't steal your soul," Tarabin said, raking a hand through his iridescent hair. "And yes, we read minds."

It was the one thing Mkasa dreaded the most, a new torture where the place of secrets and conscience had been breached. There was no stopping the enemy now. They knew every thought and every move. He held on to that.

I see Makuria in my mind, Tarabin, lord of the deadlands. I see burning huts and screaming children running towards the river. I see the fires and the bones. I see the arrows from King Ibada's bow. Does that stir your imagination as it does mine?

"So you're broken, Mkasa of Makurae," Tarabin murmured. "And you weigh yourself against your enemy. Is that why you came?"

"I came to right wrongs."

"*Kemnebi* made you come."

Shenq, strong-jawed and powerful. Mkasa wondered what the Commander would have said. Nothing perhaps. He was smarter than words.

Tarabin held up a fist without turning round. "Medicine is too precious to leave behind."

Nothing could have reduced Mkasa to a whimpering mess more than seeing the leather pouch swinging from Tarabin's thumb. Rat-Face chuckled before closing a large wooden gate behind them.

"*Kemnebi* will lose the race. He's already too far behind. You know he'll come searching for you and wasting valuable time."

Mkasa fell silent. He had too many thoughts for Tarabin to steal, too many to make him a silent confidant.

"That's right. Say nothing, my friend," Tarabin said. "I already know your heart. It's blacker than mine."

Mkasa swallowed a lump of guilt in his throat. If Shenq lost, he would lose his beloved Meryt. Who would have her then? He couldn't see Tarabin's face but he knew it was bleak.

There was a brazier of food not far from the entrance, skewers of glistening rats they looked like and jugs of spiced wine.

"Eat boy, it's a long time before dinner," Tarabin said, with a laugh to his tone.

Mkasa thrust the pouch down the front of his shúkà and grabbed a skewer. He chewed through the crackling flesh and sweet sauce. It was the most delicious thing he had eaten in days and the wine only reminded him of how hungry he was. The generosity made him feel uneasy but he refused to address it until he was sated. Even as they walked on through the tunnels for what seemed like hours, he tried to ward off the chills that crawled down his spine and the rotten taste of fear that filled his mouth.

"Lay your hand against my shoulder," Tarabin comforted, spear clunking against the ground. "We are going eight hundred feet below ground."

Mkasa was surprised by Tarabin's tone but he did as he was told. He prayed to HaShem for an escape. There was no situation so hopeless, no mind so wild, no scheme so outrageous that a man could not escape it.

Tarabin did not respond to his thoughts. Perhaps he couldn't read prayers.

It was many hours before Mkasa felt a rush of warm air against his cheeks, smelling soot and burning wood ahead. The tunnel opened into a large cavern, brilliantly illuminated with thousands of lamps and tripods with ewers of burning coals. He saw dancing shadows reflected in the ceiling and a green pool in one corner. Paths branched into nooks and passages, each carpeted with skins of the southern panther.

When Mkasa's eyes became accustomed to the glow, he saw an array of stalactites hanging from the domed roof, some whorled and pointed like kudu horns and some thick like the decorative pillars of the temples. But none more beautiful than a frail stem that rose as high as the ceiling, creamier than goat's milk, and from its branches hung stalagmites like the crown of a willow tree.

"Welcome to the Hall of Leviathan," Tarabin said, offering his weapons and armor to an attendant. "And this is Queen Ma'adia, my most beloved."

The woman that stood beside Tarabin was so beautiful, Mkasa had to lower his eyes. She wore a dress of silver beads clinging to a near-naked body and on her dark head was a crown of men's hands. Each knuckle was filled with a stone the color of a tear drop and brighter than any he had ever seen.

"Dear warrior," she said. "You are welcome to our world. I pray you come to love the twilight eyes."

Mkasa bowed his head, since all words had caught in his throat. He was already heart-sore for home but not half as sore as when faced with hundreds of men examining him with the same bright eyes as if nothing escaped them no matter how trivial. There was a natural dais in the rock where the noblest of warriors sat, breasts adorned with men's ribs, each joint dipped in silver and hideously beautiful in the firelight. Row upon row of women crouched in nests of cave pearls and their children ran in and out between the stalagmites, laughter echoing like a chorus of bells.

The cavern filled with the sound of their voices and as they clapped and sang, Tarabin leaned over and whispered. "Tell no one what you have seen, son of Ahmose. You're a dead man if you do."

Mkasa nodded, feeling another cold shiver. He dared not think how he could tell a soul if he would never again see the sky.

Tarabin allowed an attendant to take off his outer clothing as he lifted a hand to hush the murmurs, addressing the throng in his own language. He stood proud and tall in a tunic of embroidered linen and his legs were encased in antelope skin. He pointed now and again at Mkasa without any hint of hatred and the word *Kemnebi* rang out several times. It was the man that walked out onto the dais that terrified Mkasa. His chest was covered with two scapula bones melded between ribs of silver and, from his belt, hung a sword brighter than any he had seen. The burden of such armor suggested great strength and it was likely no opponent would ever get close enough to cut him down. The crowd roared his name, shouting *Saqr* over and over again.

"My son," said Tarabin. "Splendid don't you think? He needs a sparring partner for that big old sword. Can't say I'd want to fight him. Would you?"

Mkasa reeled with dread and he was convinced he would die that night. The words stuck in his mouth and he could barely breathe.

"Didn't think so," Tarabin continued.

Mkasa took the seal from behind his breastplate and as he did so there was a terrible hush in the cavern. Saqr fell back, muttering in the language of the shadow-world and Tarabin merely raised a hand.

"My people, we must accommodate this nobleman. He's a hero, a prince to fight a prince. That's how it is with bone lords. Here's what I propose. If he kills my son, the Makurae can have this underground city and he can take a wife from amongst my women. And you," he pointed at the people. "You'll have peace when I am gone."

The crowds cheered, fists pumping the air. Mkasa could hear the applause several caverns away as more people arrived, streaming through the tunnels.

"They like a bit of drama," Tarabin whispered to Mkasa, handing him a bone sword from his own belt. "So let's give them a little, shall we?"

Mkasa closed his fingers around the leather grip, tilting the hoary blade. It was straight and sharp and light as air. So magical was its sheen, for a moment he thought it was a wisp of smoke. He barely heard the scrape of bone as Saqr drew his sword, standing only six feet away and swaying on his hips.

Strike hard and fast, he thought. *Straight and sharp.*

Saqr came on with a diagonal strike and Mkasa lifted his sword to block it. The second strike was a long reach and came at his legs, and Mkasa jumped back to evade it. Every time Saqr thrust his blade, Mkasa stepped out diagonally and before he could see the attack coming, Saqr's sword struck his near the point almost knocking it out of his hand.

Both fighters were urged on by the yelling of names, caverns echoing with the ring of swords. Mkasa twisted and blocked, clothes ripping from his body and streaked with blood. But Saqr was faster, changing his grip in mid-air. The swordsmanship was unlike anything Mkasa had ever seen and he began to feel defeated. He watched each lethal move and slowly, he saw a way of attacking and defending at the same time.

Saqr came in for another diagonal attack, only this time Mkasa deflected it, crossguard catching Saqr's blade at the weakest point. Blade scraped against blade and as he angled his sword towards Saqr's face, he thrust in one last time.

Saqr took a gash to his cheek and roared loudly, black fluid seeping from the open wound. He dropped his sword and barreled towards Mkasa, face a grille of teeth. Mkasa felt himself lifted off the ground and thrust back against a rock and that's all he remembered until he saw Tarabin's face.

"Good try," he said, pulling Mkasa to his feet. "But not good enough. Lucky my son didn't kill you when he had the chance. It took six men to pull him off. Tomorrow you will fight again."

Mkasa wiped the blood from the back of his head and the pain made him wince. He could hardly walk. He could hardly see. And he had lost.

"We have work to do" Tarabin said, passing an arm around Mkasa's waist. "When the sun goes down Saqr will go hunting. Although I have a suspicion there won't be much fox and snake to shoot at."

Mkasa knew the lack of food meant the presence of man and his mind whorled with hope. Shenq's men could be up there hiding amongst the rocks and they may have seen Kanja's men in the distance with one less man to their team. They would find him, wouldn't they?

Stop thinking, he said, nursing his head. As if by an unseen signal, the caverns became silent and the Imazi craned their heads upwards at the great domed ceiling. The occasional snort confirmed a scent and Mkasa knew there was something out there, something the Imazi feared.

How can they smell through layers of rock? he thought, peering up at a thousand yellow spikes that clung like bats from the ceiling.

"He's out there," Saqr said in the Theban tongue.

"*Kemnebi.*" Tarabin unsheathed a bone dagger in one hand and snapping his fingers with the other. "Take Halensi and Akun. If you don't come back, our guest will be a comb of bones."

Mkasa listened to their guttural chatter as they scrambled away through a dark tunnel. It was the only time in his life he prayed Shenq wouldn't kill the enemy.

"You! Come with me," Tarabin said, leading Mkasa to a nook where there was a shelf carved in the rock wall, laden with the thickest of skins. The smoke from the fire curled upwards to a natural shaft in the ceiling, likely uniting the chamber to the outside world and there were hundreds of smaller air shafts snaking up through the cavern roof. Mkasa longed for an axe. They were plenty sharp enough to slice through bone, but were they sharp enough to cut through rock?

"Makurae?" A girl stood beside him, holding out a bowl of broth. Her eyes glittered in the torchlight, blue he thought they were.

"How did you know I was a Makurae?" Mkasa noticed a wet-lipped grin and there was a light in those eyes that made him feel uneasy.

"Your bones," she said, smiling. "I can always tell a southerner by his bones."

Mkasa couldn't begin to estimate her age. Twelve, twenty perhaps. She wore animal pelts and bone armor, and there was a knife in her belt that glimmered like the moon. "I won't be stirred in a pot, my lady. You'll have to kill me first."

"I can kill you just by looking at you, Makurae," she said. "I've killed others before you."

Mkasa could believe it. She had muscles under that fur-lined tunic of hers and her lips were full and meaty. "What others?"

"Are you jealous?"

"She wants you. It's plain to see," said Tarabin, looking down at him with a raw smile. "She's a half-blood, not from the same vine if you know what I mean."

Mkasa took it to mean she was a lesser caste with her dark hair and creamy skin. "I have a wife," he said ruefully, missing Iutha all the more.

"*Had* a wife," Tarabin corrected, voice gravely. "You belong to her now."

Mkasa had often wondered if the Imazi bred with the dark skins of the Theban territories but he had seen no proof of it until now. The rest of them were whiter than the rocks they leaned against, some blending completely with their surroundings.

He turned his face away so the girl would not see him redden. But her voice called out in his head, hard and strong.

"S'haila," it said.

That was her name.

SHENQ

It was dusk by the time Shenq found Blood tracks snaking through the canyon towards the northern horizon. He dismounted and led his horse south along a short gulley to a shallow cave overlooking the Desert of Tables. Imazi traps were scattered about between boulders and scree, some already filled with fox and rats. By what Shenq could see of the waning moon and its height, he estimated a clear night and a bright one for hunting.

He found a stairway in the floor of the cave, steps worn in the center by ancient feet. Metal brackets graced the walls and there were paintings of oryx and white-skinned men with bone armor. But there was no way in, not even through the narrow funnels now filled with sand and rock.

"Time to eat," Meru-Itseni said, peering up at the sky through the mouth of the cave. "Thought I saw a few geese up there."

Shenq heard the sarcasm in the warrior's voice and he saw the hungry look on his face. It was too dark to shoot up. Down was a different matter. "See our friend," he said, glancing up at a black kite circling lazily in the sky. "He knows where the food is."

He could hear the wing beats against the cliffs before the bird suddenly plummeted towards earth. A flutter of feathers and a spray of sand later and there was a fat fox spitted on a pair of talons. It was likely seized from a trap.

"You and the Captain will take the first watch," Shenq said, exhaustion creeping into his bones. "I'll take the second. And don't range too far north."

Tehute took a pack of food from Khemwese and headed off down the slopes with Meru-Itseni. They disappeared behind a thin veil of sand just as the wind picked up.

The rest of the men settled down for a meal of bread and cheese, and flagons of beer. There were jars of onions and salted ox tongue, the remains of the Farafra supplies. That was before the moon disappeared altogether and wind spiraled and screamed in the darkness, throwing rubble and sharp rock into the cave.

"Take the packs off the horses," Shenq shouted. "And cover the entrance!"

Feeling their way around the cave, they took blankets and hung them over the meager breach, calming the animals with soft words and blindfolds. Shenq waited for Meru-Itseni and Tehute, and when they didn't come back, he hoped the warriors were resourceful enough to have found a burrow.

He did not sleep well that night, not with the winds buffeting the slopes. He dreamed of an abandoned villa dusted with sand and drapes wafting in a caressing breeze. He could still smell the faint echoes of lotus blossom and the scent of Meryt's hair. When he searched for any trace of her it brought out a pain in his heart, sweet and sorrowful.

You must win, the voice urged. *You must overcome.*

And then he heard a scream.

He couldn't tie in the sound to his dream until he snapped his eyes open all the way, hearing only a sigh of wind against the cliffs. The blankets flapped in a breeze, no longer tied down as they had once been and, as he looked between them, he was surprised to see no wall of sand to dig through. There were black shadows under the boulders and a hoary light overhead and, if he was honest, he couldn't have spotted a rat from where he sat. The moon was a thin arc of light no bigger than a toe nail.

He heard the scream again and struggled to stand. This time it seemed to come from a sand gully at the bottom of the slope.

A vixen?

He held his breath and listened.

There was a plume of white smoke in the foothills, tapering into the air as if a fire had started beneath the earth. His heart began to hammer and he glanced at his men, gargling a snore here and there. Tehute and Meru-Itseni were out there near the traps and he hoped they hadn't stalked off to the foothills to roast a rabbit or two.

Stealthy sounds issued nearby and Shenq had a strange feeling something was watching them . . . something menacing . . . something evil. He could almost hear the clatter of weapons and he thought he saw the flash of a blood-red khopesh. Crescents of light seemed to dance overhead and he imagined an army of winged things, toying with his mind. His subconscious knew what it was only he couldn't put a name to it. He wanted to go searching for it but his legs were heavier than anchor weights and his arms were stuck to his sides. Instead, he stared out at the terrain, ash-gray in the moonlight and the only sound he could hear was the soughing of the wind.

The men slept on and the horses barely twitched, hind legs resting up on their toes. For a moment Shenq relished the blackness that covered them and the purling vapors below. No one could see them unless they were looking for them. His mind spun cartwheels of anticipation. He was always prepared for battle, violence was part of his world. But he would have preferred to hunt down the devil himself than go in search of a few blood-hungry Imazi. Come to think of it, he had never seen one up close.

Tehute appeared out of the darkness, placing a restraining hand on Shenq's shoulder. "Hold steady," he said, crouching beside him. "*Imazi*. Down there."

Too close, Shenq thought, narrowing his eyes in the direction of Tehute's finger where the moon cast a sullen radiance over the sands. "How many?"

"Two, sir." Tehute blew out a long breath. "They're emptying the traps by the look of it. There's no sign of Kanja's men. On a clear day, you can see all the way to the west."

Shenq sensed a prickling of unease. The ground was no longer pocked with hoof-prints and there was no way to track Kanja now. "Where's Itseni?"

"North of here, behind a boulder," Tehute said with a huff of frustration. "He says there's a tunnel in the rock, a deep one."

"Did he go in?"

"Part way, but there's only a thatch of roots and kindling. It was too dark to go any further."

Shenq wondered how many Imazi tunnels there were on this side of the canyon. It was an ideal place for an ambush and he could imagine a few of them half-shadowed in the rocky alcoves, itching for a fight.

"They know we're here. Wake the men."

A man's scream rent the air and the very sound of it made Shenq shudder. He searched the terrain with its silver sheen and he saw two shadows streaking between the boulders on rapid feet. He unslung his bow, slipping two arrows from his quiver. When the sound came again it was both loud and muffled as if a hand suddenly covered the mouth it came from.

"Kneel Darkeye!" The response was relentless, heartless, savage.

Shenq gritted his teeth as he leapt towards it. That's when he noticed the misleading echo, bouncing off the cliffs. There was no sign of them and he turned this way and that, snaking between a host of rocks.

They must be here somewhere, he thought, eyes searching each cleft and furrow.

He had stalked many an enemy through the desert, scattering them across the sandy earth and clawing the very entrails from their bellies. But this was no rootless sand-warrior. This was a demon clothed in dead flesh that stank of mold and rot.

The wind sighed, heavy with the scent of freshly slaughtered game. He couldn't see his men on the lower slopes and all he could see was sand glistening between the boulders in the waning moonlight.

It sees you, the wind murmured.

Shenq was suddenly thirsty and he sucked down what little moisture he had in his mouth, wishing he was rushing over moonlit sands with his men. Cold fingers seemed to crawl up his back, reaching for his throat and he turned seeing nothing but a pale mist in the air.

Horse-breath, he thought, not daring to stare at it any longer.

Shenq knew if he saw the thing that tormented him he would go mad. *Best not look it in the eye. Best not look at it at all.*

Halfway up the slope was a boulder waist-deep in marl and a curl of light streaked out from behind it like a drawn sword. A doorway opened in the cliff wall and a warrior stood at the threshold, hair the color of mist and salted with gray. He was stocky, well-trimmed and hideous to look upon.

There was a dry sounding rattle followed by a baleful laugh and Shenq almost fell under the spell of the performance. The warrior stared with milky eyes; chest shielded by the scapulae of elk.

"We don't take kindly to strangers," he said, hurling something towards Shenq.

Shenq watched as it thudded to the ground, a ball of hair and blood rolling towards him with open eyes. *Meru-Itseni*, he wanted to say but the words stuck in his throat. And his neck . . . Shenq had given him a fine collar of gold flies, the type all soldiers wore for bravery. It dangled across one cheek, shimmering in the brightening sky.

You were brave, my friend, braver than all of us.

He almost gasped right there on the hillside, only the crunch of footsteps on the scree made him look up. The warrior started down the slope with a swagger, hand holding a blood-soaked sword.

"Who are you," Shenq said, dropping his bow and

unsheathing his sword. He listened for every sound, every breath.

"Saqr, Prince of Ma'arav," the warrior said, puffing his outrage through black lips. He stopped a few feet away and sniffed. "And you are?"

"Shenq, Commander of the *Kenyt-Nisu*."

"Ah, the *Kemnebi*, darkest of all leopards."

Shenq wanted to bound up the slope and make a quick end to it. But the scree would only slow him down and the white-boned warrior had the upper hand as far as he could see. The anger was like a rope inside him tightening, ready to snap.

"Where is lord Tarabin," Shenq said, lips curling around the words.

"My lord doesn't care to fight the likes of you. So he sent me instead." Saqr looked down at the corpse at his feet and pushed it with his foot. "Who was that?"

"*That* was my armor-bearer."

"And why would the likes of you need an armor-bearer?"

Shenq didn't want to waste time talking. He wanted to plunge his sword inside that yawning mouth. "All commanders have armor-bearers. Where's yours?"

"Feasting with the others. My father has guests to entertain."

"Guests?"

"A prisoner then."

Shenq could see by the expression and the inflated posture it had to mean one of Kanja's team and he hoped it wasn't the boy. Probably that witless sorcerer if he could guess.

"Don't concern yourself, rival of rivals. He was an imposter, a burden. It'll lighten the load and give their team a head start. Someone has to win." Saqr gave a deep-throated laugh and looked past Shenq. "Your men are busy, I see. They're quick on their feet and lively."

It was then Shenq heard the scrape of metal and the

grunts behind him, and he turned his face slightly to see dark shapes ducking and twisting, and the flash of long white hair. From the little he could make out, Khemwese and Jabari drove them to their knees, axes slashing blow by blow.

How many Imazi were they fighting? he thought, wincing deep inside.

"Two of mine against five of yours," Saqr said, watching the butchery through wide eyes. "The *Kenyt-Nisu* are noble warriors. You should be proud of them."

Shenq was proud of them until he realized Saqr could read his mind. His anger was replaced with fascination but not enough to re-sheathe his sword. *Pity there's not a side of oryx dangling over a hearty fire and a jug of wine to wash it down. I take it we have oryx?*

Saqr inclined his head and narrowed his eyes. "We are surrounded by desert, rival of rivals. One thing we do have is oryx."

"I haven't seen any."

"Below ground," Saqr corrected. "Quartered and swimming in gravy."

Shenq noticed the two Imazi warriors were now writhing and groaning in the dirt and his men were making sport of them before lopping off their heads. He noticed a creep of uncertainty in Saqr's face and he wondered briefly how the warrior could keep his thoughts together let alone Shenq's.

It's to my advantage, he thought, watching a gash of pale yellow as it streaked across the eastern sky. Saqr and his army would soon be blinder than mole rats. *A swordsman must keep his mind focused on the fight and not on the workings of two minds.*

"You forget," Saqr snapped, "I'll pluck you up like a frail weed and drain you dry."

"None of my warriors enter a battle they cannot win," Shenq said. "That's a lesson you could stand to learn."

"You have no lack of enemies, *Kemnebi.* Kill me and ten

thousand will pour from the earth in hordes."

"Tell me, are we to stand here talking or shall we fight?"

Saqr shifted slowly at first and he sucked in a quick breath. With a loud bellow, he lurched forward, sword flashing and ripping through space. Shenq held his ground, holding his sword out in front. He knew his blade would skid off that bone-gilded armor and likely out of his hand. The only flesh he could see peeked out between strips of fur-lined leggings, a wall of thigh if he guessed correctly.

His heart pounded wildly and the instinct to kill had taken over. He stood there for a breath or two until he saw the flash in the corner of his eye and felt the current of air by his ear. In that instant, he whirled round in a half-circle, blade lowered like a farmer's scythe. He saw Saqr's eyes as he came around, shocked and wide, and tinged with disbelief. It was then Shenq swung in low, blade slicing through thigh and hide, bursting out with a rush of blood. There was a pause before Saqr toppled forward, hands mauling the air. He sank to the ground on top of his weapon, panting louder than a swordsmith's bellows.

The Imazi prince lay on his side, legs propped against each other like two logs in an open fire. He opened his mouth to speak but his lips curled back over gray teeth and there they stayed even as Shenq slit his throat. Blood wept into the sand until there was no more left inside him.

Shenq snatched the sword and held it aloft, hardly hearing the cheers of his men. "Tehute, Khemwese, cover every inch of this bloodshed. Jabari, wrap up the remains and tie them to the horses. Menkheperre, Harran, come with me. Now move!"

The sun's rays raced down the cliffs towards them like a wave of molten gold and Shenq searched for the doorway in the cliff wall. There was no sign of it and for a moment he thought he was seeing things.

"Sir," Menkheperre charged up the slope behind him, hand covering a wound in his shoulder. "My arm's cut. It's not deep, just stings a little—"

"How bad is it," Shenq said, seeing blood between his fingers.

"I can still swing a sword, sir." Menkheperre swung his arm just to be sure. "Where's Itseni?"

"Over there. He deserves all of heaven's graces. He deserves gold and silver. He deserves . . ." Shenq broke off and swallowed down a sob.

"His body should be left unadorned," Harran said, fist clenching a blue blanket. "Let me cover him."

Harran wrapped the head in the blanket before placing it beside the body. He marked it with a spear and a red banner tied to the haft. The heralds would see the place and bring the warrior home. "He should be cleansed and shrouded," he said. "I pray the heralds find him. I pray they come today."

Shenq placed a hand on Harran's shoulder and looked down at the body of his friend. "He was a good man, a brave man. He served me well."

"I hope he forgives me," Harran said, staring down at Meru-Itseni, "for any lack of honor I have shown to his body."

Shenq walked back down the slope, leaving Harran to see to Menkheperre's arm. He dreaded bringing news of a fallen friend. If he closed his eyes he could see the banner of Thoth snapping above the palace gates in a brisk northerly wind, and he could see a woman and a small boy with tear-streaked cheeks.

Fallen, Shenq would tell them though it pained his heart to do it.

There was no sign of the tunnel in the cliff wall, only smoke funnels in the ground and sinkholes to trap game. You never knew where they were until you fell in them. They were clever, the Imazi, with their hidden shafts and gateways, and halls of chiseled granite. Tarabin was at the heart of it, waiting for his son to come home. And when he didn't, the prisoner would die.

"One less to kill," Shenq muttered darkly, laughing at Othene's stupidity as he mounted his horse and snatched up the reins.

The fretful wind had subsided and the boulders stood silent against a pale blue sky. He hoped they would have covered the worst of the white desert, reaching Suhaj and the river by nightfall. He looked down at Saqr lying in the dirt and tied with ropes. It reminded him of a pig's belly all trussed up and ready for roasting.

"Sir!" Jabari shouted. "I say we ride. We're almost a day behind."

Shenq checked off his men and saw one missing. "Where's Harran?"

"Praying, sir," Jabari said, horse snorting beneath him and throwing up its head.

Shenq watched Harran, white against the cliffs, arms out by his sides. The boy picked his moments and this was the worst of them. "Does he have to do it up there?"

"God can see him better," Jabari said.

"So can everyone else," Shenq sighed.

He whistled to Harran looking back one last time at the spear and its flickering red ensign. The wind had shifted in pitch and intensity and it seemed almost calm as they set out, dragging the bodies behind them.

Gold sands spilled into a carpet of gray and Shenq surveyed a dusky dune straight ahead. It was like a static wave that seemed to stretch for miles and he continued to look for tracks as they climbed it. The summit revealed a white tableland below; boulders elevated on grooved trunks and silhouetted against a fiery orange sky. Shenq could hear Khemwese teaching Harran how to navigate by the stars and how at dawn when the sun hides the moon, there would be new shadows and shapes in the desert.

They buried the bodies beneath one of these high monuments, heaping sand and stone on top of them to equal the terrain. Shenq inclined his head towards the sky where a wall of dark clouds churned and the wind howled.

A giant plume of sand spiraled towards them, base swollen like an animal's paw.

"Take cover!" he yelled, voice tolling like a funeral bell.

They all huddled in cloaks, sand stabbing and blinding, and driving the horses half mad with fear. One packhorse bolted into the midst of it and it wasn't just any packhorse. This one was carrying a cargo of weapons.

Curse her, Shenq almost yelled, slamming a hand against his head.

Thick yellow mists filtered through natural arches and eroded stairs, coming to rest on a dry riverbed where only a trickle of water could be seen. They found a small cove within a collection of these, pressing the horses against the rocks and covering their faces as best they could. Pebbles rained down on man and horse, and the storm raged on for the rest of the day and a good part of the night.

It was midnight before the winds ceased altogether and Shenq cursed the lost time. They had hardly left the foothills of Ma'arav and now they were coughing up their guts and shaking off the worst of it. The best he could hope for was a full moon and he saw half a one, rising behind a curtain of yellow. The rocks were a ghostly white against a backdrop of gray and he wondered if the sky would soon swallow the moon.

It was time, he thought, feeling it in his belly.

"Go after that horse," Shenq said, shooting a scowl at Jabari. The wretched mare was nothing but trouble.

The drifts almost came to the top of his calves and Jabari trudged his way towards a distant rock, top sloping upwards like an upturned beak. His footsteps were heavy in the sand and he turned once and waved.

"We'll set up camp here," Shenq said, coughing up a ball of phlegm and hurling it as far as he could.

He knew Kanja was out there somewhere, hiding in a burrow just as they were. And what's more, he would soon be celebrating the return of his mare unless Jabari got there first.

"I'll keep watch, Maaz," Khemwese said as he caressed a trunk of rock expertly furrowed as if it had been shaped by a potter's hand. Dust fell from his fingers and his shaal and coat looked as if they were covered in ash.

"You could leave, you know," Shenq said, loathing to part with him. But he couldn't stop wondering why the giant hadn't run back to Kush when he had the chance. "I could say the Imazi took you underground. I could say—"

"It would be a lie, Maaz. And I won't lie." Khemwese smiled with that big-toothed smile of his. "My father was a glutton. He was like a cat with two birds in its mouth. He fought for Thebes and lost. It was just a game."

Shenq was aware of an unexpected release of tension and he was glad. "Don't ever say I led you down a road you didn't want to ride."

"I've followed worse." Khemwese sucked in his breath. "Harran leads us down a brighter path. He holds his lamp high."

Shenq spat in the sand again. "If he holds it any higher he'll blow our cover."

He went off in search of his blanket. It was a cold night and he huddled with his men, hoping he would get some sleep this time before the sky rained arrows or worse. Sometime in the night, he felt Khemwese's hand on his shoulder.

"Menkheperre has a fever," Khemwese said. "The wound is worse than I thought. It's clean and dressed. For now.

Shenq grimaced and nodded. "Anything else?"

"Jabari hasn't come back, Maaz. The watch is all yours."

Shenq relinquished his warm space to the giant and took over the watch, grabbing a bite of bread and cheese. "Stay here," he mouthed, leaving him in charge of his men.

Jabari should have returned by now with the mare and Shenq hoped the weapons were still on her back. They would have no chance against a company of shadow-hunters with the weapons they had, one quiver each and a belt of knives.

Sand blew off the crest of a nearby dune and Shenq could have sworn he heard it sing. If he did walk away from the campsite, he hoped like hell he wouldn't find anything out of the ordinary.

Between two rocks in a shallow depression he could just make out a twist of smoke and without the aroma of burning wood and a mound of ash it was hardly more than a hole in the ground. He crouched beside it, measuring six hands in width, a notched crater cut by human hands. He knew there weren't any hot springs beneath the sands and he brooded over the smoke vent, gauging it all. His father once said the caverns were vast, stretching for miles and miles. *You can only see the smoke at night and when you do, you know you're walking on the very roof of the Imazi world.*

The rattle of loose rock alerted Shenq to a presence and he turned to scan the terrain. He saw Harran still close to the camp, pointing to a standing stone to Shenq's right. Without leaning out blindly to see what it was, he unsheathed his knife and pressed his back against the rock. As he curled his face around, he saw a figure standing beneath a giant mushroom of limestone, gaunt and pale like a phantom.

Shenq jumped and almost lost his breakfast. It was Ayize and by the look of his rounded shoulders, he was more despondent than dangerous. There was no one else with him and Shenq could hear the sobs from where he stood.

"What happened to you?" Shenq asked as he approached. There was a sallow tinge to the boy's skin he hadn't noticed before.

"We were hiding from the storm. We lost two horses," Ayize whined.

"How careless. You lost two others a week ago."

"Mkasa's gone," Ayize said, sobbing and wiping the ooze from the piercing in his lip. "The Imazi took him.

They wanted me but . . ."

Shenq closed his eyes for an instant, locked in a moment of dread. Mkasa had offered himself up instead of the boy. His big heart had won through. "Better go back and find him. Save me the trouble."

"They'll skin him and eat him—."

"No they won't. Not with that big old seal flapping about on his chest. The bone lords are afraid of it. If you wait here long enough he might just squeeze out of one of these funnels."

"I *have* been waiting."

"Well, wait some more." Shenq sighed loudly and wondered where the boy's manners had gone. "Where are you camped?"

Ayize's sobbing turned to relief and he pointed to a large ridge. "Over there. As far as they know I'm still asleep under a blanket. A man has to relieve himself, doesn't he?"

"A man is entitled to pee but not too far from camp." Shenq hoped Kanja had found something to distract him, preferably an Imazi hunter with a nice sharp spear. "And you found me quite by chance in the middle of the desert."

Ayize shuddered as if he didn't know what to say. "Mkasa told me to run. He told me to find you. So I prayed to HaSher. I prayed for a way."

"*HaShem*. And yes, there is always a way. You should eat, boy. You're nothing but skin and bone."

Ayize scowled. "I'm sick of fox. It gives me the runs."

Shenq wanted to laugh but the sound would only carry and so he grinned instead. "It's time to choose sides, my prince. Make sure it's the right one."

"How do you know I'm a prince?"

"Well I didn't. But I do now."

Ayize gulped down a swallow. "Kanja's my brother. I won't leave him."

"Then go back the way you came."

"Othene said it was fate we came to Thebes," Ayize

said, backing up a little. "That it was all in the stars."

"I wouldn't call it *fate*. Othene can't read the stars. He couldn't read a book upside down even if you gave him one. No sorcerer makes good on his promises." Shenq flicked his eyes over the landscape, boulders whiter than goatskin. "He keeps secrets. Big ones."

"What secrets?" Ayize said, wincing as if he knew what was coming.

"They always say your worst enemy is the one closest to you."

"What do you mean?" Ayize looked at Shenq searchingly and there were tears in his brown eyes. But Shenq didn't want to stop. There was so little time.

"It was Othene that poisoned your father with his two whipping boys. Only they were caught and punished. You know the rest." Shenq watched the boy's quivering lips, knowing the questions he wanted to ask.

"They would never hurt Baba. They—"

"It doesn't take all the king's sons to find medicine in a far off land, now does it?" Shenq watched the boy shake his head and wipe his eyes. "Seems your sorcerer is tossing bones for the same throne."

Shenq couldn't help wondering what was going through Ayize's mind. He thought of words that would reassure him, words of support. After all, if the boy survived he would be king of a great nation one day, and by the look on his face he didn't believe a word of it.

"Your father changed the succession when he found out. I wouldn't let anyone else have that crown if I were you."

Ayize's temper flashed. "They never told me. They never said I was a king."

"Better keep a sword handy at night if you're looking to go back. Otherwise, come with me and live."

KANJA

Kanja tried to shake off the voices. He was tired of the living desert where dunes moved and sands murmured, and he was tired of being hunted by things that never ate or slept. Leaning against a trunk of rock for nearly two days, he thought he saw wild dogs in the mist, leaping between the hummocks. They had instincts sharper than his and they were faster than horses. But there was nothing there, except dunes, endless dunes.

He hated hiding out in caves. He hated the darkness and the thin stuffy air and he hated the silence. *Graves are for dead men down there below the earth.* And he wasn't dead yet. Was he? The winds had almost gone and the horses shook the last of the sand off their backs.

"They're ahead of us," Kanja snapped.

"They're not ahead of us, Mongaka," Othene said. "There are sinkholes in the sand, remember?"

"Where's the boy?" Kanja couldn't see Ayize amongst the furs. He couldn't see him amongst the men.

"He's gone. Just like the horses."

Kanja could hear the sarcasm in Othene's voice. They had lost two more in the night and his dreams were filled with swirling mists and a mare's head in a swamp.

Nura, sweet, beloved Nura.

"He's not gone. He's sulking because I left Mkasa behind." Kanja imagined the boy's sour expression, eyes wrung out as if he couldn't shed another tear.

"The boy was too fond of the Makurae," Othene said. "He was the driving wall between you two. No better than a rat in a prison cell, spreading disease and corruption. He's already dead. I saw it in the clouds."

The silence was broken by the familiar howl of a night

creature, mournful and distant. Kanja thought he could see a pair of twinkling eyes only he couldn't be sure. "Najja. Up there," he said, pointing at a flat-topped rock.

Najja used his horse to haul himself onto the summit, crouching on all fours with his bow on his back. His eyes flicked from one rock to another and he began to sniff the air. "Nothing."

"Can you see the horizon?"

"Just," Najja nodded. "The hills of Suhaj are three days away."

And then Kanja had an idea. The storm had cost them too much time and now the boy was missing. "Ride on to Suhaj and bring me that token. I'll stay here and look for the boy."

Najja leapt onto his horse and gestured for a water skin. "I'll wait for you by the eastern gate," he said, grinning. "All temples have eastern gates."

He was off before Kanja could change his mind, galloping between the rock formations where the moon cast a sliver of black shadows. All he could see now was a star streaking across the sky like a comet with a fiery tail. *Massui* . . .

There was no house for Massui's spirit to return to. So he wandered the plains for an animal to indwell. He likely crept around on four clawed feet and had found Ayize and eaten him.

Ayize is dead, Kanja thought, torn apart by wild dogs. It wouldn't be a bad thing. He just hoped it was quick.

He took his bow and stalked towards a large rock with the head of a woman. He wanted to take heart but there were storms in his head and his brow ached from the tension in his jaw.

The Imazi were brutal so Othene said, and he would know. He had studied them once in another life. He was a hawk then, taking to the skies and dodging their arrows. Tarabin had a face like a grinning skull and a great white head that wagged from side to side. He was a throat-cutter.

Kanja twirled a knife between his fingers and narrowed his eyes at a plume of smoke. It came from the snout of a dog, he was sure of it. *No, not a dog.* If it was a dog he would see its eyes, glowing in the black.

Ayize. It was Ayize, playing games.

Shadows stretched like fingers on the valley floor and a wind sighed and tugged at the rings in his ears. He wanted Ayize to appear over the brow of the dune so he could fit an arrow to his bow and kill him. It would be kinder. After all, the boy would never make a good king.

He measured the moon from the horizon, guessing it was the fourth hour. Full moons were said to drive a man to insanity and he was either a fool or an idiot to run off in the night searching for a boy. Besides, the moon had a blue tinge to it. It was unlucky.

Occasionally, he caught a sour whiff and he wondered if there was carrion in the forest of rocks and he heard the keening in the wind and a rustle behind him. He turned sharply feeling a surge of anticipation and all he could see was a mass of rocky shapes stretching as far as the horizon. But it was the same keenness every hunter felt when faced with danger. There was something moving beyond the wind-carved statues.

It's him, the stupid boy.

Kanja made off in the direction of a funnel-shaped rock. It was black when it should have been white, and the sky was yellow at the horizon as if the sun refused to set. He was grateful not to have wheels slewing about in the sand drifts and two good feet to manage the way, and he continued up a shallow slope easing himself over the summit. He couldn't see anything out of the ordinary, just thick rocks both to the left and ahead of him. It was silent except a vivid blush of color that seeped through the gullies as if a star had exploded in the night sky. His jaw dropped and then closed at the stench of a recent kill, tart on his tongue.

"Crazy bitches," he said, looking at a pile of fur on the

ground not far from where he stood.

He could almost see each hair as it twitched in the breeze and the legs curved at an odd angle. He was reluctant to touch it but he knew he had to. Leaning down he removed the pelt and gave a short, sharp jerk of his head. He cursed the orange light for what he saw. It was a boy, picked clean like a half-eaten fish and all he could see of the skull were two lips in a grimace of pain.

"Ayize," he whimpered, sinking to his knees.

He covered the body and almost gagged at the stench. He wept long and hard, spittle streaming from his open mouth.

The gods have punished me for my hatred, he thought. *They will punish me forever.*

He never looked back when he left that place, walking amongst the boulders and feeling the crunch of shells under his feet. He felt a prickling in the back of his neck and looked up suddenly. All he saw was a bird pecking amongst the rocks, eye bigger than a date pip and a packhorse pawing the sand.

Nura . . . No, it couldn't be. She was dead. He walked slowly towards the animal, whistling softly between his teeth. It was the dished face and the whinny that made him break into a run and it was the weapons on her back that made him smile.

He held out a hand to her muzzle, delighting in a snort of warm air. She shied suddenly at the capering shadows amongst the rocks and a dance of blue lights in the sky.

"Leave her," a voice said, arm grasping Kanja about the neck.

Kanja tried to squirm, but the arms were tighter than an anchor rope and he felt the jab in his ribs. He saw an arc of light like a harvesting scythe and for a moment he thought he was half-way between this world and the next.

"You're a dead man," the voice said with a Theban drawl. "Just like that half-wit brother of yours."

Kanja tried to place the face but he had never spoken

to Shenq's men. It was like some haunting entity in a very bad dream. The warrior spun Kanja around like a partner in a dance and there he was, bracelets snaking around thick arms and the stench of three-day-old sweat lingering on a fretful wind. He stared at Kanja with great curiosity—or Kanja imagined that he did—eyes unwavering like a granite statue.

"Jabari of Tungul," Kanja whispered, stepping back. He watched the warrior with interest, especially the gold on his arms. "You traitor!"

"Ah," Jabari held up his knife. "You're a smart man. Surely, you wouldn't want to call a freeman a traitor."

"I can't argue with that," Kanja muttered. The boy wasn't adorned with a metal anklet like most slaves. He was outfitted like a nobleman and the collar around his neck was a mark of honor.

I'll have that when you're dead, Kanja thought. And he'd have those bracelets too.

"So, here we are man to man." Jabari bowed his head, *shenti* rippling in a caressing breeze. "How do you like this bone-yard?" he said, spittle misting from dark lips.

Kanja had no idea he was standing on an Imazi burial ground and he felt a twinge of fear. *They bury their dead above ground?* Perhaps that was just as well. "A free man rides where he wants," he said, staring into eyes that were inky one minute and luminescent the next. He wondered what caused it.

The moon, you fool, the voices said. Yes, it was only the moon, the same moon that gave animals eyeshine at night. He had hoped Jabari would talk some more but he kept a grip on that shiny knife, playing it from hand to hand.

"Some say you're a demon," Jabari said. "So I just had to see for myself."

"Am I?" Kanja unsheathed his dagger.

Jabari hesitated as if struggling for words. "Blacker," he whispered.

Kanja wondered if Jabari was thicker than a temple wall

with that stupid grin on his face until he saw the hunch of his shoulders.

Kanja sprang forward dagger alive in his hand. Jabari jumped back, swinging on his heel and driving under to block the attack. Metal sang on metal, parrying, pressing, turning one cut and then the next and Kanja swung so hard, Jabari's dagger sparked in the darkness as it slid against his blade. He took slow deep breaths as he drove Jabari back, driving him into a ditch, driving him against rock, striking, slashing, yet somehow he couldn't touch him. Jabari whirled the blade above his head like a dance he took pleasure in and he blocked the savage downcut, fighting his way stroke by stroke.

Thrust the blade in tight, fool, the voices said. *Thrust when his arms are high.*

Kanja felt the bite as the blade raked across his cheek. He knew what Jabari aimed for and he twisted away, struggling to keep metal from his skin. He sucked on his bottom lip to cover the piercing, tasting salt and blood.

It was close. Too close.

Jabari twisted again, dodging between an avenue of boulders and thick knuckled columns. He paused for Kanja to catch up, grinning all the while and beckoning with a finger. Kanja leapt after him, grunting and panting, angry at the blood in his mouth, angry at Jabari's resolve.

How long had it been? Yet the Theban would not wear down and Kanja wondered what armor protected him, how thick the hedge was between them.

It was the slow heavy breathing that urged Kanja on, plunging into madness and savagery and smelling blood with every thrust. Raw anger flowed through him as he grunted again, hearing the dull ring of metal and the whoop of Jabari's voice.

Or was it a howl?

And then Jabari twisted again, this time slamming his back into a low saddle of rock. He hardly groaned as he fell, jerking his dagger up, punching and kicking as Kanja fell on top of him.

"I'll be a thorn in your side until one of us has had enough," Kanja snarled, slamming his blade into the soft crease of chest and upper arm. A red puddle seeped out from under the blade and Kanja pulled it free before plunging it between two ribs.

He watched Jabari's face as it turned from a wide-mouth grin to a moue of pain. And he heard his voice, loud and clear.

"Demon . . . That's what you are."

MKASA

Mkasa opened his eyes. He was lying on his back under a thick pelt and at first he thought he was dreaming. Horns dripped from the ceiling and he saw tiny specks of daylight peeking through each one. Shifting slightly on his bed of skins, he studied the rock shelf he occupied. There were plenty like it in the cavern, cut in the limestone walls and filled with men and women. Even their snores made him sleepy and he wondered where the sun was.

Throwing his legs over the bed, he looked for his bow and quiver but they were gone. All he had was a small dagger in his belt and a pouch of poisoned arrowheads. What good were arrowheads without a shaft?

The girl was his constant companion. She lay on the floor beside him, wrapped in a swathe of black hair and studying him with a disapproving eye. Girding her brow was a circlet of silver and from it hung a net so delicate it reminded Mkasa of a spider's web.

"Food?" she asked.

Mkasa nodded, hoping it wasn't any more of that thick gristly broth that put him to sleep. He glanced at an old woman straining under an armful of wood. She tossed a few logs into the pit and tongues of yellow and orange leapt into the air. He could hear it crackling from where he sat. Now and then he watched the smoke as it wafted up towards a wide funnel where the walls were grooved and deep enough for a foot.

S'haila returned with a trencher of stew, and sat on the floor beside him. "Elk" she said in that strong voice of hers.

Mkasa closed his hands around the hollowed out platter, wooden by the look of it and bleached by the sun.

"The khamāsīn has com," she said, eyes tracing the walls of the cavern. "No one can live through it. There is no sun, no moon. The sky has swallowed them both."

Mkasa felt his belly tighten. He knew no one could survive a sandstorm and darkness at the same time, and Shenq and his warriors would be buried deep in the desert unless they found a tunnel.

"You can't go outside," she said.

No, I will never go outside.

Mkasa tasted the stew. The meat was tough and gamey and flavored with herbs, and it made him want to gag. He knew he had to eat to build his strength, especially if he was going to climb that shaft all the way to the stars. It was the only way out.

"You're not going anywhere, Makurae," she said, lip raised in a sneer. "They'll tie you up and leave you for the *shakāl*. Do you know what it's like to be eaten alive?"

"No one's lived to tell the tale," he said between slurps.

She watched him through heavy-lidded eyes and something dark crept into her tone. "I see you plain enough. I see how you shame your own house. How you hate *her* that sleeps in your bed. There are two inside her, Makurae, two of you. How can a man hate like that?"

"Give me my bow and I'll show you."

"Do you think a woman's heart is something to laugh at?"

"I think all hearts are something to laugh at. Yours, mine, everyone's." Mkasa preferred silence to chatter, and the girl had little to talk about. "Hearts lie. They're all black and hard."

"Mine isn't," she said.

"You would know more of that than I do."

"You do have a heart, Makurae. Why do you keep thinking about the boy?"

Mkasa wasn't aware he was thinking of Ayize, so young, so vulnerable, so utterly alone. The two words the boy had mouthed when he last saw him suddenly became clear.

The seal.

He would need it if he wanted to survive and there it was, tucked behind his shúkà. He refused to take it off on the first night and every night after that he slept fully clothed. No sense in thinking he was staying.

"Show it to the Bonelord," she said, "and you'll live."

"Give that tongue of yours a rest," he said, stretching his legs. "He'll kill me as soon as he sees it."

"Not so. It's Imazi forged. I can see that from here. Tarabin must have admired the man he gave it to."

"My father," Mkasa muttered, wiping his mouth and discarding the bowl. "He was a great man."

"And you'll be greater," she said, staring at the floor.

"Is it day or night?"

"We light fires at sunrise," S'haila said, looking up slowly. "There's hot water and oils, and fresh skins to dress in."

Mkasa wanted to bathe in one of the hot pools but not with her standing there gawking at him. She was a scrawny slip of a girl with twigs for legs, and she had a lovelorn grin that made him sick. And as for the fire, was it a dayfire or a nightfire?

"Where's *your* bed," he said, yawning.

"I sleep where you sleep. I walk where you walk."

Mkasa leaned forward over the bed and glared at her. "I have a wife. I have a child. And I will be going home."

"This is your home," she said, standing. "For now."

Mkasa frowned and locked eyes with her. "For now?"

He had not noticed it before but the girl had a hunter's arm, packed with a knot of muscle and capable of wielding a weapon. A light weapon perhaps, but a weapon nonetheless.

"You slept well then," a voice said with a snort of disdain. It was Tarabin, standing above him with two rocks for eyes. "Prince Saqr didn't come home last night. Maybe he won't come home at all."

"Hunting oryx were they?" Mkasa asked, suddenly standing.

"Men." Tarabin stared down at him and grinned. "Saqr's more fickle than the wind. No one knows which way he blows. What do you make of it?"

Mkasa had no idea what to make of it and he hoped the lop-eared falcon had drowned in a sinkhole.

"If he doesn't come home," Tarabin said, ducking beneath a screen of limestone draperies, "I'll have your bones for a breastplate."

What a bright breastplate that would make, Mkasa thought, delighted that Tarabin saw the sense in getting some fresh air. He wanted to ask if he could go with him but the sound of wild laughter stopped him in his tracks.

"Do you know what I think, Makurae?" Tarabin said, eyes watering. "My caves are grand enough for any man and cooler than your sweat-ridden villas. Is there anything sweeter than making love to keep warm?"

"Fishing," Mkasa said, nodding, "with the sun on your back."

"There's a few pools down here and a fire for warmth. See, we look after your every need."

"Let him go with you, my lord," S'haila said. "It would be an honor."

"What would you know of honor, girl? Food is what he needs." Tarabin waggled his hand. "Just bread and cheese, mind."

The girl looked at Mkasa and neither said anything about the elk. They followed Tarabin to a long wooden table where half a dozen men sat. One rolled a lump of beeswax around a wick and proceeded to light it from the fire and another cracked an egg with one hand while slurping stew from a wooden bowl.

"Saqr back yet?" Tarabin asked a man with a sour face.

"No, my lord," Sour Face said, studying Mkasa with his pale yes. "Want me to get the spit?"

"Not yet, though I'm looking forward to that shiny

brown flesh."

Mkasa had no intention of being flayed alive and he stopped his mind before they could catch it.

"You have my leave to look around," Tarabin said, smiling at S'haila. "Take him to the green lake, girl. Take him any way you want."

The twelve men laughed and then stared with dull white eyes. There were pupils in those eyes, small black dots surrounded by a cloud of white. It was only in the sunlight those pupils disappeared altogether.

"What good is he to us? It's *Kemnebi* we want," said Rat-Eater.

"He'll come soon enough," Tarabin said, lowering his face into a cup. "This boy is sweeter than gold to him."

They're afraid of me, Mkasa thought, until the men frowned over their bowls and broke out in a round of laughter. He cursed himself for thinking it and flinched. Their eyes were still crinkling in amusement as S'haila took him to the fire pit where an old woman turned flat loaves on a stone. Grabbing a ball of cheese, her eyes flicked to an unguarded doorway. "The King's Chamber," she said, smiling.

"And where does the Queen sleep?" Mkasa murmured as he followed her.

"She never sleeps."

Mkasa stared at her with a frown and took a bite of bread. The flavor was as elusive as she was and the cheese was bitter. He gazed out across the cavern with its paths and bridges and he wondered where they led.

"To the pools," S'haila said, eating the last of her meal.

"Pools?"

A faint smile brushed her lips as she turned to face him. "They come from the rain."

And rain comes from the sky. Mkasa felt lightheaded at the thought.

She grabbed a lighted torch and headed for a trail that cut between two sparkling tree columns. An archway stood at the end of it with ancient words sprawled across the lintel.

"All the caverns have names," she said, raising the torch. "This is Boneyard."

Mkasa studied her upturned face, nose clustered with tiny brown dots. "How many times have you seen the sun?"

"Many times." She flicked a finger and ushered him on with a tilt of her head. "I saw a Darkeye once, skin like beer. He was beautiful, only he wouldn't mate with me."

Mkasa didn't care to ask why. She was rough-mouthed and too pale to take pleasure in. But her eyes were blue like the sky.

"My mother took a Darkeye to her bed. Though rocks could hardly be called a bed. She pulled him from his horse and tied him up. There wasn't much he could do."

"And you're his daughter?"

She nodded, tucking a tendril of hair behind one ear. "I'm a half-blood. I get punished more than them."

"Punished?"

She stopped suddenly and turned to face him, eyes roaming his body. "A company of Darkeyes came through here a year ago, Siwans I think they were. We were hunting fox at dusk and one of them saw us. He wanted to know what it was like to bed a milkgirl. So he pushed me down amongst the rocks and none of the women stopped him. I was punished for that. Do you know how Imazi's punish their own? They tie them over a boulder and leave them in the sun. It hurts Makurae, like knives going through your skin. Only half-bloods don't die. I ran away for a time but they found me."

Mkasa saw her smile and he smiled back. "How did you escape?"

"I can climb anything just like my mother. I can scale that wall without ropes."

Mkasa studied the wall she pointed at, sinewy like men's bones and creamier than goat curds. Sometimes he thought he saw a knee and sometimes a foot, and sometimes a grinning skull from the darkness. There would be plenty of footholds if he cared to try.

"Beautiful, aren't they?" she said, voice as sinister as it was gentle. "Ancestor's bones we call them. We don't bury our dead underground. We leave them in the sun for the *shakāl*."

Mkasa was glad to hear it. The possibility of bones in the cavern walls was abhorrent to him. All men deserved a decent burial, even the enemy.

"You'd like to kiss me, wouldn't you?" S'haila said, turning suddenly. "I think you'd like to do more than kiss me."

Mkasa had no idea where the idea came from and backed away a few steps. "My heart's already taken and yours is blacker than mud."

"Pity," she said and gave a sudden snort. "You stink."

Mkasa was hoping it was the cheese. It had a mighty bad odor as far as he was concerned. "I've smelled worse," he said, following her through a slippery flowstone passageway.

"You should bathe. You'd want me then."

I want Meryt, he thought. How many times had he imagined eyes greener than sycamore leaves and the sound of her laugh? And then he regretted thinking about her.

"I know leaves," S'haila said. "We eat the herbs the men bring back. I tried to grow them once in Spirit Cavern. But plants need sun. So they died."

Torches hung in brackets overhead, crackling and sending up a cloud of smoke. As far as he could see that same smoke went up somewhere, through a shaft and out into the clean air. The corridor opened out into a path where one side was smooth rock and the other a sheer drop, and soaring above was a domed ceiling where hanging formations reached down almost as far as the stalagmites below.

"Devil's den," she said, grinning, always grinning.

"There's a seven hundred foot drop down there."

Mkasa placed a hand against the rock, easing himself along the narrow ledge. He could have sworn he heard whispers. He could have sworn he heard his name.

"The caverns whisper," she purred, eyes searching the walls. "Sometimes they weep."

"Caverns don't weep."

"It's the twins, two Darkeyes. A gift from Pharaoh Aneru to King Tarahawk," she said. "It's beautiful here, don't you think?"

"Aneru? He was Pharaoh's grandfather." Mkasa remembered the promise, two Theban princesses for two Imazi princes. It was to seal the peace treaty between the two.

"They fell, you see," she said, pointing a finger towards the pit. "Their screams disturbed the devils and now they whisper."

"You don't believe any of that, do you?"

"No," she said flatly. "I believe they escaped."

Escaped? How? "Devil's den," Mkasa repeated, wondering how many of them lurked in that inky pit. "What do these devils look like?"

"Black, with leathery wings and sharp little eyes," she said, walking a little faster now. "They'll tear you to pieces if they catch you."

"How big are they?"

"This big," she said, raising a hand and measuring a short distance between forefinger and thumb.

Hardly worth fretting over, he thought. Bats, that's what they were. Tiny little bats. He almost hit his head on a limestone drape, hanging like soiled linen from the roof, and then he saw the lake and the glow of emerald beneath its waters.

"There's a light in the center of the earth," she said, dropping the torch into a metal sconce. "Like a fire. That's how you can see the color."

"I won't bathe," he reminded, scowling.

There was something reptilian about her eyes, bright and strange. Mkasa could have reached out and kissed her right there but his belly warned him against it. There would never be a moment's peace.

She threw off her tunic in one tug and dived in, a shimmer of white amongst the green. *She can't hear me, she can't see me*, Mkasa thought, waiting. Sure enough, there was no sign she heard his thoughts, wanting him instead to watch her. Pale limbs gyrated in a ritual dance and for a moment he was mesmerized. Not once had she surfaced to take a breath and not once did he feel threatened. He could have traced those limbs with a finger, beautiful they were like clouds at sunset, and he wondered if she was a captive too, a half-blood and hated.

I can't stay here thinking about it. He watched her for a time, glimmering like a Nile perch. Up and down she went and rolling on her back, never coming up for air.

He heard a trickle of water and his stomach churned at the sound. Unhooking the torch, he crept towards a breach in the wall, wide enough to crawl through and dark enough to hide. Water rushed in through the narrow channel and he prayed there was sunlight on the other side. Pushing the torch through, he crawled on his belly, struggling against the current and scraping his knees. He could hear the rocks groaning and sighing, and somewhere above him the wind murmured through the caves.

And then the torch flickered and died.

He cursed before letting his eyes adjust to the darkness, before the drone in his ears got louder. *Keep moving*, he said to himself and he reached up to where the ceiling almost met the floor. *Too narrow, too tight.*

He crawled as far as he could, water splashing his face and eyes, forcing his way upwards to who knows where. When he lifted his hand to the ceiling, he could feel a gradient on one side and edging his way towards it, the tunnel began to widen.

There has to be a way out, he thought, following the sound of the water. He could hear a rumbling now like a giant belly desperate for food.

A waterfall? No, wind. Where there's wind, there's a way out.

The hairs on the back of his neck began to prickle and every movement sent a shock up his legs, almost to his hips. *I won't be buried here*, he thought. *I won't be buried without a name.*

He had to grind his teeth to keep from screaming and he bit his tongue in the process. Struggling to crawl he rolled to one side, thigh cramping and muscles aching with every move. Fingernails torn and bloody, he pulled himself upward as far as he could. The space was wide enough for him to kneel and it was well he could still breathe.

Help me. He didn't recognize his own voice, the voice in his mind. When it called out again, he began to sob. *HaShem, help me!*

He had no idea if he had turned a complete circle, whether he headed back the way he came. He just knew he had to keep moving, to keep the shudder from his lips. Here and there he caught glimpses of light, smaller than a fingernail and he could hear a *swish* like a cloak whisking about a man's ankles. But it was only the wind.

His head was throbbing and the best he could do was twist sideways until he saw the light for what it was. Torches and oil lamps flickered in the distance and he found himself crawling out of the tunnel onto a flat ledge at the brink of another chamber. Below him lay a bed of fat pillars rising out of the ground and beyond that were alcoves and grottoes, and pools of the deepest blue. Statues of the ancients looked down with saintly eyes, stone fingers curled around swords and daggers. Their favorite weapons no doubt. One was named Tarahawk, another Tarawolf and on their heads were coronets of men's hands. Opposite them were the twin princesses, eyes sad as if that was the mood the craftsman captured at the time of their making.

I hope you ran away, he thought, giving them one last look.

The remnants of a hearty breakfast were littered on a flat stone, bread, tiger nuts and figs, and a stack of freshly gnawed bones. The sight of it nearly made him sick.

Hooking the torch in an empty sconce, he staggered through the scree to a fire pit in the center of the cavern. A flame rose from the ashes fanned by a sudden gust and something shimmered on the ground amongst the kindling.

An axe . . . he could hardly believe it.

Snatching it in a blistered hand, he studied bit and poll, turning it this way and that to measure its strength. When he felt a breeze on the top of his head, he looked up and saw the funnel rising towards a black sky peppered with stars.

Climb. Now!

Easing himself up on the flat stone, he saw a narrow fissure above his head. Slamming the axe down hard, he gripped onto the handle and found the leverage he needed to hang on. Stretching sideways over the fire, he swung out, easing himself up towards a narrow ledge. He grabbed a knuckle of rock at the lip of the funnel and pulled himself up into the darkness. He was half out of breath as he sat there, legs spread out either side.

At least the Imazi were hunting under the moon and not down here searching, he thought, watching a cloud of dust motes dancing in the shaft.

It was quiet for a while until he heard the crunch of gravel below. The girl was down there somewhere, waiting, thinking.

She could see through his eyes. She knew where he was.

SHENQ

Shenq heard the jingle of the harness before his horse lifted his head to snort. The warriors began to stir at the noise, some reaching for weapons, and twice he heard a sound, a blood-chilling yell.

He hoped it was Mkasa somehow freed from his underground jail, seal bouncing against his chest. But it was Khemwese that ran towards him in the early dawn, teeth white and glistening. There were tears on his cheeks and cuts on his arms, and the howl when it came was terrible.

"Mourning," whispered Harran, grasping Shenq's arm. "He's mourning."

"Mourning?" Shenq felt his stomach lurch as he stood there. He pushed Ayize behind him and nodded at Harran. "Go to him."

Harran took a blue blanket from a packhorse and a spear. His forehead was speckled with sweat and there was an odd sheen to his eyes Shenq didn't like. He ran towards Khemwese and bowed his head. They whispered for a while until Harran collapsed to the ground, tearing his tunic and mumbling *Barukh atah Adonai* . . .

"Tell me!" Shenq shouted, striding towards them both. He saw Khemwese's mouth move but he couldn't hear the name. "Who?"

"Jabari," Khemwese muttered, hanging bloody arms where he had cut himself. "He's dead."

Dead? No, not dead. Just wounded. "Take me to him."

They found him by a boulder curled in a ball, a silver knife peeking out from bloody fingers. Shenq sank to his knees and touched the flesh, colder than the man who'd killed him. He was lacking the fly collar and bracelets, and his eyes were closed as if a kind hand had made them so.

"Kanja," Shenq whispered, glimpsing the snake-like hilt. He drew it out and stared at the blood as if it was his own.

Jabari waved one last time, don't you remember? He knew. He knew something.

Shenq regretted sending Jabari after the mare and he regretted not killing her when he had the chance. All he could see was sand blowing around them, pale and silent, and the only sound was a faint sobbing, Ayize's sobbing, knees shaking under that skinny body of his.

Shenq felt Khemwese's hand on his shoulder, only it didn't stop him from shouting. "I'll have him cropped at the neck! I'll have his corpse tied between two horses and ripped apart. He won't be buried. He'll never have a name."

Shenq heard Harran's sobs and he couldn't help but shrink back. In the midst of the drone in his head, the shouts and the cursing, all he could think of were the past victories and he was lost for words. It made mourning so unbearable.

He took off his collar and laid it over Jabari's neck. There were twelve golden flies shimmering against dead skin, evidence of twelve great victories. "He will be brought home to his mother and he will be buried as a nobleman."

Harran covered the body with a blanket, tucking the extremities under Jabari's body. He drove his spear into the ground and tied a small red pennant to the hilt, watching it flutter in a gentle breeze. "Blessed is the Judge of Truth," he whispered, saying the prayer for the dead. And when he finished he turned to Shenq. "There should be a watchman. His body should not be left unattended."

"The heralds will be here soon," Shenq murmured. He leaned against the boulder and pulled himself back to his feet. He watched the sunrise through clenched teeth and the glow of orange everywhere. He wished Jabari could see it.

Snapping his fingers, he urged his men to mount. "To Suhaj," he cried. "Menkheperre needs a doctor and we need weapons."

"Mkasa," Ayize muttered, swallowing at the same time. "What about Mkasa?"

"The Imazi have a covenant with Thebes, boy. If they touch a seal bearer, they risk war."

"If he is so special then why haven't they let him go?"

"We don't know they haven't." Shenq glared at those dark eyes and wanted to shake the boy.

"We can't leave. Not until we're sure."

"Did you know their caverns are full of gold and silver?"

Ayize shook his head. Of course he didn't know. How could he?

"The Imazi trade with Thebes. It wouldn't do to lose such a powerful patron. And as for my brother, he has a hunter's spirit. We'll see him in Suhaj."

Shenq turned to Menkheperre, staring at cloudy eyes. "Can you ride?"

"Yes, sir," Menkheperre murmured, barely nodding. Weary as he looked, he had strength enough.

Shenq grabbed a horse and lifted Menkheperre onto the saddle pad. He had seen the boys staring at one another, sizing each other up. "Ayize will ride behind and Khemwese too. We will be at the village by nightfall."

Shenq swung his leg over the dun horse and tied the goatskin pack to the saddle. There were no tracks to follow, the sandstorm had seen to that. Beyond the towers of rock Shenq could see the world had turned white, covered in a soft mantle of chalk and blushed by a rising sun. Farther off, the rutted tracks the drovers used had vanished altogether, lost amidst a rolling sea of dunes. Dressed in bronze plate and grimy linens Shenq knew they were a sorry sight, hardly a riot of color against a drab sky.

Hooves clinked against shells and crystals, and Shenq

glanced up at the rock formations each its own island resembling hawks and fine-boned faces. They towered above them in sparkling white, eroded by years of sandstorms and teetering on narrow necks. It was remarkable they were standing at all.

As the sun moved across the sky, shadows shifted and the landscape seemed to change. With the white desert behind them, they galloped through flatlands of brown grass leading to a belt of the purest sand. Shenq glanced back at Menkheperre slouched on his horse and wondered how much time they had. If Kanja was ahead of them, his men could be hiding in the uplands and behind isolated rock domes that bordered the eastern edge of the river village of Suhaj.

The horses began slogging through smooth, unbroken sand, ears pricked forward and nostrils flared to the scent of water. Shenq could see the temple pylons and a rank of palm trees rising up behind a ridge, and there was a narrow road that cut between the slopes leading to the quiet dusty streets of the village.

Shenq held up a fist and the men slid from their horses, unslinging bows and slipping arrows from their quivers. Untying the goatskin wrap from his horse, he patted the stallion and let him loose. The magic box was safer with him than a stampeding herd of horses.

Khemwese and Tehute turned full circles as they proceeded towards a rocky spur pocked with boulders. As the sun sank behind them and the shadows thickened, Shenq kept a wary eye on the land around him. A black kite circled lazily in the sky and a startled sand cat hissed before scrambling into the brush.

Padding quickly along a course of sand speckled with pebbles, they made barely a sound and once Shenq thought he heard voices and stopped until it was silent again. He patted the air as they reached the end of the spur and the warriors paused, dropping slowly to the ground.

Menkheperre staggered onward, face tilted downwards

as if he would collapse and Shenq caught him before he went any further. "You'll be able to sleep all you want when we get to the village," he whispered, giving him a glare and touching a finger to his lips. "Right now, I need you to stay awake."

Shenq urged Ayize forward and handed him the Box of Heka. "Look after this and look after Menkheperre."

Shenq studied the rocky slopes some twenty feet in front of them and saw a man creeping along the fringe of the trees. "Shadow hunters," he murmured, catching a glimpse of the emblem of the cow.

Palm trees curved upwards and a faint breeze ruffled their spiny fronds. There was a dark huddle of men beneath the husked trunks, grazing on goat's cheese and roasted snake. Some wore horned-helmets and tunics of black wool, and their heads were half-shaved and painted in silver. A three-legged dog hobbled down the slope, barking and baring its teeth.

"Looks like he caught our scent," Shenq said.

And then the arrows came.

"Take cover!" Shenq shouted over the sudden whir.

They spun for cover behind the boulders, aiming and loosing their arrows at varying speeds. The air was filled with the sound of sharp cries and neighing horses, and all around were dark arrow shafts sprouting from the ground like clumps of dried grass. *Pi-Bak-Amana*, Shenq thought, dreading the priestly dwarf all the more. He had set his hunters on the ridge to attack the riders as they came thundering through.

Shenq beckoned to his men to hold their fire and, lowering himself to the ground, he edged behind them towards Captain Tehute. The enemy had already released a barrage of arrows, some punching the sand, some bouncing off rocks. Several hundred more cambered above them, slapping into the boulders with splintering cracks.

"We're safe enough until the sun goes down," he said.

"How long will they keep this up?" Tehute said, ducking as low as he could.

"Until they run out," Shenq said, narrowing his eyes at the shapes flitting between the rocks. "Wait until it goes quiet and then aim high. My guess is the High Priest is sitting in a chair just behind that knoll, drinking a cup of wine."

The arrows started up again, rattling like hail overhead. Shallow arcs glanced off the boulders above them until the barrage slackened as the shadow-hunters likely chose to save what was left of their arrows.

And then all went quiet.

"Draw," Shenq whispered, watching Tehute pull his bow up and line the bowstring with his cheek.

"Nice and high," Shenq reminded, peering over the rim of the boulder. "Fire."

The shaft rose gracefully, hanging for an instant before plunging steeply behind the knoll. There was a deep bray of pain and a shout, and then all Shenq's arrows broke loose.

He saw a man toppling down the slope with an arrow in his eye, falling in an explosion of sand. A second rolled forward holding his gut and a third swallowed an arrowhead just as he opened his mouth.

The shadow-hunters began to retreat to a greater range and there were intervals of silence as they reloaded. When the sun sank below the horizon, the shooting ceased altogether.

"Seems we've got ourselves a face-off," Shenq said.

"Not quite," said Tehute, spying a curtained litter, weaving between the rocks. "Looks like the High Priest's come to see what all the noise is about."

Shenq was surprised to see a woman's face peeking out from behind the curtains with a grin wider than a barn door. She was dressed in a *shenti* that looped at her thighs, belted with a long sash edged in turquoise and gold.

"Greetings, Commander," she said.

"Greetings, my lady," Shenq replied, standing. He couldn't help noticing a thick collar of beaten gold adorned with scarab pendants and teardrops of feldspar to hide bare breasts. "What a welcome."

"We do try to entertain our guests," she said as the bearers set down her litter. "I am Hemet-ka, Enchantress of Hathor, foremost of all women."

"A thousand apologies," Shenq said, trying to keep the laughter from his voice. In his opinion, she was no higher than a scorpion's tail. "You are the chief wife of the High Priest?"

"I am one with the master, yes."

"Just like him then."

"No one is like him," she said, fingers caressing her pectoral collar, the mark of her order. Half-closed eyes were meant to entice but all it did was make her look tired. "I can't do magic. Oh, I can conjure snakes and toads. We all can. But not the magic. Do you know Pi-Bak-Amana, High Priest of Suhaj?"

Shenq couldn't recall a time ever meeting the man. But he would have a stern word with him when he did. "I know *of* him."

"He's expecting you." She stared up at his eyes as an astronomer would an unusual star.

"How kind of him to make room for us."

"They said you were young, but . . ."

Shenq wondered why she hesitated. His body was grimy with sweat and his clothes were no better than rags.

"So beautiful," she whispered, licking lips stained with red ochre.

The statement took him by surprise and he could feel Harran flinch beside him, face knotted with anguish. He was hugging his bow a little too tightly in Shenq's opinion.

"It is a beautiful night, Hemet-Ka," he said. "Why waste it on arrows and cursing. My men need a bed for the night and by the look of it so do you."

Hemet-ka's cheeks were smooth and puce, and she

cleared her throat before speaking. "Then a bed it is."

She was larger than most women, almost muscular, and the gold around her arms and ankles would have weighed a regular man down. Part of Shenq clung to the possibility that she was the High Priest, an ever-changing persona, a phantom that assumed any character. Perhaps she hung upside down from a rafter at night, talons sharp and curled.

"Talking of beds, one of my warriors is in need of a doctor," Shenq said. "You do have a doctor?"

Hemet-ka snapped her fingers and a shadow-hunter stepped forward. One side of his face was burnished to a shine and the other was knotted in tufts of black hair. "Tell your warrior he is safe with Xonsu," she said to Shenq. "Tell him to do what the diviner says."

Diviner? Shenq thought. *He'll love that.* He gave Hemet-ka a lingering stare. "Khemwese will guard him. Pharaoh's orders."

"Whatever you say, Commander."

Shenq watched them leave with a heavy heart although he knew Khemwese had an arsenal of knives on the nap side of his belt and a mind to use them.

"Come. The rest of you will bathe before seeing the High Priest," she said, sighing heavily as if it would take energy to explain.

Shenq could see all her attention was fixed on him as if none of the warriors existed. But he refused to cower under her scrutiny, her witchcraft.

"The grooms will attend to your beasts," she said.

"If they can find them," Shenq muttered. His stallion was heading towards a water trough last he looked.

Leading the way, she sauntered through narrow alleys and flat-roofed houses. Shenq watched her broad back, naked except for the counterweight of her collar and tied with two falcon heads. He could have sworn he saw horns where her ears should have been.

Not a woman but like a woman.

The silent tread of the shadow-hunters reminded Shenq they were surrounded by a gang of angry men. He shot a glance over his shoulder in an attempt to count heads. There was no escape, not now.

The temple pylons were up ahead, lit by braziers and responding to the outlying beacons. There were torches along the walls and two large fires burning outside the guardhouse where merchants and travelers haggled. The moon was a waning face, barely visible through the trees and its reflection shimmered on the surface of the Nile beckoning them home.

"I can't go in," Harran whispered, staggering alongside Shenq. "The courts are dark and full of magic."

"You don't believe in magic."

"No, sir, but they do. We could fight them off—"

"With what? There are five dozen of them and five of us."

"There's an armory, sir, west of the sanctuary."

"Then ask her if we can be excused to find it," Shenq snapped.

It was then he saw the flames from the red beacon as they licked the air and a trail of smoke above it.

"Kanja's already here," he said.

As they entered the first court, the scent of perfumed oils were slick and captivating and there were palm gardens and orange groves, and pools of the deepest green. Sacred statues stood between papyriform pillars, *shentis* fluttered in the breeze. Shenq had never seen images dressed in cloth nor had he seen stone limbs brushed with oil. He began to wonder what manner of temple it was.

"You may have to bow to the High Priest," Shenq whispered to Harran. "I wouldn't ask if I didn't think you could. It's time those knees hit the floor."

"I won't bow to him. I won't bow to anyone—."

"His tortures are most creative." Shenq took a deep breath, sensing a chill in the air. "They're said to take days."

The very mention of torture was enough to silence Harran and he continued to walk beside Shenq with a tight-lipped stare. The great hall was dank and oppressive, mold leaching from the walls and there were long tables laden with food and goblets of sweet-smelling wine. *Three*, if Shenq had counted correctly.

"Put down your weapons," Hemet-ka said, pointing to the floor. "You need both hands to eat."

I need both my hands to wrap around your scrawny neck, thought Shenq. "We'll stand if you don't mind," he said, keeping bow and quiver slung on his back and taking the box from Ayize. He kept two small knives in his belt and the sword under his cloak.

"Seems we're not the only ones here, Hemet-ka," he said, back prickling as if a cold breeze caressed his spine. He plucked a goose thigh from a silver platter to study the sheen on its crispy skin.

"If you want the token, you must kill for it," she said, mouth widening in to a slow smile.

Sounded fair to Shenq. "Where are the Bloods?"

"Worshipping. It's Hathor's Honor Day, the day she was given life," she derided, cradling the whip as if it were a babe. Her eyes rested on the goatskin pack under his arm and she frowned. "Is that a gift?"

Shenq squeezed the box a little tighter. "For our host."

"May I see it?"

"Best not. It is for his eyes only."

Shenq watched Tehute as he chewed slices of ox flesh and desert game, and Harran lifted every flap of bread to see what was under it. Ayize's face was smeared with fava beans and his ravenousness made Shenq smile. He could hear low chants seeping like a vapor beneath the doors of the sanctuary. It was a miserable sound, a lament perhaps for the dead.

"They sound happy," he grunted, tucking the box between his knees and tearing meat from a bone with his teeth.

"You know nothing of the gods." Hemet-ka took a handful of sesame rings and tiger nut sweets, and stuffed them in her mouth. "She is the goddess of dance. This is her music."

Hardly music, Shenq thought, listening to the gurgling priests and the maddening sistra. He tasted the first promise of battle when he thought of Thutiy. He was likely schooling his snakes in a cinder pit and chanting in that out-of-tune voice of his.

The baths were steaming with oils and scrubs and they were dressed in fresh clothes. Checking their weapons, they were brought to the audience chamber by an elderly attendant and left to stand there before a gold throne. There were carpets and hangings, and cushions of the brightest hues and there was a pool in the center of the room with an open roof above it.

Shenq carried the box by a thick leather strap, swinging it now and then. He turned a half-circle to take in his surroundings, cocking his head at the mural of a coiled snake wrapped around a temple boy.

"Apepi," a voice said. "Beautiful isn't he?"

"The god of darkness and madness," Shenq said, turning towards the voice.

He saw a stunted man nesting amongst the cushions on the throne, forehead broad as if it had been flattened with a mallet.

"Not madness, Commander. *Confusion.* He is the enemy of light and truth. He likes to do battle. And so do you. Perhaps you'd like to meet him one day."

Perhaps I already have, thought Shenq, wondering how the dwarf managed to hop up on such a high chair without being seen. His feet were stretched to the edge of the seat and his face was long, finely chiseled and handsome in its way.

"Pi-Bak-Amana, High Priest of Farafra at your service," the dwarf said, hand over his chest. "You should be on your knees."

"An unmannerly position, my lord," Shenq countered. "My warriors are commanded to stand and face their superiors not lie idly around."

The High Priest laughed. "I've been looking forward to meeting you, Commander. You are a man of dignity and poise, a man of great stamina. I slaughtered an ox this morning and burned its entrails so I could see you coming. A diviner entertains so much better with a belly-full of blood. Is that a box?" Pi-Bak-Amana said, taking a hard look at the package. "If it is it's poorly wrapped."

"It might have been cleaner if it hadn't been trussed up and lashed to a saddle."

"Save your tricks, Commander. Goatskin is a shroud for dead traitors. Cunning is what you are. How is it you still breathe?"

"God is not done with me. Nor is our beloved Pharaoh."

"Pity. Hemet-ka thinks you're quite something. You know, I've often thought she'd make a good meal only I don't have the heart to do it. And I know what you're thinking. You're thinking food's scarce around here and I've eaten all the priests."

"I expect you enjoyed every bite."

"Enough!" Pi-Bak-Amana hammered the arm of his chair with his fist. "You should know the Bloods have taken the token. Their leader is on my battlements looking at stars. You can have him if you give me that box."

Shenq knew the box was good for something and he wasn't about to let it go on a whim. "All in good time, my lord."

"Why do your men refuse to kneel? You do know I'm related to the Pharaoh by marriage."

"His great aunt wasn't it?"

"The princess was such a sweet young thing. She died in childbed and so did the child. You know so much about me, Commander, and yet you stand there stiff as a rod."

Not a sane person in sight, Shenq thought, gazing at the

pool. Flotsam floated at one corner, debris he reckoned from the peristyle roof, and he could see the reflection of the moon like a giant face in a bronze mirror.

"The moon can trap a man with its sorcery. Stare at it too long and you will turn to stone."

"*This* moon is full," Shenq said, scowling at the water. "Yet the moon outside has hardly waned."

Pi-Bak-Amana leaned forward and whispered, "Its magic, Commander. *My* magic." There was a moment of silence before he spoke again. "I suggest you show me your seal if you want weapons."

Shenq walked forward and held up the Pharaoh's seal. "Your men were most gracious on the way in, my lord," he said, voice loud enough to scatter two nesting birds in the architraves. "I pray they are just as gracious on the way out."

"My men?"

"Shadow-hunters."

"They're Bull-Warriors, Commander, the best of their kind. You should have known them by their insignia." Pi-Bak-Amana bit the seal with the side of his mouth and tossed it into his belt.

"We are riders of the Kamaraan, my lord," Shenq said, half turning to his warriors. "I would have expected a fanfare."

"The Kamaraan calls for seven men, Commander. Two of yours are settling in to my staterooms and the other two . . . Where are the others?"

"Dead, my lord, and braver than Montu."

"Don't be facetious, Commander. How can anyone be braver than Montu? Look at you. Three warriors down. How do you expect to win now?"

"With as much dignity as I can muster, my lord." Shenq hated the sound of his voice, reverent as if he cared.

"Who are the survivors?" Pi-Bak-Amana said, eyes feasting on Ayize. "I was told the prince of Thebes was amongst them. But this boy looks like he's been painted with pitch."

"An ugly rumor," Shenq said, relieved the High Priest had no idea what Menkheperre looked like. "Pharaoh insisted the boy stayed at home."

"How fortunate. It would have been a burden to lug a half-wit to Farafra. I've heard he prefers a pen to a sword. And him?" Pi-Bak-Amana pointed at Harran. "Who is he?"

Shenq turned to look at Harran, distracted only by the boy's voice. He was swaying back and forth, and mouthing a prayer rather loudly.

"The Pharaoh's prophet, my lord. A seer."

"I know what a prophet is, you fool. But what's he doing in here? "

"He wanted to meet you, my lord. He'd heard so much about you."

"He's *Shasu*, a stinking breed. How can he see me with his eyes closed?"

"He can see more with them closed than open."

Pi-Bak-Amana curled his lips and spat on the floor. "I have the feeling you'd rather be sleeping in holes than in silken sheets."

"We don't wish to burden you."

"I take pleasure in entertainment, Commander." Pi-Bak-Amana pointed a stubby finger from long arms. "You're wondering where you've seen me before."

Shenq shook his head. It was the last thing on his mind.

"I'm in your thoughts. No, darker than that. In a deep well where you left me."

"News spreads fast, my lord." Shenq smiled, knowing the priest sought to taunt him. "The last man I killed in a well is very much dead. I severed his spine just before he drowned."

"But did he drown? Perhaps he still walks the earth. Perhaps he's here with us now. Everything you see is magic. Even me."

Shenq studied two raised eyebrows and pondered the remark. The priest was insane. That's all there was to it.

"You have come to the end of the line, Commander. Well, not quite. You still have to face the rising sun tomorrow. You still have to face the Pharaoh. What a shame that will be. What if I told you there are no priests, no Hemet-ka? What if I told you they are me and I am them?"

The darkness would have given the High Priest a reprieve if it had not been for the lamps. Sweat glistened at his forehead. He was playing games.

"I would naturally assume it was a mistake," Shenq said. "I saw both on the way in."

The wailing stopped suddenly in the sanctuary and all Shenq could hear were whispers as if something slithered along the ground towards them.

"How foolish to bring a *Shasu*," Pi-Bak-Amana continued. "And now I must watch him pray. One wonders how such a man wormed his way to the Pharaoh's inner sanctum when his territory is so far north."

"I've always considered his territory widespread, my lord."

Pi-Bak-Amana shuddered as if a coil of air had suddenly settled on his shoulders. The broad collar clanked as he moved, arms curled around his stomach. "Does Pharaoh allow such heresy so close to his person?"

"Pharaoh received *you*, my lord."

"My skin is much tougher than that, Commander." Pi-Bak-Amana took a slip of paper from an attendant and gave it a cursory glance. "You look at me as if I'm an ox on display, a freak."

"Then I promise not to count your teeth."

"This is no game! Soon you will be cursing the very womb you came from. And come midnight, your sweet little wife will be a widow. Come morning, the Pharaoh and his household will be a chorus of wails."

"This is good to know. What else?"

"The wounded warrior you brought in is very sick. There are snakes in his belly the size of a man's finger. And his arm? The wound has putrefied. The doctor may need a saw."

"Is this just one of your pranks to disarm me?" Shenq swung the box a little wider now.

"You are already disarmed, Commander. Dangerously so, by the look of it. What *is* that?" Pi-Bak-Amana said, pointing at the parcel.

"If you are who you say you are, then you know what it is."

"The Box of Heka. Give it to me."

Shenq felt like he was in a dungeon, airless, suffocating. He was captivated by the priest's broad collar, especially the moon at its center. It was too thick for an arrow to penetrate but a whirling throw-stick would cut a wider swathe, slamming the stumpy priest in the temple. He would be killed cleanly, stone dead on the floor.

Pi-Bak-Amana hopped down from his throne and it was then Shenq saw the deformity. He was a roundback, no more than six spans tall. He held out a hand to snatch the box but Shenq held it high.

"A token, my lord, for the box."

"Very well, then. Take the rearing cobra on the altar. Pure gold, my friend and very heavy."

Shenq stalked towards the altar without turning his back on the High Priest. He ran a finger across the great marble slab and took up the token. It was heavy. At least the priest hadn't lied about that.

"You are a hunted race," Pi-Bak-Amana said. "*Hunted* because you can't run far enough. How fast can you run, Commander?"

"Fast, so my captain says." Shenq put the cobra down, eyes never leaving the High Priest's face.

"Perhaps you would rather die than see my magic."

"Shall we toss for it?"

Pi-Bak-Amana snarled and bared his teeth. "You're not as clever as you think you are."

"Still it makes me cleverer than you."

The High Priest snapped two fat fingers on his apelike arms. "It's time to meet my beloved children, Commander. Come and see Apepi's brood."

"As much as I appreciate the tour, my lord, I have a race to run."

"Run? Oh yes, you'll be running alright." Pi-Bak-Amana raised a finger to the roof. "They're everywhere, Commander. They can smell your fear and taste your blood. Even now."

A vast ceiling spread out above them, a weave of dead trees and leaves, and red and black streamers looped from the architraves, trembling in a puff of wind. A gold star the size of a temple door hung behind the altar, edges sharper than spears. It was tied by a single braid of rope to a metal rod and creaked now and then in the wind.

Shenq started when he saw a priest standing beside a pillar, pale and stiff, and staring beneath heavy-lidded eyes.

"He *was* the serpent master," Pi-Bak-Amana said, looking in the direction of Shenq's gaze. "Sadly, he didn't deliver on his promise. I would have given him sanctuary if he hadn't brought me a stack of fish tales. He had a voice once, a singing voice. He certainly hit the high notes when they bit him."

Shenq walked towards the priest, sensing his warriors close behind. *Dead men don't stand.* Only this one did, straight as a nail. "He's maimed," said Shenq, sidling a little closer.

"*Crushed*, Commander, and filled with poison. I saw . . ."

"You saw what?"

"I saw what took him. Teeth as large as falcon's claws and twice as sharp. We gave him a draught of joyroot to ease the pain."

"Thutiy," Shenq muttered, looking at the priest. He

transferred the box to his left hand and flexed his right. "What brings you to the temple of Farafra. Don't tell me. More gold? Looks like your pockets are empty."

Thutiy moved then, eyes flicking around the room. "He attacked me . . . ," he whispered, voice hoarse. "The serpent . . . he attacked me."

"I knew a priest once with a sour voice," Shenq said, "and we all know how that ended. Tell me, who is this serpent?"

"Apepi. I brought him the scrolls. They were sacred so Pharaoh said." He tried to take a wheezing breath as blood trickled from the corner of his mouth. "There are no priests, Commander. Only him. He lies—"

Thutiy wheezed as the High Priest's knife went in, hurled from a strong arm. He scratched at his throat to retrieve it before he fell to his knees, landing breathless at Shenq's feet.

"He sold me for a promise, Commander," Pi-Bak-Amana said. "The sacred scrolls . . . well you heard him. What was in them would have delighted a throng of drunkards and a few small children. Not me. And not the gods. Thutiy was an ugly freak of a man. I should never have done business with him."

Shenq could have sworn he saw starry vapors pouring from the High Priest's mouth and he heard the same dry whispers all around. There was a dead cat beneath at the foot of the column, entrails oozing from its stomach. He would have ignored such a trivial sight had the animal not died in a grimace of agony. It reminded him of Meru-Itseni. It reminded him of Jabari.

Left like a pile of filthy rags beside the road and now they're buzzing with flies.

"Give me the box," the priest said, leaping on a nearby plinth so he was eye-level with Shenq.

Shenq unlaced the rabbit skin lashings and the goatskin case fell to the floor. He hugged the box to his chest, one hand resting on the lid.

"Don't open it!" Pi-Bak-Amana shrieked, holding out a hand. "It will be a very long night if you do."

"There's magic in it, so they say. But then of course, you knew that."

The whispers were louder now, coming from a lateral aisle that ran beneath the peristyle roof. *Whispers, dry-rattling whispers.* All Shenq could see were vague shadows and lights floating in the dark. His shoulders hunched like a stalking panther and his body was rigid. He realized his men were staring at him with wide eyes, waiting for him to tell them what to do.

The box skidded across the slabs when he threw it, turning a full circle before it stopped altogether. A trail of blue vapors poured from the lid, curling and twisting in the air.

Shenq unsheathed his sword, glancing at Ayize by his side, knife in hand. The floor began to move, a scintillation of greens and blues, and from the roof came the red and black streamers, streaking down the pillars. Thick scaly bodies, heads raised and hoods glimmering in the lamp light. There was no sound as one lunged forward, fangs digging into flesh and bone and it was Tehute's scream that echoed against the walls.

Shenq raised his sword, hacking at coil and muscle, and yelling all the while. He fought until his legs were caked in blood to the knee and sweat ran down his cheeks like hot tears. The High Priest cackled, a high brittle sound that seeped into his bones.

I'll take your arm off in a heartbeat, Shenq thought. *And then your head. I'm well oiled now.*

No sooner had they dispatched the snakes, a war horn sounded and a hush came over the hall. Shenq checked his men, seeing Tehute had suffered a gash to the leg. He shivered at the sudden chill and the first scud of rain. Droplets teemed through the open roof, filling the pool beneath and clearing the air.

A screech came from the rafters, a shadow no bigger

than a man's hand silhouetted before the silvery moon. On and on it came in a sharp-beaked dive, straight as an arrow into the High Priest's head. The shriek was like a girl who had pricked her finger on a spindle and Pi-Bak-Amana topped to the floor, head smacking against stone. Only it wasn't the dwarf that lay there but the sorceress with the thick gold collar.

Shenq unsheathed his sword and padded through blood and shards of snakeskin. He knew it was Hemet-ka by her turquoise sash and the long black hair. When her lips moved, he held his breath.

Kill one and you kill them all.

He lifted his sword, bright and wicked in the lamplight, and brought it down across her neck. Death was the sweetest release she could hope for. She lay with her arm outstretched, finger pointing at the pool and there on the surface, rippling like a silver fish, was the reflection of a man with red-painted braids.

"Najja!" Ayize shouted.

"It's a trick," Shenq said, gripping the boy with a strong arm.

He looked up. There was no sign of Najja in the sky, only a thunderhead of cloud that hung over the temple with a sputter of lightning in its belly.

"I'm over here," said a voice.

And there, standing before the altar and silhouetted by the great star, was the Bloodman, bow pointed at the floor, arrow nocked at the ready.

"He's not real," whispered Harran.

"He's real alright," muttered Shenq, seeing a hint of fear in those dark-slitted eyes. He re-sheathed his khopesh and unslung his bow, slipping an arrow from his quiver. "Take cover. And take Tehute with you."

Tehute was limping and muttering, eyes bigger than walnuts. Harran took him to the nearest pillar and pressed him to the ground with a firm hand.

"Brother!" Najja shouted, smiling at Ayize. His chin

was painted red, throat wrapped in beads. "Come. Fight with me."

Shenq saw the boy off behind a pillar and shook his head at Najja. "It's just you and me. If I win, the cobra's mine."

"You won't win," Najja said, cheeks bulging from behind a grin. He drew the bowstring back to his chin and loosed an arrow.

Shenq twisted away as the arrow clattered to the ground and, lifting his bow, he moved into range. The first arrow tore through Najja's chest and the second through his gut, and his body dissolved into a shower of red beads.

"Over here!" said a voice.

Shenq turned again and saw two Najjas now, one to the left of him, one to the right. He darted behind a pillar, arrows passing within a foot of him and hissing like the words through an old man's teeth. He returned them arrow-for-arrow and the warriors split again into a cloud of dazzling shards. Only this time six warriors formed a ring around Shenq, bows raised and primed to kill. All he could do was stare through a veil of sparks, wondering if filling the warriors with arrows was making them breed.

It was then he heard the music, if indeed it was music at all. Harran was standing before the great doors, tapping his feet. His body began to sway and then he turned slowly at first, spinning faster and faster. The prayers were louder now; strong words, powerful words, and his hands were outstretched as if an unseen energy came from each finger. The red warriors cowered and seemed to shrink to the size of worms, some flopping into the pool and evaporating in a hiss of steam.

Only one Najja stood alone under the great golden star, eyes filled with tears. "Don't kill me," he said. "Please . . . My spirit has nowhere to go."

Shenq felt no pity for the stargazer whether he was real or not. And he felt no pity for Ayize's sobs. He was about to rush on Najja with the last of his breath when he heard a groan like the toppling of a metal cauldron. Looking up, he saw the star swinging from a frayed rope, strands snapping as they unraveled. The great sheet of gold slid downward and the longest point impaled Najja through the back, ripping through his belly and entrails spilling to the floor like a rush of oily snakes.

Harran's shout brought Shenq back to the present and he dropped his bow when he saw Tehute's milk-white face, blood bubbling from his lips. He crouched by his side, holding the wiry frame he loved so well. There was a time when he knew what to say only this time his throat was choked with grief. All he could do was listen to the thin gravelly voice and remember all that he said.

"Run them down," Tehute sputtered, lungs filling with blood. "Let them dread you now."

MKASA

Are all Imazi women so curious? Mkasa thought, gripping the axe haft between his teeth.

Fumbling his way up the shaft, he could see the mouth at least ten feet above him and when he looked down he could see hard packed dirt and cinders, and he could taste them in his mouth. He was betting he could reach the top in a stretch or two.

Move! he kept telling himself, feet and hands searching the rugged walls for grooves. Just above his head where the soot had faded, he saw a series of thin gashes likely pierced by the blade of an axe. He was thankful for soft rock, thankful for an axe.

His nails were grimy and torn, and his throat was so dry he could hardly speak. The girl was down there somewhere with a knife in her hand. If she was anything like that bully Saqr, she wouldn't miss.

"Ah, there you are," shouted a voice.

It's her . . . that half-blooded wench with the sorry eyes. He looked down and there she was, climbing slowly, grinning as if she enjoyed the suspense.

"Such a handsome one," she said. "And here we are climbing rocks when we could be hanging by our bellies like two sparrows."

Mkasa had no idea what she meant and he didn't like the sound of it. He backed up the shaft with short nasal breaths, seeing a series of grooves above him, the kind climbers use. Easing the axe from his mouth with one hand, he slammed the blade into the widest gap he could find. The haft cracked almost as far as the grip and he winced as he held on.

"Makurae!" she yelled. "Wait."

Part of him wondered if he was losing his mind. But there she was, eyes filled with a primitive rage too evil to have been hidden since he last saw her. The knife glimmered in her belt and in that moment she slipped it free. It was pointed downwards as if she would change her mind and give him a second chance. Or would she just change the grip in mid-air just as he had seen Saqr do?

She moved closer, slowly now, and he felt that uncontrollable tremor in his legs, the urge to scramble up the funnel to the blue outside.

Now! he thought, gripping onto the wooden haft, praying it would hold. He had an instinctive pace of his own and looking down, he could see she was several feet below, slipping, sliding, not moving as fast as he was. It gave him the drive he needed. He could climb a sheer rock and grip it with both hands, climbing higher than anyone he knew.

"Wait!" she shouted again.

Mkasa kept moving, pausing only to check where she was. Closer, much closer than he'd hoped and he could feel her eyes burning into his feet. *Girls like her mate and kill. And nobody's eating me*, he thought.

The funnel had begun to taper the closer he got to the top. *Better be wide enough*, he thought, breathing harder now. Over his gasps he heard her calling and he felt warm breath on his heel.

"Please . . ." she whimpered, looking up through wide yes, weighing her chances.

There are no second chances, he thought as he felt the claw-like hand around his ankle. And then . . .

"Take me with you," she said. "I can help you."

Looking down he felt a moment of uncertainty. But only a moment. "You can't help me woman, any more than I can help you."

"I can smell them out in the desert long before you can see them. If I wanted to kill you, I would have yanked you down amongst the cinders by now. Please. Its freedom I want. Not love."

There was truth in her voice. She was holding his foot after all. Mkasa didn't know whether he should feel insulted or relieved. He just stared at a pair of blue eyes and a mouth twisted in fear.

"Cinders or stars?" she asked.

"Stars," he said, nodding.

Mkasa pulled on the axe, legs suddenly swinging in mid-air when he heard the crack. The gash in the wooden haft nearly split in two hanging there like a heron's open beak. He was dangerously close to panic even though the bone-girl was only two feet below him.

"Quickly," she urged. "They're down there. I can hear them."

Twelve feet below him he could see flickering torchlight and pushing his back against the opposite wall, he wedged his feet in a shallow groove.

There. Safe. Jammed like a cork.

Catching his breath, he tried to pull the axe free only it wouldn't budge. He tried again but it was stuck fast. He thought he could get around it at a squeeze but he knew there wasn't enough room and pulling down with all his weight he heard the snap.

"S'haila!" a voice shouted. "Bring him down!"

The girl responded in an ancient tongue, wheedling, laughing and playing the lover's game. But the bonelord would have none of it and nocked an arrow in his bow. Mkasa heard the girl scream and he knew there would be more if he wasn't quick enough. The arrow pierced the skin through the side of her calf, hanging there like a tanner's stitch.

"Take my hand," he muttered, reaching for her. Those sallow fingers were warmer than he imagined and he pulled her up, feeling her legs around his waist.

"Get me out, please," she begged again, eyes meeting his.

If he had enough time, he would have broken the

arrow from her leg and ripped his shúkà into strips to stop the bleeding. But he looked down and saw the bonelord kneeling amongst the cinders with a drawn bow, string pulled back to his cheek.

"Climb," he hissed behind gritted teeth. "Now!"

A second arrow glanced off the wall just as the girl scurried to her freedom and a third caught in a groove beside him, teetering as if it would clatter to the ground. Mkasa snatched it before it fell, knowing the bonelord did not have enough space in the fire pit for a full draw. Instead, he saw the white warrior scale the first three feet, legs faster than a spider. It wasn't long before he was hanging only a finger's width below, gripping to each rut and groove.

Mkasa jammed his butt into a shallow sill, hands gripping the broken axe. He slammed one foot into the bonelord's throat and plunged the arrow into his eye. He heard the scream and the snap of bone and when he kicked again, the warrior fell owl-eyed and screaming. He lay skewed and bent in a bed of cinders and that's when Mkasa saw another set of hands dragging the man out by his feet.

"I need more time," he murmured, looking down the funnel to the fire pit.

There is no more time!

Using the broken axe head as leverage, he scrambled up the narrow funnel, not caring if he ripped the skin off his back. When he tumbled over the lip, he lay breathless in the sand, gazing at a star-filled sky. His muscles were tight as he struggled to a crouch and there was a buzzing in his ears that wouldn't go away.

The girl was a few feet off with a broken arrow in her hand. How she had taken it out of her leg he would never know, but there was a foul-smelling paste over the wound and tears of pain in her eyes.

"Can you walk?" he asked.

"I can run," she said, nodding.

They staggered down the slope through boulders and scree, reaching a layer of white sand before surveying the funnel behind him. There were shadows up there, plenty of them. But nothing moved.

They continued to run for the next few hours, alternating between a jog and a walk, mouths dry from thirst. Mkasa knew they could go a long time in the desert but not without water, and he kept a sharp eye out for a well. S'haila's leg was bleeding fast now, dripping all over a carpet of white sand.

"I can smell them," she said. "To the north."

And then he saw them in the distance, three parties of twelve men clad in bone and plate with the glint of silver everywhere. He could almost tell Tarabin from the rest, antlers pressed against the sides of his head, merging with a ragged herd of oryx.

Thirty-six good men and a bonelord . . . we'll see about that.

He pulled S'haila down behind a white standing stone with a jagged head. "What were they hunting? Oryx? Us?"

"We're shadows to them," she said. "They're too busy with that carcass to care about us."

Field dressings, yes, that's what they were doing. Taking the innards out of an oryx.

"Praise HaShem they can't see us," Mkasa said aloud, crouching, panting.

"No, but they can smell us." And then S'haila moaned.

Blood . . . , he could smell it on her skin and he would need to dress that wound. Ripping his shúkà at the knee, he made a bandage, praying for water, praying for honey. A smear of it would keep it clean.

"Rest," he said gently, studying cheeks sallow in the dawn and eyes of the brightest blue.

There were tendrils of yellow on the eastern horizon and he wondered how long it would be before sunrise. The Imazi needed to get their kill below ground or risk their skins turning into bloody pustules.

He was ill at ease hiding behind that tall white rock

even though they were out of range. It looked like a rooster's head from where he sat and it was the only one high enough to hide behind. There were fox snares he couldn't see on the run and holes large enough for a man's foot. If he wasn't careful, he would be full of arrows before the night was out.

Move, he kept saying to himself. Only he hadn't slept well in two days and the thought of trekking the desert without water made his belly churn. His muscles began to relax and then his eyes flickered in sleep. He felt his head rock sideways onto a warm shoulder and that's the last thing he remembered.

Thud!

The sound woke Mkasa and he flinched, eyes narrowing against the blinding sun. How long had he been asleep? Hours?

Thud! Thud! Thud! A hail of arrows pegged in the dirt around him like a row of prison bars.

"Makurae?" the voice was hoarse and familiar all the same. All he could see was the silhouette of a man he never thought he would be so pleased to see.

"Kanja . . ." He almost choked when he saw a pendant of flies dangling from an Alodian neck and a coil of Tunguli bracelets around his arms.

"S'haila . . ." Mkasa murmured, looking for her. "The girl . . ."

"Give him root and water," Kanja said, pulling Mkasa to his feet. "He's exhausted."

Mkasa remembered little else until he woke again to the sound of a high-pitched whistle. It was a warning call, a single note. Just like the ones Commander Shenq used to give. This time he was belted to his horse, delighting in the scent of the coarse black mane. He saw Kanja ahead of him and the dim outline of Othene beside him, head cocked to one side and giving a hearty smile.

"Brother," Othene whispered. "Can you hear me?"

Mkasa nodded, narrowing his eyes at a bright sun. All

he could hear was the horses' hooves tapping against pebbles and the creak of leather. He tried to speak but his throat was tight and dry. *Joyroot.*

"How long have I been asleep?" Mkasa asked.

"A day," the sorcerer said. "We'll be setting up camp soon. There's smoke on the temple pylons."

Hopefully it was a beacon dressed with black streamers, Mkasa thought, still groggy from the drug. He looked for Ayize but there was no sign of him and he wondered if the warrior was dead like the rest of them. He tried to sort through his thoughts but his mind was a blur of images.

"Ayize . . ."

Kanja hung his head. "The *shakāl* got him. They dragged his sorry carcass out in the desert and skinned him."

Mkasa felt his heart try to beat faster and if he wasn't so sleepy he would have mourned. Instead, he hunched over and vomited.

Only two left. I can fight two, surely.

"There's no more wine," Kanja shouted. "We need wine."

"We'll get some from the temple, Mongaka," Othene said. "There's a swallow in my pack."

Mkasa could smell the smoke when they pulled him from his horse and he could see the curling flames through the palm fronds. The pylon gates were open and a handful of guards stood outside the guardhouse, eyes scanning the avenue of rams and the desert beyond.

"Where's Najja?" Kanja snapped, eyes narrowing at the beacon. "He said he'd meet us here."

"Those are Hawk ribbons, Mongaka," Othene said, pointing. "They got here first."

Mkasa felt his heart flutter only his belly growled more. They set up camp behind a sandy hummock bordered by trees and shrubs. Rusty brown vultures hissed and growled in the sky, making steep spirals and swooping behind the trees.

"We'll stay here and wait for the Hawks," Kanja said, patting his mare on the neck.

"How do you know they haven't already left?" Mkasa said, gawking at Kanja's mare. *She was dead, wasn't she?*

"Just a hunch. Better sharpen these arrows, brother," Kanja said, offering a full quiver. "You'll need them in a few hours."

Mkasa heard the swallow in his throat and he knew Kanja heard it too. He was more afraid than he had ever been in his life. What magic was it that brought a dead mare back to life? And where was Jabari? Weren't those his ornaments wrapped around Kanja's throat?

"Did it ever occur to you that Tungul is full of beggars?" Kanja said, eyes searching Mkasa's face. "They're no better than spiders and we stamp on the worst of those. Fail me, brother, and I'll have that little *Shasu* girl myself."

Mkasa let out a deep breath as Kanja stalked towards the trees. He stood with Othene, gazing at the pylon gates, fingers pointing, heads nodding. Mkasa knew it was his time to kill and he had never missed a shot yet. If he missed Shenq, Kanja would kill him. And if he didn't, he would be Nomarch of the North with a child bride.

You don't need another man's wife. Think, fool. Think! It was then he mourned Iutha, longed for her. He would make it up to her if he lived.

Slinging the quiver over his shoulder, he nestled in amongst the horses. It was cool in the shade and they were well hidden in their sandy nook. *If only I had a bow,* he thought, counting the cast in his head. Kanja was well within range even for a knife if only there was such a thing in his belt. They had seen to that too.

Vultures watch. Vultures wait. And while they wait, they take what they can.

Mkasa cursed Shenq and longed for him in the quiet times. If only he was there to tell him what to do. He sensed a wave of nausea and a rising sob in his throat, and he felt the mare nudge his shoulder, suddenly glad of her warm oaty breath.

"We could run away, you and me." Mkasa gazed at those big brown eyes and the small dished face. The mare gave a snort and threw up her head as if the idea was absurd. He would get only an arrow in his back, several, in fact.

He glanced over at Kanja crouching in the dirt and stirred the dying ashes of an old fire. If he wasn't mistaken the sorcerer was in a trance, eyes rolling into the back of his head.

Wine tastes better with a little joyroot, so the sorcerer said. *Give a man a handful and he won't live to taste it at all.*

Mkasa inched his way towards Othene's horse with an outstretched hand. The animal barely noticed him, eyes half closed in sleep. He searched for that small leather pouch amongst the packs, squeezing a half-empty wineskin with a white feather tied to its neck.

The sorcerer is in the place of dreams, fool. He'll see you.

Mkasa looked beyond the horse to the sorcerer with his low pitched wails. He looked like a pasty-faced crone with stick-thin arms raised high over his head. No one was allowed to move when the sorcerer was dreaming. No one was allowed to speak when his mind was searching.

Yet Kanja told me to sharpen arrows. So that's what I'll do.

It wasn't until he ran a finger between the animal's belly and girth that he found it, a pouch tied with leather thongs and filled with a black powder. Taking the stopper from the wine skin, he poured a fistful of the root into the nozzle and shook the skin vigorously, taking care to put each back where he found them.

It was the only wine skin left.

He turned to watch the sands where vultures fed on horse dung, some fighting over a cat-snake, and he never heard the movement behind him, only the rough hand on his shoulder.

"You're wasting time," Kanja said, tapping the quiver

on Mkasa's shoulder. "I thought I told you to sharpen these?"

Mkasa swallowed and rubbed his brow. "I was—"

"Stealing," Kanja said, lip curling over his teeth. "You took something. What was it?"

"I . . . I was looking for water."

"Liar! You tried to take the token." Kanja fumbled through his pack and found the Farafra statue exactly where he left it. He seemed to frown good and long before speaking. "Follow me."

Mkasa followed Kanja to a small clearing where fallen branches made for a good bench and a pile of cinders barely glowed. The sound of the whetstone nearly sent him off to sleep and Kanja tapped him on the shoulder twice to keep him awake.

The afternoon turned to evening and still there was no sign of Shenq. But they kept the cinders warm until Othene brought pesen bread and goat's cheese, and four skinned rabbits on skewers. The sorcerer shoved the meat in the cinders and turned them now and then so as not to wake the flame. It was getting dark and the guards would spot them from the temple gate, especially those lighting the torches along the avenue. Bull-Warriors they were, half-bald with silver heads and a shock of greasy black hair.

When they had finished eating, Kanja motioned to Othene, placing him on the opposite side of the route. He kicked sand over the coals, watching the front gate. It wasn't long before Mkasa heard creaking hinges and the crunch of horses' hooves.

"Stay close," Kanja whispered, handing him his bow. He led Mkasa to a brazier nestled between the paws of a recumbent ram. "See those merchants? I think you know who they really are. So when I tell you to aim, send a flaming arrow at their leader."

Mkasa nodded and gripped the bow. It was Alodian forged, made from the tusks of water buffalo and fish bladder, and heavier than the one he was used to. He notched an arrow and waited, studying a man with long black hair, horse prancing in a sideways gait. There were two small boys running along beside, one had a club foot and a staff to lean on and the other patted Shenq's leg with a smile.

He's already lost three men, Mkasa thought as he saw several horses devoid of their riders. Jabari, Meru-Itseni, Tehute . . . And a new rider to their ranks. A young boy with red braids.

Ayize?

Mkasa felt the hammering in his chest and he was conscious of a sharp intake of breath. Out of the corner of his eye, he saw Othene a stone's hurl away, bow drawn and aimed right at him. Whatever plan Mkasa had of turning his bow on Kanja was wiped clean from his mind and the need to survive took over.

He glanced up at the snapping ensign on the temple wall. *Wind's away from us,* he thought, almost sighing with relief. Shenq had a sharp sniffer under that brown headdress. He was bound to smell something.

Mkasa tried to think of everything he knew about the Commander, just like any other enemy. How he would fall after the arrow struck, whether he would shriek and scuttle beneath the horse, or fight until his body was pinned to the ground with arrows.

"Aim," Kanja whispered.

Mkasa dipped the arrowhead into the nearest flame and angling his shoulder towards his target, he pulled the bowstring back. *I must take the shot,* he thought, sensing a sudden lull in the wind. He trusted those yellow eyes would sense him first because Shenq's instincts were sharper than his.

So he held the bow steady and waited for Kanja's voice.

SHENQ

There was a solemn mood in the air that made Shenq jumpy. There were no crowds, only a company of Bull-Warriors roasting nuts in a brazier. None of them knew their master was headless in a pool of blood. None of them knew what he really was.

A boy and his crippled brother limped alongside, asking questions and touching the horse. "Do all horses have a whinny in them," one asked.

"All of them," Shenq said, nodding. "And some have a smile."

"Like him," the boy said, laughing at Marees' drawn lips.

Shenq threw both boys a kite of silver and Harran blessed them as he passed by. The stallion was restless, sometimes bobbing his head, sometimes shaking it. Between the recumbent stone rams more braziers smoked and crackled, flames reaching higher than a man's arm.

"It stinks," Menkheperre said, flapping a hand in front of his nose.

"Keep your eyes on the path," Shenq said, seeing vultures in the night sky.

The stench reminded him of a cow he once found on the banks of the river Nile, innards half-eaten by crocodiles and maggots. But he knew it wasn't a carcass. It was the refuse pile behind the eastern gate.

"My butt's sore," Menkheperre moaned. "Why's my butt sore?"

"I'll make it sore," Shenq said, irritated at the boy's moaning. No bottom should have been sore. They had only mounted up a moment ago.

He twisted in his saddle and looked back at the boys.

They were talking now, whispering and laughing. They were the same age, same height, same build, and there was a camaraderie Shenq admired.

He turned back and watched the stallion's nostrils flare as wide as they could go, ears tilted towards movement. There was something out there, hiding amongst the trees. And they were closing in like a pack of silk-coated jackals.

He placed a hand behind his back, drumming the air to warn his team and just as he was thinking how hot it was, an arrow slipped between the leaves, streaking towards them on a steady path. And then a second and a third, only this time they were tipped with fire.

"Drop!" Shenq shouted, grabbing his bow.

Each warrior lay parallel along the horse's flanks, gripping girth and breast straps as they galloped for cover. Arrows hummed overhead, cracking against branches and pegging into the earth. There were so many of them, Shenq lost count until the grass began to burn and flames shot up the tree trunks, spreading to the end of each limb.

He growled in pain and dropped his bow. The arrow had gone in all right, snapping off when he jumped from his horse. It was as near as out by the time he found it, arrowhead peeking like a splinter from his upper arm. He gripped the arrowhead and yanked it free. The scream when it came was no louder than a growl and he praised HaShem for the linen coat and the archer's lack of skill.

It could have been my leg, he thought, thankful he could run.

The air became thick with flame and smoke, branches falling to the ground in a cascade of sparks. Everywhere the sound of squeals and snorts, and thundering hooves as the horses fled. Shenq wrapped the fringes of his shaal over his nose and stared through the haze. He could just make out Harran, robes hitched to his knees and hurdling over a burning log with Menkheperre and Ayize at his side. But there was no sign of Khemwese.

Shenq's throat began to burn and there was a searing

pain in his lungs. He tasted bitter bile in his throat and retched.

Run!

There was no air to breathe, only thick churning smoke and Shenq staggered between the trees to a clearing where the wind had driven the smoke towards the temple. Palm fronds began to smolder and there were scattered sparks in the grass, and he took three deep breaths to clear his head. Estimating the temple to his left and the village to his right, all he could see was a dark figure some twenty feet away, darting between the braziers and the village wall. Long red braids gave him away and Shenq realized the warrior was as good as unarmed with both hands over his mouth.

He nocked an arrow, tracking his target through a light gray haze. *Kanja,* he thought, seeing a weave of light and shadow. It could be a sorcerer's trick. If he struck the warrior in the heart would he not split into a thousand shards?

Something struck him on the back of his head, bringing him to his knees. And then a blur of shadows.

When he opened his eyes he saw eight lamps burning hungrily, casting a ruddy glow over a small room. A girl leaned over him, wet rag in hand and black hair tied in a strip of linen. She had eyes the color of the sky.

"You nearly killed him," she whispered, sniffing the air. "I couldn't let you kill him."

"Who," Shenq mouthed.

"My Makurae."

"Makurae?" he croaked, before easing to one side and coughing up a ball of black soot. He felt the pain on the back of his head then and winced. "What did you hit me with, girl?"

"A branch," she said flatly.

Shenq groaned and felt the lump on his crown. "How long have I been here?"

"Two days," she said, folding a pile of fresh linens. The

bone collar clattered as she moved and so did the bracelets on her arms. "I turned you every hour in the night so you wouldn't die. You could have, you know."

Shenq did know. He had kept many a man alive the same way. "Who are you?"

"S'haila, half-blood of the Imazi, outcast, orphan. Though some say I have royal blood."

"That's what they all say."

"That's what my mother said. Before she died."

Shenq looked around, seeing a cozy house with a blackened hearth. "Where am I?"

"In a vintner's cottage on the east side," she said, sniffing again. "He went out picking this morning and left you some breakfast. Couldn't find your packhorses but your stallion followed you in. At least I think he's yours. Yellow with a black stripe down his back and a nasty bite. I tried to run him off, only he just stood there and grinned."

Shenq coughed up a second ball of phlegm with a hacking laugh. "His name's Marees and he likes girls."

S'haila frowned. "Every last man helped put out the fire. They caught the worst of it. They found Hemet-Ka in pieces and no one's seen the High Priest. There's death for the man that did it. Oh, and I cleaned your sword."

Shenq was glad she had. He already felt like the losing side.

"There are bones behind the rams and a twist of robes. A wine merchant's boy, they thought. Drink this," she said, holding out a bowl of broth. "Elk liver and herbs to clean the gut. Vintner filled your packs with fresh food and medicines. He wants you gone before noon."

Of course he does. Shenq sat up and took a sip. "Where are my men?"

"Vintner says the Bloods went south this morning. Merchants too." She sighed heavily and stared at the floor. "He never saw any Hawks."

"How many Bloods?

"Three Bloods, three merchants."

Shenq had lost his men and he had lost the boy, and all he could do now was study the girl with the death-white skin and a necklace of bones. One leg was bandaged below the knee but apart from that she was fit. "How did you come here?"

"Tarabin caught a Blood in Mara'av. Like a greasy eel he was all fidgety and longing for the stars. I thought he was beautiful."

"So you saved his life?"

"He saved mine." She studied Shenq with a slow smile, skin flushing. "And now I've seen a Hawk up close. I wonder which I prefer."

The thought was a disquieting one and Shenq swung his legs over the pallet and sat up. His mind was a fog of disappointment and he moaned. "I must ride," he said, coughing again. "I must find my men."

"I won't go back. I'll never go back."

"Nobody said anything about going back. You're safe here."

"No one's safe here, especially not a half-blood. They'll toss me out like filthy rags. I'm going to Thebes." The girl gave him a sideways look. "And you're taking me with you."

Shenq wasn't so sure. She didn't look like she could hold a spear. And what was all that sniffing? It reminded him of bush swine with their long tusks and runny noses.

"I'm good with a knife and I'm good with a spear," she said. "I can smell men a mile away. And I can tell you their number."

"And you can read minds."

"That too."

He took a final swig of broth and handed her the bowl. His tongue was numb and it hurt to breathe. And he prayed he was strong enough to ride.

"I washed you," she murmured.

Shenq stood up in that small room and saw the glint in her eye. He was naked and his skin was itchy clean. "I'll have none of that, girl. Do you hear?"

S'haila giggled and handed him a *shenti* from the pile. "I washed your hair and combed it. Thick as a horse's tail and shiny too."

Shenq ignored her and dressed as fast as he could. His belt was freshly oiled and his weapons whetted to a shine. The bow hung from a peg by the door and there were three full quivers hooked to his saddle. When he went outside to a small courtyard, the stallion rolled back his lips in greeting and nuzzled his hand. The sun nearly scorched his eyes and he squinted at the desert beneath a flat hand.

"Girl, the desert is no place for a woman," he said, swinging his leg over the horse's back and looking down from the saddle. "There's *shakāl* and Imazi . . . Let me send for you when the race is over."

She was quiet then. It came of having a lump in one's throat, Shenq supposed, or it came from knowing he was lying. She wouldn't survive a day in the hot sun with that pale skin of hers.

"I would survive," she said. "My skin's not as white as the others. I can stay out for hours without burning."

Shenq didn't want to wait and see. He thanked her and wheeled his horse to the east, galloping on a straight path towards the temple. The pylons were a smear of ashes and the trees hung like skeletons over the avenue as if winter had already come.

Kanja will think I'm dead, he thought, dismounting.

He studied a sea of bodies, Bull-Warriors and horses, and a club foot that peeked from under a log. It was charred and still warm from the fire. He prayed for the mother of the child and he prayed for the Imazi girl.

I pray for peace wherever she goes and a husband to keep her warm.

There was no sign of his men there and he sighed with relief as he mounted his horse. It was hot, devilishly so, and his chest was already a smear of sweat by the time he reached the river. He could hear the trickling current beyond the pier and the sharp screech of a bird. The bony limbs of old sycamores spread wide along the bank and the birds were thickest there, twittering to one another in their high-pitched chatter.

Vintner says the Bloods went south this morning. Merchants too.

Shenq heard the girl's voice in his thoughts. They numbered *six*. Perhaps Kanja had three prisoners?

Shenq tracked the sandy turf, studying the pockmarks of horses' hooves until he heard a shout. He could barely see a small figure behind him, riding through the gray mist.

"Kemnebi!"

Shenq waited until he could see the figure clearly and then he groaned. It was the Imazi girl, swathed in animal bones and riding a donkey.

"You left this," she said, panting. "I thought you might need it."

He tried to speak and found no words. Twice she had saved his skin and twice he had shown little more than impatient disdain. It was the gold cobra, the Suhaj token.

"There is no greater joy in this world than having a riding companion," Shenq said. He realized she wasn't as scrawny as he first thought, arms corded with muscle and back straighter than a poker. "If you mean to follow me then you'd better get on with it," he said, chuckling.

"Vintner's says the donkey's good and strong," S'haila said, throwing the leading rope to Shenq. "There's wine in the skins and figs to move the bowels."

Shenq caught the rope and tied it to the saddle, wheeling his horse around. "Watch for tracks," he said pointing to the ground.

"You Thebans are hardened warriors," she said. "More disciplined than the bloods. That's why Pharaoh chose you. You're the man he wants in front of his armies and I can see why."

"There was a captain I once knew," Shenq said, sensing a wave of sorrow. He hardly knew why he wanted to talk. But he did. "He taught me to forage and hunt when I was a boy and he taught me to throw a knife. He cared for the boys like a father would. I was afraid of pigs once so he made me sleep in the sties at night. After all that grunting and rumbling, I wasn't afraid of them in the morning. I was eight by the time I killed a fox and nine by the time I killed an oryx."

"How old were you when you killed a man?"

"Ten. It was a sand-warrior. I never looked back after that."

The road from the temple was hot and bright, crowds gathering for the markets, some waving at Shenq and some staring goggle eyed at the girl with the pale blue eyes. When they emerged at the south gates of the city, a division of Bull-Warriors marched north with fifty head of cattle. They parted ranks as Shenq rode through, eyeing him with curiosity.

"Tithes for the temple," Shenq muttered, catching the girl's wide-eyed stare. *A waste since the High Priest is dead.*

"You should never ride north again," she whispered, urging the donkey closer to the horse. "They'll kill you if you do."

Shenq knew killing a priest was high treason, only it was the bird that killed him first. There were black arrows littered about in the sanctuary and he would certainly pay for those. "Mouths are quick to blame, especially when threatened."

"This mouth is silent," she said, tapping her lips.

She seemed to stare at the river, at the boats and the palm trees. And sometimes she stared at the women, carrying babies and baskets of herbs. When a bird screeched she flinched, eyes trailing it across the sky, body trembling with every new sight.

"Keep your eyes on the road, girl, and tell me what you see," Shenq said, smelling fish and onions.

"Food," she said, looking down at a watchman's fire. "Men always think of *food.*"

Shenq saw her grinning up at him and he kept his eyes

forward, studying the shimmering waters of the river in the early morning sun. A fishing boat struggled against the current, oars lashing the waves into a foam, and a flock of bitterns rose from a sandy headland as the boat slipped past.

"Horses," S'haila said, eyes drawn to a pile of droppings and a few potholes in the sand. "They're bold to stick to the open road."

"They think I'm dead, that's what it is."

"No. They know you're not dead."

How the girl was so sure, Shenq would never know. He had inspected the temple grounds just as Kanja would have done and there were black steaming bodies beneath the trees.

The girl hummed and sometimes she sang, and sometimes she foretold the weather. They veered southeast to the desert and the gently rolling plains and it was well past afternoon when Shenq's nose caught a whiff of roasting fires. They dismounted and scanned the skyline for a haze of smoke, spotting a dusky trail above a stand of palm trees. It was half a mile or so in the distance and behind a moderate dune.

"Rabbit and sweat," she said, dismounting and crouching. "Horses and blood."

Her nose confirmed what Shenq's eyes could see, fish heads strewn about the sands and a coating of vomit. With the sun as hot as it was, the Bloods were likely holed up in that distant stand of trees, watching from their shadowy nook.

"Do you have good night eyes?" S'haila said, resting her cheek against the soil and sniffing loudly.

"I do. Why?"

"Because they're waiting for you."

HARRAN

Harran sat with his back to a tree, hands tied with ropes. The flogging had gone on all afternoon and the Makurae was close to unconsciousness. When they untied him from the tree, he fell in a crumpled heap. *Flogged once by his brother and twice by his enemy.* He prayed that was the end of it.

Shenq was dead, killed by a friendly arrow and burnt to a cinder. That's what Kanja had told them. There was no one to save them now.

Harran was numb at the beatings, watching Khemwese's black skin shimmering against the pale trunk of a tree. He was so tall, he took the lashings on his thighs and rump, and his face hardly flinched.

"Who are you?" Kanja yelled, over and over again.

But Khemwese never spoke. His dark eyes stared off in the distance, cheek pressed against the bark.

When they got to Menkheperre, Kanja teetered on tired feet and waved a hand. He was exhausted, it was plain to see. *And afraid,* said a voice in Harran's head. If the Pharaoh's son had one scratch on his royal behind, Kanja would never make Commander of Thebes.

Othene took Khemwese and sat him down in front of a tree. He tied his hands behind it, pressing his sore back against the gnarly bark. He left Mkasa where he fell and sauntered over to the fire.

"I'll watch the men and the horses," Othene said, taking the flail from Kanja's hand. "You sleep."

Kanja's eyes ran over Khemwese's body and he tensed. "He's Meroëvian, I can feel it."

"Kill him then."

Kanja wiped the sweat from his brow and shook his

head. "I'll wait for Mkasa to wake up. He's good at killing things."

Harran closed his ears to the chanting and he watched the leader of the Bloods, taller than he remembered and swathed in beads. There was a leather bag hitched over one shoulder—a bag he couldn't do without, and all he did was stare for hours through the palm fronds wrapped in a shawl and shivering all the same. The joyroot had taken over his body. It had surely taken over his soul.

"Their spirits are here," Othene said, smearing the red paint on Kanja's chin. "They watch you. They stand in glorious red with spears by their sides. The wind is rising. It's time."

"Massui . . . Najja . . .Yuku . . ." they both whispered, intoning the names of the dead.

Harran could hardly think over the din. It had been a slow endless trek across the dunes from Suhaj and he knew he could have died in the fire with those two little village boys. All he remembered was Khemwese's strong arm and his urging voice, and then he saw Kanja coming out of the woods shedding tears of joy over Ayize.

But they were false. And now the boy was neither Blood nor Hawk and no one could trust him. So he was tied up alongside next to Harran, eyes flicking this way and that. When the smoke leaned across the pond blowing ashes into his open mouth, he spat and cursed.

"At least we can see which way the wind's blowing," Harran encouraged.

The boy said nothing. Strapped to his tree, he was likely wondering why that nice warm fire was on the other side of the pool with a few griddle cakes cooking on a flat stone. His feet were speckled with filth and vomit. The rabbit they roasted for breakfast was barely cooked and he had retched it right back up.

Crack!

Harran heard the sound above his head and saw the stone drop only a foot from his thigh. Kanja was standing now at the water's edge, poised with a flat stone in one hand. He skimmed it across the surface and watched it leap towards them in three fast bounds. It hit the tree behind them and made him laugh.

Harran wondered why Kanja hated the boy. Why he taunted him and scared him with black magic. They didn't need to tie him up. He was too frightened to run away.

"Those are another man's honors," Ayize said at last. "Look at him, glittering in his bracelets and beads. He's no better than a thief."

"He's your brother," Harran said, watching Kanja sit back down by the fire.

The warrior tried to tug the pack from Othene's tight fist and when he did out spilled a gold statue. Even though Kanja was veiled behind a shower of sparks, Harran could see the anger on his face.

"I know what happened to Baba," Ayize said, lip curling over white teeth. "And I know who did it. See, his heart's black."

"His mind too," Harran said, nodding. "He's too fond of the vine. It will kill him before the arrows do."

Ayize looked off in the distance, eyes narrowed. "Mkasa told me about your HaShoo. He told me he's a great God."

"Ha*Shem*," Harran corrected. "And yes, He is a great God."

"Can he see me? Right now, I mean?"

"He sees you," Harran said, nodding. "He even knows what you're thinking."

"Then he knows how much I hate my brother."

Harran flinched. "Your brother is half-crazed with wine and root. How can he be himself?"

Harran followed Ayize's gaze through the rattling fronds. There was a dune to the west and his eyes followed the line of the summit. All he could see was a dark gray world and a patch of stars, and he wondered what the boy saw.

"I see ghosts every time the wind blows," Ayize murmured. "Baba, Ulan . . . all of them."

"They're only shadows. Sleep if you can," Harran said. "It'll be dawn before you know it."

The boy needed no prompting. His chin fell on his chest and he was snoring before Harran could count to three. Menkheperre sat a few feet off, running his rope up and down the tree trunk. It was no use. Harran had tried the same thing, only his became tighter each time he moved.

The pool separated the Hawks from the Bloods. Its margin was wide enough to walk around and littered with soft white sand. Mkasa crouched at its brink, sluicing himself with water. His face was a knot of agony and one eye was bruised shut. They must have punched him before they flogged him, splitting his lip and jaw. When the sorcerer and Kanja wandered off between the trees dragging a net for birds, Mkasa sauntered towards Harran with a cup in one hand.

"He's like a fighting rooster," Mkasa whispered, tipping the cup against Harran's lips. "All feathers and claws. I've heard him calling out to the gods. He won't hesitate this time."

"Why did they flog you?" Harran said, taking a few large gulps from the cup.

"They thought I had stolen something. They were wrong. Don't drink from the skin with the feather. You won't be going home if you do."

"Do they mean to kill us?"

"That net is too big for birds, brother. Either they mean to hang us from the trees and let us rot, or they're hoping to trap something else."

"Shenq?" Harran said, feeling a pulse of hope.

"My arrows went wide. I made sure of it. I pray he got out alive."

Mkasa staggered back the way he had come. Stripped of his weapons, he was almost as helpless as they were.

There was nothing the warrior could do to save them, not unless Kanja and Othene fell asleep.

A snapping of twigs made Harran's stomach roll as Kanja and Othene set that trap, spreading it on the ground between the dead palm fronds so it couldn't be seen. Kanja sprinted back into the clearing, pack bouncing against his back. He crouched next to Harran, eyes boring into his. "You can see things, can't you?"

Harran felt the light touch of long fingers on his arm. "I can?"

"I say you can if you try hard enough. Do I have your loyalty?"

"You will never have my loyalty."

"I'll give you some wine if it will change your mind."

Harran turned his face away. He would have no wine or root. It would only put him to sleep and then he'd wake up all bewildered with a swollen tongue.

"I admire leopards," Kanja whispered, "but I've never caught a black one. They say the pelt is for kings."

"If you admire the leopard then you may have discovered how he hunts," Harran said, fingers tingling in the ropes behind his back. "He's fast on his feet and he keeps to the shadows. You'll never find him."

"That's why I have you. Now close your eyes and tell me where he is."

Harran's eyes fluttered shut and he gave thanks to the great HaShem, drifting into the place of prayers. He wanted to pretend he was back in Thebes, not resting on a bed of tree roots. But it was no use pretending. Make-believe was for little boys.

He could see the desert and its tawny mantle and he could see a hawk in the pale blue sky. It seemed to circle for a time before falling to earth, beak open and streaked with blood.

"I see a hawk with a bloody beak," he said softly, smelling Kanja's breath on his cheek.

"What does it mean?"

Harran opened his eyes. "It means you had better run."

"Hold your tongue! You're always so useful with it." Kanja looked over at Khemwese and glowered. "I'll rip the tusks from the giant's ears if you lie to me."

Harran had grown to love those tusks and he wanted no bloodshed. "There's a world of difference between giants and regular men. My father knew a giant once. He was nearly two men tall. He could juggle knives and swords and cut a melon in half at the same time. He was sold to a slaver in Men-nefer, only he ran away. I say it was his mind. He was quick, you see."

Kanja gave a half smile. "The fast ones are always worth their weight in gold. Only that one's asleep."

"Not asleep," Harran insisted, clearing his throat. "Half-way between the sky and the earth, especially if he drank that wine of yours."

It was a while before Kanja spoke again and when he did he drew out his knife. It was plenty sharp by the look of it and he was ready to use it. "You never told me who the hawk was with the bloody beak."

"He's the sword in the shadows. He's the rising wind. He's the voice that speaks."

Kanja winced and rubbed his forehead, just as a north wind swirled through the trees, sending a flurry of sand through the oasis. He looked up at a half-swallowed moon and down again at the trees, and then he threw a glance at Ayize.

"When little boys betray their brothers, we cover them in blood and leave them in the desert. A tasty morsel for a hungry leopard, don't you think?"

"Perhaps that little boy has learned the truth," Harran said, knowing how much weight his words had. "Perhaps he's a man now."

"It would be kinder to slit his throat in his sleep."

"That would be murder."

"No. It would be taking him out of his misery," Kanja snarled.

"He doesn't look miserable to me." Harran shot a look at the leather pack on Kanja's back. "That statue's good and heavy. It might buy a kingdom or it might kill."

"Sun's going down," Kanja said, standing. "Better get some sleep."

"I'd sleep better if I had a blanket," Harran offered, feeling a fresh cold breeze on his cheeks.

"No chance, Prophet. You might fly away with the rest."

Kanja sauntered towards a tall palm tree and leaned against the husked trunk. The wind blew across the dunes, blowing the braids from his shoulders, and he stood there for a time, staring north without moving. All of a sudden, he snapped his fingers at Othene and grinned.

"Better stoke up that fire, old father. Let's bring him in."

SHENQ

"Put this shawl around you," Shenq said to the girl, wrapping it over her shoulders. "You're paler than the moon."

She nodded, slinging a bow across her back and stuffing a large piece of bread in her mouth. "Might not eat again until morning," she said, spitting out a spray of crumbs.

Shenq nodded, amazed at her appetite. He had never seen such a small woman eat so much. They shared knives and medicine pouches, and hobbled the stallion and the donkey in a trough between two dunes.

Crawling up the slip face to the summit, Shenq saw a small oasis about seventy feet or so to the south, surrounded by palm trees and interlaced with maple and brush. Three silhouettes sat before a blazing fire, warming flat loaves and beans, and skewering meat over the embers. On the other side of a pool sat three others, shivering in the cool night air and tied so it seemed at the wrists.

They're alive! Shenq thought, counting them off in his head. He wondered why Kanja had placed them so far away, but all he could come up with was the stink. Menkheperre had breath that would knock an owl off its branch and Harran was hairier than a dog's armpit.

S'haila seemed to study a tree whose crown swayed back and forth. "Looks like someone's got an itch or they're sawing themselves free."

Smart girl, thought Shenq, smiling at her for the first time. He could see a spark where the ropes rubbed the bark and he hoped the Bloods couldn't see it too.

"Three watchmen and three prisoners," she said, gripping a dagger.

"Two watchmen," Shenq corrected. "The other is your Makurae. You can see the blood on his back."

Shenq knew she was already calculating how helpless Mkasa was. "They better keep one eye open if they plan on falling asleep."

"They won't sleep. They're waiting."

It's too easy, Shenq thought. At closer range, he could pick them off with two good arrows if it wasn't for the flatlands between him and the oasis. The trees were like a standing fort, guarding its garrison from the outside world and he would be a helpless target flat on his stomach on those bright silver sands.

The sorcerer was alert, walking around the pool with a bow over one shoulder and nostrils wider than two jug handles. He gripped a curved knife, occasionally looking at Kanja, occasionally studying the prisoners.

Kanja sat by the fire, chin bobbing against his chest and twice he jerked himself awake, eyes flicking from left to right. He rocked a leather pack to his chest, head bent over it as if droning a lullaby. *The Farafra token,* Shenq thought, longing to get his hands on it. It was a gold figurine of Ptah with his dark green skin and skullcap.

"You untie the prisoners. This will give them something to fight with," he whispered, handing her two knives.

She crept down the windward side of the dune like a crab, scuttling up and down through sandy grooves and slinking down a dark hole. She was methodical, untying Menkheperre and Harran and whispering to them as she did it. It was likely they were the strongest, having somehow avoided a beating.

Something caught her eye and she retreated into the shadows. That's when Shenq made his way towards the trees, watching the shimmering pool through the leaves, bow to the ready. The brush was dry and thorny underfoot, and he elected to keep at least thirty feet between him and the fire. Othene seemed content to watch the eastern horizon from the other side of the pool, taking a few practiced slashes in the air with his knife. Black eyes flashed bright and hard, and it was impossible to tell what he was thinking.

As Shenq crept through the brush towards the clearing, he saw Kanja's eyes, narrow and cunning. They were trained on Khemwese, body angled away and lips pressed flat. *He's preparing a plan of attack*, Shenq thought, wondering why Kanja wasn't pacing around the oasis like a sentry. He'd be a sitting duck if he was. Instead, he watched the giant intently, hands clenched and jaw set. There was something different in his demeanor, fear or recognition perhaps.

Mkasa was curled up by the fire. His back was a blaze of sores and dried up blood, too frail to fight. Occasionally, Kanja looked down at him, watching the curve of his throat and the rise of his belly.

Shenq's heart raced, feeling a surge of blood that made him unusually alert. Like a leopard feels perhaps when he tracks prey and guards against predators himself. Under a bright moon, he inched forward, cursing the shadows for a bed of broken twigs. There was a path through the trees snaking towards the oasis and he could see the pockmarks of horses' hooves.

They rode through here last night, he thought, deciding the path was the least obvious point of entry. *Because it's the most obvious . . .*

Keeping the snapping flames in his sights, he saw a position to the right of the path and fifteen feet behind Kanja. He passed one small breathless moment as he raised his bow, aiming at the warrior's chest where a choker of beads looped below one breast.

A bird cawed overhead and Kanja turned his face towards the sound, jumping to his feet in an instant. Flashes of red passed between the trees as the warrior paced back and forth, muttering and cursing.

Shenq shuddered. He should never have waited. Now

Kanja was kicking Mkasa in the back, head moving in jerky twitches as he spat out a stream of foul words. Shenq slung his bow and crept forward, feeling leaves against his skin and scattered twigs underfoot. Swinging one leg over a broken branch, the crackling fire made enough noise to cover a cat-footed leap to the other side. A mosquito tickled his face threatening to sting, and he reached up and crushed it between palm and cheek.

And then he paused.

There was a rustling in the thicket three feet ahead, a bird perhaps. He looked back at the dense shadows behind him and forward to the fire where one flame danced above the embers.

Kanja was gone.

Shenq sniffed the air, keeping his head forward, eyes searching the shadows for any sign of movement. It was very quiet in the grove and if he was right, his men were in great danger. The silence did not sit right in his brain and there was a cold wind on his neck, a distant alarm.

He saw Mkasa sit up suddenly as if he heard something—a snapping twig, a horse's nicker, a sudden gasp. What was it? Shenq hadn't heard a thing.

If Kanja stepped out in the open it would be a great opportunity and just as Shenq thought it, there he was, gripping the white girl by the throat.

S'haila, Shenq murmured.

He couldn't see his men behind her and he felt a flutter of hope. A wild yell gave him a thrill of excitement mixed with dread and he watched as a grin broke across Kanja's face. "I'll cut her throat if you don't show yourself!"

Shenq nocked an arrow and drew his bow, focusing on nothing but Kanja's eye. He saw S'haila flick her eyes to one side as if something approached to his left, and he heard a snapping twig and flinched. The arrow went wide, flying just to the left of Kanja's ear.

Shenq dropped his bow under a tree and crouched beneath a cover of fronds. He was too close to whatever it was to use his bow and it would only creak when he drew it. His khopesh would be a ray of silver in the moonlight, too easy to track. So he drew his dagger instead.

Something moved.

So did Shenq.

He flicked his eyes from left to right, scanning the trees, the tops of the brush. He could smell sweat and meat and fetid breath. There, between two saplings, was a figure running at him through the gaping branches and just as he neared, Shenq struck.

Only he wasn't quick enough.

Othene brought up an arm to deflect the blade from slicing his throat. The cutting edge of Shenq's dagger slashed through Othene's forearm, splitting the flesh right down to his fingers.

Othene issued a soft grunt, swinging out with his knife hand and lips drawn back in a black snarl. Shenq jumped back into a tangle of brush, one leg kicking out from under him. Just as he regained his balance, the knife dropped from his hand and he could see it gleaming amongst the detritus. But there was no time to retrieve it. Othene came on, lurching and stumbling and, just as he was over him, Shenq kneed him in the crotch.

The old sorcerer doubled over in an explosion of pain, head lowered like a charging bull, driving Shenq into the brush with a few good blows. Shenq rolled and fell, hearing the sudden rush of wind in his ears and the scuffling of leaves. And before he knew it, he was scooped up in a net and hauled into the air.

There were shouts now as he swung there from the trees, ropes digging into his flesh. And then came the arrows, nipping and scratching and hot bursts of pain. With knees drawn up under his chin, he began to roll, pitching the net from side to side as far as it would go. It was a meager arc but it was enough to ward off the worst and get him closer to the trunk of a date palm.

Two knives glanced off the tree to his left and one

caught him in the thigh, slicing through a soft pocket of flesh. The other opened a gash in his forehead, sending a gush of blood into his open mouth. The sharp taste warned Shenq of a greater threat, as did the sound of sawing.

Othene was down there, cutting the ropes.

There were shouts as if someone was coming, whipping palm fronds and crashing through the undergrowth. It had to have been a big man with all that noise, Khemwese if he could bet on it.

And then the sawing stopped.

There were more snapping twigs and then the sound of feet, padding out to the desert beyond. He heard Harran's voice and Ayize too, and he let out a sigh of relief.

It suddenly dawned on him that he was stranded at least eighteen feet off the ground and if he cut himself away with his skinning knife, he would likely fall and break his back. And if he wasn't maimed, he'd still get a butt-load of splinters.

Never in his life had he felt so worthless, swinging there like freshly butchered swine and it would only take a whirling axe to finish him off altogether. He unsheathed the obsidian knife from the inside of his belt and began to cut the web of ropes in front of his face. He made a hole just big enough for one arm and, as he swung back towards the tree, he grabbed hold of the gnarly trunk.

"Careful now," a voice said.

Shenq looked down and saw Harran guiding him down with a flapping hand. Anchored there for a time, he cut himself away, grabbing onto the notched bark just as the net floated downwards. He planted his feet on each side of the tree and, with a series of jumps, he lowered himself to the ground taking half a dozen splinters in his hands.

"Where are the others?"

"Khemwese's gone to find the sorcerer," Harran said. "The Imazi girl is seeing to the men. She's good with herbs. Ayize has a warrior's eye, sir. He knew Kanja would run for his horse. So he took the knife the girl gave him and hurled it as far as it would go. A streak of silver under the stars, smooth and bright. It caught Kanja in his leg. He went down like a stone."

"A warrior's eye, you say?" Shenq grinned, wondering what the boy was aiming for.

It was then he saw Khemwese rushing towards him. "Your weapons, Maaz."

Shenq felt a fist of fear that clutched his guts and his throat was tight. "Othene?"

Khemwese held up a restraining hand. "I chased him as far as the dune, Maaz, and when I was in range, I threw my knife. It was too soon, too low. Just as he turned, the knife caught him in the shoulder and he staggered. Things came out of his mouth like bats, all black and cackling. I thought it was the devil himself.

"By the time I reached him, he had pulled the knife from his shoulder and he was laughing at me. 'Stupid boy,' he said. '*Stupid*, just like your father.' It made me mad, all that hissing and carrying on. So I grabbed him by the neck and shook him. He was dead by the time I stopped."

Shenq was glad. He didn't feel much like riding all the way to Thebes with a sorcerer in his pack.

"It's demons that stole his mind," Khemwese said, "like they steal every shred of a man's dignity. He was the storm sent by the kingdom of darkness to discourage us. And now he's dead."

KANJA

The river was a spray of flower petals beneath moored ships and fishing boats. Some way off, people lined the avenue of sphinx, craning their necks to see the victors. Kanja heard their frenzied screams in the distance and he knew who they shouted for.

Outrun by two boys and a girl . . . Kanja almost laughed at his own stupidity. They showed him the points of their daggers as they tied him up. Never were two boys fiercer, spitting curses and yelling *coward* as if their lungs would burst.

Kanja was a coward. He had tried to run. And now he sat astride his mare, body swaying in time to her stride, smelling the scent of her mane and the sweat on her mottled gray coat. There was a lump in his throat as he patted her, wondering if she sensed what he sensed.

There was a stand of sycamores between the horsemen and the city gates, and he could see the palace pennants rippling on their dowels. The desert had quickly become a dusty road where shrines lined the way and scattered farms lay on the outskirts, shrouded in their glorious fields of green.

Only half a mile to go, he thought, dreading it all the same.

Smoke from a watchman's fire blew across the path and in the old man's hand was a warm flat loaf smeared with chickpeas and garlic. He held it high for Kanja to take and waved away any offer of payment. The flavors were good and sharp, and Kanja savored every bite.

It was then he saw the vulture, the one he killed as a child. It stood on the embankment, staring out at the river and feathers rippling in a faint breeze. *It's alive. I only have to touch it,* he thought, reaching over his horse's neck. He could have sworn he felt those silken feathers beneath his fingers but he knew it was too far away.

Instead, he was hemmed in at all sides by the Hawks, hearing their light chatter and hating the smell of them. To his left he saw Khemwese, blacker than a horse's eye. They said he was Kibwe-Shabaqo's son. They said he was a prince, the true King of Alodia.

When Kanja remembered his childhood, he remembered the boy his uncle proudly carried on his shoulder. The child he was forced to bow to, the child they said would be king. *Why him and not one of his brothers?* he once asked his uncle.

Because he is highly favored, explained his uncle. *Because God has chosen him.*

Their God was not the Alodian snake god. It was another they blessed at every meal, prayed to every day and worshiped on their faces. The story was told to them by an old man, a wire-haired *Shasu* with one green eye. And Kanja had once loved those stories. Every word.

To his right, he saw the Prophet with his elfin features and otherworldly eyes. *They all look the same, these Shasu*, he thought as Harran sang a song about sowing a whirlwind and reaping storms, and his wavy locks of brown hair billowed about his cheeks. He wasn't so bad. He was just a prophet after all.

"Do you know HaShem?" Harran asked when he finished his song.

Kanja's mind was a churn of heartrending memories. "Ayize does. He thinks He's the flame in the fire, the seed in the soil. I think . . ." What did he think? Harran had told him only yesterday and now would be a good time to remember. "He's the voice in the wind."

"Then you know Him." Harran covered his head with his tallit. "When I pray, I call Him Adonai. Do you know what it means?"

Kanja shook his head.

"It means *Master*. He is my Lord."

Kanja felt an ache in his gut. It was like a bird locked inside his ribcage, longing to spread its wings. "Adonai," he repeated and swallowed hard. There was something in the name that made him want to sob.

Crying is for boys, you fool, the voices said. *You're in a snare of your own making. You'll never get out now.*

"I'm not a fool," Kanja murmured.

No, you're a murdering fool!

"I am Kanja, prince of Alodia, son of Ibada, King of the three nations of Kush," Kanja said loudly, eyes pricking with tears. He could almost hear the trance dances in the deep of his mind and he imagined the great hall of his father's house where a fire burned in the central hearth, warm and hazy with wood smoke. It was fleeting. It was home. "What will they do to me?"

"We have all been called to do great things, my prince," Harran said. "Often our greatest callings are the gravest as well. You need only to bend your knee and lay down your sword. Pledge yourself to Adonai and you shall rise a greater man."

Kanja gritted his teeth. "I hope I shall die well."

Shenq was at the head of them, scouting the river and the desert behind, hair wild and eyes sharp in a flash of sunlight. In the distance the pylons of the great temple of Thebes rose up through the river mist and Kanja could smell the brackish scent of torches. Small ripples brushed against the shore, silver breakers in the sunlight, and he would have given anything to feel cool water between his toes.

Almost there, he said to himself.

There were no ropes on his hands or any bonds to speak of, and he didn't have the strength to run away. He had no weapons, no hope. He watched a group of heralds beneath a thick-trunked sycamore, pulling three chariots towards them. Hawk chariots they were with black and gold ribbons and plumes for the horses.

Can't go in without plumes, Kanja thought almost laughing.

Can't go in without chariots.

He imagined the Pharaoh and his Queen sitting beneath a brightly colored awning, eating fava beans and eggs, and lemon flavored lamb. He could almost taste the flavors in his mouth. And the princess? Would she ever forgive him? Or would she just forget him like all the others?

The desert was ablaze with gold as the sun's rays spilled across the river towards them. He thought he saw a tribesman on the east bank with a spear by his side.

"Ulan," he murmured, staring at long red braids. *Yes, it was Ulan.*

Beside him was Kamara with a small boy by her side, dark-eyed and watchful and as tall as her knee. He could see Yuku and Massui, and his beloved Najja, hands wrapped around spears and necks a twist of beads. Behind them an army of four hundred men, shúkàs blood-red against that yellow sky. They were waiting.

The Hawks stopped for a time to greet the heralds and then there was whispering. Something had happened. Something that made Kanja's belly spit up bitter juices.

Shenq cantered towards him, head bowed and grim. "Your father is dead, my prince," he said. "King Ibada of Alodia is dead."

"Dead?" Kanja murmured.

Shenq nodded. "The heralds said he died a week ago. They said he died a very slow death."

Poison, Kanja thought. *It stays in the body and rots the very stomach.*

"Long live the King!" the *Kenyt-Nisu* shouted, pumping the air with their fists.

Long live the king, Kanja thought, imagining a heavy gold crown on his head. It was gold wasn't it? He couldn't remember any more. But he did remember the blood red stones around the rim and how heavy it was to hold. He was king now, only there was a sting in his joy. He had destroyed his father and he was a thief caught and punished.

"My king," Shenq said sternly. "You have a choice. Go with us to Thebes and you will be tied between two horses and ripped apart. Go home and you will be escorted under guard to Souba. There you will be tried and hanged."

Kanja could hear the crowds in the distance and he dreaded their jeers and catcalls. He reached for his pack but it was gone. Just like all his winnings, squirreled away in Shenq's keeping. What would they think of him now, these elegant people of Thebes? They would call him a savage, the scourge of Alodia and they would hurl spit and arrows.

Better get down off that horse and run! It was Othene's voice in his head, thin and reedy as if it had come from the grave.

"There is a third choice," Shenq said. "The tenets of the *Kenyt-Nisu* state that if a traitor be found amongst them, he will ride through the ranks of his own men and be shot through with arrows. It is an honorable way to die."

The grandest snare of them all, Kanja thought, turning his eyes to the horizon.

He saw Ulan and he had so much to tell him. "You fill my world," he whispered. "Come and sit with me and tell me how you are. What should I do, brother? What would you do?"

The trees seemed to rustle the cacophony of the damned and there was the terrible sound of cackling. The leaves said he was the bane that shattered all lives, the rat in a sighthound's mouth. And over it all he thought he heard another voice.

This man has asked you to join his ranks. He has asked you to be the pride of the Egyptian army for just one day. He has asked for the privilege of killing you. Do it.

"What will happen to my body?" Kanja asked.

Shenq raised his hand. "Your body will be buried with all the honors of a prince. You have my word."

It was better than being left in a ditch and wrapped in a tattered cloak. Kanja had no use for his body now and in a strange way he felt sorry. He would never feel the Alodian crown on his head or grip the gold scepter of the ancient fathers. There would be no wives to love or sons to come after him. Instead, the mourners would fill the streets with a strange and wild music. But at least he would be free.

"Do it," he whispered.

Shenq snapped his fingers at Mkasa and nodded. The Makurae held out a wineskin. It was half-full by the look of it with a white feather dripping from its strap. "Drink," he said. "It will calm you."

"Thank you," Kanja murmured. It was what Ulan would have said.

Kanja took the wineskin and looked into those sad kind eyes. There was something in the Makurae's gaze that told him half a skin would be just enough. His heart felt like a harp strung achingly tight as he patted the mare and took those last few gulps. Only his brother, his sweet innocent little brother gnawed his knuckles and darted worried glances. His skin was pale as death and his eyes ran with tears.

Kanja lifted the boy onto his mare, squeezing, rocking, crooning. Ayize gulped mouthfuls of fresh air between sobs and then he wailed. It would be the same sound he would make over Kanja's dead body when they put him in the ground.

"Make me proud," Kanja said, nuzzling the boy's neck and smelling the last of his clan. "They're fine shooters. It will be quick."

"Run," Ayize whispered. "Why don't you run?"

The thought was sweet. But Kanja had no more run in him. "You are the King of the south now, a Souban lord. Don't you want that, my brother?"

"I want you to take me home."

Kanja pressed the boy's face against his chest and heard the soft whimpering. "Do you remember what Baba said to Ulan when he chose him? Do you remember the words? Then say it with me. *You are the voice in the moon, the light in the sun and the star in my heart. You are all things to me.*"

Kanja let Shenq take the boy. He would likely try to blindfold him or tell him to look away. But Ayize was a man now. He would watch for all it was worth.

"Ayize will return to Alodia in one year," Shenq said. "He will return as a prince."

Kanja nodded. It was all he could do.

Taking up the reins he waited as the heralds assembled themselves behind him and the warriors of the *Kenyt-Nisu* in front. A long line to wave him through and bows to the ready. It was a while before the drug began to overpower him, sands a blur and far-off sounds of cheering. *I am a king for only one day . . .*

All of a sudden he was lightheaded and excited, feeling the wind in his long red braids. Even his mare pawed the ground, ears pricked forward as Khemwese blew his horn.

He wouldn't run away. That was a coward's trick. He would take the arrows in his chest, the death of kings.

I'm here, can't you see me? There was Ulan with the sun behind him, arms waving and jumping in a flurry of sand. *Ride, brother. Now!*

Kanja kicked his horse on, arms out by his sides. He was about to shout the war cry of the Bloodmen and then he changed his mind.

"Adonai!" he yelled as his head snapped back.

All he heard was cheering and the sound of his name. He never felt the arrows as they ripped into his flesh and he never saw the black kite that circled overhead.

I bend my knee and lay down my sword. I pledge myself to you.

There was no horse beneath him now and no wind in his long red braids. Up into the sky he went, higher and higher and higher.

Dear Reader,

I hope you enjoyed *The Fowler's Snare* and my first book, *Chasing Pharaohs*. Many of you have told me how much you loved Commander Shenq and Pharaoh Kheper-Re and many readers have asked if there is a third book. Well, stay tuned because the fight for the Two Lands isn't over yet.

As an author, I love feedback and you are the reason I write. So tell me what you liked, what you hated, what you would love to see happen. I am looking forward to hearing from you. You can visit me on the web at www.cmtstibbe.com.

Finally, if you would like to write a review on any of my books on your favorite bookseller's site, I would be honored to have your feedback. Reviews are hard to come by and you, the reader, have the power to make these books.

Thank you so much for reading *The Fowler's Snare* and for spending time with me.

Claire M.T. Stibbe

Author's Note

Pharaoh Thutmose II (approximate dates: 1493-1479 BC) ruled between the time of his father, Thutmose I, a brilliant military commander, and Queen Hatshepsut, known in her reign as Pharaoh Maatkare. It has been proposed that by the time he was in his twenties Pharaoh Thutmose II was in very poor health. Indeed, when his mummy was unwrapped it showed scabrous skin covered in scars as well as a body that was thin and shrunken.

It is possible given his incapacity that this young Pharaoh may have relied on his half-sister and wife Queen Hatshepsut to govern the Two Lands although there is nothing to prove this theory. However, it wasn't hard for me to imagine a sedentary character, disinterested in the day-to-day administration of his realm. From there I crafted him with a veneer of absurdity and an underlying shrewdness, the second of which he would have inherited from his father.

Queen Hatshepsut, at this stage, was no more than Great Royal Wife to Pharaoh Thutmose II. Whether she was as scheming as she was ambitious is not known. All we do know is that she later became a pharaoh in her own right. Given her status and the frequent jostling for power, I imagined her to be devoted, perceptive, judicious and with a touch of real class. This is only a small portion of her arsenal of gifts and traits.

Senenmut's best known role was tutor to princess Neferure. He earned a variety of titles, including Steward of the Estates of Amun, a position that allowed him unrestricted access to the riches of Karnak temple. He was as talented as he was ambitious and he was the beloved of Queen Hatshepsut. Just how beloved is purely speculation although the vulgar graffiti found in a Deir el-Bahri tomb gives some clues. Coming from humble beginnings, he rose to power swiftly due to relentless hard work and his determination to see Queen Hatshepsut succeed.

Commander Shenq is purely fictitious as are the warriors of the Pharaoh's most Honored Ones. His fortitude and serenity added a delicious flavor to the daily life of Pharaoh Kheper-Re and his court during the time of the 18th Dynasty.

In the *Chasing Pharaohs* series, Thutmose I is referred to as Pharaoh Ka-Nekhet, loosely taken from his Horus name *Kanekhet Merimaat.* Thutmose II is referred to as Kheper-Re, taken from his Prenomen, *Aakheperenre.* I have shortened some of these names for ease of pronunciation.

Also by C.M.T. Stibbe

Historical Fiction
Chasing Pharaohs

Suspense
The 9th Hour ● Night Eyes
(To be released 2014/2015)

Historical Sources

Hatshepsut – Joyce Tildesley

Chronicles Of The Queens of Egypt – Joyce Tildesley

The Realm of the Pharaohs – Zahi Hawass

Ancient Egypt – Georgio Agnese & Maurizio Re

Tutankhamun And The Golden Age Of The Pharaohs – Zahi Hawass

Imperial Lives – Dennis C. Forbes

The Tomb Of Ancient Egypt – Aidan Dodson & Salima Ikram

Egypt, Gods, Myths & Religion – Lucia Gahlin

Tutankhamun, The Eternal Splendor Of The Boy Pharaoh – T.G.H. James

Ancient Egypt, Its Culture & History – J.E. Manchip White

Ancient Egypt, An Illustrated Reference To The Myths, Religions, Pyramids and Temples Of The Land Of The Pharaohs – Lorna Oakes & Lucia Gahlin

Ancient Egypt, Thebes & The Nile Valley In The Year 1200 BCE – Charlotte Booth

Made in the USA
Charleston, SC
27 January 2015